"The most original vampire novel
to come along in quite some time."
–Rocky Mountain News

The BOOK of COMMON DREAD

BRENT MONAHAN

ST. MARTIN'S PAPERBACKS

This novel is a work of fiction. All of the events, characters, names, and places depicted in this novel are entirely fictitious or are used fictitiously. No representation that any statement made in this novel is true or that any incident depicted in this novel actually occurred is intended or should be inferred by the reader.

THE BOOK OF COMMON DREAD

Copyright © 1993 by Brent Monahan.

Stepback photograph by Will Crocker.

All rights reserved. No part of this book may be used or reproduced in any manner whatsoever without written permission except in the case of brief quotations embodied in critical articles or reviews. For information address St. Martin's Press, 175 Fifth Avenue, New York, N.Y. 10010.

Library of Congress Catalog Card Number: 93-691

ISBN: 0-312-95359-3

Printed in the United States of America

St. Martin's Press hardcover edition/July 1993
St. Martin's Paperbacks edition/September 1994

10 9 8 7 6 5 4 3 2 1

For Steven Gorelick—
mentor and friend

PROLOGUE

࿇

In the midst of life we are in death.

—*The Book of Common Prayer; Burial of the Dead*

Montague Fox flipped open the magazine, exposing the book concealed inside it. They were a study in stark contrast—the glossy, clay-and-glucose-sprayed magazine with its beautiful half-tone illustrations framing the small, yellow-paged book in its dull and distressed leather binding.

Fox's eyes rested with pride for a moment on the book, then shifted to the advertisement in the lower corner of the magazine's left page.

FOR SALE

RAREST ALDUS 1503.

INQUIRE BOX 460

LONDON, WCA 2 1 EN

In the year 1503, only four books had been printed by Aldus Manutius, but "rarest" signaled the one work among them which was legendary. So far three inquirers had responded to his cryptic message, none bothering to ask the subject of the book. Montague never ceased to be amazed that so many bibliophiles possessed such arcane knowledge.

Fox daubed his forehead with the handkerchief that already lay moist in his left hand. He sat in a hotel office only two levels below ground, but it seemed like an antechamber to the bowels of Hades. The office belonged to the hotel's custodian, and its back door opened into the boiler room. Through the semiopaque glass, Fox noted the hellish red glow of the boiler room safety lights, their illumination shimmering in the sweltering air. Mixed in the steam were odors of mold, rust, and decay. Somewhere beyond the glass, a pipe complained under the pressure of superheated steam.

Across the table another man sat perspiring freely, but he did not bother to wipe away the trickles. His thick, grime-encrusted fingers drummed a tattoo on the table. He stared with dark, unblinking eyes at the old leather cover. "Don't like ta read," he declared, raspily.

Fox closed the magazine protectively over the book. "I don't either."

The other man's eyebrows rose on his beetled forehead. "Yeah, right."

"Not anymore, Bertrand," Fox said. As if to prove his point, he removed the delicate, wire-rimmed glasses from his ears with both hands and blinked a smile at his companion. "I've had enough books to last a lifetime. I don't care if I never see another book again." He folded up the glasses and lay them next to the magazine and his pocket watch. "All I want now is to retire to the French Riviera, lie on the beach, eat well, and watch women wiggle by."

Bertrand laughed coarsely. It took several moments for his yellow-toothed rictus to fade and his face to remold into an expression of low cunning.

"How much you gonna get for that book?" Bertrand asked.

"Not just this copy," Montague reminded him, convinced that reminding was necessary. "This is one of eight, remember?"

"Yeah, sure."

"But only you and I must know that. If either of us slipped and let a customer know there were more, that would tear it. It's incredible enough that even one should exist. Understand?"

"Yeah, sure."

Fox hoped so, as he studied the image of Bertrand Worthington III. That this scarred and beer-bloated mass of meat in front of him should insist on being called Bert, much less Bertrand, would be ludicrous enough. He should have been called Bruiser or Smasher. His insistence on the use of his given name was a pathetic denial of the brutality the mirror showed him every morning. A boiler specialist was Bertrand Worthington III, six foot four and seventeen stone of fiery, intemperate passions, a human counterpart to the boilers he bullied about day after day.

Montague Fox, at the opposite pole, was a cool-headed relictarian. Slight of frame and delicate from birth, he had compensated by conjuring an aura of strength from his intellect. Early on, he discovered the powers in language and facts and performed his own kind of bullying, on those who could be mentally cowed. Having amassed an arsenal of knowledge, he hunted out a profession that would value his brain as much as he did.

Montague worked for no less an employer than the British Museum. His muse was literary, for he read Egyptian hieroglyphics, Babylonian cuneiform, early and middle Greek, and Latin, with varying degrees of expertise. Stone tablets, clay shards, papyrus, and vellum were all in a day's reading. At forty-six, he had studied and expounded and ass-kissed his way into the number two position in the Library Division of the Museum. His division was the repository of such treasures as the oldest piece of paper in the world (A.D. 137, Yuan-hsing period) and the oldest copy of the New Testament (A.D. 400, Convent of St. Catherine, Mount Sinai). Both relics were priceless. For many years, the value of the articles in his charge, coupled with the recognition of his own intellectual superiority, had kept the balloon of Montague's contentment buoyant.

But then, three years back, Fox chanced on commercial television. One wintry night, the fare on neither BBC 1 nor BBC 2 was palatable, and he had condescended to watch "something common." Never before exposed to the blandishments of "telly" advertising, Montague fell victim to their animated onslaught like the Hawaiians to cholera. Electronic equipment, travel, fashions, cars, all were pitched between flash-glimpses of ravishing young women, partaking, admiring, promising. He was assured that this was the real meaning of life and that he deserved it. Today.

He became a believer. But he was a child in front of the amusement park without the price of admission.

Every working day Montague was surrounded by treasures. Broken, partial things coated with grime, things not very prized when they were new but grotesquely valuable now that the patina of time was upon them. Month after month he clenched his teeth at the thought that just one of these artifacts, sold to the right well-heeled collector, could set him up for life. Unfortunately, it was all accounted for, all numbered and codified by Receiving before he was allowed to handle it. Except on one occasion.

At the request of a highly regarded literary journal, Fox had penned a scholarly piece on the history of paper milling. Not long after, a gift arrived at the museum, addressed directly to him. The donor had read his article and was sure that Fox was the man to accept the gift on the museum's behalf. The benefactor descended from a long line of magistrates and still lived in his ancestral home. While renovating the attic, he had uncovered 282 sheets of blank paper stuffed between the wall studs for insulation. As Montague's article had disclosed, the "laid marks" and the watermark proved the paper to have been manufactured in Fabriano, Italy, between the years 1497 and 1515 (before England possessed such skills). Produced from almost pure rag and with no acid, the paper had remained in a remarkable state of preservation. Although Montague wrote a florid note of thanks to the donor, he never gave the paper to the museum. He needed it, to forge tickets to the amusement park.

Few men were as equipped to duplicate an ancient book as was Montague Fox, Esquire. Almost a decade earlier, an entire font of late-fifteenth-century cursive Greek type had been proven by Montague's superior to have been a fake. Fox was instructed to "get it out of the museum." The pieces, though imitations, had been so cleverly made that he had taken them home. Only three other elements remained for Montague to parlay his knowledge into outrageous profit: a hand printing press (which he had a cabinetmaker fashion to his specifications); ink (which he himself made from charcoal, boiled linseed oil, and chemical dryers); and finally the selection of the right book.

The choice of books he could counterfeit from was limited by the size, age, and quantity of the paper. The folios were not of the large, "royal" folio sizes but rather of the "medium" dimension, intended for everyday Renaissance court work or for quarto folding, into the proportions of the portable readers then popular.

Montague settled with satisfaction on a book of exquisite obscurity and extraordinary rarity.

After many months his labors were over, and eight copies rested in his bank deposit box, sewn and bound. The only remaining questions were how to advertise his "genuine find" (he used one British, one American, and two Continental literary journals) and how to guarantee that those interested did not take one look at his frail physique, grab the offered treasure and run. Which explained Bertrand. The boiler repairman and the scholar shared a thirst for the devil's brew, generally at a common pub. The boiler man was notorious for a nature wholly in keeping with his dangerous appearance. He was also known to lay many bets and consequently ever on the lookout for opportunities to make easy money. Montague's offer to Bertrand of a thousand pounds for a successful night's work was accepted with no questions. Until now.

"Eight copies, but we make like there's just one," Bertrand parroted. "And what'cha askin' for each?"

The boiler man was like a bloodhound on the scent. Montague knew that the subject would have to be dealt with, once and for all. "I won't sell for less than ten thousand."

The alcohol-pickled abacus clicked slowly behind Bertrand's dark and dangerous eyes. "If you get more, I should get ten percent for my part," he said, carefully.

Montague snickered, in what he hoped would sound like an assured, dismissing manner. "Your part probably isn't even necessary."

"What about this here place?" Bertrand argued. "Ain't I keepin' you safe by providin' neutral ground?"

The brute had a point. In case any of the customers later discovered they had been stung, Fox did not want a way for them to find his home or place of business. Bertrand's profession provided him access keys to the nether regions of a score of public buildings.

"I tell you what, my friend," Fox acceded. "You get a thousand pounds for each sale, just for being there. If muscle is required to protect me or the book, you'll get *two* thousand on the next sale. Fair enough?"

"Yeah. That's better," Bertrand said, through a grin. He looked to Montague like the enormous, square-toothed cat who menaced Mickey Mouse.

Montague picked up his pocket watch, admiring it as it came into focus. It had been fashioned around 1838 by the watchmaker and magician Jean Eugene Robert-Houdin, and was still an accurate instrument, more than three times its present owner's age. Fox had been able to purchase it at a flea market only because its owner had no idea of its value. After the forgeries were all sold, however, he could buy virtually anything he wanted, any time he wanted.

"It's five after eleven," Fox declared, revesting his watch. "I'd better go out and wait for our guest." He stood, put on his eye-glasses, and shoved the sopping handkerchief into his trouser pocket. It had seemed odd to him that his first prospective customer should insist on coming to the hotel at such a late hour. But for all the money about to be paid, this piper who signed his name "V. DeVilbiss" could call the tune as late as he wanted.

Fox opened the door to the outer hallway. He flashed Bertrand a benign smile. "It's probably best if you say nothing."

"Suits me," Bertrand muttered, his attention diverted to the floor, where a black bug scuttled into the light, intent on regaining darkness on the opposite side of the room. Bertrand's foot came down hard; he ground the bug into oblivion with quiet satisfaction.

Fox closed the door. The elevators were just around the corner. His customer had promised to arrive there "about eleven-twenty." Fox wanted to be waiting when the time came. As he rounded the corner, his stride took a hitch.

A man stood dead center in the corridor, his aspect alert. The distance and the rear lighting that nimbused the stranger's form made his features difficult to discern. His dress, however, was quite distinguishable and clearly out of fashion. These days, nothing but opera or perhaps a royal gala would excuse a man's wearing dress tails and a three-quarter-length cape. The stark, white V of his dress shirt contrasted with several textures and shades of black.

Montague walked forward with measured step. The stranger kept his gaze leveled on Fox's face. As the scholar drew nearer, he noted that the tails were worn by a figure a little under six feet tall and probably a bit underweight. The man's shoes were patent-leather pumps with velvet bows, and the arresting cape was of a fine-woven, inky wool, lined with moiré silk. Drawing closer, Fox found a handsome visage, which did not entirely conform to what he had assumed was a French last name. Although the stranger's lips had the pouting fullness, his hair the dense blackness, and his skin the thick texture of a southern Frenchman, his complexion had a Scandinavian paleness, as if he never ventured outdoors.

And then Fox saw the eyes. Amber. Glowing as if twin candles were lit inside the man's skull. The sight stopped Fox's advance.

"I expect you're the man with the book," the gentleman declared, in a voice seductive as a cat's purring and an accent that was pure Kensington Gardens.

"Yes," Fox managed, after recovering from the sounds of the clipped king's English. "And you are Monsieur DeVilbiss."

"I am. Where is it?"

Fox jerked his head slightly, indicating the corridor behind him. "Not far."

DeVilbiss gestured for Fox to lead the way. As the scholar started off, he said, "Opera finished earlier than you expected?"

"I left before the end."

"Not a good one?"

"No. It was *Faust,*" the mellifluous voice replied. "The cast was poor."

Fox walked six feet ahead, but the flesh on the nape of his neck shuddered from a chill pouring off the man, a coldness like that which cascades out of a Christmas tree when it is first brought into a house. The winter night had been merely cool when he and the boiler man had entered the hotel, half an hour earlier. He wondered if the temperature had suddenly plummeted.

"Such a shame. To miss that final trio, and the angel choir," Montague sympathized. From the safety of his two-pace lead, he risked a private grin. This man was a buyer, couldn't even wait until the final curtain to rush to the meeting. The clothing bespoke money to burn. His polite but taciturn manner indicated a man totally focused on doing business.

Fox stopped within several paces of the office door and pivoted around. "This *will* be everything you hope for," he assured the customer, in a low voice. "But the price . . . is fifty thousand pounds."

DeVilbiss did not look daunted. "A great deal of money for a stolen book," he remarked.

"Who said it was stolen?" Fox responded, coolly.

"I don't care if it is," the man said. The hard fix of his amber eyes struck like steel on the flint of Fox's heart. "Let me see it first, before we argue price."

Fox tore his eyes from the gentleman's stare and reached for the door knob. "Very well." He gestured for DeVilbiss to enter first.

DeVilbiss moved quietly into the room, giving it an unhurried, vigilant survey. "This . . . says the book was stolen," he declared.

Montague saw that the slow-witted Bertrand had at least gotten his first instruction right and was waiting in the boiler room. He closed the door loudly behind him, as a signal for his huge partner to appear. "You're not, by any chance, a member of any police force, are you?" he asked.

A soft snort of amusement escaped through DeVilbiss's nostrils. "No. Not by any chance."

"Because, if you are, this will be regarded in a court of law as entrapment," Fox went on. The words fell smoothly off his tongue. Montague had rehearsed the speech as preparation for this particular scenario. It not only protected him in case the man were a minion of the law, but also added to the charade that this was indeed a genuine, if stolen, book.

Before DeVilbiss could answer, the boiler room door opened, and Bertrand eased himself into the office.

"Who is this?" DeVilbiss asked, without apparent alarm.

"This is Mr. Wren," answered Fox. "He's letting us use his office, and I asked him to stand guard, to make sure we're not disturbed."

Having taken the large man's measure, DeVilbiss shifted his attention to the table. "May I see it now?"

"Yes, certainly," said Fox, hastening to the magazine and flipping it open with a flourish, exposing the little book. "As you can see, the cover is old but not genuine. I put this one around it for protection. And, of course, there is no title page."

A hand with elegant fingers emerged from the folds of the cape.

Fox picked up the book. "But the colophon and printer's mark have survived. The last page has worked its way loose."

Having gotten out his recitation, Montague yielded the book. "If you feel you must verify its authenticity, I understand. Leave me, say, a thousand-pound deposit and you may take the page with you. We'll simply conclude this on another evening."

The creation of the last page, with its printer's mark and publication information, had cost Fox a pretty farthing. The careful production of Venetian printer Aldus Manutius's dolphin entwined about an anchor symbol had set him back one hundred pounds. But that famous anchor, printed on the genuine paper, was precisely the hook that would catch the most incredulous buyer.

DeVilbiss accepted the book, moved swiftly to the table and sat. As he did, he said, "I won't need to take the page. Give me five minutes, and I'll tell you whether or not I'll pay your price." As if to validate his words, the man reached into the depths of his tails and withdrew a thick stack of banded thousand-pound notes. He dropped them casually onto the magazine, then opened the book.

Montague stared blankly at Bertrand, whose bulging eyes were focused on the stack of pound notes. This was a scenario Fox had not envisioned. The man was actually starting to read the text. Montague's words, in fact, translated by himself into Greek. The last copy of the real Aldus 1503 edition had disappeared more than a hundred and fifty years before, with not even a reproduction remaining. Two eighteenth-century books had passages that paraphrased sections of the infamous contents, however, and it was from these scant roots of knowledge that Fox's imagination had flourished and blossomed into full-blown prose. He had labored hard on its invention. There was no way any contemporary could call him on the authenticity of the text. Nonetheless, he felt beads of sweat swelling on his forehead. He assured himself that it was due to the boiler room humidity; he looked at Bertrand and saw that the giant was leaking from every pore. Montague would have felt heartened by the sight had he not then chanced to look at the face of the stranger. DeVilbiss's brow, cheeks, and chin had a matte quality, betraying not even the slightest sheen of moisture. Fox dug into his clammy pocket for his handkerchief.

DeVilbiss scanned through the book as if speed reading, his forefinger weaving lightly down the center of each page. Half a dozen pages in, he seemed to lose patience and picked up the pace of his study. Long before reaching the end, his forefinger stopped. He closed the book gently and set it on the table. He rose from the chair and, with a look that seemed for all the world to be pleasure, he announced, "This book is a forgery."

The force of the man's conviction rocked Montague back a step. He realized the implication of his movement and drew up his frail frame with mock umbrage. "I am one of the world's foremost experts, sir, and the paper, the type, *and* the ink are all authentic."

"I don't give a damn about the paper, the type, *or* the ink," DeVilbiss replied, his voice still even. "The words are pure fiction. How many copies of this fabrication exist?"

Bertrand straightened up and slowly slipped his right hand behind his back. "He's a copper all right."

DeVilbiss sneered at the pronouncement. His eyes narrowed and stayed fixed on the scholar.

"No, he's not," Fox contradicted, as his throat became more parched. "But he *is* trouble."

"Not for long," Bertrand snarled. He lurched forward like a two-ton truck whose clutch had just been popped. As he advanced on DeVilbiss, his right hand arced around into view. The stiletto, though six inches long, looked puny in his hamhock grip. Red boiler room light glinted off its razor edge.

"No!" Montague screamed, frozen in place. Bertrand was deaf to his command.

DeVilbiss stood like a gazelle overtaken by a lion, as if already in shock and resigned to his fate. His hands pushed futilely against his huge attacker as Bertrand drove the knife hard into the place where the black brocade vest made a V of the brilliantly white shirt, then pivoted the blade upward beneath the skin.

Bertrand gave a grunt as he yanked the stiletto from his victim's stomach. DeVilbiss made no outcry at all. His fingers had curled into the coarse material of the boiler man's coat, and they held fast as his knees buckled. Bertrand's shoulders hunched forward from the dead weight.

"Get off me," Bertrand growled, softly.

The long, thin fingers held fast. Bertrand stabbed the knife into the table surface, then clawed the offending hands from his coat. The gentleman collapsed onto the floor, his cape rustling around him in an elegant swirl, covering his face.

"Jesus Christ!" Montague gasped. "Are you mad?"

Bertrand sidestepped around the body. "Not a bit," he answered. He lunged across the table and scooped up the banded stack of pound notes. "He was gonna get you an' me sent up. Instead, it's tough on him."

"But what if he told someone—"

Bertrand thrust up his free hand to silence his partner. "Shut yer yap! What's done is done. I'll get rid of the body." He waggled the money in his other hand. "But I also get all of this. You keep your book an' hope the next mark ain't so bloody clever."

Montague's complexion had taken on the pallor of chalk. His salivary glands had kicked back in; a string of spittle hung unnoticed from the corner of his gaping mouth. "Maybe . . . he isn't dead."

Bertrand paused from riffling through the pound notes. "Is that all that's worrying you?" He snatched the knife from the table and knelt down next to the body. His left hand sorted through the cape folds for an opening. "You're dead, rich boy, ain'chya?"

The thin fingers thrust out from under the cape with astonishing speed, splayed and curled into five hard talons, tips up. Before Bertrand could flinch, they drove up through the taut trouser material and into his groin, fastening around his penis and scrotum. Almost as swiftly, DeVilbiss's other hand thrust out and clamped over the boiler man's mouth.

"Sorry, I'm not, actually," DeVilbiss hissed, affecting a mocking imitation of his victim's lower-class accent.

Montague's mind tottered on the border of shock. He stood bolted to the floor as the caped man resurrected with a vengeance. Only Montague's eyeballs moved, drinking in the impossible sight of Bertrand's genitals being cleanly ripped from his groin. Twice, Bertrand stabbed the stiletto through the back of his attacker's cape, but the stranger was totally unfazed.

DeVilbiss's palm pressed the boiler man's quivering jaw shut; two of his fingers disappeared through Bertrand's cheeks, burying themselves up to the first knuckles. Blood spurted across the table legs. The knife clattered to the floor. Casually, the elegantly dressed man tossed the detached genitals into a corner, rose to his knees, then his feet, lifting the dying man upward as if he were nothing heavier than a stuffed toy. The muffled screams and gurglings were echoes of a slaughterhouse.

Slowly DeVilbiss pivoted, holding his victim away from him so that the outpourings of blood would not stain his evening dress. He turned so that he had Montague clearly in his line of sight. Where the knife had entered his stomach the shirt was torn, but there was little sign of blood. DeVilbiss smiled and lowered his mouth to the huge man's twitching neck, as a lover might to his beloved.

Stark white incisors gleamed in the office light.

Montague's legs lost their strength and slid out in front of him. He dropped swiftly to the floor.

DeVilbiss sank his teeth into Bertrand's neck. His eyes remained fixed and unblinking on the quaking scholar.

Bertrand stopped twitching. A low groan escaped his lungs.

DeVilbiss drew his mouth from the neck. A look of displeasure distorted his handsome face. He spat a mouthful of blood onto the already reeking floor.

Montague moaned balefully.

DeVilbiss released the boiler man. The corpse-imminent collapsed clumsily into a pool of its own blood.

"And now, sir," DeVilbiss said, after wiping the blood from his lips, "you were about to tell me how many copies of this forgery you have made."

Fox began to hyperventilate, heaving in a great quantity of air, then gasping for more before he could use what he had.

DeVilbiss walked to the crumpled figure and kicked him lightly between the legs. Montague stopped breathing altogether.

The gentleman knelt beside the scholar. "When the pain goes away, you will breathe normally," he said, in a gentle voice. "Do you understand me?"

Montague nodded. The pain ebbed, and he did as the voice and the unblinking eyes commanded. "Why?" he gasped.

"I was about to ask you the same thing. Why, of all the ancient books to forge, would you pick the most dangerous one on earth?"

"Dangerous? I don't understand."

"That's evident."

"You're going to kill me," Fox squeaked.

"Not necessarily," DeVilbiss encouraged, smiling warmly. "All I need is to be sure no copies of the book exist, either real or forged. Now, one last time, how many copies did you create?"

Montague's eyes bulged, struggling to focus on the encroaching face. "Eight."

"Where?"

"In my safe deposit box, at the bank," Montague whispered, fixing his stare on the looming mouth, needing to see the teeth.

"Where is the key?"

"At my house. I can—"

The elegant fingers caught Montague's collar and ripped it open, found the golden chain from which dangled the safe deposit box key, and snapped it from Fox's neck.

"I wear mine in the same place," DeVilbiss revealed, matter-of-factly. "Too valuable to leave lying around. I'm sure you visited the bank today, to fetch the book." He thrust his hand into Montague's inside coat pocket, withdrew his billfold, and rifled through the plastic cards until he found one. "This bank?"

The scholar nodded mutely.

"You've obviously never seen a *real* edition of old Aldus's book. You're to be congratulated. You've come close to its true contents several times. Too close."

The scholar wanted to weep for the cruel disaster that had erupted from his brilliant scheme. "What's in the book?"

"Knowledge about me," the elegantly dressed creature replied, "and those who command me."

Montague blinked at the statement. "Others command *you?*"

DeVilbiss's lids dropped momentarily, as if exhausted. "You find *me* frightening? I'm a lamb compared to . . ." He caught himself; his gaze drifted away from the little man's still-furrowed eyebrows. "One doesn't survive for five hundred years by accident. Eternal life is earned, day after day after day. Now stand, my talented little forger."

"Stand? Why?" Montague dared.

"We can't leave you in here, so close to the hallway. Someone might hear your cries for help after I leave."

"I promise, on my—"

DeVilbiss put a silencing forefinger to Montague's lips. "Stand."

Montague obeyed. DeVilbiss grasped him by the collar and guided him around the table, toward the boiler room door. As he moved, DeVilbiss scooped up the forged book and the magazine. "You are indeed an authority," DeVilbiss granted. "This is beautiful work."

"Thank you," Fox croaked. The creature who held him spoke so gently and civilly that he began to hope he might survive. A few more kind remarks and he might become relaxed enough to piss in his pants.

They passed through the boiler room door, with Montague in the lead. He remembered with rue his likening of the room to the bowels of Hades. Its pulsing red glow looked all the more hellish.

"Now what?" Montague dared.

In answer, DeVilbiss drove his incisors hungrily into the scholar's neck, clutching him in a grasp of steel so that the carotid artery would not escape his attack.

Montague yelped and twisted, calling up the last reserve of his energy in a vain attempt to avoid extinction. A bonfire of pain had been torched in the side of his neck, and its flaming tongues licked outward to all extremities. His ears thrummed with the pounding of his own heart and with a low moan of sexual pleasure that was certainly not his.

Montague's bladder let go. He quit flailing and awaited death.

But it did not come, even though the creature fastened to his throat drank for what seemed to him an hour. He was released gently, allowed to collapse face-up on the concrete floor.

Montague looked up with wonder at the towering figure dressed in black. His body felt shod in ice. He was vaguely aware through his pervading numbness that his teeth chattered and he was shivering like a wet dog.

"Sorry to borrow so much of your blood," DeVilbiss said, "but one must live as one can. Are you cold?"

"Yeh . . . yes."

"Hmm!" DeVilbiss arched his curved eyebrow even higher. "In such a warm room?"

Montague let his head loll, following DeVilbiss's stride to the mouth of the boiler furnace. The man opened the large door, letting in fresh air that made the flames roar hungrily. With a flourish, he threw the magazine and the book into the conflagration. He walked back toward Montague without having closed the door.

"Still cold?" DeVilbiss inquired.

This time, Fox's chattering affirmation broke the word into five syllables.

"Well, we can't have that!" DeVilbiss exclaimed. He scooped up Fox as easily as he had handled Bertrand, cradling him like a baby. "Not for such an artist!"

The last shred of Montague's sanity told him it was an idiotic gesture, yet something about his attacker's eyes and the reassuring tone of his voice made Fox want to thank the man. He concentrated on fixing his lips, so that he could utter a simple "thank you." Before he could manage the act, his feet had passed through the furnace doorway.

CHAPTER ONE

December 12–13

❧

He was so learned he could name a horse in nine languages,

so ignorant that he bought a cow to ride on.

—Benjamin Franklin

Simon Penn stared silently at the ocean-blue Mikasa plate. It had to be at least ten inches across, and the portion of food in its center looked like an island lost in the Pacific. Lynn had called it a "lasagna roll-up." It was undoubtedly the spawn of *The Pasta Diet* or her infernal *American Heart Association Cookbook*. As far as he was concerned, the one candle burning feebly in the center of the table, wreathed at its base with holly, was more than enough illumination.

Lynn aspersed low-cal dressing on Simon's salad as if it were holy water. Softly from the Bose speakers, Bing Crosby invited everyone to have themselves a merry little Christmas. The holiday was only thirteen days away, but this was the first time Simon had heard a Christmas song on the radio. Predictably, it was one that made no mention of Jesus.

"Oh! Remember I told you about the Schickner Collection?" Simon said, glad to have something to share. "It finally arrived. Over six hundred books, and more than half incunabula. But the most incredible part is the scrolls. Especially—"

"Have you called Kenneth yet?" Lynn interrupted, from behind his right shoulder.

Simon caught Lynn's image on the knife blade resting atilt on his cloth napkin. She looked unimpressed by his news. He knew why.

It was directly related to the free realtor's magazine she had picked up at the bank. With no regard to subtlety, she had placed the magazine above Simon's setting, opened to a page of homes "in the mid-$300,000s." He unfolded his napkin and dropped it on his lap without enthusiasm. "Yes, I called."

"Let me rephrase that: Did you *speak* with Kenneth?"

"No. He was in a meeting."

"He's always in a meeting," Lynn returned, topping her goblet with chilled Perrier, then emptying what was left into Simon's glass. "Did you tell his secretary who you were?"

"I left my name and phone number." Simon lifted his fork mechanically.

"I told you to use *my* name as well." Lynn sighed. "You'd be good at advertising, Simon. You have the imagination, not to mention all those weird facts you've been cramming into your head for the past thirty years."

As he dug a corner off the lasagna, Simon said, "The way I understand it, most clients don't appreciate imagination. And anyway, advertising's supposed to be dog-eat-dog."

"All business is dog-eat-dog if there's real money in it," Lynn riposted.

Real Money was the name of Lynn Gellman's game. Now thirty-four, she had entered the C. W. Post campus of Long Island University on the waning cusp of the Vietnam War era. But she had no affinity with students who had bought into the Great Society and the Peace Corps. Her path was too predirected to wander off into English literature or social work. Business administration was her major and psychology her minor. While pursuing her MBA with a marketing concentration at SUNY-Albany, she summer-interned at Dow Jones in Princeton, securing a job before she had graduated. A year at *the Wall Street Journal* headquarters had allowed her to ferret out better opportunities in the Princeton area. Central Jersey, she found, was the information nexus for the American psyche. The Gallup Organization and the Eagleton Institute polled political thinking; Educational Testing Service quantified learning levels;

three corporations—Opinion Research, Total Research, and Demographic Research—formed the Great Triumvirate for supplying "people knowledge" to business and industry.

Lynn became an account manager for Demo Research. She was the one who held the clients' hands and "interfaced" between them and the numbers crunchers back in Princeton. A dog-eat-dog Real Money job if ever there was one. Though she kept her finances to herself, Simon had lived with her long enough to know that her Princeton condo, her BMW, and her periodic safaris to Fifth Avenue had to be backed by at least seventy thousand a year. For two years they had split the expenses of basic necessities, shared a bed, a bathroom and even his bathrobe, but he knew that he would have to make Real Money before she shared her fiscal bottom line or his last name (the latter definitely with a hyphen). That's what this was all about. Biological clock ticking; need even at seventy thou for a second income to buy the "mid-$300,000" house, then add the in-ground pool to the backyard; enough left over to board Lynn's clone or clonette at the right private school. Past time for Simon to shoehorn himself into the Real Money game unless he wanted to be jettisoned.

"At least advertising's lively," Lynn persisted. *"You* work in a mausoleum."

"Some interesting people I know disagree," Simon answered. " 'I shall not wholly die. What's best of me shall escape the tomb.' "

Lynn again appeared manifestly unimpressed. "Which one of your dead friends wrote that?"

Simon looked at the front door, as if for escape. "Horace."

"Catchy. Too bad they didn't have advertising agencies in Horace's day." Not expecting a reply, Lynn plunged on. "You've got to start somewhere." She intensified the admonition with her fork.

"I will," Simon promised, "as soon I grow up."

"You're already too old to grow up," Lynn replied, icily. "I suggest you fake it."

They ate in silence. Her exhortation was almost a year stale, but Lynn continued to chew on it stubbornly, despite constant rebuffs. After each episode, Simon expected that she would give up and that he would find his things on the curb in front of her place the next day. But it had yet to happen.

The dessert was a yogurt sorbet. One scoop. The whole meal added up to less than eight hundred calories. Not that either of them was overweight. It was just that Lynn ate half of her meals with clients, all over the United States. Big power breakfasts, lunches, and dinners in the most chic restaurants from Boston to San Francisco. Large meals at home would jeopardize her trim figure. She was short but well proportioned, with rosy cheeks—suggesting that she got her health and shape from outdoor athleticism. In truth, she hated exercise, extremes of temperature, and anyplace where insects teemed.

"You want to go out and get a tree tonight?" Simon suggested as they cleared the table.

"Can't," Lynn answered. "I already took a Valium; I'll be asleep by nine."

"Something important tomorrow?" Simon asked.

Lynn shot him a vexed expression. "I told you last week: I'm in Chicago for three days. It begins tomorrow with a ten o'clock meeting."

"I don't remember your telling me," Simon murmured.

"It's *also* on the calendar. Your life is the same from day to day, but mine changes. Check it once in a while, okay?"

"Right. Let me finish the dishes then," Simon offered.

"Thanks." Lynn picked up the latest copies of *Forbes* and *The Atlantic* and started toward the bedroom. "Simon."

He turned with dishes in his hands.

"If you fill the dishwasher, don't run it tonight, huh?"

Simon nodded.

"What are *you* gonna do?" she asked, as an afterthought.

"Take a walk," he replied. Down on Witherspoon Street, Häagen-Dazs had all the fixings for a hot fudge cookies-and-cream sundae.

"It's raining," Lynn observed. "Probably turn to sleet before long."

Simon continued clearing the dishes.

"Well, at least dress warmly and take the doorman's umbrella." Lynn continued toward the bedroom. "It's a lucky thing you have me."

Simon fetched his rain gear. As he tugged it on, he reflected that Lynn's parting words had become the leitmotif of their relationship. But Lynn was not the only person who looked upon Simon as a lost soul. His parents and two sisters had all but given up on him. He had left Zanesville, Ohio, with such promise. Even after he had declared philosophy as his major at Princeton, his family members assured one another that it wasn't important. What would get Simon into a prestigious law or business school were high grades, the cachet of Princeton's name, and great GREs. Simon had gotten the high grades, the bachelor's degree, and good GREs. But, at thirty, he had not yet gotten around to applying to any professional schools.

Simon had paid for his room and board throughout college by working in the library. During those four years the brain center of the great academic institution had beguiled him. He had always held a scholar's reverence for books. The more he worked within the miles of stacks, browsing indiscriminately and voraciously, becoming ever more amazed by what wonders could be captured on paper, the less he wanted to work anywhere else. His resolve to secure a full-time position in the library became firm once he landed a temporary job in the Rare Manuscripts Preparation section. Over the decades, generous alumni had donated such rarities as a Gutenberg Bible, original opera scores of Richard Wagner, and original manuscripts from the estates of Emily Dickinson and the Brontë sisters. Simon's skills with Latin and Greek made him valuable for working with the ancient manuscripts that were slowly being added to the collection.

But Simon's constantly expanding store of esoteric knowledge and typical academician's salary left both the Penn family and Lynn Gellman unimpressed.

"It's a lucky thing you have me." The timbre and inflection of each syllable was etched in his mind.

He had met Lynn at the annual Bryn Mawr Book Sale, in the old gymnasium behind Town Hall. She had wondered aloud if a certain book was worth the price, and Simon had offered a quick critique of it. Looking back to those days, he deduced that her attraction to him was one of complements. Although she felt a need for exposure to the arts and letters, her single-minded drive toward business success had left little time for such subjects. Simon was an instant right brain, a living Trivial Pursuit game at her side, no matter in which direction the party conversation drifted. He knew, for example, the real reason why Citizen Kane's sled was called Rosebud, that the Eskimos in fact did not have twenty-two words for snow, and the name of the little indentation between the nose and upper lip. On those rare occasions when Lynn had leisure time, Simon was always free to attend McCarter Theatre or the University Guest Lecture Series. He was also appreciated and liked by the powerful people behind the scenes and, from part-time literary and theatrical pursuits, frequently ended up rubbing shoulders with the famous. Simon was sufficiently good-looking—fairly tall and wiry, with an intelligently attractive face and a head of thick, sandy-colored hair. He was four years her junior. He was also mild-mannered and malleable. Except in the matter of taking just any job to leave the library.

Simon stepped into the rain and raised the oversized orange and black umbrella. Across the street, the fortresslike redbrick walls of Princeton High School glistened in the streetlamp light. He started briskly toward the center of town, a quarter-mile away.

It was not that Simon anticipated working at the library for the rest of his life. He ached to be what he called "productive instead of just reproductive," perhaps to write books that others would catalogue and analyze. Or maybe he would enter a totally unrelated profession that uniquely served mankind in an enduring way. Whatever it might be, someone surely had written about it, and he was counting on serendipity and all those miles of book-filled shelves to lead him to the answer. Once that happened, he would shed the library like a chrysalis. Perhaps he could begin his metamorphosis sooner than that. He had become inured to Lynn's same old song to the point that he all but tuned it out, and yet lately he had become so personally dissatisfied with his life and so melancholic that even he had noticed it. Maybe tomorrow he'd leave Lynn's townhouse carrying more than an umbrella in his hand. Her absence was the perfect opportunity. That way he wouldn't have to hear how unlucky he was about to become.

The shortest path to Häagen-Dazs was through Princeton Cemetery. As American burial grounds figured, it was an old one. Pre-Revolutionary War by decades. It was also fairly impressive by dint of its inhabitants—a signer of the Declaration of Independence, a pair of governors, and one U.S. president lay under the rough grasses. It occupied five square blocks, bounded by an oft-painted black wrought-iron fence. Simon passed through the back gateway, still thinking about leaving Lynn.

Diffused light cast an eerie pall across the densely ranked headstones. The rain had softened to a cold mist. From the verdigris mottling of the copper-clad cathedral spire to the burnt green of the close-cropped grasses, the cold fog had stolen all color from the town and bleached it into a Steichen monochrome. The fog muffled the fall of Simon's feet and the sudden beating of a surprised dove's wings. Simon paused, to watch the bird vanish into the gloom. As his eyes drifted back toward the earth, his gaze fixed on a white figure. For an instant his mind believed it to be a memorial statue, a beautiful weeping angel he had once admired on a sunny day. Then his eyes told him the figure was not of stone but of flesh, and wrapped within an ankle-length white robe. The robe had arm slits on either side and a capuchin hood which hid the face within its shadows. From the shape and length, Simon judged the wearer to be a woman. Whoever it was, the figure stood statue-still, focused on one particular, massive gravestone. The flight of the dove had failed to distract her.

Simon sensed that the encounter held the potential to make a melancholy night memorable. Forgetting the hot fudge sundae, he moved forward with stealth and eased into a crouch. As soundlessly as he could, he collapsed the umbrella and propped it against the tombstone that concealed him.

The figure stretched a slender hand toward the gravestone in front of it. Fingertips brushed the granite as if with fear, then inched across its upper surface until the palm rested flat. The other hand appeared, rising to brush the hood back.

Simon held his breath. He knew the profile well. It was indeed a worthy model for an angelic statue, one to which a Michelangelo's skills would do justice. She pivoted in slow motion, straining to pierce the gloom and assure herself she was alone. Once she had turned a full circle, she stooped in front of the stone. From his vantage point, Simon could not see what she was doing. A soft noise accompanied her activity, too faint for him to identify. A minute later she stood and began working her way through the markers toward the walk. Her arms were again within the cloak, drawn up so that her elbows winged the material out on either side.

If she turned right, Simon could not help but be discovered. He knew where she lived, however, and he held his place, betting that her destination was home. She turned left and glided away until her white robe was lost in the fog.

Simon waited a moment, then stood up and raised his umbrella. He had lost the exact location of the gravestone that had held her interest. He was fairly certain, though, that he would find it by the carved name. As he scudded forward, he watched the sea of grass undulate over his shoetops, dropping dew and soaking through to his feet. Suddenly, he found the grassy carpet vandalized. A large divot had been torn out of the lawn and thrown aside. The hole beneath the spot was deep enough that Simon could not see its bottom. He considered plumbing it with his hand, then realized with real apprehension that this would put part of his anatomy into the world of the dead.

Simon peered up at the gravestone. The name was expected— another of the cemetery's noteworthy residents.

FREDERIK A. VANDERVEEN III
6/28/29–9/25/79
STATESMAN, PEACEMAKER
REQUIESCAT IN PACE

The stone was flanked by Vanderveens. Although many were too ancient and weatherbeaten to read, half the row's markers had the same last name. So did a street several blocks away and a wing of one of the university's halls. Among Simon's eclectic readings had been a history of Princeton. He knew that the Vanderveens were one of several Dutch families whose settlement predated and made possible the incorporation of the town. A long and venerable family tree, and the last living member of this particular branch had just left the cemetery.

Simon looked again at the hole. The strange sound he had heard was digging. He found an abandoned flowerpot and dropped it into the hole; it was only a few inches deep. There was no sign of the dirt. Simon had hoped for an interesting incident when he had first spotted her. He had gotten his wish. But now he expected to be eternally haunted by the mystery, because he knew he could never bring himself to ask Frederika Vanderveen why she stood cloaked in the cemetery, digging dirt from her father's grave in the dead of a December night.

The next morning, as Simon stepped off the curb at the corner of Jefferson and Wiggins, he was nearly crippled by a Mercedes. The driver had made a token gesture of stopping at the red sign, then used his engine's impressive horsepower to speed around the corner and beat the pedestrian to Wiggins Street's asphalt. Simon jumped back, but not far enough to avoid the spray of water puddled from the previous night's rain.

"Bastard!" Simon yelled, with anger but not surprise. Such get-out-of-my-way-I-own-the-road driving was commonplace in Princeton. If it wasn't a Mercedes, it was a BMW, Porsche, Jaguar, or perhaps even a Rolls-Royce. Princeton not only boasted the highest per capita percentage of Ph.D.s in the country but also had the densest concentration of millionaires. It was among a handful of chic commuter enclaves within reasonable distance from New York City. It was also surrounded by enough university-spun-off think tanks and research labs to make it a big-salary town in its own right. Though the town proper had only about five thousand residents, it offered a Laura Ashley shop, an outlet of The Nature Company, three bespoke tailor establishments, and seven investment firms with seats on the New York Stock Exchange. Businesses ten miles away borrowed its cachet, calling themselves Princeton Photo, Princeton Supplies, Princeton Park. Businesses twenty miles away used Princeton post office boxes for the same reason. People walked through the town wearing the zip code—08540—brassily silk-screened across their sweatshirts. At a New Year's Eve party a decade before, actress Julie Christie had remarked to Simon, "It's a snooty little town, isn't it?" When he asked her to elaborate, she said, "You'll never find a McDonald's on Main Street, will you?" Powerful financial pressures had eventually resulted in a Burger King invading Nassau Street (the town's "Main Street"), but it operated behind understated brown tile, and the only outward sign of its existence was the name, spelled out in restrained, ten-inch letters.

To the ancien régime, anyone not born in the town could never be considered a True Princetonian. That did not seem to daunt the influx of New Yorkers or the French industrialists, Iranian oligarchs, and Hong Kong plutocrats who poured in, driving the price of housing so high that Princeton was among the ten most expensive places to live in the United States. They needed another sweatshirt, Simon thought acerbically: PRINCETON: HOME OF THE ATTITUDE PROBLEM.

"Merry Christmas!" Simon yelled at the disappearing Mercedes, which had a wreath tied to its front grille. Even though he knew that preoccupied Princeton pedestrians were potential emergency-room candidates, his mind continued to ponder leaving Lynn, as well as to puzzle out the strange occurrence in the cemetery the previous night. Both subjects had kept him awake past midnight and were responsible for his waking up late. He had solved neither by the time he reached the front doors of Firestone Library. In spite of his hurry, as he crossed the yawning entrance area he slowed his pace and turned his head expectantly to the left, where a two-story wall of glass separated the foyer from the reference room like a modern-day cathedral screen. Frederika Vanderveen stood, engaged, on the opposite side, bathed in a wash of morning light.

29

Frederika's enthralling beauty emanated from more than the perfect features, figure, coloration, and carriage which made both men and women stop in the street and stare at her passing. Through his adult years, Simon had seen perhaps a score of women with her caliber of physical attractiveness. The others, however, seemed to radiate an aura of self-assurance that made common men call them bitches in their despair. These others knew their worth in the dating and marriage market. Their stares were challenging and assessing, while Frederika's eyes were usually unfocused in thought or downcast; their smiles were calculated and hard-edged, while hers were gentle and unsure; their dress was smart—hers was merely in style. The others were distinctly unapproachable, yet every man could imagine that his undying affection and sincere attentions could rescue Frederika from the sadness beneath her gentle smile. Other exquisite women worked at their allure; Frederika just didn't. Which made her the deadliest man-eater in Princeton.

A dark figure walked into Simon's line of sight and stopped. Simon could see that Frederika had captured another eye. He glanced at the man and found him, in his own way, almost as riveting as the woman. He was about five-ten, elegantly thin, and looked to be about forty-five. He wore L.L. Bean boots, tailored brown wool pants, a classically beat-up leather jacket, and a scarf that matched his pants. His large-pored skin was unnaturally pale, even more incongruous when Simon noted the blackness of his hair, except where gray tufted his temple. Simon angled himself for a better view. The man's eyes were hidden by silver-coated sunglasses. Long, thin fingers held a Dutch-boy cap in one hand and a European men's purse in the other. He radiated an aura no less potent than Frederika, except that his was one of power, pride, and intense force of will.

Simon turned away. He did not want to seem rude to the stranger. Nor did he want Frederika to see him standing there; she had caught him staring too often already. Simon turned to the right and walked briskly toward the Rare Manuscripts Preparation section.

A moment later, the pale-skinned man unfroze and crossed with purpose to the guard who oversaw the main turnstile.

"Excuse me," the man said, in an upper-class British accent. "Is access to the library free?"

"No, sir. There's a charge," said the guard. He waved a lethargic hand. "Ask at the desk."

The man pivoted around. His hand went up to his sunglasses. He looked at the winter light filtering in through the front doors and the reference room. He left the glasses in place. He approached the front desk and asked again about access.

"Twelve-fifty for a one-week pass," the librarian told him. "Twenty-five for a month. Access only; no checkout privileges."

"For a week, please," the man said, opening his purse.

"I'll need some kind of identification," the librarian said.

"Certainly," the man responded, through a dazzling white smile. "Will my international driver's license do?"

"Yes." The librarian accepted the license and studied it. "This will only take a minute, Mr. DeVilbiss," she said.

Because he was late, Simon took a shortcut through the Exhibitions Hall's showcases. He carried a standard Swiss army knife as a key ring. He dug it out of his pocket and blindly fingered through the half dozen keys until he had the one he wanted. Unlocking the nondescript wooden doors that concealed the entrance to the Rare Manuscripts Preparation section, he was confronted by a forbidding gate of woven steel wire. He hurried through the gate's unlocking procedure and entered his domain, the cluttered and musty-smelling warren where things rare were codified, analyzed, and preserved. The caged-in bookshelves on both sides of the passageway were crowded for the first time in Simon's recollection. The bequest of Abraham Schickner was huge—more than six hundred books, the majority either hand-scribed or printed before A.D. 1500. Simon could not help shortening his stride; his eyes insisted on sweeping along the cracked and wizened spines of the special books. Most were written in Latin or Greek. From the titles it was obvious that Schickner's preferences ran to religious books and their antitheses—volumes on magic, the occult, superstition, and the supernatural. Histories, philosophies, and eloquently phrased yet

31

benighted scientific tomes peppered the collection. But the greatest prizes were stored in a pair of special, airtight cases. Made of stainless steel brushed to a satin sheen, the cases were roughly the size and shape of coffins, their lids incised with curving windows of tempered, shatterproof glass. Inside, under pressurized inert gas, rested thirty papyrus and vellum scrolls, some dating from hundreds of years before Christ walked the earth. The security lights of the case nearer the wall winked on and off, because its contents had been removed. One of the two persons who had taken them out had to be Dr. Gould, Simon's boss. By default the other keyholder was the Reverend Wilton Edward Spencer, Willy to his friends.

Reverend Spencer had grown up as the only son of a well-to-do Virginia landowner, had served for decades as the pastor of an equally well-to-do Presbyterian church, and had picked up the unusual study of Akkadian and Ugaritic grammar. Upon retirement, he spent several years in Syria and Iraq, becoming a world authority on the two dead languages. Now almost seventy, he taught at the venerable Princeton Theological Seminary, passing on his rare knowledge to other religious scholars.

Willy Spencer's residency at the seminary had had a great deal to do with the Schickner Collection being bequeathed to nearby Princeton University, because the crown jewels among Abraham Schickner's treasures were a unique pair of Akkadian scrolls with a mysterious history. The scrolls had been discovered in a cave near the Caspian Sea and had been carbon dated back to about 600 B.C. The country they had been smuggled out of was never specified, for fear that its government would some day learn of the discovery and sue for their return. The loss would have been painful even for the multimillionaire, since he had won the treasures in 1957 by bidding $600,000 in an ultrasecret, ultraexclusive auction. His prizes were made of calfskin, both wrapped around cedar rollers. The author's real name was unknown, but the Greek who had translated the work into his own language in the early fourth century B.C. dubbed him Ahriman. In the Zoroastrian faith, Ahriman was the Devil. Tucked among both prescient and fantastic statements was a pointed denunciation of the beliefs and practices of many religious groups of that time, particularly the Zoroastrians who dominated the south-land around the Caspian Sea.

The scrolls were titled *Physics* and *Metaphysics,* the latter for things that Ahriman claimed to exist beyond the physical world. Scholars had only had the Greek translation to work with, as published in 1503 by the great Venetian printer Aldus Manutius. All earlier, hand-scribed copies seemed to vanish around the beginning of the sixteenth century. While some were of the opinion that Aristotle had read the work and patterned his own encyclopedic *Physics* and *Metaphysics* after it, most dismissed the Ahriman texts as the ravings of a brilliant but insane mystic. Those few scholars who had read the book had little time to form their opinions: less than a month after Aldus had printed the book, legates of the pope descended on Venice, confiscated all unsold copies, and ordered under threat of excommunication that Aldus never reproduce the work again. Pope Alexander VI had apparently found Ahriman's lack of faith as disturbing and threatening as the Zoroastrians had. Forty-eight copies had been sold. The Church's agents tracked down thirty-five and burned them. The rest went as safely underground as the Christians in the catacombs. Through the centuries single copies emerged in public; they promptly disappeared. On separate occasions, a library and a museum and all their holdings had been totally destroyed by fire within days after receiving a copy of the book. Each had had, for its time, a redoubtable security system. The museum, in Leipzig, had been consumed in 1823. Since that time, no other copies had publicly surfaced.

This, as Willy Spencer had related it to Simon, was the bizarre background of the two scrolls and their translations over the last twenty-five hundred years. Now Willy had been given access to what were possibly the originals of those scrolls. In 1958, soon after secretly purchasing the treasures, Abraham Schickner had brought in the great German scholar of Akkadian, Professor von Soden. Von Soden had taken only three days to declare that even though the calfskins were ancient, the purchase was nevertheless a clever forgery. He gave three reasons for his opinion: All other Akkadian texts of that period were written on baked clay tablets; the Akkadian

33

grammar was imperfect; and the science on the scrolls was far too advanced for six hundred years before the birth of Christ.

There was no greater authority for Schickner to turn to for dispute. In disappointment, he stored away what he assumed was a very expensive mistake, and the world remained ignorant of the scrolls' existence. Then, six months ago, Willy Spencer had published a scholarly monograph that showed the limits of von Soden's understanding of certain Akkadian local dialects. In excitement, Schickner had written to Reverend Spencer and included transcriptions of portions of his Ahriman scrolls. Spencer had written back from a summer dig in Turkey that he would be honored to examine the scrolls when he returned. Then Schickner learned that he had cancer of the brain and only weeks to live. He had willed his entire book collection to Princeton Library, with the stipulation that Wilton Spencer do a complete translation of Ahriman's *Physics* and *Metaphysics*.

Word of such a spectacular bequest was not long in leaking out. *The Journal of Written Antiquities* was first to announce it, followed swiftly by *The Chronicle of Higher Education* and the *New York Times*. Even before the books arrived, scholars and journalists were besieging Spencer for information on the mysterious Ahriman scrolls. So far, he had refused to release a single word of his work.

Simon approached the reverend with a purposely heavy tread. He knew how adept the old man was at masking out the rest of the world while working and how angry Willy became when jolted from his concentration.

Spencer looked up and smiled. "Morning, Simon!"

"Good morning, sir," Simon returned. The old pastor bore a vague resemblance to Albert Einstein, a former Princeton U. professor who still commanded godlike reverence on campus. Willy was bald on top but sported a wild victor's wreath of white hair above his ears. He wore wire-rimmed glasses which perched perpetually on the tip of his nose, and when he smiled he displayed a slight gap between his two front teeth. The weight of years had pressed his frame down a couple inches, to five foot seven. His trousers and shirt changed from day to day, but he always wore the same paisley tie,

34

the pattern of which varied slightly, depending on the viscosity of Willy's recent lunches.

"I'm not seeing any more visitors," Willy announced, suddenly removing his smile. "I've given enough interviews and gawks," he muttered, swinging his hawklike gaze back at the scroll rolled out before him under protective glass. "I'll never get this translated otherwise."

"I understand. How's it coming?" Simon asked, stealing a glance at the ancient treasure. For their age, the mottled buff and tan surfaces had retained a remarkable resiliency, cracked in places and corroded at the edges, but still largely intact. The ink had not survived as well, and Simon wondered how Willy's old eyes distinguished many marks, despite his magnifying instrument and ample light.

"It's coming fine, fine. Just beginning, of course. But I don't believe it's a fake."

"No, huh?"

"In spite of being on vellum rather than clay. Don't know what to make of that, but then again, the materials aren't my concern; only the words." Spencer pushed the spectacles up to the bridge of his nose, for yet another slow run down the slope.

"And the words are convincing you?" Simon prompted, fascinated by the man's mind almost as much as the magnificent scrolls.

"They are. I can understand why von Soden rejected it. Great as he was, he didn't have the knowledge we've gained since his time. Semiotics has taken a quantum leap in the past two decades. It's not only the peculiar blending of ideogrammatic and phonetic usage but also a unique form of unpronounced determinatives." Spencer babbled on in his jargon, assuming that Simon understood every word. Simon wasn't even trying. He had no interest in Akkadian and would be happy when he could read Spencer's translation along with everyone else. His attention was instead focused on the shape of the characters. To him, cuneiform writing looked like a pick-up-sticks game played with large-headed concrete nails. How the detective-scholars had deciphered this lost language in the first place astonished him.

35

Simon waited until Spencer lost some steam and was catching his breath before he said, "I don't want to be as annoying as the visitors, sir. I'll let you get back to work."

"You can interrupt me any time, Simon," Willy offered, winking. "Any time."

Simon thanked Willy, took a printout from his desk and left the room by the main exit. With his nose buried in the report, he was unaware of the sounds of the self-locking gate and doors as he walked out to the main catalog section. His objective was to see if any of the items in the Schickner Collection were already owned by the library. He seated himself at one of the catalog desks and became so engrossed in his task that he was completely unaware of the person who had come up on the opposite side.

"Excuse me," Frederika said.

Simon lifted his eyes from his work. The voice was not immediately familiar to him, but he placed the dress and the figure instantly, so that his head snapped back and his eyes rolled wide, like a doll suddenly uprighted.

"Oh! I'm sorry," Frederika apologized, now equally startled.

"That's all right," Simon assured, rising from the chair with instinctive civility.

"I'm Frederika Vanderveen."

"Yes, I know. Reference. We've talked . . . on the elevator. And you were on the gurney next to me during the last blood drive."

"Oh. Right." Her voice sounded huskier than he remembered, although he had not had an opportunity to hear it for several months.

"I'm Simon Penn."

"I know. I'd like to ask you a favor," Frederika said, in a timid tone.

"I hope you don't want to see the Ahriman scrolls," Simon replied, honestly.

Frederika shook her head. "But it is about another of the Schickner books. I understand the *Memphis Grimoire* is part of the collection."

"Is it?" Simon asked. "I don't know, offhand."

"Yes." Frederika leaned forward and set her delicate hand on the exposed page. "I've seen a copy of this printout." As her finger traced slowly down the list, her fine, golden hair gradually cascaded around her face. Simon inhaled the delicate fragrance of her.

"I don't even know what a grimoire is," Simon admitted.

Frederika's forefinger moved on. "A book of rites and incantations. Magic."

"Oh."

"Here it is."

Simon moved his eyes unwillingly from Frederika and looked at the information below her finger. "Yes. What about it?"

"I'd like to see it."

Simon offered her an apologetic mien. "Sorry. Dr. Gould doesn't like unauthorized people in our section under ordinary circumstances. With those scrolls in there, everyone with pull has been finding an excuse, so an edict was made."

"I see. Well, could you bring this one book out for me?"

Simon shook his head. "Nobody outside the section can handle it until it's deacidified and theftproofed."

"That's a shame." Frederika winced and glanced forlornly in the direction of the Rare Manuscripts section's closed doors.

Simon eased back onto the stool. It occurred to him that this was now the longest conversation he had ever held with the woman, and that his refusal threatened to bring it to an abrupt end. "Is this for you?" he asked, to keep it alive.

Frederika laughed. "For me? No. It's for an old college roommate. She's doing graduate work on medieval history, and her thesis is on witchcraft. This grimoire's very rare, so she can't have it sent through interlibrary loan. When I told her we were getting a copy she freaked out. It would really complete her research. There's one at the Library of Congress, but she can't get down there for several weeks. By then her advisor's on sabbatical. It'll delay her graduation half a year." Her words tumbled out with remarkable fluidity, as if she were reciting the Pledge of Allegiance.

Simon missed the rote sound of Frederika's reply; his thoughts focused on the many negative things he had heard about her, trying

37

to reconcile them with the image of innocence she projected. "I assume she reads Latin."

"No," Frederika answered.

"Rather shortsighted for a medievalist." Simon scanned the basic information on the book and whistled softly. "Two hundred and five pages!"

"She doesn't need the whole thing," Frederika said quickly. "There's supposed to be one chapter on necromancy."

Simon's eyebrows lifted. "Raising the dead?"

"Exactly. That's all she wants out of it."

Simon registered the intensity of Frederika's expression. Her former roommate had to be some fast friend to have commanded this kind of concern on Frederika's part. Seated behind the large desk, with Frederika standing on the other side, he felt like a high school principal. Her Alice in Wonderland look, in a blue dress with white pinafore, only made him more uncomfortable. "Maybe I can help."

Frederika brightened. "Really?"

"But I also need help," Simon ventured. He hoped to God he could keep his face from turning crimson. Rather than dangle a silence that invited limitless assumptions, he plunged on. "You rent a room in your home. I suddenly need a place. It would only be for two weeks."

"I don't understand," Frederika said. "What happened to the place you've been living in?"

"It's my girlfriend's. My ex-girlfriend's." His face begged her not to push for further explanation.

"How did you know I had a room?"

"How?" She was sizing him up as he spoke. Thanks to his friend, Neil, he knew the room was empty. It was a struggle to keep an ingenuous look on his face. He felt the dreaded blush rising. "I overheard a girl student mention it last year. Is she still renting from you?"

"No. The room's vacant," Frederika said, still thinking. She lifted her hand to her mouth, to cover the gentle clearing of her throat. The reason for the rougher quality in her voice registered on him.

"Sounds like a cold coming on," he said.

"You don't intend to share my toothbrush, do you?" she asked, sounding only slightly sarcastic.

The pent-up blush suffused Simon's face. "I didn't mean . . ." He became aware that Frederika's helpless little-girl look had gradually transformed into that of an assured woman.

"I'm sure you didn't."

"I'll pay you whatever's fair," Simon pushed. "Say three hundred for the rest of the month?" Her sudden shift in attitude unnerved him, compelling him to increase his intended offer: "I could have the passages translated by tomorrow night."

Frederika glanced again at the Rare Manuscripts section doors. "She'll need the ritual part—you know, the words the magician speaks to raise the dead—translated *and* in Latin," she told Simon.

Simon's elation lifted him from the stool. He extended his hand. "Deal. Just as long as I don't have to work with hieroglyphics."

Confusion pinched Frederika's face. "Excuse me?"

Simon's arm hung in midair like a railroad crossing gate. He had gotten what he wanted, and yet he found himself pointlessly prattling on. *"Memphis Grimoire,"* he said, sheepishly. "I assume it . . . originally came from ancient Egypt."

"Ah. Yes." She sniffed once and squeezed her eyes shut. "I think you're right about that cold."

"I have a surefire remedy," Simon offered.

"That's okay," Frederika answered. "The translation and the rent will be enough." She put her hand gently in Simon's. Neither of them made an effort to shake. "I live on Hodge Road."

"I'll find it," he said, although he knew where she lived.

Frederika's warm smile brought dimples to her cheeks. "Till tomorrow night, then." She swung around abruptly and walked toward the Reference section.

Simon stared for two minutes at the printout, then took out his keys and reentered the Rare Manuscripts chamber. He moved quietly past the engrossed Willy Spencer and on to the storage cages. Keys still in hand, he unlocked the door that opened onto the occult and supernatural works. His eyes swept along the shelf just above his head, reading the spines of *Le Tarot des Bohemians*, *De Arte Cabalistica*, *Malleus Maleficarum*, the *Sefir Yetsirah*, the *Kabbalah*, and *Fama Fraternitatis*. On the shelf below, a clutch of crack-spined works huddled together as if in dark conspiracy: the *Testament of Solomon*, the *Sword of Moses*, the *Grimoire Verum*, *Lemegeton*, *Hell's Coercion*, and finally the *Memphis Grimoire*. Simon knew they were all just so much ancient foolishness, but when his fingers touched the *Memphis Grimoire* a shiver ran up his arm and into the base of his skull. He drew the book gently from the shelf and locked the cage.

As Simon walked back to his desk, he thought about sharing the same roof with Frederika Vanderveen. Reason warned him it was just a place to stay for a while, possibly the unexpected chance to learn something about her digging dirt from her father's grave. Nothing intimate could or would happen between them. The first woman for whom Simon had ever fully lowered the drawbridge of his emotional defenses had been almost as beautiful as Frederika. He had been a teaching assistant in philosophy and she a student in his "precept" section who made clear her interest in extracurricular activities. He had knowingly betrayed ethical standards by dating and bedding her on the sly before she had finished the course, but he redeemed himself by giving her the final B grade she deserved. When she ended their brief relationship at the start of the next semester, Simon assumed it was out of anger. He learned only after months of futile pursuit that lowering her panties for successive teachers was her peculiar stratagem for raising her grades. When Simon moved in with Lynn it had been a deliberate decision of head rather than heart, and now he knew it to be just as great an error in judgment. He refused to allow his heart's compass to spin back wildly toward physical magnetism. He resolved that when the next two weeks had passed, he would have nothing to regret.

CHAPTER TWO

December 13

∽

. . . A good book is the precious life-blood of a

master spirit, embalmed and treasured up

on purpose to a life beyond life.

—Milton, *Areopagitica*, sec. 6

Y ou want ketchup?" the waitress asked, as she set down the plate.

"Yes, indeed," her customer replied, flashing a smile that was inviting in spite of his slightly long incisors.

The waitress grabbed a bottle of ketchup from the only unoccupied table in the restaurant and plunked it down in front of the neatly dressed man. "Anything else?"

"Not right now, thank you," DeVilbiss said. He inched the plate to one side to make room for his newspaper. When he looked up again, the waitress had disappeared. DeVilbiss beamed at his food. P.J.'s Pancake House had been a find. By far the best hamburgers in Princeton, and especially the version in front of him now—medium rare, topped with melted cheese and chili. Big steak fries on the side, smothered in ketchup. A wedge of lettuce and a slice of tomato for balance. American cuisine at its simple best.

DeVilbiss spooned a steaming heap of chili into his mouth, then turned his attention to the other diners. The cozy eatery was brightly lit, seeming to reflect the cheery mood of its customers. Many still wore ruddy glows from the December cold outside. To his left, however, one woman's face, wreathed in her own cigarette smoke, looked as pale as the haze that enveloped it. Past her left shoulder, DeVilbiss saw a man who appeared to be in his sixties, wearing an obvious hairpiece and without eyebrows. Probably in the throes of cancer therapy, DeVilbiss guessed. Other than those two, the rest of the crowd appeared healthy, especially the college kids filling the booths, pink-skinned with sparkling eyes and thick, shiny hair.

But looks were deceiving, DeVilbiss knew. Autopsies on hundreds of Vietnam War fatalities had proven it. Even by their teenage years, the seeds of destruction had been sown. Deposits of fat had already begun to build up in their veins. Death had written its name on all of them, everyone in this restaurant and out on the streets beyond. Everyone except him.

DeVilbiss returned to his burger with gusto, savoring the rich marbling of fat that made it so tasty, wolfing down the deep-fat-fried potatoes. There was no danger to him here. As he ate, he leafed through the pages of the *Princeton Packet,* scanning the columns. At last he found the advertisement he had placed. Below his name and lettered pseudocredentials was the announcement of his recent establishment in Princeton and his services. Astrologer, herbal health counselor, and channeler with the departed. It was more than a front; even the Undead needed the means to stay alive. These were also services that people most often sought after dark. Most important, as ridiculous as they were, they gave him an excuse for being here.

DeVilbiss divided his attention between his food and the teenage couple at the table squeezed beside him. They were earnestly engaged in the subtle business of verbal courtship, neither too skilled nor too inept at it. Precisely right, he judged, for persons their age. DeVilbiss swallowed his last fry and glanced at his wristwatch. Time to be going. Firestone Library closed in forty minutes. He did not want to get there just before closing. Too much chance of someone wondering why they hadn't seen him leave.

DeVilbiss paid his check and stepped into the night air. It was, a radio weatherman had informed, an unusually cold December for New Jersey. DeVilbiss had smiled at the news. The weatherman had obviously not been around in the late 1880s, when the snow in December had drifted to the tops of telegraph lines, or even in the 1920s, when the Hudson River had frozen solid from bank to bank.

He had. He'd seen more than five hundred winters, from a hundred different locales throughout Europe and North America.

Entering the library, DeVilbiss moved without hesitation to the Microforms Reading Room. Together with the Reference Room and the Exhibitions Hall, it was one of the three areas that could be used without entering the main part of the library. And the only way into the main area was strictly regulated by both a narrow turnstile linked to a counter and a guard who scrutinized all access cards. A dozen feet away, another guard checked all outgoing bags and brief-cases and made sure that an exit turnstile ticked off each departure. DeVilbiss was not about to have the two turnstiles disagree in their counts at closing time. He noted that the Microforms librarian was well occupied in answering a student's question. He glided past, unnoticed, selected a roll of microfilm, and moved to a reading machine in the farthest corner of the room. He was well versed in using such a room; it had become one of the requirements for his existence. At ten minutes before closing, he rewound the film and took it back into the long line of shelves that held the complete records of the world's most important newspapers. At the back of the shelves, in a dark corner, sat a reading machine with an OUT OF ORDER sign taped to its lens housing. DeVilbiss drew a reshelving cart in front of the machine and crammed himself under the little table that supported it. He listened to the public address announcement about the library's closing, made no movement as the librarian walked down the rows flicking off the lights, and remained statue-like as the room became engulfed in darkness.

DeVilbiss trained his acute hearing on the sounds of the library, sensing sounds from far down corridors and around corners as the last of the staff exited the building. His pupils swelled until the amber color of his irises all but disappeared. The feeble beams of a single outdoor lamplight filtering through the windows made the room as bright as midday to him. He focused Zenlike concentration on his watch's second hand as it swept ten times around the face. Then he rose from his cramped concealment and walked with silent assur-ance toward the entry hall.

After purchasing his access pass that morning, DeVilbiss had

44

planted himself in front of the seven-level floor plan in the card catalog section, sweeping his eyes back and forth until he had it roughly memorized. Next, he had made an unhurried circumambulation of the building, verifying doors and exits. As he did, he noted with dismay that the library had extensive door and fire alarms and fire dousing systems.

From the entry area DeVilbiss exited right, heading through the Exhibitions Hall. The floor plan had shown him that the Rare Manuscripts Preparation section was only one door secluded in that direction as opposed to two doors distant through the center of the library. These were the only two means of access; the repository of the library's most precious documents sat as insulated as any ancient fortress's inner keep.

Every few seconds DeVilbiss paused and listened. Satisfied, he moved on until he reached the unmarked double doors. His fingers pressed against them, feeling for the telltale pulsing of electricity. He sensed nothing. He withdrew a set of picks from his coat pocket and knelt before the lock. He was surprised to see that the apparatus was somewhat old-fashioned. He rummaged among his pockets for less-used tools. The noises he made masked the crepe-soled footfalls of the approaching guard until escape was impossible. He barely had time to stuff the lock-picking tools back into his pockets, stand and present a confused face.

The guard turned the corner and stopped dead. His hand rose automatically; his finger flicked on the flashlight in mid-movement so that the beam swept across DeVilbiss's chest and onto his face. DeVilbiss offered a sheepish grin.

"My God, I'm glad you happened along!" he exhaled, moving forward slowly, palms open and up. "I thought I'd be locked in the dark all night."

The guard's tense face relaxed a fraction at the amiable English accent. He kept the flashlight on DeVilbiss's face, however. "Didn't you hear the announcement?" he asked, peevishly.

"As a matter of fact, I didn't," DeVilbiss said, stopping about ten feet from the guard. "Absent-minded professor, what? Over here on sabbatical from Oxford. Political science department?"

The guard nodded noncommittally. His eyebrows were still knit.

"If you could show me the quickest way out, I'd be ever so grateful," DeVilbiss continued. His eyes fixed momentarily on the thick ring of keys hanging from the guard's belt.

"Do you have some identification, professor?" the guard asked, backing carefully toward a small table set against the wall.

"Why yes, of course," DeVilbiss gushed. "In my inside jacket pocket. All right if I fish in?"

The guard nodded.

DeVilbiss moved toward the desk as he withdrew his billfold. He flipped it open and set it gingerly on the desk. "My library access card's the very top one."

The guard moved forward, keeping the light in DeVilbiss's face.

"I say, this is rather rude treatment," DeVilbiss complained, shielding his eyes from the glare, "especially after I almost had an accident coming down that stairwell over there." He gestured broadly with his left arm. As he did he took a small step forward. "I trust you know there's an iron bar standing out from the wall, about this long." His right hand went up as a distance measurer. The guard glanced away from the billfold, which he had just picked up, to follow the sweep of DeVilbiss's hand. "A person could—"

With an unhuman quickness, DeVilbiss thrust himself forward, grabbed the guard by both ears and gave his head a vicious left-hand twist. The neck snapped noisily. The guard's eyes and mouth flew open, but no sound came forth. The flashlight dropped from his grasp. DeVilbiss caught it deftly in midair with his left hand and taloned into the guard's jacket with his right, preventing the dead weight from hitting the floor.

"—break his neck," DeVilbiss finished. He lowered the heavyset man easily to the floor and reclaimed his fallen billfold. His head swung slowly from one side to the other, his eyes darting in thought. He squeezed them shut for a moment, remembering. There were fire alarm boxes in every room, but one set into the wall two rooms away was particularly useful for his purpose. He hefted the guard over his shoulder and strode to the place. After he dumped the body on the floor he entered the nearest stairwell, which was in the pro-

46

cess of being painted. He was relieved to see that the tall stepladder he had observed in the morning had not been moved. He carried it back to the place where the guard lay. He lifted his black turtleneck sweater and unwound twenty feet of rope he wore around his middle. Such ropes had provided escapes for him a score of times in the past. He needed it now for another purpose. After listening to the library and assuring himself that no more guards moved nearby, he scaled the ladder and tossed the rope over a sprinkler pipe that ran just below the line of the ceiling. He climbed down and tied a noose, which he slipped around the corpse's broken neck. Then he hauled the body upward, until its shoes dangled three feet off the carpet. He tied off the rope and tilted the ladder at a wild angle against the wall, as if the guard had kicked it away. He stepped back to survey his handiwork, then took the guard's right leg and swung it lightly toward the wall. He satisfied himself that if the "suicide" had been alive and struggling with a last-minute change of heart, the toe of his shoe could reasonably have punched in the fire alarm glass. He exited the room wearing a smile of self-satisfaction.

Holding the guard's ring of keys, DeVilbiss walked back to the doors that concealed the Rare Manuscripts Preparation section. A subring held a single key which had seen much use. DeVilbiss selected it and fitted it easily into the lock. He turned the key and pulled the door fully back. Just beyond lay a gate formed of bars and heavy steel mesh. Before he could examine this new obstacle, DeVilbiss noticed a triangle midway up the small space of wall between the door and gate. The triangle was formed of three small plastic buttons, one green, one yellow, one red. The red button abruptly winked on and then began to flash.

DeVilbiss's head snapped back in surprise. The damned library already had daytime guards, turnstiles, security patrols, locked doors, and steel gates. Why did it also need an interior entry alarm system? Could anyone be that paranoid over books—even rare ones? Caught unprepared, DeVilbiss cast his eyes frantically around the entryway for a means to disarm the alarm. The button stopped winking and glowed a hot, threatening red. A moment later, a bell's persistent clang ripped through the deep silence. DeVilbiss conceded that the shutoff switch was in another location. He refocused on the greater problem before him. His sensitive eyes peered through the bars and wire at the rows of ancient books, stored behind yet more steel mesh.

DeVilbiss heard sounds of entry, echoing from the main hall. Growling in frustration, he shoved the wooden doors inward and assured himself that they locked automatically. He sprinted through the rooms, returned to the corpse, and reattached the ring of keys. His fist punched into the fire alarm, shattering the glass and sending up more strident clanging that merged with the din of the alarm behind the Rare Manuscripts area's doors.

The library extended three stories below ground level and three above. The top towers rose into a rough cruciform shape above the main structure, like the central keep of a castle. Staying barely ahead of the rapid footfalls, DeVilbiss entered the nearest stairwell and climbed. Memory told him that it ascended all the way to the highest part of the structure, where the elevator machine room and the hot-air draw fans were housed. The clanging of the alarms was just as loud near the top, reverberating through the long shaft. DeVilbiss reached the top level and moved toward the door. He found it also wired to detect entry and exit. He could leave no evidence that anyone had left the building after the alarms were tripped—not with the scrolls still secure.

DeVilbiss looked up. Twelve feet directly above lay a trapdoor, secured with a simple draw bolt. On the wall just below it were two grab irons. Farther down, the wall was smooth. A ladder was evidently carried up when access was needed, no doubt a precaution against free-spirited students. DeVilbiss climbed onto the rail at the top of the stairs. He stretched up his hands, coiled his legs and jumped. His catch was sure and two-handed. He pulled himself up to the top iron, hung by one hand and undid the bolt. Monkeylike, he kicked the trapdoor open, then swung up and out into the night. He lowered the trapdoor and dug into one of his many coat pockets. His hand came out holding an alnico magnet, wrapped with several feet of twine. He put his ear to the trapdoor and ran the magnet along its surface until he heard the bolt slide into place. He repocketed the magnet and duck-walked to the edge of the tower.

Official vehicles idled close by on two sides of the library. Their bubble-gum lights whirled brightly but their sirens were mute. The alarms, so strident within the library, could barely be heard. Just across the roofs and over a small stretch of lawn lay Nassau Street, Princeton's main thoroughfare. Street traffic and a throng of moviegoers leaving the Garden Theatre flowed along quietly, unaware of the turmoil on campus. It was as if the university did whatever it could to shelter its problems from the outside world. What amazed DeVilbiss most was the absence of fire engines. He wondered if the library's fire system was sufficiently sophisticated not to alert the firehouse unless the sprinkler mechanisms were opened.

Several Gothic stone spires decorated the tower's parapets. Any one of them would have provided a perfect belaying point for his rope, if he had still had it. DeVilbiss estimated the drop to the lower roof to be about thirty feet. He moved to the darkest side of the tower, scanned the campus below, then vaulted confidently over the parapet. He repeated his feat from roof to roof until he landed on the ground behind a clump of holly bushes. He straightened up and brushed himself off.

"Hey, you! Come out of there!"

DeVilbiss turned. A campus policeman stood ten feet from him, with the thong of a wooden nightstick wrapped around his right hand. DeVilbiss obeyed his command.

"What were you doing in there?" the policeman demanded.

"I was looking for my dog," DeVilbiss replied, this time without the amiable persona he had affected for the library guard. "Have you seen a black and white mutt, about this big?" DeVilbiss advanced, holding both hands up.

"No. I—"

"Damned cur!" DeVilbiss spat. "I just tripped over a root or something in there. Nearly tore my pants."

"You'll have to call for him out on the walks," the policeman said. The nightstick lowered to his side.

DeVilbiss brushed himself off again, this time dramatically. "I'm not going to call him at all, Officer," he said, with injury in his voice. "He can jolly well freeze to death for all I care."

The officer labored to hold back a smile. It was precisely what DeVilbiss had hoped for. Character role accomplished, he turned his back and walked with a dignified pace toward Nassau Street. He counseled himself that the best thief in the world would not have anticipated such an elaborate security system, that even despite this his foray had not been a total disaster. He had learned that he needed a key and an alarm access code . . . or a person who had both. As he rounded the corner onto the sidewalk his eyes fixed on the huge library. His next offensive would be foolproof.

CHAPTER THREE

December 14–15

❧

Thou hast power until the word is spoken;

then it gains mastery over thee.

—*Saki, Bustan, ch. 7 (ca. 1252)*

Simon parked the borrowed pickup truck in front of the mansion and just stared. The whole of West Princeton was mildly obscene in its affluence. The average house sat on an acre and a half, had twelve rooms, three full baths, and three chimneys and went on the market at three quarters of a million dollars. The Vanderveen house was larger than average. Like most of the manses in the area, it had been built at the turn of the century and was more impressive for its size than its aesthetics. If his eclectic memory served him, Simon remembered this particular style as Federal Greek Revival, defined by Doric-columned pediments, white stucco exterior walls, half-moon-topped, ceiling-to-floor windows, and cracked, clay-footed pots awaiting summer planting.

Darkness had begun to claim the cold earth. A bluish tint washed across the dusting of snow on the lawns. Simon glanced at his watch. Not even five o'clock. It was no wonder so many people became despondent around the winter solstice. He had once browsed a copy of *Smithsonian* that touched on the physiological effects of lack of light. Winter depression now had a clinical name—Seasonal Affective Disorder, or SAD for short. Scientists had recently discovered that humans need a minimal amount of natural light striking the eye's retina in order to suppress the release of a depressant hormone called melatonin. Maybe that was what Tommy Wheeler, the night guard at the library, had needed. Simon had been shocked at his suicide. Tommy had enthusiastically shared plans for his retirement with Simon only a week before. Maybe he had gotten bad news about his health. Now Tommy was part of the high December suicide statistic. Simon gathered up the sheets of notebook paper that lay on the passenger's seat and climbed out.

It was difficult to imagine that this entire house was inhabited by one person. Simon found it even more difficult to picture Frederika as its mistress. It was a masculine dwelling, like a temple for a male deity. Her father had also lived in it alone, but that seemed proper. Frederik A. Vanderveen III, after all, had been something of an earthbound god. Simon vaguely recalled his death, sometime just before Simon had graduated. Vanderveen held an endowed chair at the university, which meant that his teaching load was minimal. As with Joyce Carol Oates in the program in creative writing, one of the main purposes of his appointment had been to enhance the already awesome prestige of the institution. Nominally a full professor in the Woodrow Wilson School of Public and International Affairs, he had spent far more of his time on meridian-chasing jets. His expertise was in world hunger and its relief. He had been for a time the United States' representative on the Council of FAO, the Food and Agricultural Organization of the United Nations. He had also served as a longtime advisor for Oxfam. His obituary had listed a spate of honorary degrees. The *Daily Princetonian* and the *Princeton Packet* had both expended great quantities of ink in praising the man and deploring his untimely death from a massive heart attack. From the cemetery marker, Simon remembered his age as merely fifty. Your basic beloved humanitarian and superhero, Simon thought, as he passed under the shelter of the massive portico.

Simon noted that the house held no sign of the holiday season, not so much as a wreath on the front door. He reflected that it would have cost a small fortune in wreaths, lights, garlands, or whatever to turn this somber structure into a festive home. He rapped with the brass door knocker. A cough sounded from a distance within and then another, closer. Frederika opened the door. She wore jeans and a turtleneck pullover under an Icelandic sweater. A mid-length leather coat hung from her hand, dragging on the floor.

Simon thrust forward the sheets of paper, like a teenager presenting his first prom corsage. "The translation."

"Thank you." Frederika folded the pages carelessly with one hand and stuffed them into her pants pocket. "Let me help you with your things."

"No, don't," Simon said. "You'd better not come outside with that cold."

"It's okay," she insisted. "Anyway, I have to show you your entrance." She dug into her opposite pocket and took out a shiny key.

"This *is* a furnished room, isn't it?" Simon asked. "Because I put my furniture in one of those public storage places."

Frederika pressed the key into Simon's hand. "It's furnished." She pulled on her coat and headed for the pickup.

Simon followed at a slower pace. His buddy, Neil, had made no mention of a separate entrance. Then again, Simon had no reason to suspect he would have free run of the place. He reminded himself to have no expectations, that the more he remained an aloof observer of Frederika Vanderveen the happier he would emerge from the episode.

Frederika lowered the pickup's tailgate and hefted Simon's thirty-five-pound television set, one of the variety the Madison Avenue ad men had facetiously dubbed "portable."

"No, that's too heavy for you!" Simon exclaimed.

Frederika shot him a withering glance. "Do I look like I'm made of porcelain?"

She looked precisely like that to him, but he made no further comment and let her stagger with the television toward the house and around its side, to the bottom of a steep set of iron stairs. There she set down her burden, to rest her arms. Simon lowered the pile of clothing he carried, surveying the climb. He studied the large wing over which the stairway ran. The walls were largely of glass, but draperies cloaked the inside from view.

"Living room?" Simon inquired.

"Ballroom," Frederika answered.

Simon made no effort to conceal his awe.

Frederika gamely hauled the television up the stairs to a balcony above the ballroom. Simon saw that the large room had an enormous skylight incised into its roof. No light came through its twelve panes, whose upper surfaces had not been washed in years. Just beyond the balcony rail, a downspout hung precariously from the wall, unattached to the gutter. Up close, Frederik Vanderveen's temple was not quite so impressive. The taxes on the place had to be close to Frederika's take-home pay. It seemed a Jumbo-sized white elephant. No wonder she accepted boarders from time to time, Simon thought.

"I had the lock changed today," Frederika informed him. "The girl who last rented from me never returned her key."

"That's very thoughtful," Simon acknowledged.

Frederika looked as if she had more to say, but instead covered another cough with the back of her hand.

Simon pushed the key into the lock and opened the door. "Thanks for your help, but I can bring in the rest of the stuff. You really should stay inside."

Frederika lugged the television into the room and lowered it to the floor. She turned on the light and stepped aside. Simon entered. The room was of modest size and furnished with modern, utilitarian furniture. No antiques, no gigantic four-poster bed, as Simon had imagined. But it looked clean enough.

"This was the nanny's room," Frederika revealed, moving to the opposite side of the bedroom. "The bathroom's out this door and to the right. It's all yours."

"We didn't say anything about kitchen privileges," Simon pointed out.

"Whatever you eat you bring in yourself. If you use the pots and pans, clean them immediately. You can use the washer and dryer if you're neat."

She spoke in a hurried monotone, as if annoyed at the trade he had engineered and anxious to be done with him. He felt like a transient in a flophouse, but he said, "Sounds fair to me."

Frederika walked out the hall doorway. "Good night."

Simon returned the wish, watching her departure with appreciation. Her blue jeans were not of the skin-grafted variety. She did not require the obvious to mesmerize. Simon reminded himself that having this room for a time was like viewing the shark at the aquarium. Totally safe, so long as he resisted diving into the tank.

Frederika was twenty-four years old. That was one of perhaps a dozen facts Simon knew about her. She had gone directly from a Swiss boarding school to Vassar. She had held a few jobs in the Boston area directly after school, then returned to Princeton, where she had not lived since she was ten. She had worked at an entry-level position in the Firestone Library for a bit more than two years. The job had been offered to her, it was rumored, by a forty-seven-year-old assistant dean with whom she had slept, but Simon doubted that a mid-level administrator in Arts and Sciences had much hiring influence in Simon's corner of the campus. That she had slept with another member of the faculty Simon was sure, but the gossipmongers set the total in double digits. The same tongue-waggers had singled out prominent men in the town as well. All shared the characteristics of being at least ten years her senior, influential and self-assured. Most, it was rumored, had been one-night stands. The difference between Simon's precept-class lover and Frederika was that apparently the reference librarian wanted little tangible from any man. The longest relationship Simon knew of was with his friend, Professor Neil Yoskin, and that, by Neil's reckoning, had lasted six weeks. Simon credited the extra weeks to the psychologist's professional id-handling skills. In every case, to Simon's knowledge, Frederika had been the one who ended the relationship. Simon had heard her called every manner of name, by envious and judgmental women and by men who despaired of receiving even her invariably fleeting attention. Slut, tramp, whore, bitch, and nymphomaniac were all epithets that people had attached to her behind her back. Neil's term was "vamp." He meant it not as an old-fashioned euphemism but in the original meaning of "vam-

56

pire." She had an unquenchable hunger, he observed, that compelled her to drain attention and affection from each man as quickly as she could, then move calmly on to the next. He judged it "an infectious sickness," one that deeply scarred every man she touched.

To her credit (and also unlike Simon's coed lover), Frederika Vanderveen had never been "the other woman"; all of the men she beguiled had been unmarried at the time. Simon had pressed his friend for his opinion on what caused her notorious behavior, but Neil had been professionally close-mouthed about her, even though she had not been his patient. It was obvious that the psychologist bore his particular collection of permanent scars. Neil did volunteer his certainty that it had something to do with her father. Whenever Neil had tried to unzip her mind, she became sullenly defensive and ultimately silent. She wanted nothing of his healing art.

Great beauty, great pain, and great mystery. The proximity of it gave Simon a vicarious thrill. He realized just how boring and lonely his own existence was, how stagnant he had become while quietly waiting for the purpose of his life to find him.

Simon walked to the door that connected his room with the rest of the Vanderveen house. He put his hand to the knob but changed his mind and left it open. He stared out at the barren, white hallway wall for a moment, then turned for the outside door, to finish relocating his things.

Simon had been thinking about Frederika when the phone call came into his office. It was hardly a coincidence. He had thought about her fifty times before lunch. When he had left his rented room, he found no sign of her. The kitchen was spotlessly clean, with not even the lingering smells of food or coffee. He wondered if she took breakfast out or just skipped it. The library wasn't open at that hour. Perhaps she went out for a morning walk. He hadn't heard her coughing. He wondered if her cold was better. He had not seen her when he performed his morning ritual in front of the Reference area. He worried where she was. And on and on throughout the morning.

Simon half-shifted his attention to the phone, lifting the receiver and muttering his name into it.

"I deserve better than this," Lynn's voice came through. A controlled but furious edge was in it.

"You probably do," Simon answered.

"Not probably. Definitely. You shit."

"Look, did you read my letter? It's all—"

"Yes, I read your letter," Lynn interrupted. "The relationship was going nowhere because *you're* going nowhere."

"Possibly. At any rate, neither of us is really happy."

"You won't be happier just because you leave me. You'll see: six months from now you'll be twice as miserable. *I'll* be happier."

"Then it'll still be for the good."

Lynn sighed. "Simon, don't you understand that *someone* has to push you? Somebody's got to be the heavy, since you're clearly incapable of it yourself."

Simon looked around the office self-consciously. Mercifully, neither Dr. Gould nor Reverend Spencer had yet caught the distressed tone in his near-whispers. "No, I don't see that."

"Where are you staying?"

"With someone on the university staff," he evaded.

"Thanks for being so goddamned considerate. Half the living room's missing, and I have to run out in the dead of winter and buy a bathrobe. You couldn't wait until after the holidays to walk out?"

"I just thought—"

"Bullshit. You didn't think at all. For example, what is tonight?"

Simon felt himself clearly on the defensive. The heat was pouring off his forehead. In another second the sweat would start to bead. "Tonight?"

"I knew it. The J and J Christmas party, remember? My biggest account, and you want me to go alone."

"I'm sorry. Can't you get a date? Barry?" Simon suggested.

"Right. And I explain to him what you've just done. It's one-thirty, Simon. The party's in six-and-a-half hours."

It was precisely what Simon had hoped to avoid. Instead of a

58

clean, postmortem-free break, he was going to be subjected to a full evening of rancor and recrimination. "I'm really sorry, Lynn. If you need me to go I will."

"Thanks so very much."

"What time should I be over?" He hoped to God she wouldn't offer to pick him up, since he didn't own a car. The Vanderveen mansion would have her playing twenty questions with a vengeance.

"Seven-thirty. That'll make us fashionably late."

"I'll see you then."

"Simon."

"Yes?

"Try to dress like you're *somebody*."

The phone went dead. Simon exchanged the receiver for an original edition of Thomas à Kempis's *Imitation of Christ*. The retreat backward five hundred years was sorely needed.

When Simon opened the inner door of his rented bedroom, he found the hallway dark. Light reflected faintly from downstairs, and the aroma of cooking pasta wafted up. He descended the curving oak staircase, nodding his respect at the long line of ancestral portraits. There were seven (all men), with Frederik the Third's, at the bottom, the largest. Kitchen light spilled along the central hall onto the foyer's Carrara marble floor. Simon followed it back toward its source.

Frederika stood at the restaurant-sized stove, fishing a strand of spaghetti from a pot of boiling water. She turned as Simon entered. Her face was the color of the pasta.

"Are you feeling okay?" he asked.

"No, not really," Frederika replied, nasally. She tossed the spaghetti strand against the tile that backed the stove. It stuck.

"I didn't see you at the library today," Simon observed, off-handedly.

Frederika lifted the pot from the flames and dumped the contents into a colander in the sink. The steam gushed upward, and she lowered her face toward it. Without turning toward Simon, she said, "I had some Christmas shopping to do, so I took the day off. You're not the mother hen type, are you?"

"No. Sorry."

Frederika kept her face lowered. She inhaled the steam noisily, through a partially blocked nose. Simon was about to comment on that and her pale color but thought better of it. "You look quite handsome," she said, head still down.

Simon glanced at himself. He wore the black velvet dinner jacket Lynn had given him the previous Christmas, along with a matching bow tie, a good cut of black woolen pants, and patent leather evening pumps. "Dinner party in New Brunswick," he explained. "Obligations."

"You'll be out late?" she asked, finally looking at him again.

Simon smiled. "Now who's the mother hen?"

Frederika raised an imperious eyebrow.

"I'll be home by one," he said. "I know . . . it's a school night."

Frederika's laugh, although hoarse, was a strong, happy sound. "Have fun."

Simon took one last look at her, then retreated.

The walk across Princeton was a cold one. Simon had been unable to find his earmuffs, and the wind had his ears stinging a quarter mile from Hodge Road. He drew his greatcoat up tightly and plunged on. He found himself in front of the cemetery. He started across it, thinking of the night he had seen Frederika standing before her father's grave. He still had no idea what the significance was. Nor could he imagine how just renting a room in her house might shed any light. In the bleak night, with wisps of snow circling them, the grave markers were all the more soul-chilling.

Simon's teeth chattered lightly as he knocked on Lynn's door. It opened almost immediately, swinging inward with force. Lynn appeared, looking attractive in a full-length lamé party gown. She smiled grimly; her right hand remained on the doorknob.

"Right on time," she said. "Punctuality is one of your few virtues."

"We're not going to have the gloves off all night, are we?" Simon asked. He started forward, but Lynn gave no indication of allowing him inside.

"No, we certainly aren't," she answered. "Because *we* are not going together."

Simon took a step backward. "What?"

"I took your advice and spoke with Barry. He was quite eager to escort me. So I have no more need of you." Lynn's smile broadened into wicked stepsister proportions. "He'll be along any minute. I'd really appreciate it if you get lost. Thank you." At last she retreated. She gave the door a push. "Merry Christmas." The door slammed shut.

Simon laughed lightly. If he had thought about it, her actions were not unpredictable. Barry was another of the account managers at Demographic Research, and from Lynn's descriptions a back-stabbing climber. He was only twenty-eight and looked like a minor Dickens character, and Simon could count on her to translate his youth, physical shortcomings, and admiration for her into sure signs of malleability. He figured they would either be married within six months or end up killing each other. He turned from her door still smiling. God bless Barry. He was about to learn just how lucky he was to have Lynn.

By the time Simon reached Witherspoon Street, the glow of his relief had worn off and he was colder than ever. The wind bit icily at his face. He turned onto Spring Street and jogged to Chuck's Café, for dinner and thawing. He ordered Buffalo wings and fries, with a giant Coke to slake the fire of the wings' spices. He made only a token gesture of protecting his evening wear; without Lynn to escort he had no idea if he would ever need such heavy-duty threads again. He hung around the café for an hour, shooting the breeze with his friend Rich, a graduate student in physics. Then, warmed inside and out, he decided to brave the cold as far as Nassau Street, to shop for a small "thank you" Christmas present for Frederika—definitely not too expensive, lest she get the wrong idea. One of the few things he knew about her was a fact that Neil, the psychologist, had mentioned: she loved to garden and had taken it upon herself to redesign and personally replant the mansion grounds. At Micawber

Books he found a beautiful volume on English gardens. By the time he reached the head of Hodge Road it was a quarter past nine.

The street was dark and deserted. Tendrils of snow gusted under the feeble streetlamps, appearing like Walpurgnisnacht souls in flight. Simon lengthened his stride. The Vanderveen house stood a mass of solid blackness. He wondered if Frederika had wisely taken her cold to bed. He cut across the lawn and hugged the house, wanting out of the wind. As he rounded the corner, he took a hitch in his step. The faintest hint of light penetrated the ballroom draperies. More strangely, it seemed to shimmer and pulse. Simon made a detour around the wing, searching in vain for an opening in the curtains. Then he remembered the skylight. He climbed the iron steps almost as far as the landing. His high vantage gave him a view down through the glass onto the far third of the ballroom floor. He saw four white lit candles, which formed a large, downturned arc. He could see no one from where he stood, but his mind formed a vivid and disquieting image. During his college days, incense and candlelight had helped him seduce more than one young woman in his cramped and common dorm room. The effect of many more candles, in such an opulent open space, had to be far more libidinous. He fought with his conscience for all of five seconds, then clambered over the iron railing and down onto the ballroom roof, to spy Frederika's latest conquest.

The roof was slightly canted, angling up from all four walls toward the skylight. Simon duck-walked cautiously over the gritty tarring and dropped to his stomach when he reached the skylight. Slowly, he peered over the edge of the glass frame. Now he saw virtually all of the room, illuminated by a great ring of twelve thick candles. In the room's center lay three concentric white circles. He judged the outer diameter of the shape as eight feet. To the north side of it, almost touching, lay another circle with a diameter of about four feet. The smaller circle had been completed, but the larger figure needed considerable work. Simon recognized both immediately. He had, in fact, laboriously copied them just the day before. They were called mandalas, and their purpose was nothing less than raising the dead.

The practitioner of the black magic was Frederika Vanderveen. She was alone. She knelt at the outer edge of the larger circle, dressed in the same white robe she had worn in the cemetery, carefully pouring powdered chalk into complex forms. Her request to have him copy the necromantic section of the *Memphis Grimoire* had raised a characteristic curiosity in Simon that led him to also page through *Lemegeton* and *The Key of Solomon*. Further research informed him that in medieval times the latter two volumes were considered the ultimate in black ritual arts, but the intricate magic circles of the rarer *Memphis Grimoire* made their mandalas look like hopscotch courts. Frederika had evidently been slaving at the circles since Simon left the house, and she still had more to lay down. She had completed the innermost ring, with its pentagram and five names of God; she had also finished the second circle, containing the signs of the zodiac and other magical symbols. Now she worked on the hieroglyphic names of the gods of ancient Egypt. Every few seconds she consulted one of the pages that Simon had provided her.

Simon shuddered, from more than the December cold. His trembling brought him back to his surroundings. Frostbite threatened if he lingered outside dressed as he was. He rose to his knees and worked his way back to the staircase. Transferring weight with a cat burglar's stealth, he moved up the steps to his bedroom door. He entered without noise and waited until his eyes adjusted to the dark. The heat of the room stung his ears and hands. He stripped off his coat and jacket, crossed to his closet and began indiscriminately pulling on layers of clothing. He tied a flannel shirt around his head, knotting the sleeves over his forehead. On his way out the door, he grabbed his bed quilt.

When Simon returned to his post on the roof, Frederika was laying down the final names. She had ingeniously used a baker's cake decorator for applying the powdered chalk. Her reproduction of Simon's drawings was an artistic improvement. As she worked, Simon's lips silently mouthed the names of Edjo, the cobra goddess; Horus, the falcon god of the dead; the sun god Ra, in both his old and young manifestations of Ra–Atum and Ra–Harakhte; and his wife, Hathor. Largest of the names was the ancient god Ptah, protec-

tor of the holy city of Memphis. To Frederika's side lay a black
wand, a hairbrush, a small, shiny key that looked like the twin to the
one she had given Simon, and a silver box. The wind made a sudden
plaintive moaning through the trees. Frederika's head turned upward. Simon pulled his face back an instant before her eyes lifted.

Simon drew the quilt over his head and risked another look
through the skylight. Frederika stood with the hairbrush in her
hand. Her fingers pulled through the brush's teeth, plucking out
hair. He was not surprised by her next motions; his painstaking
translation of the Latin had fixed the ritual in his mind. When she
had gathered all she could, she placed the ball of hair in the center
of the smaller circle. The text required at least some part of the
departed's body to be contained within the "calling ring." She set
down the brush and began the task of moving the twelve candles in
until they almost touched the outer edge of the larger mandala.
Finally, she picked up the silver box, Simon's translation, and the
black wand and stepped into the innermost circle. She reviewed the
pages, pulled back the opening of her robe, and stuffed the pages
into an inside pocket. Simon's coldness vanished for a while, after he
saw that she wore nothing underneath.

Frederika opened the silver box and pulled out a pinch of glistening powder. She tossed it onto the candle pointing directly south
and mouthed several words. The candle's flame flared briefly in
yellow-orange. She had begun blessing the four corners of the earth
and invoking the protection of the spirits of earth, wind, fire, and
water. Simon felt another shudder course through him. He knew it
was all ridiculous mumbo-jumbo, and yet his most primitive in-
stincts kept insisting that he should be terrified. Frederika's intense
observance of the ritual added to the eeriness. She was clearly
behaving like a believer.

The beautiful sorceress set the box of powder on the glazed
wooden floor and lifted her wand. After consulting the translation
again, she recited three prayers to the One God of All, turning every
few moments to face a different quadrant of the room. Each time she
did, she glanced down, to be certain she had not strayed out of the
inner circle. To do so, warned the book, meant the risk of being

snatched directly to hell by the very demons she sought to control.

Frederika paused in a wracking spasm of coughs. When she had recovered she spoke again, in a voice much louder. Her words were faintly audible through the glass. With the final page held before her eyes, she uttered the magic syllables that would summon six of Lucifer's most dread angels to her bidding.

"Berald, Beroald, Balbin, Gab, Gabor, Agaba, arise!" Frederika commanded. The wand trembled in her outstretched hand.

Simon pressed his ear to the glass. Next she would utter the name of the dead soul she wished to raise.

"Bring to me the shade of Frederik Vanderveen the Third, departed on the twenty-fifth day of September, nineteen hundred and seventy-nine."

Simon felt his heart thumping painfully at the base of his throat. His eyes, which had been watering slightly from the cold, pumped out an involuntary gush of astonished tears.

"Venite," Frederika intoned. *"Venite! Ven-i-te!"*

Each from his and her own vantage point, Simon and Frederika stared expectantly at the smaller mandala, waiting for the smoky materialization of her father's shade.

"Come," Frederika bid, this time in her own language. *"Come!* COME!"

Only Simon heard her. She lowered the wand. Her shoulders slumped, then heaved spasmodically. She sank onto the polished oak floor, unmindful that her hands had broken past the boundaries of the protective mandala. No howling devil appeared to snatch her into the underworld, but Frederika's soulful sobbing proclaimed the torments of a very real inner hell.

Simon rolled onto his back and stared up at the unwinking stars. Watching the young woman's disappointment for another moment was too much to bear. Casting the spell had not been a silly schoolgirl's adventure with her. He suspected that this furtive attempt at necromancy had also not been her first. Several of the grimoires stipulated that the grave of the summoned soul must be opened at midnight and the corpse tapped three times with a magic wand. One he had not glanced through, however, must have allowed only a mound of dirt from the gravesite for success. Simon had his answer to the cemetery mystery, but he felt no satisfaction. He had traded one answer for a dozen questions. More than roof, glass, and an expanse of air separated him from her, making the sympathy he wished to offer an impossibility. The wind gave another mournful moan as he slowly made his way back to his rented room.

CHAPTER FOUR

December 16

᯽

A faithful friend is a strong defense, and he that

findeth such findeth a treasure. A faithful friend

is beyond price, and there is no weighing of his goodness.

—Ben Sira, *Book of Wisdom (ca. 190 B.C.)*

The Saturday morning light pouring through the little window added welcome warmth to the bathroom. Simon plodded to the mirror and yawned at his tired-looking image. He had been awake far into the night, long after he stood sentry at his bedroom window, watching until the flickering ballroom light died. That had been toward midnight. He had sympathetically imagined Frederika on her hands and knees, wiping up all her carefully drawn chalk lines by guttering candlelight, mopping as well tears of frustration and perhaps humiliation. He had lain awake to hear her climb the stairs and scud to her room with a weary tread. For a long time afterward his mind revisited and pondered what he had seen, until finally sleep caught him between thoughts.

As Simon dragged a disposable razor over shaving cream and stubble, he heard a series of coughs. Frederika sounded sicker than she had the day before. He lowered the razor and listened. The coughs worsened into short, rasping barks. Simon scowled, angered at how badly she was treating herself. The house had an electronic thermostat, which automatically set back to 62 at ten o'clock. She had worked for two hours in the unheated ballroom, wearing only a robe. He put down the razor, crossed the hallway to her closed bedroom door and knocked.

"Are you all right?" Simon called.

He was answered by a forceful sneeze. He opened the door and peeked his head in. Frederika's bedroom was as he had imagined his rented one might be—appointed with expensive French provincial furniture and set off with a feminine floral pattern repeated on wallpaper, curtains, and bedspread. Frederika was bolstered nearly upright by several pillows. She wore a different bathrobe now, this one quilted and ratty, buttoned all the way up to her throat. Her hair looked like a misused straw broom. She sneezed again, more forcefully. Her hand flailed toward a large Kleenex box at her side, found a tissue and covered her red nose.

"Gesundheit," Simon wished.

Frederika blew. The noise was unwholesome. She made a revolted face. "Thank you."

"I know I'm not your mother," he said, "but if I were, I'd keep you under those covers all day."

"If you were my mother you wouldn't give a damn," Frederika replied, in an oddly matter-of-fact tone. "But thanks for the good advice. If I promise to listen to it, would you do me a favor?"

"Name it."

"I've got one slug of cough medicine left. Could you pick me up one of those 'itchy eyes, runny nose, feverish, coughing, you need your rest' syrups?"

Simon laughed lightly. "I'd be glad to. And as long as I'm at your beck and call, I'd like to get you breakfast. What'll your stomach hold?"

"Black coffee and buttered toast would be fine." Frederika eased partway down under the covers. "Oh, and the *Princeton Packet?* It's on the kitchen counter. I'm sorry to be such a bother."

"It's okay," Simon said. "I probably shouldn't have stuck my nose in. Do you want me to call someone to help you? A girlfriend . . . or whatever?"

Frederika coughed and shook her head. Simon had no idea who she would ask for if she had said yes. From what he knew of her, she was a loner. She had no special friends at the library, and whenever he saw her on the streets of Princeton she was by herself. Except for the fireworks relationships she built around sex, her existence might be that of a hermit. Hermitic and hermetic, he thought, wryly.

"I'll get breakfast," Simon said.

"You might want to finish shaving first," Frederika suggested.

Simon took her advice and hurried through the rest of his bathroom ritual to get to the breakfast preparations. He realized that it felt exhilarating coming unexpectedly nearer to her, like jumping up on the ledge of a high rooftop. He hunted up a breakfast tray and arranged the coffee, toast, napkin, and newspaper into an esthetic composition.

"This is embarrassing," Frederika told him as he set the tray down over her lap. "I hardly know you."

"That can be remedied," Simon said. "Ask me a question."

Frederika stopped raising the coffee cup and looked directly at Simon. "How was the party last night?"

"Uneventful."

She laughed, making the air in her chest rattle. "Great beginning."

"Sorry," Simon apologized. He was not about to tell her he had come home early enough to witness her attempt at necromancy.

"All right," Frederika retracked, "tell me why you work in the library."

Simon sat on the edge of a chair placed near the bedroom door. While she sipped and nibbled, he gave her a capsule summary of how he had chanced on library work, grown to love it, and still lingered on, in hopes that it would lead him to his "great and unique purpose in life." As he spoke, another part of his brain sat in silent judgment of what he said, weighing each word in light of his audience. He was surprised at his own candor but credited it to a subliminal desire to yield something of himself in exchange for what he had learned of her by spying.

Frederika had rested her cheek on her fist as she listened. When Simon finished, she said, "I find it hard to believe that translating old Latin texts will give you direction."

"It got me out of my girlfriend's house and here, didn't it?" he replied, smiling.

Frederika raised her forefinger. "Touché!"

"Speaking of Latin," Simon said, "do you know if your roommate got the translation yet?"

"I haven't heard from her." Frederika's face betrayed not the slightest hint of her lie, exquisite in its artful, wide-eyed innocence. Simon made careful note of her skill.

"Incredible, that black magic stuff," he remarked.

"Is it? I would think it was all superstitious nonsense."

"And yet some people still believe. Just the other day, I read about animal sacrifices in a park outside Philadelphia. In modern times, why do you think people still try it?"

Frederika shrugged. Her eyes cast restlessly toward the window. "Boredom. A . . . dramatic way to rebel against society. Or against the mainline religions."

"Some people must really believe in it," Simon persisted. "I think maybe they're looking for a sign."

Frederika looked back at him. "What kind of sign?"

"For an afterlife, good or bad. Anything to convince them that there'll be something after death." Simon's pupils dilated, as he concentrated on picking up the slightest trace of a reaction on his landlady's face. He could not tell if he had failed to hit the mark or if she was again using consummate muscle control, because she betrayed no emotion at all. Yet he sensed that he had pushed her as hard as he should. He stood.

"I have a tennis game at nine," he apologized. "Can you hold out for that cough medicine until noon?"

Frederika seemed mildly interested at his mention of tennis. He pictured his two-dimensional image taking on a little bas-relief in her eyes. "Sure. Thanks again," she said.

Simon backed out of the room as one might for royalty, pulling the door shut. Walking down the hall, he became aware for the first time that the adjacent bedroom door had a new knob. It was an outside lock model, identical to the one that Frederika had had

71

installed in his room. He tried it and was not surprised to find that the handle would not turn. Simon was positive of its purpose. This was the lock for the key he had seen through the skylight. The room beyond was Frederik Vanderveen's. Before last night it had held a brush with traces of the man's hair. Frederika obviously did not want her boarder in the room. He wondered idly if his key might fit into the lock. After only one brief interview, he suspected that an inanimate room might reveal more than Frederika Vanderveen ever would.

The ball bounced on the serving line with little pace. Simon approached it at a dead run, swung his racquet hard and pounded the ball into the net cord. He watched without expression as the ball popped off and landed out of bounds.

"Set!" Neil Yoskin called out, trotting toward the net. "Six–two. You're playing like a demon, Penn, but your concentration's all off."

"Thank you, Bud Collins," Simon returned.

Neil glanced at his watch. "We still have five minutes. You want to just rally?"

Simon looked around the cavernous Jadwin Gymnasium tennis area. It was hard to believe that something this big was a few stories underground. As members of the staff and faculty, he and Professor Yoskin had court rental privileges. Neil had been his most frequent partner for the past three years. Generally Simon won, but Neil-the-psychologist hadn't needed professional insight to realize Simon was preoccupied and at a disadvantage.

"No, I've had it," Simon declined.

Neil grabbed his towel off the net post. "Something big's happened to you; what is it?"

Simon made no attempt at evasion. He was sure Neil's questions would lead right into the subject he wanted to broach. "I left Lynn."

Neil grinned with approval. "I make it a rule never to offer unsolicited advice regarding relationships. Once a knot's been severed, however, I'm Dear Abby: It's about time you walked out on that bitch. What was the deciding factor?"

"You just said it; it was time. So I moved out while she was on one of her trips."

Neil reached across the net and gave Simon's shoulder a congratulatory shake. "Attaboy. Just because you're mild-mannered, she thought she could shove you forever. I know better. Remember that time we were playing doubles and Koether hit you intentionally with that overhead?"

Simon smiled in memory but needed no reply, as Neil pushed on. "You broke his serve twice and practically emasculated him on set point. There's Bengal tiger inside that pussycat exterior, Penn."

"I wouldn't go that far," Simon said, walking off the court.

"But you *did* go that far," Neil returned jovially. "All the way to . . . where did you move to?"

The opening had appeared even sooner than Simon expected, but he dashed smoothly through. "I took a room on Hodge Road."

Neil blinked in astonishment. "Freddie Vanderveen's house?"

Simon nodded. That was another of the few facts he'd known about her, one that he'd forgotten: she always invited her paramours to call her Freddie. "You were the one who told me about it."

Neil dipped one eyebrow and cocked the other. "Did I? How stupid of me."

Simon picked up one of their balls, which lay beside the net, and started squeezing it. "Just for a couple of weeks, until I can find something permanent."

Neil's upbeat mood had vanished. It was replaced by a professionally constructed wall of impassivity which, Simon was sure, hid a garden of weedy emotions. Simon had not been surprised when he had discovered that Neil-the-psychologist was one of the most volatile people he knew; among Simon's former high school classmates was a volunteer fireman with proven pyromaniacal tendencies and a policeman who had been the class's biggest juvenile delinquent. Neil validated Simon's theory with his next words.

"Well, that was a stupid thing to do! I mean, if it was only for a few days, why the hell didn't you move in with me? You'd have had the place to yourself starting Thursday. Remember, I said Cinda and I'll be in Martinique?"

Simon shook his head. "If it were just you, I'd impose; your relationship with Cinda isn't quite stable enough to bring me on board."

"Oh, that's a load of horseshit," Neil snorted.

"There's no point in arguing; thanks for the offer, but it's a done deal. You *can* give me your help in an even more important way, though."

"How?" Neil asked, suspiciously.

"I'd like you to answer a few questions about her. Do you mind?"

Neil wiped his towel a few times across his face, but his eyes never left Simon's. "You didn't engineer this move just to get close to Freddie, did you?"

"No," Simon answered.

"Because my example should have been enough for you. She's poison, Penn. Poison pen. That's pretty funny, but neither of us is laughing." Neil moved toward the chairs that held their equipment bags.

"Is she mentally ill, Neil?" Simon asked, following. "That's all I really want to know." Neil turned and looked at Simon over his shoulder but did not seem about to reply. "I don't want to hear all the psychological equivocation. Do *you* think she's the kind of person who should spend some time in an institution?"

"Maybe," Neil said, quietly. "Not because she can't function in everyday society. Obviously she does. But there are deep-rooted personal problems that should be brought to light. What makes you ask?"

"I think she's turned to the occult, to try to contact her father."

"You mean like séances?"

"Yes. That sort of thing."

Pinch marks formed at the corners of Neil's eyes and over the bridge of his nose. Simon was sure Cinda, Neil's live-in girlfriend, would not be happy to know how much Neil still cared about Frederika. "That's too bad."

"What do you know about her relationship with him?" Simon asked.

"Not enough. I think it was a love/hate thing. She told me her mother abandoned the two of them when she was six." Simon remembered Frederika's bitter remark about her mother but did not interrupt Neil's words to share it. "A short time after leaving them, she died. So it was just Freddie and Big Fred living together under the same roof, until he shipped her off to a private school in Switzerland."

"It couldn't have been just the two of them," Simon said. "Not with him traveling around the world all the time. She said my room belonged to the nanny. Was that—"

"She mentioned an aunt who lived with them. I can't recall her name. But she's probably a minor player in the tragedy. Take my advice: back off and be a good tenant. If you don't want to be out on the street the next day, don't press her about Daddy."

"I understand." Simon set his racquet on the chair and rubbed a knot in the back of his neck. "I'm thinking maybe she's after something practical. Frederika's a smart woman. She'd have to be pretty desperate to turn to the occult."

Neil pulled on his warm-up jacket. "What do you mean 'something practical'?"

"Well, she rents out that room, right? And her salary can't begin to cover the cost of the house. Maybe the old man dropped dead without telling her the names of the banks he had safe deposit boxes in."

Neil scowled at his considerably younger tennis partner. "Give me a break."

"But surely she knows this occult stuff is nonsense. I figure she either has to be incredibly desperate to know something or else she's just plain gone off the deep end."

Neil zipped up his equipment bag. "Why don't you figure nothing at all? You *are* getting emotionally close, Penn. You're thinking because she looks like a fairytale princess and is obviously in distress that you can slay some dragon for her. She is not—I repeat not—some helpless femme. Down deep, Freddie Vanderveen is tough as nails. Her problem is that she's her own dragon. She has to want to stop punishing herself . . . and using men to help her do it. Until that happens, any unwitting bastard who gets too close'll be chewed up like he stepped in front of a threshing machine. *Capish?*"

"Okay, Neil," Simon said, simply.

Neil smirked. "Okay, Neil," he imitated mockingly. He looked at his watch. "Well, Freddie just blew five minutes we could have used to improve our game." He picked up his bag and started toward the exit. "Get away from her as fast as you can. That's my professional opinion, free of charge. She ruined my fall last year; I'll be damned if she ruins my court time as well."

"Soup," Simon announced, carrying a tray into Frederika's bedroom. "Just Campbell's. But it was in your cupboard, so you'll probably like it."

"I'm sure I will." Frederika lowered a paperback titled *The World as I Found It* and slid up against the pillows.

Simon folded the tray legs down and placed it over Frederika's lap. "You want a little company while you eat?"

"That would be nice," Frederika said. The tone of her reply lacked conviction but her smile seemed genuine enough.

Instead of sitting on the chair near the door, Simon put himself at the foot of her bed. "You feeling better?"

"A little."

"Good."

Frederika picked up the soup spoon. "What did you do today besides play tennis?"

"Last-minute Christmas shopping. I want to mail my dad a gift. It'll never arrive in time, but he's used to that. I got him a flycasting reel. Need I tell you flycasting is not a major sport among Princetonians?"

Frederika labored to keep the amusement off her cheeks. She sampled the soup.

"I hitchhiked to that sportsman's den in Rocky Hill. Very macho place. They don't want you inside unless you look like Tom Selleck." He paused for reaction, but Frederika was content to eat while he talked. He continued on, steering in a purposeful direction what he wanted to sound like an idle monologue. "Anyway, it's more than a flycasting reel; it's a thank-you for all the time he spent with me when I was little. I hated the fishing and camping trips. I never let him know, because I understood he wanted to teach me and share the things he loved, you know?"

Frederika nodded, without lifting her eyes.

"Anyway, maybe this will make up for the time I caught more trout than he did . . . with a baloney sandwich." Frederika's eyebrows raised; he had set the hook. Simon embellished his boyhood experience with a raconteur's ear for hyperbole, metaphor, and regional dialect. It was among his favorite tales, honed during numerous recountings until it was shiny and sharp. Phrases had been repeated until they were more real to him than the actual memories. The ease of the telling let him play a private game, stealing careful glances at Frederika when she lowered her eyes to dip the spoon. He studied her as he once had a particularly engaging portrait by Renoir, not content to stand back and absorb the totality of its beauty but wanting to step up close and analyze how the subtle underlying strokes of blue, red, and green brought the pink skin to life. He noted for the first time the half-dozen shades of gold and yellow that contributed to her beautiful hair, the bone structure that dictated the shape of her eyes. He also noted that, when she brought the spoon to her mouth, her right eye drifted a fraction. Her exotropia proved to him that there was at least one frailty to her physical perfection. He pondered the depth of her concealed mental frailties, wondered how much he could learn up close there.

"But he was good-natured about it," Simon concluded. "He's a special guy. I suppose you have similar stories. Your dad was special to thousands of people."

Frederika nodded again, and kept spooning soup.

"Did he spend a lot of time with you?"

"Not fly fishing," she answered.

"No, I meant—"

"He was a very busy man." She pushed the tray toward Simon. "that's all I can take, I'm afraid."

Simon accepted the words as double entendre. Not unprepared for her reaction, he downshifted smoothly. "Listen, you'll probably be in bed all weekend, and Christmas is just a few days away. You don't have a tree. Do you want one?"

"Oh, that would be too much—"

Simon stopped her with his raised palm. "No trouble at all. I'm helping my friend Rich choose his tree. That pickup I arrived in is his. It'd be nothing for us to get a second tree and bring it back here."

"Tonight?" Frederika asked.

"Yes. He's coming by later in the afternoon."

"Okay." Frederika affixed a warm smile, as if the soup or the prospect of a Christmas tree had suddenly instilled some health. "Just add the cost to my medical bill, Doctor."

Simon grinned back. Neil was right: she did have a vampire's power to seduce, even when she had no designs whatsoever. He picked up the tray and retreated from her beguiling aura.

Simon tried the mansion's front door, found it unlocked, and waved for Rich to drive on. He pushed the door open and muscled the eight-foot Douglas fir into the entry. He knew that bringing the tree directly into the house's heat would shock it badly, but there were so few days until Christmas that he didn't have to worry about it shedding needles.

"Ho, ho, ho!" he shouted up the stairs, instantly regretting his outburst. Frederika already thought of him as a meddlesome big-mouth and mother hen; he didn't need to add jackass to her list. He leaned the tree against the door and bounded up the stairs two at a time, to ask his landlady where she kept her Christmas tree stand. He knocked on her door softly, in case she had fallen asleep. There was no answer. He knocked again, put his ear to the door and heard nothing. He tried the doorknob, found it unlocked, and risked a peek inside.

The bed lay unmade and unoccupied. The bedside lamp was lit, but the bathroom was dark. Simon called Frederika's name into the hall. The echo made the house seem even emptier. Simon saw the *Princeton Packet* lying on top of the rumpled bedclothes. It was turned back to one of the center pages. He crossed to the bed and picked it up. The article in the center of the page was the previous week's police blotter. Sandwiching it were six ads. Four of them he could not imagine would hold any interest for Frederika. The fifth, a long shot, was for Persian rugs. The last one held Simon's attention. It promoted a Vincent DeVilbiss, who followed his name with a blizzard of initials that meant nothing to Simon. He announced his recent arrival to Princeton and touted himself as an expert in astrology, herbal health, and channeling. Simon smirked at the advertisement, thinking that the man would probably make a living. Hand in hand with its exclusivity, Princeton was a place of eccentricity. Many people in the local area had forsaken mainstream religions for the New Age religion of Self. Not long ago, Simon had read that the directory of the Holistic Health Association of the Princeton Area listed 130 holistic practitioners. Acupuncture, transpersonal counseling, transcendental meditation, yoga, shiatsu, rolfing, crystal focusing, polarity, macrobiotics, Gestalt, biofeedback, t'ai chi, and Zen were all readily available. The more metaphysical and occult arts could be found as well, conducted by enough practitioners to fill a coven. There was at least one psychic healer, a "depossessor," three fortune tellers, and one self-proclaimed witch in the area. Mr. DeVilbiss would no doubt be welcomed. But not by Simon Penn.

It dawned on Simon that there was no real evidence that Frederika had gone for the man's counseling; an opened page was circumstantial. What short of desperation would drag Frederika from a sickbed on such a cold night? Simon stared at the man's phone number, then at the telephone on the bedside table. He lifted the handset and looked at the buttons. It was a new model, with ★ and # characters and an automatic redial.

Simon pressed the redial button and listened to the burst of musical noise. After the second ring a connection was made.

"Vincent DeVilbiss," the sonorous voice answered.

"I'm sorry," Simon said. "I must have dialed the wrong number."

"Quite all right," the voice forgave, in a clipped English accent.

Simon dropped the phone onto its cradle and flung the newspaper onto the bed.

* * *

Vincent DeVilbiss opened the front door and blinked twice at his visitor. He bowed slightly and swept his hand inward, to cover his surprise.

"Please come in. So sorry to keep you waiting. The phone rang."

"Yes, I heard it," Frederika said, entering the house. The porch creaked as she left it. The place was an aged duplex on Park Place, a weatherbeaten remnant of the grand Victorian era. She, too, showed a degree of surprise at the person she confronted. He was as pleasant looking as he sounded. He dressed in dark woolen pants and a quality white broadcloth shirt, which was partially covered by an unbuttoned ecru cable-knit lounging sweater. Her gaze swept upward to study the tufts of silver hair at his temples but was arrested by his penetrating amber eyes. "I hope I'm not early," she added.

"No, no!" DeVilbiss assured. His hand fluttered up like a frightened bird, flying on the wings of his elegantly long fingers. "Eight o'clock precisely. I apologize for the condition of the house; most of the furniture is rented. I own very little myself."

Frederika shrugged out of her winter coat, allowing DeVilbiss to help her. "You don't stay long in any place?"

DeVilbiss's laugh was joviality personified. "In other words, 'Are you as fly-by-night as most charlatans in your profession?' "

Frederika turned and leveled her gaze on the man. "Are you? Because I'm not here for entertainment."

"I promise to make it easy for you to judge."

Frederika opened her mouth to speak but was overcome by an unexpected paroxysm of coughing. The sounds became increasingly deep and hacking.

"My, my!" DeVilbiss sympathized. "That's a nasty cold. This problem I can help immediately. Follow me, please!" He led the way through a living room weighted down with threadbare, overstuffed furniture. Except for the soot-faced fireplace, the room was the color of aged newspaper. An effusive bouquet of fresh flowers brightened the room more than the tassel-shaded bronze floor lamp. A Scott Joplin tune cartwheeled through the house.

"I travel constantly by choice, not necessity. The world is so big;

80

so much to see in so little time, that I can't bear to grow roots," DeVilbiss imparted, as he entered the dining room. In its center sat a round oak table and four matching chairs, solidly made, at conspicuous variance with the two maple chairs, sideboard, and china closet that filled the rest of the space. On the table lay a pack of splayed-out tarot cards. The sideboard held nearly a dozen bottles of unique shapes and pleasant colors, all filled to various levels with ingredients. The remainder of the sideboard's top was hidden by hardcover books, as was the seat of one maple chair. On the other chair sat a large doll—a clown of the traditional French variety, with black and white silk costume, white stockings, and pointed cap and black pumps, both with red pom-poms. The face and hands were of porcelain and beautifully painted.

"Have a seat if you will," DeVilbiss gestured. He continued on into the adjoining kitchen, much of which Frederika could see from where she sat. Along the far wall hung homely bundles of dried herbs. DeVilbiss moved to one and plucked a handful of leaves. He turned off the music but continued to hum the tune. Frederika listened to water running hollowly into a kettle. She was relieved to find no heavily draped curtains on the walls, no crystal ball, burning incense, or wind chimes—the kind of props that screamed fakery.

"Is the clown yours?" she asked, to fill in the silence.

"As much as I am his" came the reply.

"He looks old."

"Indeed. He's been with me a long time." DeVilbiss appeared in the kitchen doorway. "Pierrot Lunaire and I are a team. A matched pair of dummies, I say." He told his joke without smiling and retreated into the kitchen without waiting for a reaction.

"Are you brewing me a cure for my cold?" Frederika asked.

"You know there's no such cure. Yet. But give the men of science enough time and there shall be," DeVilbiss declared. "I have absolute faith in them."

"Then what *are* you brewing?" Frederika asked.

"Merely something to relieve all the unpleasant symptoms. Something far better than the drugstore nostrums."

"Do tell," Frederika muttered. She was not pleased by the abrupt detour the gentleman had made. Her cold was a minor annoyance, one she would gladly endure if only he could live up to his other advertised promises.

"The amazing thing is that so many effective medicines have been known for hundreds of years," DeVilbiss remarked, loudly. "But only by a chosen few. Just as foxglove has been known to help the heart, so a rare few have possessed the knowledge of this remedy for the common cold." From the amount of noise he made, DeVilbiss seemed far busier than merely the preparation of herbal tea. A spoon clinked several times following the sound of a bottle being uncorked. Frederika glanced at her wrist and remembered that she had left her watch on the bedside table.

The kettle whistled. Frederika started in her chair.

"One more minute," the man called out. Frederika peeked under the table, then rocked it up to examine the rug directly under it. The sound of pouring water cued her to resume her patient, hand-folded posture.

DeVilbiss entered the room carrying a tray that held a hand-painted English teapot, a pair of matching cups and saucers, and nothing else. He set the tray down on the edge of the table, placed both cups in the middle and poured them three-quarters full. As he did, he pointed out, "Cream or lemon would dilute its potency. I shall drink with you if you don't mind. As a preventative."

Frederika's apprehension at being offered the tea evaporated with the man's desire to share it. DeVilbiss lifted his cup first and sipped, closing his eyes as if in mild euphoria. She followed his example and found the taste delightful. She told him so.

"I'm so glad you approve," he replied. "Please drink all of it, for its full effect." He was polite and mannerly to a fault, but his mien was not in the slightest effete. Frederika detected a quiet confidence in his movement and bearing. "And now to the point of your visit," he invited.

"I wish to contact my father," Frederika stated flatly.

"How long has he been dead?"

"Ten years."

DeVilbiss frowned.

"Is there some problem?" Frederika inquired.

"It is more difficult with the passage of time," the self-professed channeler replied. He swept the tarot cards up with one hand and tossed them on the sideboard. "Have you attempted to contact him before?"

"Yes. Several times, with no success."

DeVilbiss lifted his cup and drank to the dregs; his brows knit as if in thought. "Your mother . . . is she alive?"

"No."

"Perhaps it would be easier to contact her."

"No!" Frederika said firmly. "She's been dead even longer."

DeVilbiss set the cup down and indicated with his forefinger that Frederika should finish hers. "My sympathies. So much tragedy for one so young."

"I'm not that young," Frederika countered. She lifted the cup and drank. DeVilbiss watched without comment as she finished. When she had, she said, "What is your usual price for such an *unusual* talent?"

"I charge thirty dollars, to see if we can become attuned. If it's possible, the fee varies with what is demanded."

"You promised to make it easy for me to judge if your talents are worth anything at all," Frederika reminded him.

"So I did." He cleared the tea service onto the sideboard. As he did, Frederika blew her nose. Mucus came out in a flood, and suddenly she found it much easier to breathe. She attributed the unstuffing to the warmth of the tea. DeVilbiss dimmed the dining room's chandelier lights to a feeble orange glow and reassumed his place directly across from the young woman.

"Your father's name?" DeVilbiss requested.

"Frederik Vanderveen the Third."

"His place of burial?"

"Here in Princeton."

"Very well." DeVilbiss stretched out his hands, palms up, silently inviting Frederika to place hers on top. She obeyed. He wrapped his long, thin fingers around hers, and she felt the strength in them. "I channel through the spirit of a criminal named Roderick Miller. He was hanged in London for horse thievery in the year 1548."

"Not the most savory soul," Frederika commented.

"Neither beggars nor channelers can be choosers," DeVilbiss returned archly. He closed his eyes and let his facial muscles go suddenly slack. His body became totally tranquil.

It seemed to Frederika that she had been holding the man's hands for five minutes without his moving. She was about to speak when the table began to tremble, as if a minor earthquake passed through Princeton. Frederika eased her feet forward, to test the man's actions under the table. Simultaneously, the toes of her shoes ran into those of his. His feet were well away from the table's single pedestal leg and firmly planted on the rug. He seemed oblivious to her contact. The trembling stopped abruptly. The ceiling's color shifted subtly, taking on a bluish tint. A streak of white light dodged along the lines of the walls and vanished. DeVilbiss's hands had not moved in the slightest. A rasping sound issued from his throat. His lips did not move.

"What . . . do you . . . demand of me?" the whispered voice asked.

The hackles raised on the back of Frederika's neck. She stared at the motionless channeler, wondering if he or she was supposed to answer.

"Woman . . . what do you demand . . . of me?" the voice repeated.

"I wish to speak with my father, Frederik—"

"I know his name," the voice hissed. "What would you have me . . . ask him?"

"Ask him what happened to my first teddy bear," Frederika said. Her eyes watered with dread, but as soon as her question was out, her jaw set resolutely.

"Teddy bear?" the voice said. This time DeVilbiss's lips moved. "Yes."

Silence hung in the room like motes of dust. Finally, the voice began to laugh, at first the barest puffs of air, then with increasing sound, taking on a more robust quality by the moment. In the instant that Frederika recognized DeVilbiss's natural voice, his eyes opened and his mouth curled up into an expression of mirth. Frederika felt the heat of embarrassment burning onto her cheeks. She pulled her hands violently from his.

"Good question. I have no idea what happened to your bear, but isn't this show worth thirty dollars?" he asked.

Frederika's sudden rising upset her chair; it clattered backward noisily to the floor.

DeVilbiss's smile shifted to a look of genuine concern. "I apologize profusely," he said, getting up. "But isn't that all you expected to see: the parlor tricks of a circus sideshow performer?"

"No," Frederika answered, darkly. "I told you; I did *not* come for entertainment. I can't *believe* this."

DeVilbiss leaned back against the sideboard. "But now I believe *you.* I've shown you the nonsense I feed the dolts. Now we can get to the real magic."

"You have an accomplice," Frederika said, too unnerved and angry for his words to register.

DeVilbiss shook his head. "They were necessary in the old days. The days of magic lanterns and flash pot lightning."

"Then how did you make the table move? And those colors?"

"Electronics. I have a little box taped to one knee, with a button protruding. I simply press my knees together at the proper time, and the rest happens automatically. No use of hands or feet. The table has an agitating motor in the pedestal." He strode to the wall that separated the kitchen from the dining room and pointed up to the air return. "A miniature projection unit here. Remote speakers also, if I need the aid of sound. People today think they're so much more sophisticated than their grandfathers, but if they come to me they're usually as ready to make themselves blind as in any other era."

"You actually fool people with this?" Frederika asked.

"Those willing to be fooled. I give them peace of mind, hope of an afterlife, communion with their loved ones. All at a reasonable price."

"What do you think is reasonable?"

"As I said: thirty dollars for the first session. That's when I find out who they wish to contact and why. Then I do as much investigating as I can. I always start with the obituaries. Depending on how much information I uncover and how much time it takes, I charge up to several hundred dollars. Often, they're so pleased to hear what they already know that they give me a generous tip."

"And why bother showing this to me?"

DeVilbiss dug his hands into his trouser pockets. He took a casual, almost errant step in her direction, but his eyes were fixed hard on hers. "I already told you. Because I want you to understand that I am capable of *both* the illusion and the reality. For the average person, the illusion is sufficient. But not for you. Now, I *can* help you contact your father, but only if you can help me."

Frederika took a step backward. The fallen chair prevented her retreat. "I don't understand."

"You work in the university library. I saw you there two days ago, when I was purchasing an access card."

"So?"

"I told you that there are many wonderful arts which have been discovered but which only a few have shared."

"Go on."

"For example, that cold remedy. How does your cold feel now?"

Frederika turned her awareness inward. She realized that she felt fine.

DeVilbiss strolled the length of the sideboard. "No coughing or sneezing. No tightness in the sinuses or tickle in the throat. Not a hint of fever. Am I right?"

"Yes," Frederika admitted.

"That remedy is one among many wonderful secrets that I've unearthed. But there are so many others that I'd love to know. How huge stones were moved hundreds of miles to build Stonehenge. The lost formulas for making the stained glass of the great cathedrals. These may be beyond recovery. But they're only idle curiosities on my part." DeVilbiss continued his stroll, circling toward Frederika. He leaned his torso forward in a theatrical manner. "The one secret I am *obsessed* with is contacting the dead. This is the real reason why

I travel so much. I've learned a great deal, and shortly I'll prove it to you. But as far as I know, there is only one source that can give me the final answers I seek."

"The *Memphis Grimoire?*" Frederika guessed.

DeVilbiss stopped short. "You know this book?"

"Yes. It just came to the library. In the Schickner Collection."

DeVilbiss sucked in his cheeks and let them out. "You're a quick woman. The *Memphis Grimoire* looks impressive, but it's completely useless."

"I know," Frederika said. "I already tried it."

This time DeVilbiss bowed. "You are indeed the one I seek. No, Miss Vanderveen, while I *have* come to Princeton because of the Schickner Collection, it has nothing to do with the *Memphis Grimoire*. The source I seek is the pair of scrolls attributed to Ahriman."

"Oh. Yes. What do you know about them?"

Now that anger and fear were replaced by amazement on the woman's face, DeVilbiss approached her and righted the chair. "Much," he said, indicating with his hand that she should sit. "I know, for example, why every translation that's been made since the time of the ancient Greeks has been utterly destroyed."

"Why?" Frederika obliged.

"Because they alone teach how to speak with the dead. And the dead tell things about religion that at least several major faiths cannot allow to be believed," he lied, with consummate ease.

"Such as?"

"I promise to tell you what I know another time. What *you* must know right now is that agents of the Catholic church have destroyed every copy of this precious work. That I can prove, and I assure you they *will* get to this one as well. If I'm ever to reach all the way into the next world, I must learn the scrolls' secrets before they're erased for all time."

"But you need my help," Frederika filled in.

"Yes. Your library is like a fortress."

"I never thought of it that way, but I suppose it's true," Frederika granted. "Unfortunately, those scrolls are as inaccessible to me as they are to you."

"No. I can't believe that," DeVilbiss said in a seductive tone, as he stepped directly behind the young woman. "Those with access to the scrolls are men, aren't they? A woman of your beauty and intelligence can surely have her way with them." His fingers came to rest lightly on her shoulders.

"Even if that were true, no one has the authority to remove those scrolls now." Frederika glanced at her right shoulder but made no effort to free herself of his touch. "However . . ."

"Yes?"

"I have a friend in that section. He might be able to copy part of the scrolls without removing them."

"By photocopying?" DeVilbiss's fingertips began a gentle massaging.

"No. It's not allowed. The intense light can damage the ink. I meant copying by hand," Frederika said. She rolled her head back at his relaxing manipulation.

"Does he read Akkadian?"

"I don't think so."

"Then he wouldn't know what to copy. Even if he did, with no knowledge of the language he'd certainly make errors which might be critical." DeVilbiss's fingers stopped moving. "There is one other way. If I could be given access to the scrolls for an hour."

"You read Akkadian?"

"I have acquired the skills necessary for my quest," DeVilbiss lied.

"Why should I believe any of this?"

"You shouldn't. Yet." DeVilbiss moved around the table and sat again on the chair directly across from her. "But, as I promised, I will make it easy for you to believe me. Are you ready for *real* necromancy?"

Frederika's eyes watered at the prospect. "Yes."

DeVilbiss set his elbows on the table and raised his forefingers to his temples. "Then I'll take you as far as I can without the scrolls."

"What will I need to do?" Frederika asked.

"Just look into my eyes," DeVilbiss instructed. "There is no reciting of words, no holding of hands. Not even the fictitious

Roderick Miller. Stay perfectly still and look into my eyes. Think of your father, but say nothing. I will do the calling silently. His image will appear between us. Are you ready?"

Frederika nodded. DeVilbiss's eyes held hers without blinking. His forefingers described slow, continuous circles around his temples. Gradually, his eyelids lowered. Frederika's eyelids did the same. They sat across from one another like sleepwalkers at supper.

Suddenly, Frederika's eyelids popped open. Her eyes strained from their sockets, to drink in the apparition that shimmered before her on the table. There, in perfect miniature, was her father as he had looked the last time she had seen him alive. He smiled. It was an unaccustomed expression, filled with love. And forgiveness.

"Daddy!" Frederika gasped. "Daddy, tell me please! You promised!"

The image lost its opaqueness, dissolving as if smoke.

"Daddy!" Frederika wailed.

DeVilbiss shook himself from his trance. His hands left his temples and thrust out toward Frederika. "Stop! Say no more!"

"What happened?" she demanded.

"I told you not to speak!" DeVilbiss looked as angry as he sounded. "My powers can only bring the dead to you; I have no skill to let them communicate. If you try that, they're frustrated and vanish. It is always the same."

"Was it really my father?" Frederika asked, shaking from the experience.

"Only you can tell that," DeVilbiss answered, in a gentler voice. "I can see nothing when I'm in the trance."

"It was a trick," she said, with wavering conviction.

"You called only two hours ago, and you said nothing of who you wanted to contact," DeVilbiss replied, shaking his head as if rattling brains back into place. "I have no idea what you saw, but ask yourself: Would I have been able to create such a thing on such short notice? And for what? Have I asked for money? No. All I wish is more power such as that you have just witnessed. Power to make them speak." DeVilbiss stood and drew himself up erect and proud. "It's well to be a skeptic in matters of the occult, but one may also

89

be so worldly wise as to be stupid. Shall we help each other or not, Miss Vanderveen?"

Frederika looked hard into his eyes as if into windows. She could read nothing behind them. "I think we can help each other. I can tell you for certain very soon."

"Excellent."

"When I called, you said you stay up late into the night."

"I do. People think it's necessary to conduct séances during the witching hour. It doesn't pay for me to challenge their beliefs. So I sleep during the day."

Frederika stood. "I think I'll be able to call you later."

DeVilbiss got out of his chair, went to the dimmer and turned up the lights. "That's fine, but you'll get my answering machine. I have other business, you see." Frederika started toward the living room, but he moved in her path and reached gently for her right hand. "You asked if I had an accomplice; I do now. The most desirable accomplice possible." He raised her hand to his face in the Continental manner and pressed his parted lips against it. She felt the pressure of his teeth, and a sensuous thrill coursed through her. "To our mutual conquest of death," he said, smiling broadly, displaying both rows of gleaming white teeth, the upper incisors not quite long enough to raise suspicion.

Simon had seen enough even before DeVilbiss had restored the room's lighting. He had turned from the window and strode up the alley that disgorged onto Park Place. Disgust overwhelmed him, disgust for Frederika, for the man she had visited, and for himself. Simon had watched what he could of the dining room display, filtered as it was by half-shut blinds and gauzy curtains. He had witnessed enough to see that the annoyingly familiar yet unplaceable Mr. Vincent DeVilbiss had gotten enough of Frederika's confidence to put his hand on her shoulders and work his fingers into the cloth of her jacket. He noted well that she had allowed it. He had seen the strange staring contest they had afterward and Frederika's mesmerization. But the thing that had finally driven him from the window was his revulsion at his own voyeurism. Within the space of one week, he had found himself standing out in the cold three times spying on her. He obviously had a problem no less pitiable than hers. Lynn was right after all. Reading about life and watching it was not going to get him anywhere. It *was* time to grow up.

The walk across town to Hodge Road should have taken fifteen minutes. Simon did it in ten, coursing along the pavement with the drive of an express train, blowing similar steam in his exertion. He felt anger beating inside him like a second heart, and he was not even sure where it came from. He wanted to rip down the Christmas lights from every home he passed.

When he reached the Vanderveen mansion, Simon was surprised to find Frederika's Mazda back in the driveway. The hood was expectedly warm to his touch; the engine still made cooling noises. He walked around the house and trudged heavily up the stairs to his room. After the door was closed, it occurred to him that he felt dirty. He stripped off his clothes and tossed them in a heap on the floor. He was tugging on his bathrobe when he heard a knock on his inner door.

"Simon?" Frederika's voice came softly from the hall.

For a moment he contemplated not answering, but when she called again he replied.

"May I come in?" she asked.

Simon opened the door. Frederika stood in the hall holding a plaid wool blanket. She thrust it forward, along with an engaging smile. "I was worried about you. It's really cold out."

Simon heard her words clearly, but he took his time responding, studying the outfit she had so nimbly changed into. It was not the ratty bathrobe she wore the last time he saw her, but rather her infamous white capuchin robe. She had it cinched loosely enough so that it parted just above her knees, hinting that she again wore nothing beneath it. Because he knew what he was looking for, Simon detected faint discolorations of chalk on the robe's sleeves and dirt and grass stains on the lower hem. Gold slippers covered her feet.

"It *is* cold out," Simon answered, his lingering anger overcoming the surprise that ordinarily would have left him speechless. "But the one you should be worrying about is youself, with that cold."

When he failed to accept the blanket, Frederika walked around him, undeterred. She dropped the blanket on the bedcover and turned. "But I'm much better." She took his right hand and put it to her forehead. "See? No fever."

Simon nodded and took his hand back. "Quite a recovery. But it could return by morning. What was so important to get you from a sickbed out into this night?"

The admonition produced neither the customary scowl nor the accusation of mother henning. "I was way behind in my Christmas shopping before I got sick; I couldn't wait any longer." Uninvited, she sat down on his bed. "I also came in to say thank you for going to the drugstore and for cooking for me. It's way beyond our agreement."

"You're welcome."

"Oh, and the Christmas tree! It's beautiful." She sat looking up at him, waiting.

"That reminds me. I need to fresh-cut the trunk and get it into water."

"Now?"

"Someone has to do it, Frederika." Simon picked up his trousers, then stared at the beautiful woman on his bed, unmoving.

Frederika looked nonplussed by Simon's actions. The smile left her as she rose. "There's a saw in the garage. You can call me Freddie, you know."

"Do you have an extra blanket on your bed?"

"Yes." When Simon said no more, Frederika walked to the door. "Good night, Simon."

"Good night." He refrained from using her proper first name, for fear that she would insist on her nickname. He had no desire to become a member of that sad club. After she had vanished, he exhaled deeply and continued to stare at the space where she had been. He wasn't buying either her solicitous blanket or her expressions of gratitude as the real agenda of her visit, and that alone had preserved him from her awesome closeness. Bizarre as it seemed, he felt her crossing of the hall to him was somehow linked to her visit with Vincent DeVilbiss. Earlier, when Simon was making the trial advances to know Frederika, he felt in control of the danger. With her now approaching him, for friendship or more, he felt unsure. And yet he would not run from this.

Simon slipped off his robe, buckled his belt, and bent for the rest of his clothing. He realized his anger had vanished. He also realized with a sudden revelation what his first act of growing up must be.

CHAPTER FIVE

December 16

Evil does not always realize itself immediately;

indeed sometimes it never realizes itself at all.

—Max Picard

The Rent-A-Wreck sedan coughed consumptively, sputtered, and died. DeVilbiss swore under his breath and turned the key in the ignition. The engine revived begrudgingly, backfiring once before it settled into a chugging rhythm. DeVilbiss anticipated the change of the traffic light, easing his foot onto the accelerator pedal. He had no intention of being in New Jersey any longer than was necessary, so putting out dollars for a long-term Hertz or Avis car rental made little sense. Especially with his funds dwindling rapidly. The trip from England the previous summer had taxed his resources enough, but he had been completely across the continent and settled in Seattle when news of the scrolls' resurfacing had broken. Bad enough to have to dispose of them; having received the extra duty of disposing of the scientist added insult to injury.

For the ten thousandth time he shook his head at the popular romantic notion of his existence. Allegedly, all he needed was a coffin, a handful of native soil, and a nightly bellyful of blood. The truth was that he required clothing, food, and drink, shelter, transportation, entertainment, and a hundred other bothersome items, not to mention the cost of dragging around the props of his professional "front." His Undead life consumed much more than he found in the purses and wallets of his victims. And then there were the considerable expenses attached to funding his secret pharmaceutical research. Supernatural though he might be, he was almost as much a slave to the cost of everyday living as any normal human. At least, he mused with grim humor, he was spared health and life insurance.

DeVilbiss followed the winding road over a bridge that vaulted the Pennsylvania Railroad's tracks, through the sleepy town of Plainsboro and back out to suburban sprawl. Across the midnight horizon loomed thousands of identical townhouses. Driving beyond them, he was confronted by hundreds of single family homes, stamped out as if by cookie cutter. DeVilbiss sighed. The current state of civilization. He made a left turn and pulled over to the curb. His memory had gotten him this far. He opened the folder that lay below the scribbled address and pulled out a map of the area, hoping it was recent enough to show all the streets. He hated such tracts, for their pseudogentrified names—invariably some image evocative of Merrie Olde England, such as Fox, Hunter's, Squire's, Heather, Willow, Coventry, Nottingham, or such, teamed up with an equally picturesque setting—Crossing, Landing, Walk, Run, or Chase, Hollow, Greene, or Glen. Such grandiloquence, for a collection of densely packed, unimaginative boxes erected on what was formerly a farmer's field! He hated these developments' winding, confusing roadways, which hindered escape. Most of all, he hated the owners' pet dogs—rarely dangerous but noisier than the proverbial hounds of hell.

DeVilbiss consulted the map by the glow of a distant streetlamp, his amber eyes gathering light with owllike sensitivity. The hour was just past midnight, and few lights burned other than forgotten Christmas displays. He closed the folder and steered the car around the corner and down the length of a block. Lettering on a standard steel mailbox informed him which house belonged to M. McCarthy. He drove three houses past it and parked behind a line of vehicles. A holiday party had yet to sputter out in one of the homes. He shut off the engine and reached over the seat for his indispensable greatcoat. When he had bought it years before, it weighed six pounds. Fully laden with his trick-pocket addition and tools, it now tipped the scales at twelve pounds, four ounces. DeVilbiss stepped out into the crisp, gelid night and slipped the coat on.

The McCarthy house lay dark. DeVilbiss strode brazenly up the driveway and to the front door. By ambient light he found the clues he needed for easy entry. A sign stuck to the entryway window declared not only that the home had an alarm system guarding it but that the product had been created by Antisocial Security, Inc. Thanks to the gratuitous information, DeVilbiss knew that cutting power to the house would be purposeless: the alarm system had a battery backup. He also knew that the alarm was silent and worked by automatically phoning a distant security monitoring company, who called the local police. To defeat the security measures, he merely needed to cut the telephone lines.

DeVilbiss carried one of the garbage cans around to the back of the house, climbed on it and leapt onto the garage roof. From there to the second-story roof required another leap, no challenge to his muscles. He tightrope-walked along the roof's ridgeline, found the phone line on the northern wall and quickly severed it with one of the tools from his coat. In less than a minute he was back on the ground, again digging into his pockets, this time for a suction cup and a diamond-tipped glass cutter. He chose the back door for his entry, applied the suction cup to one of its panes, etched around it and popped out the circle of glass. The door had a knob lock and a deadbolt. DeVilbiss slipped on a pair of plastic, disposable gardening gloves, undid the lock, then felt along the upper doorjamb molding until he located the deadbolt key. His slender fingers had no trouble fitting it into the keyhole and turning back the bolt. After DeVilbiss scanned the neighborhood, he entered the house. He found himself inside a utility room. He slipped off his coat and let it collapse into a blunt pyramid on the floor, then paused and listened. The house and household slept; even the heater had stopped blowing Btu's through the ductwork.

The utility room entered onto the kitchen, which lay in a state of chaos. Dirty dishes were piled in and around the sink. Shopping bags stood gutted on the counters, their bottoms still packed with non-perishable groceries. A stack of pizza boxes leaned precariously beside the overflowing garbage pail. Seven vases of various shapes filled the table in the breakfast nook. Only one held flowers—the all-but-mummified remains of chrysanthemums. DeVilbiss inhaled the air deeply. Not more than a week earlier, the house had held many floral varieties.

DeVilbiss glided toward the front of the house, through a formal dining room (in nearly as profound disarray as the kitchen), and into the foyer area. The second-story staircase ran parallel with the front door. On the wall directly below it hung many award plaques. DeVilbiss read with no surprise the national and international commendations of McCarthy's genius in laser optics. The only greater award McCarthy could garner now was the Nobel Prize. It was he who had made practicable the "Star Wars" laser for killing intercontinental nuclear missiles, prompting one reporter to call him "the Cold War warrior whose work broke the back of the Soviet military economy." Now he worked on matter and antimatter aspects of light waves, research that hinted at dimensions beyond those of normal human senses. How and how much this threatened the Dark Forces, DeVilbiss could only guess at. Perhaps if the Ahriman scrolls had not surfaced in Princeton, McCarthy might have been allowed to live, but it cost nothing for those who controlled DeVilbiss to tack a murder onto his trip. Most of the wall plaques, like the articles in DeVilbiss's folder, also held the name "Dieter Gerstadt." Vincent told himself he should be grateful that they hadn't ordered both scientists' extermination.

DeVilbiss's attention shifted to the Parsons table under the awards. The table was filled with sympathy cards. He picked one up and read it. When he returned it to its place, he discovered a Mass card lying facedown. He brought it up to his eye level and strained to read the fine print in the near-total darkness. The name of the deceased was Kathleen McCarthy. Martin McCarthy's wife. By the dates not quite thirty-six, and dead only twelve days. Her image was captured in two framed photographs on the table—a wedding picture with Martin and a family portrait that must have been recently taken.

DeVilbiss set the card down on the table and gazed up the stairwell, toward the upper hallway. Through the doors beyond slept a thirty-eight-year-old widower, twin eleven-year-old sons, and a seven-year-old daughter.

DeVilbiss grimaced and swept back his hair in a nervous, repetitious motion. He lowered his hand and started toward the stairs. He stopped on the first step and looked back at the sympathy cards. This wasn't working.

DeVilbiss retraced his path into the kitchen, but instead of continuing to the back door, he noiselessly entered the family room. He found a wall unit filled with high-tech consumer electronics and disconnected the compact disc player and a Nintendo game computer. Because he had cut the phone line, he felt the scale of the robbery had to be greater. He grabbed as well the family's camcorder, but made sure that he unloaded the tape inside it before he left. On the way out, he closed the door against the December cold.

The stolen property was dumped carelessly onto the backseat of the rented car. DeVilbiss thrust himself behind the steering wheel and twisted the key in the ignition. The old Ford Escort whined and threatened to play dead. He smashed his fist into the door. The window crank snapped off and clattered to the floor. DeVilbiss winced and lifted his hand to his view. His middle knuckles were split open and bleeding freely. He watched without emotion as the blood staunched and scabbed and his severed flesh closed into smooth skin, all within the space of sixty seconds. He rammed the accelerator to the floor and turned the key again. The engine caught life and mustered strength. DeVilbiss pulled away from the McCarthy house as quickly as the motorized junkyard would allow.

Vincent assured himself that there was no way he could have known from the other side of the country that Martin McCarthy's wife had died. It had nothing to do with shoddy intelligence gathering. The material he had collected in the folder informed him of every aspect of the man's educational background, his full professional achievements as recently as November, and even the fact that he was married and had children. Not that family mattered to those who controlled Vincent. The last thing that would motivate them was humanitarianism. For more than four hundred years, Vincent had refused to think about that. Lately, however, he thought about it more and more. And sometimes, as now, he acted. Because this time there was a way for the young father to live. McCarthy's partner, Dieter Gerstadt, could substitute as the sacrificial lamb. Truthfully, DeVilbiss felt pleasure in his decision to play Grim Reaper at Gerstadt's house instead. Reading between the lines of numerous journal, magazine, and newspaper reports, DeVilbiss had gleaned that the naturalized German was McCarthy's professorial mentor but probably not his equal partner in the team's dramatic scientific breakthroughs. Gerstadt was childless and in his mid-sixties and had shown little evidence of individual genius before taking McCarthy under his wing, first as a graduate student, then assistant professor. But the mentor had made himself the spokesman of the team, hogging the limelight and consequently relegating McCarthy to undeserved shadow. The valuable reputation Gerstadt had established for himself was the only reason Vincent could disobey with impunity the order for McCarthy's death. *Pride goeth before a fall, Dieter,* DeVilbiss thought with cold satisfaction, steering out of the housing development, never considering how aptly the adage might apply to him.

Dieter Gerstadt might have lacked inventive genius when it came to physics, but his talent for earning money was evident from the house he owned. It was a fair imitation of a Frank Lloyd Wright creation, thrusting out over a steep decline that plunged into Princeton's Carnegie Lake. Like Wright's Fallingwater, it was situated among dense woods and craggy outcroppings, two hundred feet from either neighbor. The view across the lake, to the canal and hills beyond, was spectacular enough to have commanded a premium price. Dieter and his wife, Greta, had occupied the place for more than twenty years and intended to die there some day. Except for a much accelerated timetable, Vincent DeVilbiss shared their desire.

DeVilbiss parked the car out of sight of the house and walked back along the quiet street. He stared up into the cloudless sky and admired Orion and Cassiopeia. The constellations hardly twinkled in the cold air. With the moon below the horizon, even the fainter stars shone brightly. DeVilbiss drew oxygen deeply into his lungs as he strode. The more he thought about the night's change of plan, the better he felt. He pictured Gerstadt as a hyena, a scavenger who preferred to eat from the kill of nobler beasts but who was nonetheless deadly on his own. Proper prey for the King of Predators.

When DeVilbiss entered the Gerstadt driveway, his smile vanished and his face hardened into a death mask. He removed his fur-lined winter gloves and substituted the plastic gardening pair. The white driveway gravel crunched under his step. He softened his tread, beginning a silent circuit of the house. Houses were easy hunting grounds for him; the arrangement of doors and chimneys and the placement and sizes of windows invariably betrayed the interior layout. This structure was a modified one-story, with a lower level created in the back by the land's sharp plunge toward the lake. The rear of the upper part was cantilevered out, leaving a sheltered space below, which had been finished with a wooden deck and barbecue pit. DeVilbiss crossed the deck and peered through the lower level's glass wall. Within the darkness lay a large study and recreation area, dominated by a regulation-size billiards table. Beyond stood two doors, which DeVilbiss supposed led into the utility room and either a bathroom or storage. Before he had put his nose to the glass, his amber eyes detected the infrared glow of an optical alarm system. Gerstadt had put his academic skills to practical use; several pencil-thin red beams crisscrossed the study. He had obviously intended the beams as a second line of defense, because the sliding glass doors onto the patio had a key lock, upper and lower bolts, and a stout iron bar shoved into the slide track for good measure. DeVilbiss's smile returned as he continued his reconnaissance; after his failure at the library he needed a kill with some challenge, to restore his confidence.

DeVilbiss stepped out onto the grass and shed his greatcoat. Unencumbered, he coiled his muscles and sprang with catlike strength and agility to the upper-level balcony, hands grabbing the rail tightly. He hauled himself over and surveyed his clothing. His sweater had snagged badly on the wood. He shook his head and retrained his attention on the rooms beyond the upper glass wall. Again he detected infrared beams, knifing across the expensively furnished living and dining rooms. Beyond, he could see part of the kitchen via a pass-through. A hallway led back toward the bedrooms. The upper sliding doors were as pickproof as the lower ones had been. Nor could he use his suction cup and diamond-tipped etching tools again; the misfortunes at the McCarthy and Gerstadt houses had to appear to be completely unrelated incidents. Here could be no indication of break-in whatsoever. Nothing he couldn't solve.

DeVilbiss looked through the sliding door to the living room ceiling. Cut into it were a pair of skylights. He vaulted over the balcony rail, picked up his coat and retraced his path to the car. In the trunk lay his seldom-used equipment. The kills he made for his own sustenance rarely required more than speed and strength. But old Dieter was a hyena. DeVilbiss had decided to reequip himself. He folded the coat and dropped it into the trunk, pulled up his damaged black sweater, and strapped on the special equipment.

Again, a garbage can provided access to the top of the garage. From there he surveyed the entire length of the house's flat rooftop. He noted four skylights in all—the two at the far end, which he had already seen, and two more just past the garage. DeVilbiss treaded noiselessly to the nearest skylight and stooped to peer through it. The plastic had weathered to a cloudy sheen. From what he had seen on the balcony he calculated that this skylight illuminated the back end of the hallway. The final skylight would surely not be located in a bedroom, where unimpeded sunlight might spoil an afternoon nap. DeVilbiss was confident it brightened a bathroom.

DeVilbiss knelt beside the fourth skylight and felt around its fastenings, testing their strength, calculating how much power he needed to exert and how long its removal would take. His fingers found the tops of four round-headed screws. In his belt he had shoved a hammer and a cold chisel. He set the chisel against the first screwhead and gave it a hard tap. The head snapped off with a sharp, metallic noise. DeVilbiss put his ear to the skylight and listened. He heard nothing. He set the chisel to the next screwhead and swung the hammer again. This time, after the striking, he caught sounds from within the house. Wasting no more time, he clawed his fingertips under the skylight lip and wrenched upward. The plastic bubble tore away with the groan of a falling tree. DeVilbiss tossed it aside, peered down to orient himself, then dropped into the bathroom. The reek of stale cigarette smoke assaulted his nostrils.

"Go, Greta, go!"

The imperative voice echoed from the other side of the bathroom door. Hearing the muffled sounds of feet scudding across carpeting, DeVilbiss wasted no time in plunging through the doorway. He entered the dark master bedroom, quickly taking in its dimensions. The damned thing was the size of a squash court. He focused his attention on a small, bald-headed man who had boxed himself between the bed and the wall on the far corner of the room. The man had his back to DeVilbiss and was reaching into the open drawer of the bedside table behind him. He was dressed in flannel pajamas which failed to cover his lower back and upper buttocks. He spun around; his hand gripped a revolver. DeVilbiss recognized the pudgy face from several magazine photos. Dieter Gerstadt groped blindly behind himself for the bedside lamp's switch, unaware that he had nudged the telephone handset cockeyed on its cradle as he did. His face defined terror, eyes bulging from the effort of picking the intruder from the darkness. DeVilbiss surveyed the distance to his quarry and debated his next move. At the other end of the house an insistent alarm went off. Greta had interrupted one of the infrared beams. Dieter jumped at the noise and uttered a yelp of fear. The gun barrel traced an erratic figure eight.

"I have a gun!" The professor's voice at least was authoritative and determined. The bedside light flooded the room. As Gerstadt's eyes involuntarily squeezed shut, DeVilbiss took his chance. He threw himself across the length of the chamber, keeping his chest on line with the weapon's muzzle.

The revolver's report echoed sharply in the enclosed area; the bullet's flame flashed bright. DeVilbiss's momentum was vectored abruptly, so that he spun completely around, fell against the side of the mattress and collapsed to the ground. His left leg folded under him and his right arm came to rest against the wall, fingers curled down like those of the crucified Christ. His eyes stared up at the ceiling, unblinking.

Gerstadt coughed lightly but seemed unaware of the acrid gunpowder smoke floating in front of him. He focused on the blood sprayed across the eggshell white wall and the elliptical hole where the bullet had dug in at an angle. The trembling of his gun hand redoubled.

"Mein Gott!" the professor murmured, reverting in shock to his native language. *"Mein Gott!"* Having defended himself with obvious success, he thought next of escape and realized his choice was either over the high bed or past the corpse. He chose the latter, advancing slowly, with the gun pointed. He took one step and paused, making sure the body remained motionless.

On Gerstadt's second step, DeVilbiss's free leg swung up fast and hard, catching the man's groin a glancing blow. Gerstadt's hand twitched and the revolver went off again. Lead flew into the meat of DeVilbiss's thigh. DeVilbiss screamed out his rage as he sat up. His left hand batted the revolver roughly from the professor's hand and his right grabbed the material of the pajama bottoms. He yanked down and took his prey's falling weight upon himself. The terrorized face came nose to nose with his own. Gerstadt's hands windmilled feebly to fend off DeVilbiss's attack. DeVilbiss ignored them, grabbed a hank of the professor's white hair and drove his head hard into the wall. In spite of his pain and rage, he reined in his strength so that none of the professor's bones would be broken. When the man continued to struggle, DeVilbiss rammed his head again. Finally, his victim went limp.

DeVilbiss tossed the body off himself and dived for the telephone. The instant he had the handset he swept his finger across several buttons. Then he listened. He heard it ring and prayed he had not been too late. He heard also the ragged breath of the woman who had made the call. On the third ring a connection was made.

"Hello?" said a sleepy voice.

"Is this the police?" Greta Gerstadt beseeched.

"No." The answering voice had come awake enough to be angry. "You dialed the—"

DeVilbiss dropped the phone, not waiting to hear the end of the conversation. With the bedroom handset off the switchhook, the woman could not hang up and redial. DeVilbiss pulled himself up and started doggedly toward the hallway. The phone book had listed only one telephone for the Gerstadt residence, but he knew that Dieter might have an unlisted business number. He redoubled his efforts, guiding himself by the hallway wall, hopping forward on his good leg and letting the wounded one drag. He longed to sit still and rest, to at least clean out the hole in his side. Bullet damage, to flesh or organ, took at least an hour to heal completely, but he had not a second to spare.

The hallway opened onto the kitchen and dining area. DeVilbiss saw no one. He held his breath to listen. On the lower level the sliding door was being unbolted. He aimed himself at the top of the stairs and limped forward. The infrared alarm was an inside warning system; because of the distance between properties, the neighbors were unlikely to be awakened by its pulses. But DeVilbiss was quite certain that the woman's shrieks were capable of waking the dead once she got outside the house. Halfway down the stairs, he heard the scraping sound of the sliding door being shoved back. He worked his way lower and got his head around so he could see the door. The wife was stumbling out, unaware of his presence. The noise of the alarm had masked his clumsy advance. She paused for a moment, debating which way to run. DeVilbiss noted that, like her husband, she was dressed in pajamas. Hers were silk, and they swirled around her as she halted. DeVilbiss swung past the newel post and lurched across the room. As he reached the open doorway, the woman turned and saw him. Her hand flew up across her open mouth. She made no outcry but concentrated her energies on pivoting around and sprinting away.

DeVilbiss stopped favoring his leg. He came down hard on it, moaned in agony, and pushed off. As the night air hit him, he caught sight of the woman rounding the corner of the house, stumbling slightly over the ice-slick grass. He blocked out the agonizing pain and raced after her. With each stride, a neural explosion went off inside his wounded thigh. Halfway up the slope he caught the professor's wife and tackled her. Finally, she attempted to call for help, but the force of her landing had driven most of the wind from her. Clawing along her clothing, DeVilbiss drew his weight fully on top of her. She flailed wildly to turn over, but she lacked the weight and strength to succeed. DeVilbiss grabbed her as he had the husband, fingers clawing up a fistful of hair. He shoved her face hard into the cold, brittle grasses. She tried to scream again, but her sounds were muffled. She was still getting air. Montague snaked his hand around her face, found her nostrils and pinched them shut with his thumb and forefinger, using the heel of his hand to dam up her mouth. For a time the fighting became even more frantic. Then her muscles relaxed. DeVilbiss released his hold, wanting her unconscious rather than dead. He rested a moment, then stood up.

DeVilbiss flipped the woman over, grabbed her again by the hair, and dragged her down the slope. Her foot caught in one of the deck step's open risers and had to be released. Then her pajama bottoms snagged on the doorway track. DeVilbiss kicked her inert form in frustration. He leaned against the glass and counseled himself back into control, then worked the body into the house, leaving it beside the open door.

With the two occupants incapacitated, DeVilbiss turned his attention to the alarm. He found the reset switch in the utility room and reflected that the restored silence was golden indeed. DeVilbiss dropped himself into Dieter's tufted leather study chair to catch his breath. He gingerly lifted the sweater to examine his torso wound. It lay one inch under and half an inch to the side of his antiballistic Kevlar vest. Even his cautious measures had not protected him from a man too nervous to shoot straight. Over the decades, several of his victims had owned guns, keeping them in their houses, their cars, and even on their persons. Despite their precautions none of them had survived, even the swift and the sure of aim. None had anticipated dealing with the Undying.

DeVilbiss guessed that the bullet had torn through his right kidney. He felt his back for the exit wound. His forefinger fit into the hole, which was already smoothing over. He didn't want to think how large the wound had been five minutes before. It would heal completely and undetectably in time; time itself had assured the fact, over and over. Neither time nor any other man, however, could teach him the limits of his invincibility. He was certain that there was such a thing as a killing wound, something as final as decapitation, for example. But he had a disquieting suspicion that death could be brought on by far less grisly insult. Perhaps a knife blade severing the spinal cord at the base of his neck. Or a bullet shattering his aorta, so the healing blood could not pump through the heart and make him whole again. Which was why he took state-of-the-art precautions such as his bulletproof vest whenever he anticipated a dangerous opponent.

DeVilbiss tugged down his sweater and struggled out of the chair, groaning. Even if he were completely invincible, burns, punctures and even the scratches of frantic fingernails were as painful to him as to any other human. He had merely learned to master pain over the centuries. Once he knew it would pass quickly and his body would not be permanently scarred or disabled, he taught himself to block out injuries that would have shocked the ordinary man into unconsciousness within seconds.

Greta Gerstadt lay faceup where he had left her. DeVilbiss was grateful for the linoleum flooring beneath her. The trail of dirt and blood could be easily cleaned. The woman's ruined and soiled pajamas were of no concern; soon they would not be in any condition for examination. DeVilbiss drew in several breaths, testing to see if he had regained enough strength to carry the woman back to her bedroom. He approached her and kneeled.

The iron doorstop bar arced into DeVilbiss's field of vision as if from nowhere. Somehow, without making noise, the professor's wife had found the bar and concealed it alongside her length. Vincent thrust up his arm to protect his face, but she had picked another target. She had seen the bullet hole in his pants and swung the bar directly into the wound.

DeVilbiss howled and fell over backward, grabbing his thigh in agony. Greta rolled away, clutched the handle of the sliding door and pulled herself up. Before DeVilbiss could dominate his pain, she had swung around the door and was out into the night once more.

This time she did not reach the corner of the house before DeVilbiss had hauled her down. She flipped herself over, not about to have her face shoved into the earth again. As her attacker drew his weight over her, she came at him with a Harpy's fury. Her mouth yawned open, and she buried her teeth in his neck. DeVilbiss felt the clamp of her incisors and was struck by the irony of the act. This was one tough human, fighting with every fiber to save her life. He was the last man on earth to belittle her struggle; he had been doing the same for five hundred years, at people's throats with as great purpose. But her death was required for his life, and so their mutual rights devolved to survival of the fittest.

The contest was over almost before it began. DeVilbiss drew the woman's mouth from his neck, clamped his hand again around it, twisted her body inexorably until he had her in a comfortable feeding position, then drove his incisors deeply into her throat. Her gushing blood tasted hot from her efforts, adrenaline sweet from her panic. He sucked deeply, until her struggles ceased. Regretfully he lifted his mouth. He had not opened a throat for a full week. But he knew that she must not be killed by blood loss. He lifted her unconscious form and carried her into the house and up to the bedroom.

Dieter Gerstadt lay where he had been tossed. DeVilbiss studied the room. The bed was high and sturdy, covered with a thick eiderdown comforter. An armoire stood in one corner, despite a large walk-in closet. On the wall hung a mass-produced oil painting of a Bavarian chalet, with Alpine mountains thrusting up behind. The room looked like it belonged to the house in the painting and not as part of the imitation Frank Lloyd Wright extravanganza. The other rooms were contemporary Americana; this inner sanctum, it seemed, was the Gerstadts' last hold on their roots.

DeVilbiss tucked Greta under the comforter, then pulled Dieter into place. The uneven sag of the mattress proved that the man slept on the side where the gun had been concealed. DeVilbiss checked in the open drawer and found the expected pack of cigarettes and matches. Camels. It was interesting, he noted, how a man who would kill another man to live smoked such a deadly brand. He lowered himself to Dieter's neck and tested his blood. Its tang was not that of the dreaded B type, which gave him an allergic reaction akin to hives. He drank his fill, assured that both the man and woman would now be too weak to rise from their deathbed. He fetched the revolver, methodically cleaned and reloaded it, and placed it back in the drawer. Then he went downstairs and cleaned the floor, relocked, bolted, and barred the sliding door, and repositioned the professor's chair. He paused on the main level to admire the Christmas tree. It was a blue spruce, at least nine feet tall. It was tastefully decorated with white velvet ribbons and beautiful crystal ornaments that caught even the faint light from the hallway. DeVilbiss wondered if the couple's predilection for crystal had anything to do with Gerstadt's dealings with optics. Under the tree lay mounds of presents, expensively wrapped. DeVilbiss lost count at twenty. He was not curious enough to see how many were meant for others. They should have been, he thought, as he looked around the living room. What more could the professor and his wife have wanted? They owned the best furniture, thick carpeting, magnificent brass lighting fixtures, handsomely framed out-of-date German posters. Within the wall unit, top-of-the-line components bore the names Sony, Panasonic, Bose. The kitchen boasted every labor-saving device imaginable, including a trash compactor. On the counter sat an immense, seven-tiered Christmas candle windmill. But there was no sign of the *Christkind* anywhere.

DeVilbiss retreated into the hallway, where he found the arming switch for the infrared alarm. He turned it on and continued to the main bathroom, where he found isopropyl alcohol for his wounds. Experience had taught him that it helped the mysterious healing process. His teeth clamped together at the sharp sting, but he did not cry out. He returned to the master bedroom. The eiderdown comforter proved a perfect material for burning. DeVilbiss first lit a match, transferred the flame to a cigarette, placed the cigarette between Dieter's unresisting fingers and touched it to the cover. Within thirty seconds the bed was aflame. For good measure, DeVilbiss trailed a terrycloth bathrobe from the bed to the drapes. Clutching a water-soaked washcloth to his mouth and nose to filter the smoke, he watched from the master bathroom doorway until the fire had crept into the carpeting. By that time, the professor's hair had already been consumed in flame. DeVilbiss climbed onto the sink counter and boosted himself up through the skylight opening. He shoved the skylight down tightly and bounded along the roof toward the garage. He smiled broadly; his leg and side were feeling considerably better.

CHAPTER SIX

December 17

Woe unto them that call evil good,

and good evil. . . .

—*Isaiah 5:20*

The main stairs of the Vanderveen mansion creaked like a set of old bones. Even over the sizzle of butter in the frying pan, Simon heard each step of Frederika's descent. His stomach tensed with the expectation of the first moments, but the sight of her relaxed him. She was again bundled in her ratty old bathrobe and had her hair pulled up into a ponytail. He faced the stove quickly and busied himself sliding the turner under the pancakes.

"Smells great," Frederika said.

"Thanks. You want some?"

He heard one of the kitchen chairs scrape along the tile floor. "That's okay. Maybe I'll eat this."

A large lazy Susan sat in the middle of the table. On the side away from Frederika, a solitary fudge-topped walnut brownie beckoned from under a glass bubble. When Simon turned, he saw her inching the dessert toward her with the tips of two fingers. He reached over, stopped the lazy Susan's circuit and removed the brownie.

"Wrong," he said. "Physical laws make bad breakfasts."

"Physical laws?" she obliged.

Simon piloted the dessert and its container onto the kitchen counter, well out of her reach. "Surely you've heard of Brownian movement?"

Frederika's expression was pure blank. "No."

114

"Some guy named Robert Brown discovered the random motion of molecules in a liquid. Brownian movement. Ergo, this is *brownie* in—"

"I get it," she said, resting her head on her hand. "It deserves death, but don't torture it."

Simon went back to his pancakes.

"You are *strange*," Frederika pronounced, after a moment of silence.

Simon glanced over his shoulder at her. Her chin still rested on the back of her hand, as she studied him. She looked like one of the placid young matrons in Mannerist paintings. He realized that this was the first time she had bothered to truly see him. The relationship had changed. In spite of her pronouncement about him, her expression was relaxed and mildly curious.

"Strange . . . *c'est moi*," he admitted.

"That's all right," she granted. "So am I."

"There's plenty here," he offered, flipping two silver-dollar-sized pancakes at once. "I always make extra. Did you know you can freeze batter?"

"I'd heard. You didn't seem to believe my gratitude last night I meant it."

"You're welcome."

"I didn't see your shining armor when you moved in."

Simon flipped a pancake high into the air, made a sloppy catch and watched it land cooked side down on the griddle. "That's because I don't own any. Don Quixote was the last true knight. I'm just an ordinary madman."

"Mad perhaps, but not ordinary," Frederika returned, rising. "Where's the syrup? What kind of a greasy spoon diner is this?"

The breakfast conversation continued with tea—specifically the cure which Frederika finally admitted having visited an herbalist for the previous night. She belittled the herbs' powers, however, guessing that what she had had was "one of those viruses that last forty-eight hours and disappear." The brew had probably quieted her cough and opened her nose long enough for her to get the night of sleep she needed. Simon made no comment.

Once she had amended the explanation of her disappearance, Frederika moved immediately to the subject of the university's main library, prodding Simon into dialogue with innocuous questions. Looking for a reason behind her changed attitude in him, he waited in vain for a charged topic which never came. They were like strangers attempting a first dance together, stiffly formal and behind tempo. Before the subject had exhausted itself, however, shared tastes in books and reverence for the printed word started a free flow. The rhythm of their dialogue accelerated. Eventually, Simon's growing ease prompted him to enthuse about the Schickner Collection.

"It really is a coup for the university, isn't it?" Frederika asked.

"Yes. Especially the Akkadian scrolls. Reverend Spencer . . . he's the expert translating them . . ."

"I think I saw him waiting in front of the doors the other morning. An old man with frizzy white hair?"

"He's the one," Simon said, captured again by her blue eyes but noting this time the depth of intelligence radiating from them. She was not the only one seeing afresh with the new day. "He . . . what was I saying . . . oh yes. He calls them the Ahriman scrolls."

"I'd heard of them," said Frederika.

"From *The Chronicle* or the *New York Times*," Simon supposed.

"No. From my roommate . . . the one you made the translations for . . . she told me about them."

"Really?"

"They're supposed to have a passage on necromancy somewhere in them."

Her words, though casually delivered, fell on Simon's ears like a mallet blow. He held on to his smile with difficulty. "That's interesting. When did she tell you this?"

"Yesterday," Frederika said. She lied with the effortless grace of a deer eluding a clumsy stalker. While he enjoyed the improvement in their relationship, he also saw that she was not about to invest trust in him. At least not right away. She was steering the conversation purposely into the Stygian waters of necromancy, her quest for dialogue with the dead undeterred.

116

"She called when you were out, to thank me for the translation you made," Frederika continued. "Then she told me she'd read about the scrolls arriving at the university. I don't know how she knows about the necromantic passages, but she ended up begging me to do whatever I can to see if she can get a copy."

"What about her advisor going on sabbatical?" Simon asked.

Frederika's reply was immediate and unhalting. "She's willing to push back her graduation for this. She's sure her thesis would be publishable if she could get the passages."

Simon shook his head gravely. "Reverend Willy's a nice man, but he'd never allow his thunder to be stolen by a girl pursuing a master's degree."

"What if she could persuade her advisor to come here on her behalf and read the passages?"

"That's even more remote."

Frederika's bright demeanor dimmed. "I'm sure it's only a couple paragraphs in the whole thing. You don't read Akkadian, do you?"

Simon shook his head impotently. "Not one word. Even if I did, it's Reverend Spencer's baby. Besides, I can't even open the storage vaults without him or Dr. Gould. The system requires two keys and two people simultaneously pressing buttons on opposite ends of the room to take them out."

"Damn." Frederika looked crushed.

Simon enjoyed his newly gained favor too much to lose it so soon. There was also the possibility that a few well-chosen words from him might keep her waiting for a skeleton key into the next world rather than running back to the man on Park Place for help. Before that happened, he hoped to know considerably more about her and her mysterious need to speak with her dead father. "Maybe Willy wouldn't mind," he retrenched. "He and I are getting to be fast friends. At least I could ask him if he's found any spirit-summoning passages. If he has, I'm sure he'd show me his translation."

"That would be wonderful!" Frederika enthused. Even without makeup her skin glowed. She possessed naturally a blush that less blessed women emulated with rouge. The blue of her irises seemed flecked with sparkling slivers of ice, making them fiery and cold at

117

the same moment. Simon decided that she had perhaps not given enough credit to the herbal tea's curative powers. He could not remember seeing anyone so imbued with health.

They chatted on for a while longer about books, each wanting to end with something less charged than the subject of the Ahriman scrolls. Frederika volunteered to scour the griddle if Simon did the rest. While they worked, Simon remembered the Christmas tree, leaning in a bucket of water in the foyer. They decided to decorate it immediately.

Frederika brought Simon down into the basement to fetch the tree base and lights. While he finished securing the lights to the upper branches she descended again, for the last of the ornaments. She had still not returned when Simon finished, so he refocused his attention on the Steinway grand near the front window. He sat, lifted the lid, and, with his forefinger, plunked out the melody of "Lo, How a Rose E'er Blooming." In spite of the magnificent piano's exquisitely maintained exterior it was badly out of tune. Its insides had evidently not been cared for since Frederik Vanderveen had died. Or, Simon mused, perhaps since the father had shipped Frederika off to school in Switzerland.

Simon unboxed decorations while Frederika did the hanging. He found a cache of genuine Victorian ornaments. They were meticulously painted blown glass, imported from Germany and Italy in his grandparents' day—silver-scaled fish, fat-faced cherubs, angels, lambs, faded St. Nicholases, and mirrored balls shameless with glittering detail. Then, while he secured the last of them on the tree's upper branches, Frederika sat on the floor patiently stringing popcorn. He turned on the ladderstep with a thought. "I assume you're Christian."

"I was raised Dutch Reformed," she answered, not looking up from her work.

"And do you still practice?"

"No."

"This is just a celebration of season."

"At least for now," Frederika said. "God will have to come to me if he wants my attention. And you?"

118

"I don't deny God's existence; it's just that right now I feel the need to seek earthly things much more than heavenly ones. The same as you, I expect."

She did not deny his supposition, but he was convinced her obsession took no earthly fix at all.

The glowing cheeks, flowing blond hair, and graceful arms of the Italian crowning papier-mâché angel presented more than a passing resemblance to Frederika. Simon had almost secured it to the top of the tree when the telephone rang.

"It's for you," Frederika announced.

Simon accepted the outheld phone sheepishly. He muttered a hello.

"Simon, it's Rich." His doctoral candidate friend from the physics department.

"Yes, Rich."

"I want to let you know I'll be hanging around town for the holidays." Rich's voice had a disquieted edge.

"Really? What happened?"

"Professor Gerstadt died in a fire last night." Gerstadt was Rich's advisor.

"My God!" Simon reacted. "How horrible!"

"Somebody in physics knows a volunteer in the fire department. He said it started in their bedroom. Probably from a cigarette. Gerstadt smoked like a chimney. He wasn't the easiest guy to get along with, but he didn't deserve that. His wife died, too."

"Terrible. What does this do to your dissertation?"

"I don't know," Rich said. "I'll just keep slogging through the holiday. I could have some definite results by New Year's. Maybe Professor McCarthy will take pity and pick me up."

"Merry Christmas," Simon wished, ironically. "Is there anything I can do?"

"Just be willing to hear me bitch. I'm gonna need to pause and unwind every few days. Will you be around?"

"Sure. Count on me. Let's have dinner tomorrow night."

"Sounds good. At the Annex, so we can drink."

"The Annex is fine. Let's make it six-thirty." Simon watched

Frederika sitting crosslegged like a squaw, stringing popcorn and pretending not to listen. "Call me tomorrow at work," Simon suggested. A few moments later the conversation reached its natural conclusion and he hung up.

Simon picked up one of the decoration boxes and gathered the strewn tissue paper into it. "I gave a couple people your number," he admitted. "I hope you don't mind. It didn't seem to make much sense getting my own phone for two weeks."

"It's okay," Frederika said. "You couldn't get a phone installed quickly this time of year anyway. What happened?"

Simon summarized the conversation. Frederika clucked sympathetically. For a time, each worked within the silence of private thoughts. Simon mused on the sudden, violent deaths of two university employees. Tommy Wheeler's suicide had not yet made the biweekly *Princeton Packet*, but it would. Gerstadt's death and life would no doubt be chronicled. Simon had a bad feeling about the deaths. Common superstition predicted such ill-fated events occurring in threes. He had chosen a new path for his efforts just the night before. Linking himself to Frederika Vanderveen, even tenuously, seemed a dangerous undertaking. He hoped fervently that while she was seeking the dead, Death was not even more relentlessly seeking her.

DeVilbiss turned the page of the Sunday *New York Times*. On the floor next to his easy chair lay editions of the London *Times*, *Le Figaro*, *La Stampa*, and *Die Zeit*. The most convincing evidence of little Princeton's global urbanity was the international news gazebo on Palmer Square. The Dark Forces required two perpetual activities of DeVilbiss: the first was to report on the rise of any individual who might contribute significantly to peace and the betterment of the human condition (which made that person likely prey); the second was to watch for the appearance of any book that translated, quoted from, or even mentioned the contents of the scrolls attributed to Ahriman. For his own very private purpose, he also needed a daily copy of the most influential newspaper of the particular country he happened to be in.

The page that DeVilbiss scanned was filled with news of the former Soviet Union and the violence that arose from its restructuring. He was certain that thousands reading the same article would be telling each other they had not dreamed of living to see this day. Such a phrase would never spring to his lips; he expected to outlive not only Soviet communism but United States democracy and whatever regimes replaced both. He had lived through the culmination of the Renaissance, the discovery of the New World, the Classic era, Biedermeier culture, the French Revolution, Napoleon, Romanticism, the Industrial Revolution, Darwinism, the Jazz Age, Hitler, and the Cold War. Every race and age strove mightily, driven mad by the relentless ticking of clocks—both natural and of their own fashioning. He watched the human tectonic upheavals— violent revolutions springing from hope and despair—and waited for what he trusted would be the most important of ages: that of his inevitable freedom. He patiently rode the waves of the decades, anticipating the discoveries of those few more bits of knowledge that would free him forever.

From the kitchen, the relentless *Fortspinnung* of Bach's d minor piano concerto unwound. The music made him yearn for his grand piano, stored in Zurich. The fingers of his left hand tapped out the bass line of the piano part. Of all the languages he had learned, music spoke the truest, the most eloquently. In spite of his own athanasia, he often found himself jealous of the immortality a work of genius earned its creator. He was certain that, in spite of his gift of incorruptibility and his own particular genius—survival—the works of Bach, Shakespeare, and Michelangelo (and therefore part of each of them) would outlive him

The telephone rang. He lifted the receiver and identified himself.

"Vincent, it's Frederika."

"Frederika, my dear," he purred. "What glad tidings do you bring?"

"I'm almost positive I can get what you need. Eventually."

"What *we* need," he corrected. "How?"

"My friend in the Rare Manuscripts Preparation section is becoming close to the scrolls' translator."

"We don't need the translator. *I* can find what we need," DeVilbiss affirmed. "Can you at least play on your friendship enough that he'll get me inside?"

"It wouldn't be possible when the translator's there. And after hours they're locked in steel cases. The safeguards are unbelievable," she told him. He believed. "You'll have to be patient. It will take time."

"I have time," he assured her. *"You're* the one who needs to relax. Why don't you let me help? May I take you out to dinner and a movie tomorrow night?"

"That would be nice."

"Any time after six," he said. "I shall be here." They said their good nights.

Replacing the phone handset, DeVilbiss thought about Miss Frederika Vanderveen. He knew that he wanted more than the scrolls from her. And he would have it. Hers was a classic physical perfection, transcending the tastes and biases of particular countries or centuries. His greatest weakness had always been for things of timeless beauty, a concupiscence beyond that of normal men to touch, to possess, to surround himself with nonpareil objects. In his youth he had mortified his flesh to sublimate the desires, hoping to substitute visions of invisible, intangible perfections. But the pleasures of the flesh had proven too irresistible. This woman also possessed a rare reach of intelligence, but one hobbled by something he did not yet fully understand. It was a need that mastered her and impelled her on a naïve (and what he knew to be a futile) search. It was true that his paramount need for her was as the latest guinea pig in his quest for freedom. But he also *wanted* her, for both the rareness of her physical perfection and the mystery of her spiritual imperfection. She, as much as any other thing on earth, represented the reason why he still lived. And why he still paid the terrible price. When he was young, the writer of Ecclesiastes had told him that "desire shall fail" when man grows old. He had lived twenty-five score years, but his desire, if anything, had increased. When he was three hundred and fifty, Lord Byron had written, " 'Tis very certain the desire of life prolongs it." It was because he had chosen the philosophy of the English rake over that of the biblical poet that he had lived to read Byron's words.

DeVilbiss went back to his newspaper. He yawned grandly and stretched out like an old tomcat; every day, life was going more his way.

CHAPTER SEVEN

December 18

ⱺ

To live long is almost everyone's wish,

but to live well is the ambition of few.

—John Hughes, *The Lay Monk*

❧

Simon walked out of the library, heading in the direction of the Woodrow Wilson Building, which lay one block down Washington Road. His purpose was to learn all he could about Frederika and her formative years. The psychiatric couch approach was clearly not possible, as both his personal experience and that of his tennis partner, Dr. Yoskin, had proven. Simon would have to reconstruct the shaping of her mind indirectly, through the help of persons who had surrounded her when she was young.

Early in the morning he had gotten through to Stanley Krieger and arranged a brief appointment. Krieger had for three years served as dean of the School of Public and International Affairs and had been a professor at the university for twenty-two years before that. The pretext of Simon's request was a proposed Exhibitions Hall display on celebrated Princeton University professors. Simon told the dean that Frederik Vanderveen was to be one of the first subjects, and it was his job to begin gathering information. Stanley Krieger had been Professor Vanderveen's closest friend on campus.

The Woodrow Wilson Building was an easy landmark to spot. Its futuristic World's Fair lines, fashioned of whitewashed concrete, contrasted unhappily with the rest of the upper campus's stolid, Gothic limestone structures. In the plaza that faced it, the shallow

126

reflecting pool had been drained for the winter season. Its crazed, age-stained walls made the open space seem all the more bleak. Simon crossed the plaza, entered the building, and took the elevator to the top floor.

Dean Krieger was fifteen minutes behind schedule. When he finally appeared, he prefaced his brief apology with his guest's first name. They knew each other initially from a course the dean had taught. In the years that followed, a number of occasions had woven their lives tenuously together. Simon had little expectation of answers shedding sudden, revelatory light on Frederika's dark secrets; Stanley Krieger was above all things a diplomat, volunteering little in conversations and choosing his words with great care when he did. Nevertheless, his closeness to both Frederik Vanderveen and Vanderveen's daughter demanded that he be interviewed.

Krieger looked hale to Simon, in spite of advancing years. He was a short man but maintained an ideal weight through diet and exercise. The hair on his crown had thinned considerably in the past few years, but he had not succumbed to the common trick of growing side hair long and torturing it over the void. In compensation, his eyebrows grew thick and fierce, but these, too, the dean manicured to a fashionable length. His dress was always impeccable, proper and dignified. Today he wore a navy blue pinstripe suit, set off by red and blue regimental tie and red handkerchief. His shoes were black wingtip oxfords, shined to a fare-thee-well. Simon noted the crisp, boiled-white cuffs lying neatly just above the liver spots and protruding veins on the backs of his hands. His dress stood out especially on the Princeton campus, where most professors wore sports jackets without ties and worsted, gabardine, or denim pants over loafers, symbolizing the laid-back attitude of the true intellectual.

Krieger motioned Simon into his office and indicated their informal relationship by seating himself at one end of his tufted leather couch. Simon put himself down at the opposite end. On the coffee table in front of them sat a three-foot-high white artificial Christmas tree sporting two dozen golden balls, equispaced in four rings as if by a machine.

"I've got access to all the factual data," Simon assured, after the amenities. "What I'd appreciate from you, Dr. Krieger, is the benefit of your close friendship with Professor Vanderveen."

"The human element," Krieger interpreted.

"Exactly."

"I know very little of his boyhood or school days," Krieger began. "That you can get from his sister, I'm sure. Katerina . . . what's her married name? Callahan. Shouldn't be hard to remember, should it? Katerina Callahan. Brutal combination of names, don't you think?"

Simon nodded politely and took down the name on his notepad.

"She lives . . . or did the last time I communicated with her . . . in a suburb of Chicago." His eyes unfocused in thought. "Let's see . . . God, it's hell getting old. Don't ever do it, Simon. Elmhurst, I think. Yes, that's it. I'm sure she'll be happy to speak with you. Now, what can *I* supply? As a professor he was a font of knowledge but not an especially good teacher. He lacked the desire to entertain, to make the material fun. I suppose he expected everyone to be as motivated by public affairs as he was. And then he was also hard-nosed about grades. Could never accept the notion of grade inflation. To him, a C was a perfectly acceptable mark. For others, naturally. Certainly never for himself. Very high standards."

Simon was mildly stunned. He had not expected such candor, much less criticism, virtually from the dean's first remark.

"He dressed beautifully," Krieger continued. "Took me under his wing and transformed me from a tweedy old ragbag. And his speech! More impressive even than his dress. Every word was chosen with care, and when he lacked for the precise one, he'd pause until he had found it. No y'knows, ums, or ers. He'd stand there in complete silence for several seconds—it never took longer than that, he was so fleet of mind—and then would fall *le mot juste*. Often like a headsman's ax. His wit was beyond caustic. Acrid might describe it. Like Oscar Wilde and James Whistler rolled into one. He was at his wickedest behind closed doors, especially when someone opposed his will on hunger relief. I recall him referring to one foreign cabinet minister as an earlobe. When I later asked him why he'd

128

used the word, he said, 'Because an asshole has a function.' Don't you dare quote me on that. In the public eye, however, he was urbanity and mild manner personified. Few could resist his charm, especially since he cut such a handsome figure. I can recall several *quotable* instances."

Krieger's eyes looked beyond Simon's shoulder into the past. Using pithy anecdotes and direct quotations, he labored well to reanimate flesh on his dead friend's bones, characterizing the consummate diplomat who worked his humanitarian way with men of greater power but lesser will.

"He was a pragmatist as well," Krieger shared. "He wanted the family planning and the birth control right alongside the food relief, but he wasn't blind to religious, cultural, or ruling-class motives."

After several minutes of hearing nothing but praise and positive words, Simon decided that Krieger's early criticism was isolated and unique and that the remainder of his words would be purely eulogistic. The dean glanced at his watch, which Simon recognized as a Rolex. Simon knew that securing a second interview with Krieger on this subject would be considerably more difficult. He plunged into his true agenda.

"I need to know about the family man," Simon said. "How did his good qualities extend to his family?"

"I'm not certain they did," Krieger answered. For an instant his eyes met with Simon's, catching his former student's surprised look. Then he glanced away, made a loop of his thumb and middle finger and gave a fillip to an imaginary piece of dust on the back of the couch. "Frederik married late in life. The girl was considerably younger. Let's see . . . I guess it was twelve years' difference. Her name was Alice. She worked at the United Nations as a secretary, lacking any of his education or background. But she had charm, native intelligence, and great beauty. I'm sure her beauty was the first thing that attracted him. But I believe what convinced him to marry her was her commitment to world hunger relief and her unquestioning adoration of him. Closest thing to hero worship I'd ever seen. Not a partnership of equals."

"They had a daughter," Simon steered, hoping for more unexpected candor.

"That's right. Only one child. Frederika. She works in the library; you must know her."

"I've spoken with her, but I don't know her at all," Simon dissembled. "How did she and her father get along?"

Krieger's brows furrowed deeply. He stared thoughtfully at his interlaced fingers. "On the surface it seemed wonderful. He'd wanted a son, but he was soon pleased with her. She was such a beautiful little thing. The best combination of her mother and father's genes. Got his brains. Whenever he threw a party, he'd display her as the apple of his eye. Had her recite and play the piano. That sort of thing. He'd smile at her and she'd beam back. But I always thought I saw a glimmer of fear in her eyes. Not that he beat her, of course. No physical abuse."

"Fear from what, then?" Simon jumped in, too afraid Krieger might sail off on another tack.

"I believe it was his expectations. As I said, he set rigorous levels of behavior for himself, and he expected those around him to do no less. Especially, I'm sure, his own flesh and blood. Just too much for a child. If she played a sonatina for us and missed only two notes, those notes were what he would comment on. 'Very good, Freddie, but . . .' You understand?"

Simon nodded. His hand had stopped jotting words. "And her mother?" he asked, intentionally vague, inviting whatever response memory evoked.

"She did her best. Played the perfect hostess. Even dogged around the world with him for a time, languishing in hotel rooms while he worked. But I think she just got tired of trying to please him. One day he returned from Africa and found her gone. Moved out."

"Without her daughter."

Krieger stared at Simon, and the interviewer knew the dean was reconsidering his intimacies. "I don't see that any of this could be of value to your exhibit."

"I'm just trying to be exhaustive," Simon said, honestly. "But I suppose such questions are better put to Miss Vanderveen."

"I've done you a favor today," Krieger said, pointedly. "Do me one in return: leave Frederika alone." Krieger got up from the couch and walked slowly around the coffee table. He stretched across his desk and fetched a pen and pad. "She's a troubled young lady, and I'm sure much of it has to do with her family. She'd be little help to your project, but you may cause her great harm if you open up old wounds." He fell silent as he wrote several lines, finished with a flourish, ripped the paper from its pad and folded it in half.

The dean offered the paper to Simon. "Take this. I've written the names and phone numbers of two officials at the UN. They can tell you excellent stories of Frederik's skill as a diplomat. Stay away from Vanderveen the father and husband. Concentrate on the public man." He snapped the halves of his pen together.

Simon closed his notebook. The dean's words had the weight of finality. Simon expressed his thanks and ushered himself quickly out of the building.

The cold winter air felt good against Simon's burning cheeks. The dean had lost his wife six years ago. He was an older man, a man of power and authority, her father's best friend. Simon imagined Frederika returning to Princeton, Krieger offering the help of his influence and receiving in turn an invitation to her bed.

Simon shook his head at his wild speculation. His time was better spent amassing pieces of Frederika's formative years. He was sure the jigsaw puzzle was a vast one, and he had only begun to assemble the frame.

"If anybody calls, I'll be at the Annex," Simon sang out as he walked through the upper hallway.

"Fine," Frederika called back from her room. "Have fun."

Simon bounded down the creaking stairs and slammed the front door. For appearance's sake, he walked out to the sidewalk and turned in the direction of the town. He slowed his pace as soon as he was out of sight of the Vanderveen house. The huge colonial mass of bricks on the next lot lay dark. Simon jogged up the driveway and put himself in its shadows, from where he could see the entire side of the Vanderveen mansion.

Five minutes later, Frederika hurried out of her back door. Gone were the jeans she had changed into when she had gotten home from work. He saw an expanse of shapely leg between knee-length coat and high heels. She disappeared into the garage and emerged a minute later driving her white Mazda sedan. She backed down the driveway and onto Hodge Road as if she were late for an appointment.

Simon glanced at his watch. Twenty minutes past six. He was not meeting his friend Rich until seven-thirty. He had changed the hour of their dinner rendezvous that morning, when the physics student had called the library. Frederika had not surprised him. She was off to see the physically intimate herbalist on Park Place again, and she didn't want Simon to know. If the mystery that surrounded her was still far from solution, the woman's behavior was at least growing predictable.

Simon shouldered through the bushes that separated the properties and strode around the rear of the mansion to the stairs that climbed over the ballroom. Once inside, he made straight for Frederika's bedroom. He found the door unlocked. Her trust gave him only a moment of guilt; his purpose outweighed lesser moral restraints. He was looking for a diary. It was admittedly a long shot; Frederika did not seem like the type for longhand introspection. The thought of such a psychological Golconda, however, was hard to ignore. Simon poked carefully through drawers, across shelves, into closets and under her mattress. Among the many books he found (she seemed to be as voracious a reader as he) was her private phone book. He spent precious minutes furiously copying information. Otherwise, the room kept her secrets well. He had found far more of her personality in the cellar, where a row of college notebooks, essays, term papers, and even a thin book of her poems were stored, sandwiched between school yearbooks of herself, her father, and her mother. Simon meticulously restored her unique style of dishevel and retreated into the hall.

The door to Frederik Vanderveen's study stood effective sentry against Simon's curiosity. Hoping against hope, he tried his key in the lock. The keyhole took a different set of brass peaks and valleys. He gripped the knob hard and gave a quick twist. Neither the door nor the locking hardware was cheap; they held as if expecting invasion. Simon stepped back and looked up and down the hall. The study had no connecting doors. But it did have its own window; at a certain hour each afternoon, hard sunlight spilled under the door.

A large wooden ladder hung on one of the garage walls. Simon fought it off its hooks and set it flat on the concrete floor. He got the hang of raising it a rung at a time after twice catching his fingers. Only after he had it extended far enough to reach the mansion's second story did he realize how unwieldy he had made it. But the damned thing was too much trouble to collapse and reextend, so he dragged it along the driveway and did an impromptu circus clown act of struggling to get it upright, discovering he had it at the wrong window, rocking it along and getting it caught on the rain gutter, dropping it noisily onto the study window's mullions, finally getting it flush on the window stool. The one saving grace, he figured, was that no neighbor could possibly suppose such a clumsy exhibition would be performed by a burglar.

Standing near the top of the ladder, Simon pressed his face to the study glass. One light burned within the room, too feeble to be seen either from under the hallway door or from the driveway. It was a night-light, wed to an outlet that was set unusually high in the wall. The light shone like a votive candle, illuminating seven framed photographs spaced across the surface of a large wooden desk. Each picture was of Frederik Vanderveen and his daughter. In the picture on the far left he held her as a day-old bundle. Moving toward the right she grew progressively older until, in the last photo, she looked to be just entering her teenage years. The image of her mother was conspicuous by its absence.

Simon pushed up against the mullions. The window was locked into place. He peered through the glass again. The room was crammed with books, overflowing the built-in bookcases onto the floor. Manila folders and large envelopes buttressed the desk legs.

Under the photo frames, a number of typed pages were fanned out. An expensive fountain pen lay atop them, uncapped. Except for the glass covering the photographs, the corner of the room lit by the night-light was cloaked in a cerement of dust. Simon wondered if this was the scene of Vanderveen's fatal heart attack. He became aware of his rising gooseflesh. He climbed down and eased the ladder to the ground. Just as he had it collapsed and stored, the clock of nearby Trinity Church tolled out seven. He dusted himself off and headed for the street. Another day of his short-term boarding agreement with Frederika had flown, with little knowledge gained. Time did not favor Simon Penn.

The time was quarter to six, and the evening primroses obeyed their genetic clocks and continued to spread their petals fully open. Vincent had watched the process since the first fading of the winter sun, almost two hours before. He had not moved from the hardback chair set in front of the plant, had barely blinked in his concentration. It was not an act of self-discipline, although he had made exercises of similar situations. Nor was it for understanding; he left that to the inventors of time-lapse photography. It was simply for appreciation. If he had been a normal man, knowing that every beat of his heart, every breath he drew measured a sliver off his lifespan, he would have considered such use of time profligate, even absurd. He had had such thoughts, back when he was mortal. But time was now largely an abstraction to Vincent, a tool he could use, abuse, or ignore at will. He owned it, and not the other way around. Vincent considered himself more blessed than any creatures that knew only mortality or immortality. He had spent the first thirty-six years of his existence as a mere man, losing enough strength, speed, and wind to realize the preciousness of time, to appreciate the crushing weight of accumulated seconds upon all mortal endeavors. He wondered what would motivate a being immortal since birth, since there was always infinite time to accomplish any act, even the drawing of one breath if that being so willed.

Vincent heard the footsteps on the porch. He replaced the chair and moved to the door, opening it only a moment after the knock.

134

He stepped back to make way for his exquisite visitor. He was surprised to find that she was no less perfect than his memory conjured her. She was that rare embodiment of feminine beauties that compelled the ancients to invent goddesses, that turned vulgar men into poets. It had been almost five years since his heart had been so smitten; he had begun to wonder if it had finally become jaded. But here she was in the dead of winter, an early spring to his soul.

"My herbs worked well, I see," Vincent said, consciously working his English accent. "Yet even without their help, I suspect you are that rare beauty who grows more lovely the more one looks."

Frederika stared back boldly at his intense gaze. "And I suspect you are that class of charmer who grows bolder with each successful compliment."

Vincent laughed. "Are you hungry? I thought perhaps something simple to eat and then a movie."

"That sounds fine."

Vincent pulled his coat off a hook next to the door. "Shall we go?" he invited.

"Your radio or whatever is still playing," she pointed out.

"Let's leave it on," he said. "This ill-spirited house needs it."

In spite of their semiformal dress, Vincent suggested that they eat at P.J.'s Pancake House. Frederika agreed enthusiastically. He ordered his usual cheeseburger, fries, and Coke, and she followed his lead. He had been offering his impressions of Princeton when the food arrived but immediately fell silent and concentrated on his plate.

Frederika's laugh halted Vincent in mid-chew. "What is it?"

"You. My father used to tell a story about me when I was six. He, my mother, and I went to a very chic French restaurant. I supposedly said, 'I can tell when grown-ups really like food; they close their eyes.' That was over escargot. You're doing it over a cheeseburger."

"*Chacun à son goût,*" Vincent replied, shrugging. "Besides . . . this is not just any cheeseburger."

"You really enjoy life, don't you?" Frederika observed.

"That's . . . an understatement. Don't you?"

135

"Sometimes."

Vincent set the remaining burger on his plate. "And what could possibly prevent you from enjoying life as much as I do? Did you *really* come to me because you fear death?"

"No," she answered, and he saw a duplicate of the unhappy face she wore when she came seeking answers from the dead. This was her secret he was circling, and he did not mean to; tonight was for lightness, laughter, and lethe.

"I thought not," he said. "People your age think they're immortal. That's why so many die in automobile accidents."

"I hate that expression: 'people your age.' Just how old does one have to be before one's entitled to wave it about?" Frederika asked.

"In my case, forty-four. To a person *your* age, does that make a difference?"

"No."

Vincent had known the answer with proud confidence before asking it. He attracted women of all ages, had had dozens younger than this one. "Eat," he directed, affably. "The movie begins in five minutes."

They walked to the Garden Theatre, virtually next door to the eatery, where Paddy Chayefsky's *Marty* was playing. Vincent said, "I was never one for the epics. Give me a 'little people' movie any time. Regular people solving everyday problems. *The Apartment, The Goodbye Girl, The April Fools.*"

"And *Casablanca,*" Frederika said.

"Absolutely," Vincent agreed.

"They're also all love stories," she pointed out.

"So they are. So they are." He took her hand in his and she offered no resistance.

Even before they reached Vincent's front porch, he said, "Won't you come in for a drink? I bought a bottle of the most wonderful French Burgundy. They say it's excellent for the blood."

" 'They' being the wine sellers," Frederika remarked, answering his invitation at the same time by climbing the porch steps.

"Yes, of course. But I was thinking of the monks who nurtured and bred the vineyards into the treasures they are today."

"Then let's drink to the monks," Frederika said.

They entered the duplex and walked into the kitchen. By hallway light only, Vincent opened the wine bottle and decanted it. "We must give it room to breathe," he said, moving close to the young woman, inhaling the seductive scent of her perfume. He drew the coat from her shoulders by slowly insinuating his fingers across her collar bones and around her neck.

"And what about me?" Frederika asked. "Shouldn't you give *me* room to breathe?"

"No," Vincent answered. He let the coat fall to the floor. His eyes roamed the features of her face possessively. A wicked smile crept into the corner of his mouth. "I'll breathe for you." He trailed his lips lightly over her cheek, across her eyelids, down the opposite cheek to the angle where her jaw met her neck. Her skin felt silky smooth. He felt her heat on his mouth, kissed her directly over the pulsing of her carotid artery. She moaned softly and lifted one hand to the back of his neck. He trailed light kisses along the line of her jaw and up her chin. He felt the expulsion of her breath on his cheek, and he lifted his lips to hers. She turned her face at the last moment and explored his ear with the hot tip of her tongue. Abstract wooing of eye and ear was abandoned for the direct pleasures of touch, arousing through texture, curve, and resistance. As his fingers explored her shoulders and lower back, hers combed through his thick hair. She sighed encouragement into his ear.

To one of Vincent's experience, Frederika had immediately telegraphed sexual awareness. He was surprised, however, to find her so soon in his arms. Women of such beauty rarely yielded themselves because of mere physical attraction or intangible promises such as he had made. He had been willing to play the seduction game for her, although he had not wanted to. Sexual gratification was a life force almost as compelling as blood. He had foregone sex for almost two months. He had not coupled with a woman as beautiful and intelligent as Frederika in perhaps twenty years. Someone who possessed the still undefined qualities of soul and spirit he intuited in her he had chanced upon only once before, and that had been during his brief invasion of the court of Louis Quinze.

137

Vincent was vastly thankful for Frederika's receptiveness, and he worked his accumulated lovemaking skills on her to prove it. Her dress unbuttoned in the back. He worked the buttons open from the neck downward, as Frederika tugged impatiently at his tie.

"There's a better place for this," Vincent murmured. "Take the bottle and the glasses."

"And what will you take?" Frederika teased.

"You." Vincent scooped her up into his arms and carried her along the length of the age-browned hall, up the stairs, and into a large and very dark bedroom.

"I can't flip the light switch—my hands are full," Frederika said.

Vincent continued into the darkness with a bat's assuredness. "We don't want that light anyway," he told her. The bedstead creaked metallically as he lowered her gently onto the mattress. "Please remember I'm renting a furnished house," he said. "This is not my taste."

The furniture was old enough but too shabby to be called antique. The banker's lamp on the clipper captain's desk across the room had a low-wattage bulb. Its weak yellow cast made the room look all the more decrepit. The furniture—chipped, white-painted iron bed with massive finials, smoky pier glass mirror, hideous Victorian étagère with porcelain wash basin and pitcher, and turtle-backed chair—might have been positioned by a stage designer with a skilled eye, but there was no duplicating the patina of the pegged board floors or the cabbage-rose wallpaper, dessicated everywhere except beneath the ancient print of The Seven Ages of Man.

Frederika had arranged herself in a provocative state of dishabille, one shoe already dropped on the floor, golden hair fanned across the pillows, one shoulder and upper arm exposed and the hem of her skirt high on her thighs. "It's not so bad," she judged.

Vincent looked unconvinced. "Just pretend we're in Act One of La Bohème." He walked to the chair and picked up the clown doll that had been in the dining room on Frederika's first visit.

Frederika twisted around to place the glasses on the floor and fill them with wine. "Where are you going?"

"You've heard of putting the cat out?" Vincent replied. "I can't stand a voyeur."

Frederika giggled giddily. "Even one made of porcelain and stuffing?"

"The part you can't see isn't stuffing," he corrected. "It's very solid wood. No, I want no prying eyes, real or not." He dropped the doll unceremoniously on the floor and closed the door.

Frederika offered a filled glass. "Here. *À votre santé.*"

Vincent took it and clinked with the one Frederika held. "My health is perfect," he said. "Let's drink to yours instead."

They resisted each other for several silent sips, then set the glasses down and collapsed together onto the pillows. Each was impressed by the other's skill and hunger. An unvoiced battle ensued, both vying to give the other more pleasure. Thorough as their explorations and ministrations were, they soon settled into the primitive rhythm, pausing only to change position. Vincent filled his mouth with wine, lowered his face to the valley between her breasts, and let the red liquid dribble down and across her stomach, to pool in the indentation of her belly. His lips sensed the aroused beating of her heart. He longed to fill his veins with the very liquid that made her flesh throb so lightly but he resisted, smiling with pleasure at his self-control. He had drunk only a few days before, at the house of the old professor and his hot-blooded wife, so the desire was not difficult to master. Moreover, he needed her for more than desire; his survival depended on hers. As soon as he had sucked the last of the wine from her belly, Frederika urged him on with her heels. When he began pistoning into her again she uttered little sounds which were of pain, pleasure, or both. She used no words to spur him; when he reached his climax he cried out sweet agony into her shoulder, but she only trembled in silence.

After he lay drained and his breath had returned, Vincent became again aware of the music, floating up from the kitchen. It was Ravel's *Pavane pour une Infante Defunte.* Before his death, Ravel had admitted that he had proclaimed the infanta dead only for the euphony; what he had really imagined when writing the piece was a

Spanish princess dreamily dancing a pavane in a large, empty salon. Vincent closed his eyes and saw Frederika swaying, in a gown of pure white tulle. He opened his eyes and looked at her. She was awake but content to curl up in the hollows of his body and enjoy her afterglow. He turned his head and glanced at what he could see of them in the pier glass. He was as visible as she was in the mirror. He smiled to himself at the superstitious fools of past generations who imagined him sleeping in a narrow pine box, cowering at the sight of crosses, seeking out human company for nothing but their blood. Who in his right mind would choose to endure such an existence through the centuries? Would not the greatest lover of life not soon expose himself to the instantly killing sun of these same superstitions just to be done with the unending monotony? Men who invented a monster even more dangerous than themselves did so only from the viewpoint of their own fears. Who would choose immortality unless he had some chance at enjoying the pleasures of the world? Tonight alone, the food, the walk through a lovely town, the movie, the company and body of a beautiful, intelligent young woman were enough to justify the present limitations of his existence, enough to sustain his willingness to murder for blood, and for the elixir that kept him young. But soon, he hoped, the limitations would shrink drastically; soon, he hoped, he would need to kill merely for his own needs.

Vincent ran his hand lightly along Frederika's flawless flank. Then he eased himself away and twisted so he could reach the pocket of his trousers, lying in a heap on the floor. In masking shadow, he stealthily withdrew a small plastic vial and uncorked it.

"What are you doing?" Frederika asked, in a languid voice.

Vincent dumped the contents of the vial into Frederika's glass, then set the empty container under the bed. "Pouring you another glass of wine," he answered. He reached for the half-empty bottle.

"Are you trying to make me drunk?" she accused, playfully.

Vincent handed her the refilled glass and smiled. "I'm trying to make you *much* more than that."

Frederika drained the drink to the dregs.

CHAPTER EIGHT

December 19

ᭂ

Remember too those angels who were not content to

maintain the dominion assigned to them, but abandoned

their proper dwelling place; God is holding them bound

in darkness with everlasting chains, for judgment on the great day.

—*Letter of Jude 6*

Simon set down his pencil and pinched the bridge of his nose. He glanced at his watch. There was so much material available for review and all of it seemingly useless. In the morning he had scanned through twenty years of *The Reader's Guide to Periodical Literature,* the span of time from Frederik Vanderveen's first public attention in 1959 to his death in 1979. His work had been chronicled in thirty-eight different magazines and journals, in a grand total of 311 articles. His private life had rarely been alluded to. Simon found the names of only four persons who might shed light on the familial aspects of Vanderveen's past. In the afternoon, Simon had hauled down twenty years of the *New York Times Index,* using its stories on Vanderveen's accomplishments as the surveyor's points from which to explore other world newspapers' articles, whenever Vanderveen had had on his seven-league boots.

Through the microfilm articles, the picture of Frederik Vanderveen as consummate diplomat came into increasingly sharp focus. There was no question that tens of thousands of the world's least fortunate people owed, if not their very lives, some improvement of their existence to him. But Vanderveen the private man remained an enigma. Not that Simon was surprised that reporters had not scrutinized his personal life. The diplomat was not, after all, a movie star, rock singer, or even a high-level politician. Understanding the fact failed to relieve Simon's frustration.

Because of limited time, Simon had chosen twenty magazine and fourteen newspaper articles by headline and length and skimmed them for personal references. In truth, he borrowed the library's time, researching when he should have been cataloging the Schickner Collection. A diligent and honest worker, Simon had rarely stolen hours, and it bothered him. What bothered him more was the uncertainty of the length or direction of the path he had set himself off on. If he found a cousin, what could he say besides "That little girl who visited you one summer . . . why did I find her digging dirt from her father's grave?" Or, to an uncle: "Remember Frederik Vanderveen's girl . . . the one you dandled on your knee? I'd personally like to know if you're the reason for her sexual preferences, or was it her father's fault?" What could he possibly ask if he didn't know what she was seeking?

As he wound through reel after reel, Simon felt increasingly uncomfortable. He genuinely sympathized with Frederika's sufferings, but he questioned his motivation for investigating the private life of a virtual stranger. He suspected that seeking to cure her unhappiness was an excuse; he needed a quest right now, an opportunity to show himself and Lynn that he could act rather than just watch life go by. He also doubted that he was maintaining the objective distance his psychiatrist friend had admonished. He wound the microfilm off the spindle and reached for another spool.

DeVilbiss's face went slack. He drew in a deep breath, then sighed it out. His eyelids fluttered momentarily. Then he seemed to come to himself, staring across the table at the woman who held his hands so tightly.

"Did I make contact?" DeVilbiss asked.

Behind her thick lenses, the woman's eyes glowed. "Yes, yes you did! It wasn't much, but it happened! The table shook, and strange lights flashed around the room." A sheen of perspiration bespangled her forehead, just below her headband. Her head jittered with excitement, making the huge golden hoops of her earrings dance beneath the tight curls of her impossibly red hair. She called herself "Mrs. Raymond," and although she had pointedly avoided mention of her age during her tedious dissertation on the reason for her visit, she was sixty-five if she was a day.

"That's all?" DeVilbiss asked, screwing his face into a mask of deep disappointment. "If that's the case, I've failed. You owe me no—"

"No, that wasn't all! You spoke in another voice," Mrs. Raymond assured. "It must have been that criminal you mentioned."

"Roderick Miller."

"Yes. He spoke with a low-class English accent, and his words were like those in a Shakespeare play. But real, I mean."

"I'll take your word," DeVilbiss said. The woman continued to squeeze his hands with her plump fingers, and he did nothing to break their contact. "When I'm in a channeling trance I'm completely out of it, as you Americans say. Did he have contact with your husband?"

"He said that he knew no Arthur Raymond, but that he would search." The furrows above Mrs. Raymond's eyebrows grew even deeper. "If your contact is a criminal, Mr. DeVilbiss, isn't he in hell?"

"Not according to what he has told others," DeVilbiss answered. "Evidently hell is reserved for souls who have done far worse than stealing horses."

Mrs. Raymond nodded her understanding.

"Of the three hundred or so contacts I've tried to make," he went on, "Roderick's been able to search out almost half. He's in purgatory, I believe. Evidently, far more souls go there than directly to heaven or hell."

"Well, Arthur was a good man but certainly not perfect," Mrs. Raymond confirmed. She gave DeVilbiss's thin hands a good squeeze, then lifted her own thick ones to primp her hair. "So then, I should come back again?"

"Most definitely," DeVilbiss said, rising. "And I'll do my best to place you in contact."

"Wonderful!" Mrs. Raymond picked her purse off the floor and dug into a side pocket. "How much do I owe you?"

"Just thirty dollars." While the woman produced a pen and her checkbook, he offhandedly said, "I don't know why, but some questions are easier for the dead to answer than others."

"Really?" Mrs. Raymond bit. "Shouldn't I know that, so I can plan what to ask next time?"

"Well, tell me now precisely what you wish of Mr. Raymond, and I'll tell you what chance you have of being answered." For all of her tedious dissertation on wanting to reach her husband, she had neglected to specify what she wished to ask him.

The woman's blush was swift, coloring her almost as pink as the muumuu that tented her ample form. "You said you don't really hear people when you're in a trance."

"That's right."

Mrs. Raymond looked relieved. "It's a personal question, about a member of my family. I'm too embarrassed to say."

DeVilbiss made a small bow. "I understand. Then by all means say nothing more. My only interests are your complete happiness and peace of mind."

The blush faded into her relief. "That's wonderful." She handed the check over and grunted up from the chair.

DeVilbiss backed unhurriedly toward the front door, holding his smile fast as he watched her stumpy legs waddle in his direction. When they reached the entry, he took her hand and kissed it lightly. "It's a pleasure helping you, Mrs. Raymond. Shall we try again in two nights; nine o'clock again?"

"So soon? Oh, that would be wonderful, Mr. DeVilbiss," she gushed.

DeVilbiss opened the door. "Vincent, dear. Call me Vincent."

"Good night, Vincent," Mrs. Raymond obliged with pleasure.

It was all he could do not to wince at her simpering smile. DeVilbiss closed the door and leaned on it. For thirty dollars. It might as well have been thirty pieces of silver. The only thing that made it bearable was the anticipation of hearing her question. He was sure he had heard it before; he was betting on an unquenchable curiosity at whether Arthur had ever slept with her sister, mother, or daughter. Arthur very well might have, but whatever the secret it was safe in the grave along with his remains.

DeVilbiss walked into the kitchen, filled the tea kettle and set a flame under it. The voice spoke just as he was taking a teacup off the shelf. He nearly dropped the cup in his surprise. After five hundred years, he was still jarred by the perpetually unheralded sound of it.

"You killed the wrong man," the voice said. The abruptness of the accusation added to DeVilbiss's unnerving. He didn't bother to face its emanation point; there was nothing to see. There had never been anything to see. Just a whispering voice, always during the night, from a place without air.

"I did not kill Martin McCarthy," Vincent admitted, in measured syllables. He set the teacup down on the counter. "But I *did* kill the right man. The genius behind the discoveries was Dieter Gerstadt, not his protégé."

"We do not believe that," the voice said, in equally measured cadence.

DeVilbiss placed both hands on the edge of the counter and leaned forward, head down. "Then why don't I get the folder and lay a few of the articles out on this counter? In every one of them Gerstadt is the prominent figure."

"This is not the first time you have failed to destroy the one we named," the voice reminded. "You are to obey our will without question."

"Even if you are mistaken? I move among my kind; you cannot. That's the first reason I've lived so long. And then there is my ability to recognize the good ones before they've done much good. If I sacrifice my judgment to your will, you do yourself a disservice." DeVilbiss had hardened his tone, until its angry edge was unambiguous.

" 'No man can serve two masters.' If you felt so strongly, you should have destroyed them both," the voice countered. "Waited until they were together and created a single accident."

"They would not be together until school began again." With-

146

out turning, DeVilbiss made a small obeisance. "Sir-reverence, but may I remind you that a holy day approaches?"

"You may not." The whisper was now a hiss.

"Be reasonable for once. Killing McCarthy was *your* afterthought to *your* original purpose in ordering me here. He wasn't home; Gerstadt was. I needed to be done with it so I could concentrate my energies on destroying the scrolls." He was prepared for silence; often it tortured him with no response. "I tell you, McCarthy will be lost without his mentor."

"Time will tell," the voice replied. In the beginning its whisper had seemed seductive, almost sensual to him. Now he knew it as furtive, a spirit throat perpetually filled with the smoke of brimstone, the messenger of absolute Evil.

"Speaking of time, I trust the elixir will be delivered soon," Vincent said.

"It shall."

"Because I have only enough for four days more," he said into the cabinets. "I gave a young woman one dose, to cure her cold."

"I saw you give her herbs," the voice said. "Nothing more."

It had observed him at the mock channeling with Frederika. At night it came and went as it pleased, watching him as undetectably as if it stood behind a one-way mirror, banished from the daylight world but all-seeing in darkness.

"Then you either visited at the end of my preparations or else you're lying."

"We never lie," it lied.

Vincent went on, inured. "Together with the elixir, I gave her a mixture of kava and dried teonanacatl mushroom, to induce hallucination. Her father was already foremost in her thoughts; there was little chance she would see anything else." He returned to his agenda. "Despite your doubt, I will need an extra day's worth next month."

"Your self-seeking generosity does not obligate us to anything," said the voice.

Vincent spun around. "My generosity was to gain her confidence! This girl works at the library and is my only access to these cursed scrolls with no name. After all these centuries I have earned the right to know who's responsible for them."

"Ahriman."

"God damn you!"

"That has already been accomplished."

"Was the giver of the words a traitor, hoping to return to the light?"

"This girl works at the library and is your only access to the scrolls," the voice echoed.

Vincent abandoned his questions. "The Ages of Enlightenment and Reason have passed," he argued. "This era will believe that if the science in the scrolls is true, then the supernatural passages must be also. We flourish only because of disbelief. Nothing is more important to our mutual survival than destroying the source of this information once and for all time."

"Agreed."

"The university's library is a fortress. There are fire and security alarms everywhere, as well as guards, vaults, and steel gates. I've tried the frontal assault and failed. The scrolls must be reached obliquely. I used your elixir and my herbs to gain the woman's trust. She had to believe in me and in another plane of existence, and now she does." As he spoke, he realized the irony. He had made her believe in a false Other World and, in so doing, she had pledged herself to serve the real one.

"When will she procure the scrolls?"

"Soon enough," DeVilbiss promised. "They have only one scholar translating them. Whole teams have been working on the Dead Sea scrolls for more than thirty years, and still they're unfinished. Long before he's begun the metaphysics section, I'll have them. Have I ever failed?"

"You will have your powder when you need it." The voice left DeVilbiss's other question unanswered. Tomorrow or the next day a package would arrive in daylight, either in the U.S. mail or by overnight courier, while DeVilbiss slept. Its source was maddeningly untraceable. Once and only once had Vincent made the effort to follow the thread backward, to seek the place of the elixir's formulation. Under deep hypnosis, the delivery man had revealed that he knew nothing of value, having picked up his package from a place rather than a person. Vincent imagined some ten-thousand-year-old Tibetan monk manufacturing the elixir for a small corps of Undying scattered throughout the world, the monk's perpetual loyalty guaranteed by something as absolute as insanity. If Vincent did more than daydream, if he made a concerted effort to find the elixir's source, he knew he would either be summarily annihilated or else cut off and allowed to wither slowly and die.

The tea kettle started to whistle. DeVilbiss ignored it. "I have aged at least a year waiting for packages that arrived late."

"Why should we care about that? You have allowed yourself to age more than a decade of your own free will."

Vincent turned and smiled. "I grew tired of being forever in my thirties. I decided that I wished to spend eternity in my forties."

"There is no going back," the voice declared. "Trespassing beyond the darkness will be your death yet. The water boils."

Vincent whirled around and whisked the kettle onto an unlit burner. "Do you drink?" he inquired, turning around. He waited for an answer. "Are you there?" He got no reply. That did not mean it wasn't still in the room. Its coming and going defied even DeVilbiss's heightened senses. He had found that personal questions were invariably the way to silence it, for it had steadfastly refused to volunteer a single fact about itself. After five hundred years, Vincent did not even know the voice's name. This did not surprise him. The kabbalistic Hebrews affirmed that knowing the name or the number of any entity, tangible or otherwise, gave one power over it. Vincent drew in a slow breath, brewed his tea and took his cup out of the kitchen.

One thing was certain: even if it was still in the house, it could not read his mind. If it could, he would have been dead almost a hundred years ago. In the second half of the nineteenth century, drug companies began evolving out of local apothecary shops; first in Germany and then the United States, universities and hospitals started to create research branches. In the course of his required reading on "good men," Vincent learned of the advances being made at these places, in chemistry and pharmacology, of their scholars' ever-expanding abilities to analyze compounds and reproduce them. The same year Queen Victoria died, Vincent approached his first organic chemist, presenting him with four days' worth of the precious elixir that maintained his youth, that gave him superhuman powers and was intended to keep him forever a slave to his Dark Masters. That night he had told his first lie to the voice—who, inside the sanctuary of Vincent's skull, he had long ago begun calling *Piccolo Niccolo* or *Little Nick*—telling it that he had spilled much of the dark brown bottle's contents down a sink drain. The chemist was gifted, but the state of his branch of science was still primitive. He admitted that he could decipher only a few links of the molecular chains. For his trouble, he died. Twenty years later, Vincent had hoarded up another four days' worth and offered it to an equally gifted scientist. This man professed to have "solved the major secrets of the mixture" and presented Vincent with a batch reproducing his findings. The human to whom DeVilbiss fed the mixture died in agony on the second day. But Vincent did not despair. If he was careful, he had forever to wait, and forever would not be necessary. Each decade of the twentieth century brought swifter and more amazing advances in science. He felt growing confidence that his original race would free him from his chains. On that great day, in thanks, he would become the new Prometheus, broadcasting to the world not only the information contained in the Ahriman scrolls but the little extra he had personally learned over five hundred years. In one gesture, he would expiate all his sins and repay every ounce of blood, every life taken, by warning mankind that the fear they harbored for the "ancient foe" ever since leaving the Garden was absolutely justified.

Frederika would be his lucky talisman; Vincent felt it in his bones. Ten years before, a woman he had hypnotized and then fed the latest reproduction of the elixir had gained great strength and sensual acuity. After she took the elixir for a month DeVilbiss had shot her point blank in the stomach, and she had survived. Her skin had completely healed over after only a day, but she died of septicemia after a week of unimaginable suffering. Ironically, the latest pharmacologist to contribute her knowledge to the accumulated pool worked for Bristol-Myers Squibb, whose laboratories lay just down the road from Princeton. Vincent had been corresponding long-distance with the woman for almost a year, but now he was able to visit her in person on his second evening in town, exchanging a bundle of thousand-dollar bills in exchange for her formulae and a large bottle compounded from their symbols. If this version failed, he vowed to disembowel the moonlighting pharmacologist. But not by moonlight, because Piccolo Niccolo must never suspect.

The other dangerous game Vincent played he had begun shortly after World War II. His first deliberate decision to defy Little Nick was made in June of 1948. The designated victim that month was a thirty-year-old Southern Baptist preacher who had turned to traveling evangelism. Through various ruses, Vincent contrived to avoid the man until, by 1949, the charismatic fellow was speaking to tens of thousands of thirsting souls each week and had become far too well-known to terminate without the expectation of a major investigation. Why Vincent had begun sparing lives was, after more than four decades now of such acts, still somewhat a mystery to him. He credited it partly to his cautious return to daylight. For hundreds of years he had moved almost exclusively at night, and the denizens of darkness were largely the immoral and amoral elements of society, from the drunks, gamblers, thieves, and whores to the tomcatting rich and titled, with their demimondaines in tow. In comparison to his own opinion of himself, these creatures who called themselves humans were lower than vermin, more like cockroaches or water beetles, needing the darkness to conceal their foul existences. But when he returned to the daylight he rediscovered the kindly policemen on their beats, the innocent and uncorrupted children, Salvation Army workers with their Christmas charity kettles, mothers nourishing babies, scores of honest workaday tradesmen, all but a few of whom reacquainted him with the nobler side of mankind.

Vincent also attributed his sporadic acts of altruism to the overall advancement of humanity. Although he had been born after the so-called Dark Ages, his time was nonetheless black—when slavery

151

was common, the mad were chained in cellars, children under ten clapped in mines and dark factories from dawn till dusk, and debtors thrown into prison until someone paid their debts. A time when major faiths condoned persecution and massacre of those with different beliefs. Yet, he had witnessed man growing gradually kinder. To him, the worst villains were members of the media, who prospered by feeding the public a diet of negative news and inciting the wicked. If he had his way, he would have drunk exclusively from the fourth estate's veins. Men like Martin McCarthy, however, compelled even these insects to write positively. And so Vincent had scored another point in his second game.

The problem was that both games only worked if Vincent made all the rules and so long as his opponent had no idea either game existed. Taking the double risk made Vincent feel good about himself and gave him sound reason for anticipating the days, months, years, perhaps decades to come with something other than jaundiced ennui. He drained the last of his cup of tea and looked around the living room for the novel he had been reading. He smiled to the walls, in case Little Nick was still present. Powerful as you are, he thought, you can't exist in God's light or God's air. And you can't read my mind. If you could, you'd know that I do serve two masters. But not forever.

CHAPTER NINE

December 20

He is a slave of the greatest slave who

serves nothing but himself.

—*Thomas Fuller, Gnomologia, no. 1909*

I t's about time!" Willy Spencer carped. His crooked, arthritic forefinger pointed at the clock mounted high above the card catalog cabinets. The library would not officially open for another six minutes, but the reverend had once again wheedled his way inside. As soon as he had graded the semester's final exams, Willy had taken up virtual residence in the Rare Manuscripts Preparation section, a fixture from first opening to as late as he could cajole Simon to stay, which was usually a few minutes past five. It was Simon's habit to arrive for work a quarter hour early, giving him time to put on the coffee and glance at the *New York Times*. He had spoiled Willy, but he didn't begrudge the old scholar his impatience. Simon had never known anyone so revitalized by research.

"Sorry, Willy," Simon said.

"Lazy layabed." Even as Willy mumbled, he grimaced apishly, in way of apology for his curmudgeonly nature. "Just don't let it happen again." He scooped up the Thermos and lunch pail he brought each morning and impatiently shifted weight from one bowed leg to the other while Simon unlocked the door.

Simon moved through his routine like an old milkwagon horse: he pressed the sequence of lighted buttons that released the steel gate. The precautions seemed paranoid until one learned of the scale of rare-book thievery throughout the country. Few stole books for profit; the vast majority were mentally unbalanced persons with unnatural lusts to possess rare and beautiful volumes. The sickness had its own name: bibliomania. Perhaps the arrival of the Schickner Collection had focused Simon's attention on the problem, but in the past two months he had read about the apprehension of three bibliomaniacs. A woman who had worked in the University of Pennsylvania's main library since 1982 was accused of stealing six classic works valued at $1.5 million, including a 379-year-old edition of Shakespeare's *Hamlet*. A man from San Gabriel, California, had cut sections out of books worth more than $6 million, from universities throughout the country. But the most incredible of all was a man from Iowa who had amassed fourteen thousand stolen books in his house, with an estimated total value of $20 million. Princeton University had had its share of losses through the years, but far fewer since the installation of guards, embedded magnetic strips in the book spines, outer windows that could not be opened, and several sets of imposing steel-barred doors.

After closing the gate behind them, Simon thumbed through his key ring for the smallest of his keys. Meantime, Reverend Spencer had set down his lunch and scuttled anxiously to the other side of the room. He produced a key similar to Simon's and moved to a metal box mounted on the wall.

"Ready?" Willy called out.

Simon fitted his key into the electronic wall box.

"One, two, three!" Willy cued. He and Simon turned their keys simultaneously. In the center of the room, the metal and glass lids of the two stainless steel cases popped open. Inert gas hissed out. Reverend Spencer rushed to the cases to claim his prizes.

Simon withdrew his key. He felt like half of a Minuteman missile team inside a Great Plains launch silo. In spite of the bibliomaniacs, a fail-safe theft system for the Schickner Collection's scrolls seemed a bit much to him. He put it out of his thoughts and went for his coffee.

By the time Simon returned to the work area, Willy had unrolled one of the Ahriman scrolls and secured it under Plexiglas on the long, canted ledge slightly above his workbench. His notebooks, reference books, a sheaf of blank paper, and a Mason jar filled with sharpened pencils were meticulously arrayed across the bench. Willy offered a collegial grin.

"So, how's it going?" Simon inquired.

The old scholar's bushy eyebrows floated upward. "Ah! I was beginning to think you'd lost interest." His tone indicated injury at Simon's inattention.

"Not at all," Simon protested. "I've been working on a difficult project myself."

Willy was too benignly self-absorbed to inquire after another's interests. He acknowledged Simon's words with a sympathetic nodding of his head and said, "Let me fill you in on what I've learned since we last talked. Did I tell you the scrolls are formatted like an encyclopedia?"

"No."

"They are. The author treats a subject exhaustively, yet each subject may have no relationship to the one preceding or following it. I suspect there's a logic, but I can deal with that once the whole thing's translated. For now, I'm skipping around, translating sections that look less difficult . . . or with subjects that interest me."

"Nice to be your own boss," Simon said.

"You bet. I'm like a kid in a candy shop, sampling pieces of this and that. In the end, I'll have translated it all just the same."

"Tell me about some of these candies you've sampled," Simon prompted. He was not being merely polite; the old professor's enthusiasm was definitely infectious.

"I can see why von Soden refused to believe the work was authentic," Willy said. "It's incredible to believe that one man—even a genius—could be so far ahead of his time. For example, the theory of atoms. Ahriman reasoned that the sphere is the perfect shape and that all matter is made up of invisible but not infinitely *divisible* spherical units. He also posited that there was a finite 'alphabet' of these units, which the Aryans thought of as earth, water, wind, and fire, but which he declared was not right."

"And this was six hundred years before Christ," Simon said.

"The tests say so."

"Unbelievable!"

Willy shrugged off Simon's incredulity. "As early as 2772 B.C., the Egyptians had determined one revolution of the sun to be 365 days. By the year 1000 B.C, the Chinese knew root multiplication and could solve equations with one and more unknown quantities. At the same time as Ahriman was writing his words on vellum, King Assurbanipal had amassed twenty-two thousand clay tablets in his library. These were not cave dwellers, Simon."

"Apparently not."

"Western civilization credits either Democritus—who lived about 420 B.C.—or Leucippus—about 450 B.C.—with first imagining the atom. But I believe they borrowed the concept from these writings. I've also discovered that Ahriman developed a theory of evolution. This may be the source of Anaximander's theory that all higher forms of life developed from amphibians." Willy waggled his forefinger pedantically. "I suspect von Soden's failing was too narrow a knowledge of the era. If he knew these facts, he might have been more willing to accept the scrolls as authentic."

Simon smiled warmly and waited for the digression to end. Willy Spencer could out-pontificate the pope.

Willy grabbed one of the notebooks. "You want to hear my favorite passage?" he invited.

"Sure," Simon accepted.

Willy adjusted the wire-rimmed spectacles on his nose, then held the notebook aloft, at a considerable distance from his face. " 'From simple observation of the gases rising from a fire or from the hot land in summer, one may see that air which is heated always goes up. Also from observation, one knows that cold air always falls to fill the space the heated air occupied—the air around us being no less of an ocean than that which the fish swim in, except that it is imperceptible.' " Willy paused. "He actually said 'not to be seen by eyes' but my version flows better, don't you think? He goes on: 'We know that the bladders of certain large animals may be made airtight and inflated, so that warriors may float across stretches of water to gain the element of surprise against their enemies. In like manner, if a much larger bladder could be fashioned, sufficient to enable a fire to re-

157

main burning under it, the rising air would lift the bladder, the fire, and the one tending the fire to a great height.' " Willy beamed with admiration at the words. "And here's the incredible part, Simon: 'From such a height, one would be able to observe that even the great earth is a sphere, no less perfect in shape than the sun and the moon.' " Willy lowered the notebook and looked to Simon for reaction. "He also claims that the earth and other planets revolve around the sun *and* that the seasons prove the earth's axis is tilted in relation to its orbit! History will have to make a much larger place for Ahriman, I think."

Simon looked at the unrolled vellum. "Where exactly is that passage?"

"It's on the other scroll," the reverend answered. "This is *Metaphysics*. Since he's been so damned accurate in his worldly theories, I couldn't wait to translate his ruminations on things 'beyond the physical.' His heliocentric theory alone offered enough reason for the Catholic church to have hunted down every translation and destroyed it. Look what they did to Galileo for proving the same theory. And that was *a full hundred years* after the last translation of Ahriman's work! I can hardly wait to see if he's got words even more damning." Willy pushed the glasses back up on his nose and leaned in toward the scroll.

Simon laughed to himself. Trust the retired Presbyterian minister to manage a few licks at the Roman Catholic church. Simon knew that Willy was merely practicing on him, preparing for the furious scholarly debates that were sure to arise after the scrolls' published translations. He excused himself and went to his desk, where he found a scrap of paper he had left the night before. The paper reminded him to find the telephone number of Frederika's aunt. Simon decided to do his research immediately, so that he could give the university an uninterrupted day's labor.

Most of the major metropolitan telephone directories were kept in the Reference section, close by the glass wall that separated it from the main foyer. Simon entered the Reference area, saw with relief that Frederika was busy at the far end, and quickly located the Chicago and Suburbs directory. He found four listings for Callahans

158

with Elmhurst addresses. None had the initial K. in front of the name. He scribbled all the information onto a notepad, waited until Frederika's back was turned, and headed rapidly for the glass doors.

Simon stopped so suddenly that he nearly fell on the smooth marble floor. Almost directly in front of him stood the handsome herbalist and channeler Frederika had visited. Simon finally recalled the first crossing of their paths, in the very same spot. They had been staring at Frederika simultaneously. He could not remember exactly when, but he knew that had been at least a full day before Frederika had left her sickbed to visit DeVilbiss. Simon was reasonably convinced that she had come to him of her own volition, after seeing his newspaper advertisement. Which meant that his initial visit to the library had nothing to do with her. Then what had brought him, neither a student nor a scholarly researcher, here two times?

Intent on orienting himself, the man missed Simon's awkward antics. His eyes seemed to be adjusting to the indoor lighting, squinting even though he wore silvered sunglasses. He pivoted smartly to his right and walked with purpose toward the Microforms room. Simon followed.

DeVilbiss delivered a verbal bouquet of pleasantries to the Microforms librarian, then asked for the names of all the local newspapers. After the list was recited he continued into the microform stacks and selected three boxes, each containing microfilm copies of newspapers. He carried them to a viewing machine and began the process of winding the top one onto an empty spool.

Simon forgot his obligations to the library. He wended slowly through the stacks, pretending to search for a particular box, watching the man out of the corner of his eye. He had noted the places from which DeVilbiss had taken microfilms. He inspected each area and noted that the boxes covering September 1989 were missing. He selected a box at random and took it to the machine catercorner from DeVilbiss.

DeVilbiss sensed the librarian's stare after only seconds. He paused from his reading to regard his audience dead on. For a moment their eyes locked. Simon's contempt hit DeVilbiss like a backhand slap. He answered it with an easy smile.

Simon lost the staring contest. He looked away, but not before he had burned the man's unusual face into his memory. What lingered was not only the image but a deeply disquieting feeling that he had met this face long ago. Eyes the color of amber—the fossil resin that trapped insects and then hardened into stone around them—were not easy to forget. He saw no profit in lingering, so he stood up and returned his microfilm. He kept his eyes pointedly averted as he left; he did not need another look.

DeVilbiss watched the librarian go. He, too, had a disquieting feeling. He did not know how such an amiable-looking young man could threaten him, but he would not be unguarded if he chanced on the face again.

The nearby Roman Catholic church's bells tolled out five o'clock. Vincent sat in the safety of a dark corner, out of the light that cast shadows across the living room wall. December shadows, they were neither hard nor crisply defined. Their fuzzy edges, however, warned him just as effectively of the sun's lingering presence. He noticed that the arcing path of light had crept across the floor and cast a glow on his right shoe. He jerked his foot away as if it had been scorched, even though it was well protected by wool and leather. The cross-country journey to destroy the scrolls, he calculated, had already forced him into enough sunlight to age him several weeks, and he had gotten as old as he ever wanted to look.

Vincent set down the pen in his hand, closed the diary in his lap and hid it in the fold of the day's *New York Times,* waiting for sunset. He watched the natural light's progress across the floor, thinking of how much he loved it, and how dangerous it was to him. Somehow, whether passed down via the Ahriman scrolls or learned through encounters with others of Vincent's unnatural kind, men had learned of the Undying's inimical relationship with the sun. Like most truths known about vampires, however, it had been so exaggerated by fear and distorted for effect by storytellers that its knowledge became less than useful. For man, a creature nearly blind at night and victim of nighttime predators for all but the last few thousand years, light was a powerful symbol of good. It only stood to

160

reason that Evil's earthly minions should be reduced to ash instantly by the merest touch of the blessed sun.

Mistaken as they were, Vincent knew that for him, a cloudless summer day spent lying unclothed on some beach would produce far worse than a sunburn. A flaw existed in the formula of the life-prolonging powder that Little Nick doled out. It either caused or triggered a weakness similar to the rare human genetic disease called xeroderma pigmentosum. From only minimal exposure to sunlight, human sufferers of the disease developed rashes and blisters. Longer exposures produced unhealing sores, then melanoma cancers which metastasized to vital organs, killing nearly all victims by the onset of adulthood. The only chance of prolonging life was to hide behind roofs and walls, curtain all windows, and avoid ultraviolet artificial light as well. This had been Vincent's existence for more than four hundred years. The elixir's shortcoming had been explained to him by Nick only after he had been using it to the point of no return. He suspected the true purpose of the powder's weakness was to limit his activities to the night, the only time when those who controlled him could operate upon the earth and invisibly supervise.

For 450 years, Vincent had been forced to hide himself from the sun he had once so loved, never forgetful of the irony that these same rays were the bringer and sustainer of life to his planet. Brief, obligatory exposures, especially during travel, had aged him some five years over that period, judging from his image in the mirror, but there had been no way to prevent it. Then some ingenious men had invented suntan lotion and potent sunscreens. For the past half century, slathered with cream, Vincent dared the outdoors, also heavily cloaked, never more than a few times a month and never for more than an hour at a time. Once he had begun this practice, however, he had become almost as needful of it as he was of blood. After more than a week of only moonlight, he craved the overwhelming wonder of the world's colors, the warmth of day.

But not today. For him the light could not vanish too soon. Vincent needed to open someone's artery. Before that, he needed to hide his secret diary from Nick. Although he recorded his traitorous thoughts and deeds in a code he felt confident not even creatures of the Darkness could decrypt, he knew that the very presence of such a possession would be damning. He had no illusions that he was indispensable. He had not been the one who had destroyed the museum and the last library that had held translations of the scrolls. There were others who had made Faustian deals for immortality.

Vincent had never chanced upon another vampire, but that only meant their numbers were few. The legends sprang up and flourished long before he had been born. Perhaps at one time in the remote past, Nick and his unholy brethren had polluted the whole earth with the Undying but then found such acts counterproductive. Once regular commerce among the tribes of the world began, word of Undying commonly roaming the night would remove all doubt of their existence and make *vrykolakas* hunting a worldwide sport. By his time, Vincent reasoned, if the number had once been large it was now reduced to a dozen or less.

Perhaps he had been offered his chance precisely because someone who had ransomed his or her soul in the year 1000 A.D. had eventually tired of living as the scapegoat, the focus of men's loathing, and had attempted acts of reconciliation. A foolhardy act . . . unless one possessed a brain of his quality.

Just as the last sliver of light disappeared from the floor, a distant bell chimed the half hour. Vincent rose with the *New York Times* in hand and exited the house. He stopped at his rented car only long enough to toss the newspaper and the diary within its folds into the trunk, then slammed the lid and looked up into the sky at the pink wash of dying light. He adjusted his dark-blue camp sweater, purchased out of the L.L. Bean catalog (another wonderful invention of the past hundred years, especially in light of his shut-in nature). Beneath the sweater he wore charcoal corduroy trousers, a gray river driver's shirt and black mile walker shoes, also from L.L. Bean. He smiled at the knowledge of how well his wardrobe fit the local style.

Vincent walked briskly. He never jogged or ran if he could help it; he found such exercise undignified for a man of his age. Moreover, when he really needed to exert himself (running for several miles at speeds up to thirty miles per hour if need be), perspiration matted down his carefully combed hair. He focused diligently on outward grooming and propriety, fixed on it with an unwavering tenacity so that neither his eye nor his mind would stray to behold the meanness, the selfishness, the abhorrence of him. He crossed the university campus, passing the Gothic grandeur of the chapel, skirting the Victorian pavilion overlooking the tennis courts. His mind flashed back to other times and places.

Most of the university's undergraduates and a large part of the faculty had found excuses to desert the institution early for the holidays. He crossed Faculty Road, nosed around the boat house and regarded Carnegie Lake, dredged out from a meandering stream at Andrew Carnegie's expense after Harvey Firestone beat him out for the honor of underwriting the library's construction.

Faculty Road was bisected by Washington Road. Opposite the boat house lay a jogging trail, which wove through a small woods that bordered the lake. Vincent had found the trail during a previous postsunset amble. On that occasion he had had the trail all to himself. This evening, just as he was about to enter the trees, he was overtaken by a young woman, dressed smartly in a neon-colored, body-molded suit of nylon material and wearing a pair of fashionable and expensive sneakers designed specifically for jogging. She moved with good speed, but Vincent's hearing gave more than enough warning for him to turn and see that her face was quite pretty. He judged her either a college senior or perhaps a graduate student. In place of earmuffs, she wore a pair of headphones, attached to a tiny radio clipped to her suit. Vincent heard the wail of guitars and the crashing of drums as she passed and knew she would be half deaf by the time she was fifty. She passed him with no acknowledgment of his presence and sprinted into the woods.

Vincent paused to admire the young woman's lithe figure, then turned his attention to the moon reflecting on the surface of the lake, long enough for the coed to run directly into trouble. Vincent was not more than a hundred paces into the woods, watching with his special vision for the movements of night creatures, when he again spotted her. She lay about thirty feet off the path, on top of a coarse blanket. She would have seemed asleep had it not been for the

163

blood oozing down her forehead and temple, for the blood-stained rock lying beside the blanket, and for the man kneeling over her, wrestling her sneakers off with demonic energy.

Vincent redirected his attention to his own feet. He watched the ground intently as he moved closer, avoiding the dried leaves and branches, circling the rape-imminent with silent stealth. The attacker's face came into profile, the cold moonbeams acting as DeVilbiss's floodlight. The man had Levantine features. He was hardly older than the woman, and he wore a nondescript sweatshirt and cotton warm-up pants. Vincent had seen all manner of nationalities on campus and around the town. He guessed that most were there to study at the university. He had read that thousands of foreign graduate students attended American universities under their governments' subsidies, but funding was not provided to bring along wives. Consequently, the young men's levels of sexual frustration were high, and campus rape by foreigners not uncommon. As he grew closer, watching the man rip his stunned victim's pants roughly down her legs, he saw another weapon lying on the edge of the blanket, catching the glint of moonlight pouring through the leafless trees. It was an old-fashioned straight razor, the type Vincent had refused to abandon until Bic made his affectation ridiculous even to him. Nevertheless, he never traveled anyplace without at least one such instrument in his luggage. Like the rapist, he carried the razor for something other than shaving.

While the rapist yanked up the unconscious woman's top and bra, Vincent hunted up a half dozen small rocks. He waited until the man had hauled the woman's bottoms off and had his own pants around his knees before firing the first missile. It landed two feet from the blanket.

The man jerked around at the sound as if he had been doused with water. He grunted his surprise and thrust out one hand to steady himself. Then he listened intently.

The second rock struck him squarely between the eyes. He went over backward, his pant legs collapsing around his ankles. He rolled off the blanket, yanking his warm-up pants up with both hands, dragging leaves and twigs into the crotch as he did.

"Who is there?" he cried out.

DeVilbiss laughed, just loudly enough to be heard.

The man grabbed his razor and brandished it in front of him blindly. The third rock caught him in the left ear. He screamed and ran down the slope and onto the jogging path, stumbling northward.

Vincent followed; the small sounds he caused were more than masked by the rapist's crash through the winter brush. He smiled when he realized his prey was heading deeper into the woods. About a tenth of a mile down the trail, the rapist stopped and whirled around, listening as best he could through his ragged breaths for what he assumed would be a pursuit as noisy as his flight. When he had listened for perhaps thirty seconds and heard nothing, he straightened out of his crouch and turned to find the path.

Already ahead of his quarry, Vincent saw that his second rock had drawn blood. It would be nothing compared to the blood about to flow. He tossed another rock far over the man's head, so that it sounded from behind him. The man rushed down the path, away from the noise and toward his torturer.

DeVilbiss gave the cry of a large, angry wolf. The now-frantic rapist shrieked and left the path, stumbling west toward Faculty Road. As Vincent hopped noiselessly from one mossy mount to another, he watched with delight as the man happened into a patch of brambles, their thorns grown winter-hard and sharp. Vincent stepped down into the thickly fallen leaves and glided though them, sending up a constant hissing noise. The rapist, fighting out of the thicket and making his own commotion with the branches, leaves, and his own heaving lungs, heard the other sounds but was too panicked to stop. He cleared the thorn bushes after many painful stops and starts, lowered his head and set his legs pistoning up the steep slope.

Two stones struck in quick succession, striking the rapist on the chest and the hand that still clung tenaciously to his razor, inflicting more psychological than physical damage. The man's momentum failed.

"I shall kill you!" the rapist screamed, both his accent and fright very clear.

From a high-ground vantage, DeVilbiss saw that the brambles had dug long, crisscrossed scratches into the man's face and hands. Pieces of broken branches clung to his clothing, thorns deeply embedded. DeVilbiss angled down the slope toward his target, calmly hurling the last of his arsenal. The hunted animal turned tail and retreated, waving his arms blindly to prevent running directly into a tree. His precautions were useless when he reached a little ravine, dug into the slope by decades of heavy rains. His body hung for an instant in air, feet expecting solid earth and churning comically in their disappointment. He landed headfirst and turned a somersault before coming to a sudden stop, the wind knocked from him. The handle of the straight razor lay on the crest of the ravine where he had finally let it go; its blade dangled over the precipice.

DeVilbiss picked up the razor, closed and pocketed it. He hopped into the ravine and squatted above the rapist, whose body suddenly remembered how to breathe. The man whooped air into his lungs. Shortly enough oxygen reached his brain to remind him of his peril. He sat bolt upright and threw his head left and right.

"Back here, sport," DeVilbiss whispered, twisting the screw another turn.

The rapist staggered to his feet and, bellowing his rage at having been tormented to his limit, threw himself at DeVilbiss.

Jujitsu, the ancient Japanese art of self-defense, had been imported to England in the late 1920s, quickly becoming a fad. Vincent had taken it up with enthusiasm, regretting his ignorance of such skills for the first four hundred years of his existence.

DeVilbiss calmly rocked back on his palms as his assailant encroached, drew up his leg and uncoiled it like a cobra striking, catching the man's knee, snapping it like old kindling. He howled in agony and collapsed to the ground.

DeVilbiss stood with no haste and brushed himself off.

"Got your blood up, have I?" he asked. "I hope so." He took his thoroughly beaten quarry by the hair and hauled him upward. "Like to get your bodily fluids into strangers? I'll be glad to help you." The rapist had one last ounce of fight in him, but it vanished when DeVilbiss kicked him again in his broken knee. DeVilbiss got no resistance when he pushed the head back, exposing the length of the swarthy, bramble-gouged neck. He sank his teeth deeply with a single thrust.

The first taste of blood told DeVilbiss that this was not type B, with its acidic taste and the protein that made his skin itch until he wanted to crawl out of it. Moaning with pleasure, he sank his incisors deeper, ripping from side to side to increase the flow. The carotid artery severed. Blood spurted hotly into his mouth.

A few minutes later, the lack of blood flowing into his brain sank the rapist into a coma. He was young, however, and his heart continued to pump with vigor for some time. DeVilbiss drank on, feeling the anger drain from him as his stomach filled. While he sucked, he gazed up at the impassive, unjudgmental moon.

When he felt the heart begin to falter, the beating grow feeble, DeVilbiss withdrew his mouth. He lifted the man's limp arm and wiped his teeth clean with the sweatshirt material. He rolled up his sleeves, reached into his pocket and took out the straight razor, giving it a flick that made the blade snick through the air. Again he took the rapist's head by the hair, yanking it back so that his neck was fully exposed. He gave the hank of hair a twist, bringing the two puncture marks into direct moonlight. Then, with a cello virtuoso's elan, he drew the blade across the neck in one swift, deep stroke, obliterating the puncture marks within the larger, more gruesome wound.

Sometimes Vincent covered his marks with one among many stab wounds, occasionally erased them with a shotgun blast, or in more remote days, when beasts of prey roamed in greater numbers, lugged the corpses bare-necked to favorite nighttime watering holes and let other hungers protect him. He reasoned that only a fictional Carpathian monster would possess enough hubris to leave behind his double-puncture-wound calling card. A few times in the distant past he had experimented by cutting victims' throats before drinking, to leave no tell-tale punctures. It was a thrill letting the warm stream shoot into the recesses of his mouth. But they died long

167

before most of their blood was expelled; their death throes were disturbing, their limbs jittering and quaking like wind-up dolls gone mad as their brains suddenly became deprived of oxygen. The staining liquid also had a nasty habit of spraying on expensive new apparel. Old ways were the best ways. His victim's body hung limply, blood welling feebly from the long cut. For a moment, DeVilbiss regarded the dark rivulets pooling into the depressions above the man's collarbone. He had no desire to watch for the final pulsings, so he let the body fall. He wiped the razor clean on his prey's sweatshirt, then folded it up and stuck it back in his pocket. He patted along the would-be rapist's flanks, rolled him over and checked his backside in vain for a pocket which might hold a wallet. The man had been careful, perhaps practiced at rape; he carried not so much as a key. Grabbing the near-corpse by the ankles, DeVilbiss worked his way down the ravine, toward the mass of concrete that he had seen on his previous walk and which had been on his mind since first spotting the rape attempt.

The barrel shaft of concrete, poking up through the ground for only three yards, revealed a large storm sewer that emptied into the lake. Access inside it could be gained via a waffle-faced iron manhole cover, the type only a physical specimen with a hook-ended tool could lift. DeVilbiss removed it by inserting his fingertips, dropped the body in headfirst and resealed the cover. Perhaps, when a heavy March snow melted in a hurry, a strong and persistent torrent of water would wash the corpse out into the lake, but by that time identification would have to be made by dental charts.

Vincent hurried back to the scene of the attempted rape. He would have to make an anonymous phone call to the police if the woman still lay unconscious. He had rescued her without reflection, but he now weighed the risk of making his presence known in Princeton, linking himself to a violent crime. If she hadn't seen her assailant, he might even be considered as a suspect. The more he thought about the incident, the more foolhardy his altruistic act seemed. Two hundred years before, he would have watched the rape with the disconnected dispassion of one watching a spider devour a fly. Although he felt somewhat disquieted by this evolution in behavior, what he did made him feel so good that he refused to weigh its source or consequence.

When DeVilbiss reached the blanket, he was relieved to see that the young woman had found her sneakers and pants and walked off under her own power. He was sorry that she would never know the fate of her attacker, but at least he knew that justice had been meted out. He strode down to the jogging trail and away from the storm sewer, in the direction of Washington Road. A little beyond the place of the attempted rape he came across the rotted trunk of a tree. He wiped the straight razor clean of fingerprints and dropped it down the trunk's hollow core.

Destroying the well-protected Ahriman scrolls, while simultaneously preserving the life of a local scientist, was proving to be the greatest challenge of Vincent's long life. Killing Dieter Gerstadt had been a satisfying but physically painful triumph. He had needed an easy kill, to prove to himself that fate had not turned against him. Even better, this time he had slaked his bloodthirst while feeling supremely self-righteous about it. Vincent started to whistle "O Holy Night" as he walked out of the woods, but it was difficult; his smile was too broad. He glanced at his watch. The night was still young. As soon as he regained Nassau Street he would make a telephone call.

DeVilbiss turned for a last look at the moonlit lake. In the dark sky beyond the water a flaming meteor plummeted earthward. He remembered the old superstition of making a wish on such a shooting star. His wish had already been formed minutes before. It centered on one blue-eyed, blond-haired Christmas angel.

Simon was first to total his points. He took the idle moments to adjust his throw pillows closer to the blaze crackling within the mansion's living room fireplace. No stockings were hung by the chimney with care, but only an hour earlier Frederika had brightened the mantel with a red apple pyramid and festooned its white-enameled face with an intertwining of holly, plaid ribbons, and brass bells. Even earlier, she had come home burdened with other sym-

169

bols of the season—a German nutcracker soldier, brass coronet candleholders, and a dappled wooden rocking horse whose hollow torso held greeting cards. Before lounging on the Persian rug in front of the fire, she had illuminated the Christmas tree and lit several candles. Yet even before the firewood crackled, her face had glowed. Simon knew from the dust gathered on the old decoration boxes that Christmas had not been celebrated in the old house for years.

"Seventy-three points!" Frederika said, underscoring the number with a flourish of her pencil.

One prize among Simon's few possessions was a word game called Got a Minute. It had the alphabet distributed among the faces of seven dice. These and a one-minute egg timer were encased inside a clear Lucite cube. The object of the game was to flip the cube and, in sixty seconds, combine the letters that faced upward into as many words as possible.

Frederika's eyes darted to Simon's score. "Eighty-four?" she said skeptically. "Let me see your list!" She scooped up his writing pad and rolled onto her back. *"Qat.* Who are you kidding?"

"It's an archaic spelling of *k-a-t,"* Simon explained. "An Arabian plant used for tea. I can show you in the dictionary."

"What kind of dictionary . . . Arabian?"

"Don't be a sore loser," Simon said, peeking over the top of her head and holding out his hand for his pad.

Frederika thrust the pad out of reach. "And what in God's name is *tain?"*

"Very thin plating, used to back mirrors." Simon grabbed the pad and crab-walked back to his pillows.

Frederika flipped over and regarded her opponent with narrowed eyes. "I've heard of weird fetishes, but you're some kind of word freak . . . aren't you?"

"No. I read," Simon returned. "You oughta try it sometime."

"I'll bet I can beat your smart ass at poker or pool."

"I'd be glad to give you a chance." Frederika threw a pillow at him. Simon added it to his bolster. "Thanks. Had enough or are you still game?"

"Game? I'm more like prey. I flipped it last time." Frederika snatched up the game and held it out. "Here."

A moment after Simon set the shook cube down, the telephone rang.

Frederika clambered up from the rug. "Darn it! I could have flown with those letters." She stepped to the telephone and answered it.

"Hello?" she greeted brightly into the phone. "Hi. No, nothing special."

Simon's shoulders slumped.

Frederika glanced at Simon as she said, "Well, sure. When?" She was in role again, impossible to read. "No, no problem. Fine. Goodbye." After she hung up, she turned to Simon and offered a mildly apologetic smile. "You won for the evening. I've got to go out."

"Emergency?" Simon asked, through his own expressionless mask.

Frederika scudded into her shoes. "Yes. I teach reading for the Literacy Volunteers of America. One of the teachers got hung up somewhere and I've been asked to last-minute substitute."

Simon glanced at his watch. "At quarter to nine?"

Frederika shrugged. "We have to accommodate the learners. A lot of them have to work odd hours—the only jobs they can find."

"Where do you teach?"

"Trenton."

"Downtown?"

"Yes, downtown."

Simon scrambled up from the pillows. "I'd better come with you."

Frederika stopped him with a traffic cop's gesture. "It's perfectly safe, and there's no place for you to wait. Stay, Fido!"

Simon leaned unhappily against the fireplace.

Frederika grabbed her purse. "Bye." She disappeared into the hallway. Her car engine rumbled only seconds after the back door slammed.

Simon waited until the motor noises faded into the night before

171

he picked up the telephone directory and found the number of the LVA's Trenton office.

"This is Literacy Volunteers of America," the recorded voice imparted. "Our office will be closed from Monday, December eighteenth until Tuesday, January second. Happy holidays, and keep reading!"

Simon replaced the pillows on the couches. He told himself that just because the office was closed did not necessarily mean all tutorials had been suspended. He knew Frederika did not lie about her affiliation with the organization; he had found evidence of her association when he had ransacked her room. The knowledge reassured him. It would be nice to be able to mention that to the next person who tried to paint her all black. But Simon felt no pleasure now. She lied with such consummate skill that her words could just as easily have been responding to an invitation from the evil-auraed Vincent DeVilbiss. Simon sighed. He rejected the impulse to take another walk to Park Place. He had already spied on Frederika too often, and each time it had confused or saddened him. Jealousy had never been his weakness; he would feel especially stupid if he succumbed to it now. He did not own her, never would. He carried his game into the hallway and up the stairs. He decided he wouldn't leave the house tonight, but he would also not sleep until she had returned. If she came in later than midnight, he would know where she had been.

Simon looked down at the letters in the cube. They spelled nothing.

Frederika knocked on the now-familiar Park Place door, loudly enough to be heard over the classical music playing inside. She combed her fingers self-consciously through her hair, aware that she did not look her most alluring. Once she lied to Simon, it had been impossible to change out of her jeans and cotton sweater. She let her arm down. Don't sweat it, she told herself. The careful makeup and seductive clothing were no longer necessary with this man; she and Vincent were past that part of the dance. If her dress-down clothes and lack of makeup dampened his desire for sex, so much the better.

172

Once she knew she had a man, she rapidly lost her taste for it; it had always been that way. Her enthusiasm for accepting Vincent's late-night invitation was to report the information on the Ahriman scrolls Simon had shared with her over dinner. She knew that was his priority as well. If his skills as a necromancer were genuine, she did not want him losing heart and leaving town or, worse, devising some way to get to those ancient rolls of vellum without her.

Almost half a minute had passed since Frederika knocked. As she raised her fist again the door flew open. Vincent labored an easy smile; he was slightly out of breath.

"Sorry," he said. "I didn't expect you so soon."

"Then I should be apologizing," Frederika said, as she entered the house. "I should have allowed you more time. You called me from a pay phone, didn't you?"

"Yes," he admitted. "I was out for a walk and found myself missing you." He had not changed out of his corduroy pants and sweater.

"Isn't that nice?"

Vincent lifted his hands to help her remove her coat. "Yes, having a someone to miss is quite nice," he said. "I'm brewing us tea."

Frederika pulled her hands out of the coat sleeves. "No, thanks. It's too late."

Vincent walked energetically toward the kitchen. "But you must. This tea has no caffeine, and it's important as a preventative against that cold returning." As if on cue, the tea kettle whistled.

"I have news about the Ahriman scrolls," Frederika reported, following him into the kitchen.

"Good news, I hope."

"Yes, very good." As Vincent gathered cups and saucers, Frederika put herself down on an old chair. "Reverend Spencer—he's the man doing the translating—is skipping around the scrolls, working on the parts that are easiest. He's spent the past few days in the section called *Metaphysics*." She watched the channeler pause, holding the tea kettle directly over one of the cups as if he were afraid to miss the next syllable. "He's found passages that speak of angels!"

Vincent poured slowly; the water made almost no sound cascading into the cup. "And has he found any passages about devils?"

"If he did, he must not have told my friend."

"Your friend works directly with the reverend?"

"In the same room," Frederika explained, "but he has nothing to do with the scrolls. Oh, except that he has one of the only keys that can unlock them from their case. There's a security system. Two keys have to be turned at the same time to get them out."

Vincent set the cups and saucers down at the little kitchen table and sat. "Interesting. Evidently, they know what a treasure they possess."

"Evidently." Frederika picked up her cup. "Tell me now why certain religions can't let these scrolls exist."

"Some other time. Does—"

"Now."

DeVilbiss blinked at Frederika's force of will. "Are you testing me?"

"And what if I am? It's very easy to be made a fool of in matters of the occult."

"I'm not making a fool of you."

"I meant *you* might be a fool. Just because these scrolls are so rare and hunted by major religions doesn't mean they hold occult truths. What's so dangerous to these religions?"

Vincent regarded the young woman for several seconds, reassessing her strength of will and his ability to control her. "I have an answer, but it alone can't convince you. If it turns out I'm a fool, so be it. You either have to take that chance with me or not. The way I see it, you have no choice." Instead of answering, she took a generous sip of tea. He saw in her eyes that he had won this round. Staying on the offensive, he asked questions about what Simon had related to her.

Frederika could honestly tell DeVilbiss nothing, but what he asked at least proved to her that he had knowledge of the scrolls beyond that of any layman.

"We have to be patient about getting the information we want," Vincent conceded. "But I would so love at least to look on them, even through layers of glass. Could you persuade your friend . . . ?"

Frederika pursed her lips apologetically. "I'm sure I'll be able to, but not before Christmas."

"No, of course not," Vincent said, amiably.

Frederika became aware that, unlike her first visit, he had not drunk any of his tea. As she wondered idly if this was cause for concern, the music stopped. Vincent's head swung toward the stereo system. Frederika noticed a brownish-red stain just below the hairline on the side of his neck.

"What's this?" she asked, leaning close.

"What's what?"

Frederika touched the stain. It flaked off from her touch. "Blood. Dried blood!" she exclaimed, exploring his hair. "You don't have any bumps or cuts."

"That's good."

"Here's more, on your sweater. Do you know what it's from?"

Vincent tugged on the collar and attempted to look at the stains, hidden in the sweater's dark material. "I believe so. A chicken," he answered, calmly.

Frederika rocked against her seat back. Vincent's eyes met hers with no hesitation. "You killed a chicken?"

"Yes."

"To eat?"

"Not myself, no. Actually, I sacrificed it for a Haitian séance earlier today."

"That's disgusting."

"No, it's commonplace voodoo," Vincent countered. "I happen to be a qualified *hungan*. I spent three years in Haiti, among my wanderings."

Frederika had not taken her eyes from his since he examined his sweater. She knew from personal successes how difficult it was to catch a truly accomplished liar. She also knew from her first visit to him that he was a liar by profession. She knew him to be a dangerous man. Not the kind who might find an excuse to hit her when he got too many drinks into him. Not the underschooled surgeon or the overschooled advisor to presidents. She had slept with all three of

175

that kind, had found them intriguing for those reasons, and, for the same reasons, easy to discard. This one was much more dangerous to her, however, because the subjects of his obsession were, literally, life and death. Before this visit she worried that he might either be crazy or else use her and forget his half of their deal. Now her worries deepened considerably.

"What can I tell you?" Vincent continued, mellifluously. "I require money to live. I was recommended by friends of friends. *They* demand the sacrifice, not I." His hand went to his chest. "Would you cast such a dismayed look at your butcher for doing his job?"

Frederika labored a smile, thinking he was probably seeing through to her feelings. To compensate, she touched his hand sympathetically. He took hers and stood, compelling her to rise.

"I should have looked in a mirror after the session," he said. "I scoured the kitchen until not a drop was left, but I failed to be so thorough with myself."

"And where's the remains?"

"They took it with them, naturally. You think they would throw away a perfectly good dinner?"

"But it was a sacrifice."

"You sound as if you don't believe me."

"No, of course I believe you." She looked at her watch. "It's late; I have to go."

Vincent backed into the dark, brown hallway, gently dragging her after him. "Not yet. Now you've made me feel dirty. I must shower. For your penance, you will accompany me."

Frederika leaned her weight backward. "No, thank you. I don't need a shower."

Vincent whirled around and scooped her into his arms. "Who said anything about need?"

Frederika struggled against him. She was amazed and more than a little frightened by his strength, far greater than she imagined a man of his size and age could possess. He carried her straight into the bathroom, slammed the door behind him and only then did he flick on the light.

"I can't stay late," Frederika insisted.

176

Vincent set her down and inched her backward against the wall. His smile was gentle and playful, contradicting her fears. "Why not?"

"I have a friend visiting who worries·when I'm not back by eleven."

"Your friend sounds more like your nanny," Vincent observed, bringing his face close to hers.

Frederika smirked. "That's the truth." The image of Simon in front of the fireplace floated pleasantly in her mind, but she had trouble holding on to it. Vincent's strong and handsome countenance was almost upon her, his lids dropping and lips parting as he prepared to kiss her. She tugged lightly on his earlobe with the tips of her teeth, exhaling warm air into his ear, making him groan with pleasure. Her tactics never failed to satisfy men. She knew males were seldom, by nature, interested in kissing. No man had ever complained when Frederika evaded their lips and immediately moved toward coitus, and that was fine with her. She avoided the hot lips and snaking tongues whenever possible. Nor did she want protracted hand-holding, moon-eyed stares, or protests of undying love. But, inevitably, the less interest she showed in the aspects of romance that men expected women to desire, the more emphatic each man's romantic attentions became. Within days or weeks, she reached her tolerance level and expunged them ruthlessly from her life. For eight years—since the beginning of her sexual experiences—it had been so. She accepted it, simply, as her nature. Her passion for this man had certainly withered, but from fear rather than boredom. She determined to give him a token of what he wanted, so that she could get away and think clearly about whether or not she should have anything more to do with him.

While Vincent tugged single-mindedly at Frederika's sweater, she became anxiously aware of a lassitude creeping through her. Her expanding physical and mental enervation was countered by his growing sexual excitement. He tossed her sweater onto the counter, roughly unsnapped her bra and lowered his mouth to her breasts. She responded mechanically.

Vincent stripped off his own sweater, revealing his well-muscled chest and abdomen, as well as the golden keychain that hung around his neck. He removed the chain, passed it over the shower curtain rod, dropped the items hanging from the chain through its loop and set the chain swinging.

"You said the scrolls are kept locked with two keys," Vincent said to her. "Little keys like these?"

Frederika realized through the rising fog that he was trying to hypnotize her. She turned her face forcefully toward the door, but he brought it back with a relentless pressure.

"Look at the keys," Vincent whispered.

Frederika squeezed her eyelids shut. A moment later they snapped open, from the pain of her pinched nipple. The moment she focused on the pendular chain, glinting and glistening as one section and then another caught the light, her eyes were locked to it. The pain in her breast disappeared. Her pupils followed the moving items at the chain's low point as they described a graceful arc, back and forth, back and forth.

"Little keys like these?" Vincent repeated.

"I don't know," she murmured. "I've never . . . seen them."

DeVilbiss released Frederika, keeping his hands raised until he was sure she could stand without toppling over. He yanked off his shoes and socks, watching the young woman's rolling eyes, her lids drooping lower and lower. "Do you recognize the other things?" he asked, softly.

Frederika leaned toward the chain. "An ankh, a . . . cross and a circle."

"Yes," Vincent said, as he unbuckled his belt and pushed his trousers and underwear toward the cool tile floor. "All symbols of eternal life. That's what we both seek, isn't it?" She nodded and continued to follow the lessening arc. He unbuttoned her bluejeans and shoved them and her panties down, kneeling in front of her, guiding her clothing over first one foot then the other. He tossed the bunched material aside and pressed his face into the golden curls of her pubic mound.

Now it was Frederika's turn to groan. Vincent intensified his skillful contacts. Past experiences using drugged tea and a swinging

178

chain had taught him that the trance he induced would also increase the woman's sexual appetite, robbing her not only of volition but also of inhibitions. Squeezing and fondling her own breasts, Frederika writhed as one possessed.

DeVilbiss guided Frederika backward into the shower stall, then pressed himself hard against her, forcing his erect penis between her legs. He turned the shower on and took the cold stream upon his own back until the temperature had adjusted. Then he angled her into the spray, placed his hands under her buttocks and lifted her against the slippery tile wall. With his groin he coaxed her legs apart and began a slow but persistent grind. He tried to kiss her lips, but she turned her face away, as she had before the drug took effect. He trailed his mouth instead down her chin, along the line of her jaw and to her throat. He sucked hard on her flesh with his lips, then let his teeth press furrows in her flawless skin. Had he not drunk from the rapist earlier in the evening he would have been incapable of resisting his bloodthirst.

DeVilbiss quickened the pace of his plunges. He and the water made similar hissing noises. An unbidden thought flashed through his mind, about one of the more idiotic superstitions—the legend of creating more vampires simply by drinking until the victims die. He was grateful that no such transmogrifications occurred. Otherwise, over the course of five hundred years, he alone could have initiated a chain-reaction plague that would have turned the entire human race into vampires. Yet if he could make the legend true, just once, he would have chosen Frederika Vanderveen to become his instant kindred spirit. What he truly hoped for was an even more selfish solution. She had responded well to the dose of genuine elixir he had laced in her tea the first time she visited the house. And she had not even sickened from, much less been poisoned by, the imitation elixir he had slipped into her wine forty-eight hours before. In fact, he thought he felt a definite increase in her physical and mental strengths when she had just resisted him. At long last, he had reason to hope that the elixir's secrets had been decoded. He would force her under a prolonged hypnotic spell to continue a daily dosage for at least six months. She could not stay with him; Little Nick would surely recognize her changes. But when he was compelled to leave Princeton, he would make her follow at a distance. During the daylight hours, when he was safe from scrutiny, he would teach her what else she needed to survive. She would learn about her need for human blood to complete the regimen, and he would kill for her. After six months, he would try to destroy her. If she survived, he would be halfway to freedom. Then he planned to send her away, supplying her with formula just as he was supplied. If, in ten years, she had not aged, he would know for certain that he need no longer be a slave. He would release Frederika then from her hypnotic indenture. She would discover what she had become, what he had made her. She might hate him at first and flee from him. But soon enough she would feel, as he did, a hunger for companionship and understanding. Then she would be truly his, and they would walk through the centuries together.

In order for all this to come to pass, zombielike servitude was demanded of the woman. DeVilbiss needed to induce a deeper and more abiding hypnotic state than any other he had yet created. But first things first. Roaring out his release, he climaxed into Frederika, pinning her against the wall, his muscles hardened like steel and rippling with tension. When he recovered, he realized that she had not been satisfied. Still rampant and aroused by the conquest of her and the hope of his freedom, he determined to fornicate until she screamed out a release as unbridled as his. He wanted her subconscious mind to remember his skill, to create a slave physically as well as mentally dependent on him. He drove on and on, until her weight grew too much even for his inhuman body. He carried her into the bedroom without toweling either of them off, set her on the bed and stoked into her with abandon until he could not resist releasing again. Several times he felt her tensing for climax, then pulling back, forbidding it to happen. He began to stimulate her gently, guessing that her neural circuits had been overloaded. Her responses were as wanton as he could desire, and yet she somehow maintained the force of will to stubbornly refuse to elevate beyond a certain euphoric plateau. He exhausted the myriad sexual positions of the *Kama Sutra* and added even more exotic maneuvers that invariably brought women to shrieking orgasms. Each time he was met with failure. He refused to place the blame on his technique; in his five centuries he had taken by his estimation at least four thousand women, beggaring the legendary Don Juan's "thousand and three in Spain." If he had been forced to pay the terrible price for the continued joys of the flesh, then by God he would master those joys to the fullest.

Grudgingly, Vincent withdrew himself from Frederika and lay down beside her, gently stroking her hair. He was convinced now that she had faked orgasm during their first coupling. She was a true challenge. Did it have something to do with her desperation to contact her father? He was too tired to wander through the labyrinths of her mind via tedious questioning. He also had yet to program her and get her home before her unnamed houseguest called the police. He wanted no history of a connection to her when the two of them quit Princeton after destroying the scrolls. After that, there would be ample time to plumb her mind and shed light on her sexual dysfunctions.

Vincent swung off the bed and lit the banker's lamp on the desk, giving Frederika just enough light to see his eyes. Looking at her caused an aching inside him. He sat again on the mattress.

"I am your friend," he said. "The truest friend you have. Do you understand?"

"Yes," Frederika replied. Her face was serene; her eyelids did not blink.

"I want what you want. You will never speak with your father unless you obey me. Never, unless you obey me. Do you understand?"

"Yes."

"You must do whatever I tell you, even if it does not seem to make sense. Do you understand?"

"Yes."

DeVilbiss took Frederika's hand gently. She allowed it to be held, returning no pressure of touch.

"You will continue to do your normal work, to live your normal life. Everything just as always. You will also report everything you learn about the scrolls. Do you understand?"

"Yes."

"Repeat what I have just said," he commanded. She obeyed, exactly. "Good," he praised. "What is the name of the professor translating the scrolls?"

"Reverend Willy Spencer."

"What is the name of your friend who works in the Rare Manuscripts section?"

"Simon Penn."

"Simon Penn. Have you tried to seduce him to get his help?"

"Yes."

"What happened?"

"Nothing."

"Nothing? Why?"

A look of confusion swept across Frederika's face. "I don't know. He's a . . . gentleman."

"Perhaps he's no kind of man at all," DeVilbiss murmured to himself, glancing along Frederika's naked length.

"He just left his girlfriend," Frederika added.

DeVilbiss registered the words, although he was not sure how they provided explanation. "You will telephone me every day, at the noon hour and in the evening."

"Yes."

DeVilbiss paused to arrange his thoughts precisely. "On Friday you will draw all but one hundred dollars from your checking and savings accounts and take the money in large-denomination bills. You'll stay in your house and wait for my phone call. Pack two suitcases for a long trip. Do you have a valid passport?"

"Yes."

"Bring it also. Let no one see you drive here. Do you understand?"

"Yes."

"Repeat what I just said," he commanded. She obliged. DeVilbiss leaned close to her face and noticed for the first time that one of her eyes drifted slightly outward. "Kiss me," he ordered. "On the lips."

At last Frederika's eyelids blinked, not once but several times in rapid succession. Her lips squeezed tightly together and curled in one corner, betraying the resistance in her mind.

"You will obey me *without question*," DeVilbiss prompted, "or you will never speak to your father. Kiss me!"

Frederika obeyed, touching her lips to his. She had stopped resisting, but she also gave nothing.

DeVilbiss rose from the bed. "Get dressed, go home, go to sleep. You feel very good. You will remain in this pleasant state for a very long time. Only when I say the words 'your lost teddy bear' will you come fully awake. Do you understand?"

"I understand."

"Good. When I snap my fingers you will remember nothing after our sex in the shower. Do you understand?"

"Yes."

DeVilbiss snapped his fingers. He saw a flash of puzzlement sweep across Frederika's face. Then the hypnotic suggestion locked in. She smiled at him and rolled off the opposite side of the bed, moving gracefully to the bathroom to retrieve her clothes.

DeVilbiss waited until Frederika had driven away before closing the door. He tightened the sash around his robe and walked toward the kitchen, to prepare himself a cup of unadulterated tea. He would will himself to sleep in a few hours, but for now he preferred to relax and gloat over his conquest of the strong-willed woman. Even more deliciously, if Little Nick had been getting his invisible, voyeuristic jollies over the episode, from the bathroom to the time Frederika left the house, he could not have guessed that the session was anything more than unbridled concupiscence and the creation of a hypnotic trance purely to help get the scrolls. If Nick interrogated him and asked why Frederika needed her passport, he could say that he wished to keep her his sex slave for a few months and then kill her. A good pot of tea would also help him figure out what to do with the speed-reading reverend, who might momentarily skip exactly to the passages that could undo not only Old Nick and Company but Vincent as well. He glanced around the room but, as always, he saw nothing.

Simon's ears perked up at the sound of the automobile engine, as they had at twenty others that had driven by in the past hour. This one, however, turned into the Vanderveen driveway and pulled into the garage. Simon snapped his novel shut and hastened into the kitchen. Relief surged through him, lightening his stride. He lit a flame under the pot he had already half-filled with milk and set to work popping the lid on a tin of cocoa. The back door opened and Frederika entered.

"Hi," Simon said, as casually as he could.

"Hello," Frederika greeted neutrally. "Midnight snack?"

Simon glanced at his watch, as he had done ten times in the past hour. "Actually, it's just eleven."

"I told you I wouldn't be home late," she said, shrugging out of her coat.

"I've made enough for two if you'd like some."

Frederika stepped close to the range. "No, thanks." She inhaled deeply. "But it smells delicious."

Simon stared at the hematoma on the side of her neck, a hickey of classic proportions. With her eyes closed to the pleasure of inhaling the chocolate, Frederika missed the slackening of his jaw and the veiling of his eyes. Simon turned away, ostensibly to fetch a cup and saucer.

"I'm very tired," Frederika told him. "I think I'll turn in. Good night." She took a couple steps, then turned. "I said 'good night,' Simon."

"Good night," he answered.

Frederika's eyebrows furrowed. A trace expression of guilt clouded her face. She noted the sudden heaviness of his movement. "See you in the morning," she added.

Simon nodded with his back to her. He listened as she climbed the stairs. He snapped the lid back on the cocoa box and dumped the milk down the drain.

CHAPTER TEN

December 21

⌘

Knowledge is of two kinds—we know a subject ourselves

or we know where we can find information on it.

—*Samuel Johnson*

＊

Simon hurried into the empty room, shut the door and locked it behind him. The owner of the office had left town for the holidays, but he had given his librarian friend a duplicate key to the space more than a year earlier. Even so, Simon's attitude was furtive. The professor whose name was on the door was unwittingly lending not only his office but his identity.

Simon opened his wallet, took out a sheet of paper with a telephone number and several lines of dialogue on it and flattened it on the desk. He dialed the number and waited tensely for an answer.

"This is Katerina Callahan." The voice belonged to a woman of some years, dry and with a slight tremor.

Simon labored in a breath and set his forefinger on his script. "Mrs. Callahan, my name is Neil Yoskin. I'm a friend of your niece, Frederika Vanderveen."

"I see. Is she all right?" the woman asked.

"As a matter of fact, she isn't. I'm a professor of psychology at Princeton University, and a therapist in private practice here." During his undergraduate days, Simon had acted in both the university's Theatre Intime and Triangle Club. In later years he played bit parts for the McCarter Theatre repertory company in town. With his script in front of him, he was confident he could play this role. He was also thankful that he possessed a naturally low voice, which over the telephone lent him added years and an air of authority. His ear told him he had kept the nervousness from his voice; he hoped his pseudoprofessional jargon sounded equally convincing.

"While Frederika is a friend and *not* a patient, I can't help registering serious professional alarm," Simon continued. "I've noted signs of suicidal tendencies, a—"

"Suicide!" Mrs. Callahan exclaimed. "Has she hurt herself?"

"No, ma'am," Simon said. "I said tendencies: growing periods of depression, an avoidance of friends, and so forth."

"Has she been hospitalized?"

"No. I'm calling for your help before that becomes necessary," Simon pushed. "I'm convinced this isn't a passing thing, such as Seasonal Affective Disorder syndrome." He paused, but the woman seemed willing to listen. "I realize this call is irregular and, in fact, unprofessional. Ordinarily I'd ask you to visit my office if you lived closer, or else would write a letter of inquiry. However, your answers to my questions would no doubt generate more questions and more correspondence. I'm afraid we may not have that luxury of time."

"I see. May I call you back in a few minutes, Professor?" Katerina asked.

"Certainly," Simon said. He gave the woman the office telephone number and hung up. She might have been in the middle of something. More likely, she would phone back through the switchboard, checking on this alleged professor of psychology. Simon stood and paced the little office. He was beginning to wear a path in the rug when the telephone jangled.

"Hello," he answered simply, in case the call was from someone unexpected.

"Dr. Yoskin?"

"Yes, Mrs. Callahan." Simon sat and grabbed his script. "Thanks for calling back so promptly."

"Do you have many questions?"

"That depends on your answers," he returned, carefully.

"Because, frankly, I haven't seen or talked ot her in . . . four years."

The admission jarred Simon. Considering that Frederika had so few relatives, it seemed strange that she would make no attempt to keep in touch with her aunt. He mastered his surprise and said, "I believe the problem arises from long before that. Did you see your niece much when she was young?"

"Constantly. Before I married, I lived in my brother's house."

Katerina had probably been the "nanny" whose room Simon now occupied. Dean Krieger had directed him to potential paydirt. "In your estimation, was Frederika a happy child?"

"I would say so. She wasn't an *easy* little girl, but then that would be normal for an only child who happens also to be beautiful and intelligent, wouldn't it?"

"How do you mean 'not easy'?" Simon said.

"One minute she was off in her own world, nonresponsive to conversation. The next she'd be chattering like a monkey, impossible to shut up. And she was unreasonably timid."

"Do you have any idea why?"

"No. As I say, it was unreasonable; just her nature."

"So she *was* basically a happy child."

"Yes."

"But did she have a happy childhood?"

"Can one be one *without* having the other?" the woman countered. Her early sounds of concern had diminished.

"Yes," Simon assured. "But, in your assessment, this wasn't the case with Frederika?"

"Not to my knowledge."

"Did she suffer any serious childhood illnesses?"

"What do you mean?"

"I mean the sort that might have caused permanent neurological damage."

"No." Her reply was curt. Simon had no idea when she would reach her limit of patience. He rushed on, to deny her time to think.

"Your brother traveled frequently," he prompted.

"That's right. His wife often accompanied him. That was my reason for living in the house . . . to take care of it and Frederika."

"Did they travel often when she was very young, before she was six?"

"Yes." Now her voice was clearly becoming irritated.

"How did Frederika react to this?"

"She understood."

"She's mentioned more than once, often with emotion, her father's demands for perfection. She seems fixated on the subject. Did you notice a fear of displeasing him?"

"Fear? Of course not! Their relationship was very loving," she said, with icy vehemence.

"I'm sure you love your brother still," Simon pushed, "but preserving his good memory ought not to outweigh his daughter's safety. I'm talking about the possibility of *suicide*, Mrs. Callahan. I must ask you, did your brother traumatize his child in some way?"

"Frederik was not the cause of *any* problems his daughter has," Katerina snapped. "She was traumatized because she was abandoned! If you want to know who hurt her, ask her mother!" Immediately, there was a sharp intake of air on the woman's end of the line, as if she were trying to suck back her last words.

Simon's surprise startled him upright in the chair. "Frederika says her mother's dead. But she's alive?"

"No." Her tone had made a mercurial change. "Of course she's dead. I was . . . only speaking figuratively." Then she was silent.

"Figuratively," Simon echoed, to fill in the gap.

"That's all I have to say. If Frederika isn't your patient, then send her to a colleague and mind your own business," the woman snapped. Her delivery was harsh, but a thread of fear was woven through it, destroying her intended effect. She hung up an instant after her last sentence. Simon was glad; her words had rendered him speechless. Speaking figuratively indeed! He didn't have to be the real Neil Yoskin to hear the truth behind her denial: as far as Katerina Callahan believed, Alice Vanderveen was alive.

As Simon ran across campus to the library, his mind outraced his feet. What was most incredible was not the secret itself but that it had been preserved from both sides. Frederika's mother must have made no attempt to contact her child in all the years since abandoning Frederika, even after her ex-husband had died. Had her silence been maintained for the same unknown purpose as the Vanderveen family's? Simon resolved to put aside speculation and concentrate instead on finding the real answer. He dashed into the library's Microforms room and hunted up the index for the *Princeton Packet*. Frederika was twenty-four. He guessed that her parents had married a year before her birth—1964. He quickly found the reference for the wedding and then hauled out the proper roll of microfilm. The ceremony had been held on the second Saturday in June. The bride's maiden name was Lydell. She came from Chestnut Hill, on the outskirts of Philadelphia, and had attended Girls' High School. She had a mother, Janet, a father, Thomas, and a sister, Jennifer, who had been the maid of honor. Her occupation was cited as secretary for the FAO office of the United Nations. The wedding was celebrated at Nassau Presbyterian Church. The remainder of the column was devoted to the famous Princeton resident and groom, but Simon felt certain that the eight facts given about Alice Vanderveen would be enough for any detective worth his salt. He went to the place in the Reference room where the telephone directories were shelved, not bothering to conceal himself from Frederika. She saw him, smiled, and returned to her work. Simon took the Philadelphia and Suburbs directory to a desk and flipped it open. Three of his leads evaporated. The only listing for Lydell was an inner city address, for someone with the initials G. A. A row of pay phones was tucked into a corner of the foyer. Simon paid his toll, dialed the number, and after three rings heard the hollow, mechanical sounds of an answering machine.

"This is Arthur Lydell," the decidedly black voice greeted. "I'm not able to come to the phone right now, so please leave me a message."

Simon declined, setting the handpiece back on its cradle. Alice had to be nearing fifty; her parents were likely dead or retired to sunnier climes. Her sister, Jennifer, no doubt had acquired a new last name. Simon stared through the glass wall at Frederika, who had her back to him. What would Mike Hammer do now, he asked himself. His half-serious thought dredged up the memory of two books Simon had chanced upon in the library, books that were sure to be common detective reference works. They were obverse and reverse sides of the same coin, entitled *How to Find Almost Anyone* and *How to Create a New Identity*. The latter's author wrote about getting oneself successfully lost, applying for a driver's license and Social Security card, and establishing credit. The former was an ingenious primer on getting information out of telephone directories, the post office, county and state records offices, public utilities, and all sorts of other resources for finding persons who had hied for parts unknown. Simon had found both books abstractly fascinating but had never dreamed he would have occasion to use either one.

Simon looked up the books' reference numbers in the card catalog and found that both were shelved on the B floor. He took the Catalog area's elevator and immediately regretted not having run around to the staircase. The library's elevators were built for holding great weight and not for speed. He once overheard a wag declare that "I fell in and out of love with a woman between C floor and Two." Simon glanced at his watch. He had already used up fifty minutes of his lunch hour making the telephone call and researching the wedding. He stepped out of the elevator and turned left.

All around him lay a maze of shelves, filled with books. He worked in no ordinary library. In size and importance both, this one ranked among the top twenty in North America. Its floor space rivaled that of most shopping malls. One corridor on C level ran 400 feet in an uninterrupted line. For someone without Simon's degree of expertise, it was overwhelming. He moved surely through the stacks, in and out of the deep shadows. To conserve energy, only those shelves in use were lighted; he had once estimated that the library had at least five thousand on/off switches. Simon turned into the aisle that held the first book, his eyes sweeping along the numbers, praying it had not been borrowed. But as he found it and reached out, another approach came to him, as if his consciousness had been strolling the corridors in the vast library of his mind and had switched on a light, illuminating something. He left the book untouched and hurried out of the library's core, taking the main stairs two at a time. Simon darted his head into his superior's office, pulled it out as quickly and looked at Willy Spencer, who sat at his perpetual perch in front of the Ahriman scrolls.

"Have you seen Dr. Gould?" Simon asked him.

Reverend Spencer's face swept up, wearing a scowl. Then he recorded that the interrupter was Simon and became less severe. "Dr. Gould? He said he was going to lunch at Prospect House. Went about ten minutes ago, I think."

"Would you tell him I won't be in this afternoon?" Simon asked.

"Of course." Willy stared over his reading glasses at Simon. Concern deepened the fine webbing of wrinkles around his chestnut-colored eyes. "Come here," he bid. When Simon had, he placed his hand on the librarian's forehead. "Definite fever," he judged, "and you look flushed. Get right to bed, son, or your whole holiday'll be ruined. Scat! I'll tell Dr. Gould."

Simon thanked the old scholar and grabbed his coat. On the way out he felt his forehead and found it unusually warm.

At a few minutes past one o'clock, Simon stood in the Vanderveen mansion basement, thumbing through the senior yearbook Alice Lydell had left behind. He found Alice's photograph and, beneath it, what passed in such books for a biography.

ALICE Q. LYDELL

"Lizzie". . . . one of Mr.
Cheswick's rowdies . . . oh,
those baby blues . . . that
puke green Bel Air . . .
Queen's Court . . . headed
for NYC . . . 50 Bayberry Ln
Social Science Club 3,4;
Chorus 2,3,4.

Simon paged carefully through the book, searching for more information. A color photograph of the Senior Ball Queen and her court had been hand-pasted in. Alice stood on the step just below the queen and to her right. The queen was a girl named Robin Geisel— perky, petite, and with a winning smile, but not nearly as beautiful as Alice. In the informal photos section he found a snapshot of Alice and Robin arm in arm, sticking their tongues out at the camera, with the Washington Monument in the background. Simon paged to Robin's biography. She was described as "the future Mrs. William Agress."

Simon carried the yearbook up to the kitchen. Frederika had brought home several out-of-date telephone directories discarded by the library. In the Philadelphia and Suburbs book he found a listing for a Mr. William Agress, living in Mt. Airy. He dialed the number and rapped his pencil impatiently against the edge of the counter until the connection was made. A woman answered.

"Hello!" Simon said, enthusiastically. "I'm Richard Stern, from the counseling office at Girls' High. May I speak with Robin Agress?"

"This is she," the voice replied. Her tone was pleasant and expectant.

"Hello," he said again. "As you may know, your class's thirtieth anniversary is coming up next year."

Mrs. Agress laughed ruefully. "Do you have to remind me so soon?"

Simon relaxed at the happy sound of her voice, a welcome contrast to his conversation with Katerina Callahan. "I'm sorry," he offered. "They say misery loves company. That may be why reunions were invented."

Robin laughed again. "Maybe. How can I help you?"

"I wonder if you may still be in touch with some of your classmates whom the committee can't find."

"I thought we'd put together a pretty exhaustive list for the twenty-fifth," Robin remarked.

Simon swallowed hard, then said, "Do you by any chance still have a copy of it, because we don't."

"No, I sure don't." She was not testing his identity after all.

"That's okay," Simon said. "Whatever you can provide will be appreciated."

"Well, I'm not the social butterfly I once was, but I'll give it the old high school try."

"Great." Simon opened the yearbook near the front. "Donna Anderson," he read.

"Donna's dead. Killed in that big plane crash at O'Hare some years back, going to a book convention."

"I'm sorry to hear that," Simon said, startled by the unexpected answer.

"I'm surprised nobody in the school knew," Robin mused aloud.

"Lots of turnovers and retirements in thirty years," Simon excused. "What about Dee Appleby?"

"I don't know. Didn't even know her in school."

"Alice Lydell?"

"She's now Mrs. Thomas Niederjohn," the woman obliged.

Simon pumped his clenched fists in silent triumph.

"Let me find her number and address," Robin said. "Here they are."

Simon scribbled down the information. It was an effort to reel off two more names at random. He thanked Robin and promised to "say hello to Alice" when he called her. Hanging up, he could see why the least outwardly beautiful girl in the Ball Court had been elected queen.

A glass jar on Simon's dresser held his spare coins. He changed into grungy jeans and stuffed a fistful of silver into his pocket, then traded his white broadcloth shirt and P.U. tie for a checkered flannel shirt and a real Air Force bomber jacket he had inherited, working within the limits of his Ivy League wardrobe to create a *machismo* look. He had planned to visit DeVilbiss directly after work, risking a chance meeting with Frederika. Instead, he could have the confrontation when she was sure to be in the library.

In front of the town post office, while shoppers rushed by carrying festive, bulging bags, Simon paused at a pay phone and called the number Robin Agress had supplied. The phone rang, but no one answered. He collected his change, then leaned against the phone

194

box and collected his courage. He was bigger than DeVilbiss but that hardly compensated for the aura of evil surrounding the man. More frightening, Simon was convinced that he had known of this man's evil nature even before meeting him face to face. He decided he didn't care. He grabbed several lungfuls of cold air and trudged toward Park Place.

In the daylight the duplex house, squeezed tightly between similar old buildings, belied the New York image that the street name suggested. It looked not at all like the sort of residences Frederika's former lovers inhabited. Simon wondered about the cause of such a change in her routine and was subconsciously rattled by the prospect that it might suggest she had locked into a more realistic and lasting relationship.

Simon rapped loudly on the door. While he waited, he looked up and down the street. Other than the mailman walking his route, Park Place was deserted. The trees poked up bony branches; bushes huddled naked and dormant against the dreary dwellings. The music of an ancient Christmas carol with its lines "in the bleak midwinter/ frosty winds made moan" cycled repeatedly in his head, like a skipping record.

Simon knocked again, then moved to one of the front windows, to risk a peek inside. A tiny face stared out at him. He started back in surprise, then realized he was looking at the painted porcelain head of a French Pierrot doll.

The door started to creak open. Simon hurried to put himself in front of it. Vincent DeVilbiss appeared, digging dried mucus from the corner of his eye. The red wrinkles on his left cheek further suggested that Simon had interrupted more than a catnap.

DeVilbiss's eyes went wide. He lowered his hand and raised a toothy smile. "Ah! The intense fellow from the library," DeVilbiss remembered. "What might I do for you?"

"You might invite me inside," Simon said. He instantly regretted the harshness of his tone and resolved to moderate it.

"Certainly." DeVilbiss stepped aside cordially. He wore a stylish silk dressing gown over pajama bottoms. His feet were bare, as was the part of his chest the gown failed to cover. His clothes reminded

Simon that the man was a creature of the night—like a panther. He was doubly glad he had arrived at midday, catching DeVilbiss in his sleep, so the man would be less alert and less inclined toward violence.

Simon made a turn into the living room. He found himself staring at the clown doll in profile. It sat on the stuffed upper curve of the old couch, looking out the window as if on sentry duty. Simon pivoted to address the channeler.

"Do you intend to stay long in Princeton?"

DeVilbiss grinned. "I take it you're not from the Welcome Wagon."

"You're right. My name's Simon Penn. I'm a friend of Frederika Vanderveen."

Instead of the expected defensiveness, DeVilbiss's grin grew even wider, showing rows of even, white teeth and a pair of incisors too big for his mouth.

"Simon Penn. No wonder you were in the Microforms Room; you work in the library with Frederika!" DeVilbiss exclaimed, brightly. "She speaks well of you."

"She speaks nothing of you," Simon countered. "She thinks you're her big secret, but she's wrong. The people close to her know she's going through a bad time, even though she won't talk about it. She's looking for answers from the dead, answers she can't get."

"Perhaps she can," DeVilbiss suggested.

"Don't try your bullshit on me," Simon said. "Frederika's obviously allowed herself to fall for your mumbo jumbo, and we want it to stop."

Laugh lines appeared in the corner of DeVilbiss's seductive eyes. He seemed amused that someone thought he could be threatened.

"Or what?" he asked, lowering himself to the arm of the couch.

"You think because you move often your past can't be traced?" Simon bluffed. "We already know you're dangerous."

DeVilbiss raised his eyebrows. "Is this a royal We, or perhaps a concerned coterie of librarians?"

Simon ignored the barb. "I mean the people who care about Frederika . . . some of them influential people."

196

DeVilbiss covered a yawn with his hand. "Do tell. You have no faith in my skills, so you want me gone. You realize that deprives me of my livelihood? How do you propose to compensate my moving costs?"

Simon knew DeVilbiss might be toying with him, but it was also likely that he had pressed the right button suggesting "they" knew his dangerous history.

"We'll give you five hundred," Simon offered.

DeVilbiss's attitude of amusement continued. He stared out the window and gave a little snort of derision. "That wouldn't get me out of your godforsaken state. The press might pay that much for a story of prejudice, persecution, and bribery, committed on a poor newcomer by those of . . . *influence*."

"One thousand. Take it and run." Lynn had charged Simon only $250 a month for the privilege of staying in her townhouse. Ever since Simon had come to Princeton, he had lived simply. He had almost ten thousand squirreled away in liquid accounts. He hoped the man was greedy and a small-time con artist, not gutsy enough to force Simon to set a monetary ceiling on how much Simon cared about Frederika.

"A thousand dollars," DeVilbiss remarked, standing. "She *is* a pearl of great price."

"Well?"

"I'll have to think about it."

"Think quickly," Simon added. "The offer's good until Christmas Eve. It's also invalid if you have another session with her."

"Session, eh?" DeVilbiss held out his right hand. "A gentleman's pledge to give your offer serious consideration."

Simon knew an unfailing trick to subdue morons who enjoyed showing off their strength through viselike handshakes. He took DeVilbiss's hand high in his grip and tightened around the knuckles that connected DeVilbiss's fingers to his palm. He knew he had done it correctly, and yet the man was able to return his pressure with a force that made Simon want to cry out with pain. Their eyes locked, as they had in the library, and, despite the carpal war they waged, they both maintained an easy smile. After a long moment, DeVilbiss let go.

"You obviously took the day off from the library," he observed. "Will you be there the rest of the week if I decide to contact you?"

"I don't know. I'll call *you*. It's not that long a time," Simon replied. "Tell me: What exactly does Frederika want from her father?"

"Sorry. That would betray my professional trust."

"I don't think she's told you anything. Probably because you haven't given anything to her."

DeVilbiss cracked his evil leer. "You'd be surprised at what I've given her, and vice versa," he said. "Then again, maybe you wouldn't. There's the door, Mr. Penn."

Simon left the house without looking back. The door slammed shut as he descended the rickety porch steps. He found himself staring at the same beat-up Ford Escort he had seen the night he came to spy on Frederika. He wondered if it belonged to DeVilbiss. Then he noted the Rent-A-Wreck sticker on its bumper. Perhaps the man had only intended a short stay in Princeton, without outside prodding. Each time Simon had seen the man, he was dressed expensively. He carried himself with a self-assurance that made it hard to believe he would drive such a car, or make a living in such a disreputable fashion.

Walking slowly down the street, reviewing their conversation, Simon realized he could trust neither the man's promises nor his pretenses. The image of the eyes, wicked smile, and raven hair with silver tufts had existed in his memory far longer than DeVilbiss's stay in Princeton. And the clown doll had something to do with it as well. Something. Such an unusual pair, and yet Simon could not dredge the source of his disquiet out into the light. It was bad enough being betrayed by a stranger; it was hell to be betrayed by one's own mind.

Simon moved restlessly through the shelves of the Princeton Public Library. Ordinarily, he couldn't walk two feet along library stacks without stopping to examine some intriguing title. Now nothing interested him. He was merely keeping warm and biding time until five-fifteen, when he would make his next quarter-hourly phone call attempt.

Simon found himself in the travel section, staring at books on the British Isles. He thought about the trace of upper-class British accent in Vincent DeVilbiss's voice. Simon had been out of the country once, but to Japan; he certainly hadn't met the man abroad. He wracked his brain for a television image of the handsome face even while he doubted he had ever seen it before this week.

"Can I help you find something?" a librarian asked him.

"No, thanks," Simon replied. "I'm afraid what I need isn't in your library."

"Then you might try the Princeton University library, up the street," the woman suggested. "It's huge."

Simon thanked the librarian and walked toward the pay phone. He of all people knew what Firestone Library held, but for all the knowledge reposited there it could not shed any light on the mystery of Frederika Vanderveen.

He dialed the Philadelphia number for the dozenth time. At last the connection was made. More important, a woman answered.

"Mrs. Alice Niederjohn?" Simon asked.

"Yes?" From the soprano timbre of her voice, Simon found it hard to believe she could be in her late forties.

"My name is Simon Penn. I'm calling on behalf of someone who desperately needs your help."

"We don't give to charities over the——."

"This is the kind of charity that begins at home," Simon said, cutting her off. "I'm a friend of your daughter, Frederika."

There was a stone-hard silence on the other end. Simon heard a male voice asking "Who is it?" in the background. Then came the muffled voice of Alice telling the man it was "someone asking for money."

"I'm sorry, I can't help you," Alice said, firmly. He heard the tension in her voice.

"And *I'm* sorry to tell you that you have no choice," he countered. "I have no personal desire to dredge up your past, but your daughter may suffer a mental breakdown unless she gets some answers. Answers I think only you can provide. If you won't talk with me now, I'm coming to your house and camping on your doorstep."

"Please, don't! My family knows nothing about this," Alice said, dropping her voice to a half-whisper.

"Meet me somewhere," Simon suggested. "Anytime tomorrow."

"That's impossible."

"Then Saturday. No later."

"All right. Where?"

"Philadelphia. I have no car, but I can take the train from Princeton Junction."

"There's a French bakery on the corner of Chestnut and Eighteenth. I can't make it any earlier than four o'clock."

"All right, four o'clock. Please . . . don't disappoint me," Simon said. "I'm as protective about Frederika as you are about your present family." He marched the words out like mourners in a funeral procession, making his veiled threat unmistakable.

Alice hung up without reply.

On the way to the exit, Simon crossed paths with the librarian. "Did you find something after all?" she asked, helpfully.

"Yes, I did," he replied. "I did indeed."

Vincent's eyes swept back to the top of the paragraph and tried again to understand it. He sighed in frustration. This was the third time he had assayed James Joyce's *Ulysses,* and it wasn't getting any easier. He had heard some years back of the author's declaration that the novel must be read several times. Joyce considered his narrative a gestalt, and demanded that the reader have all parts of the work simultaneously in his mind in order to understand fully any single passage. During his second assault on the work Vincent had used a heavily annotated copy, but the esoteric references had not stuck with him. He was determined to get his mind around *Ulysses,* however, since so many of the world's acknowledged authorities had declared it a work of genius and de rigeur for any learned man's reading. This last was vital to Vincent; his pride allowed nothing less than that he be among the most cultured and urbane men of the Western world. Vincent favored the old Arab saying, "He who travels lightest travels fastest." Yet he always carried at least two of the "Hundred Great Books" with him. He always made sure that the clothing and jewelry he wore had been displayed in an internationally known magazine or respected newspaper's fashion supplement.

Vincent closed the book and glanced to the other Great Book at his elbow. It was Marcel Proust's *A la recherche du temps perdu*, the most vexing read he had ever attempted. He was about ready to dismiss it as snob literature, celebrated purely because of the sophisticated unintelligibility of its language. Where was its story? He anticipated the day when his own published remembrance of things lost would push this pretender out of the top hundred. For the time being, Proust was secure. To "come out of the coffin," Vincent would have to wait until synthetic blood was commonplace and inexpensive and he no longer needed to open carotid arteries. He would also wait until several generations after his last victims' vindictive offspring were dead and his capital crimes had been committed in a past so remote no country would demand his life. And he *could* wait; his secret diaries would insure against any memory lapses.

Vincent set the book down and glanced at his wristwatch. The delivery should have arrived by now. Little Nick was cutting it very close this time, perhaps "yanking his chain," as an American would put it, for not having destroyed the scrolls. If that was Nick's plan, it was working. The pounds of imitation elixir in the trunk of the rented car reminded him of the phrase from *The Rime of the Ancient Mariner*: "Water, water, everywhere, / Nor any drop to drink." Not for years would he risk letting his synthesized duplication pass his lips, even if he found himself without any real elixir. Let others risk their lives for him. Mrs. Raymond would waddle in for her revelatory séance in another three hours; that would take his mind off the magic powder. Then he'd walk to P.J.'s Pancake House and calm his nerves with a chili cheeseburger and the caffeine jolt of a Coke Classic.

201

The windows rattled with the rumblings of a heavy vehicle. Vincent got up and opened the curtains. Outside the house sat a UPS truck. He moved quickly to the front door.

A young woman stepped down from the truck, carrying a parcel of familiar size. She was small and pixieish and looked like a brownie in her chocolate-colored uniform. She smiled as she ascended the stairs. Behind her, the truck's blinker solenoids clicked on and off noisily.

" 'Evening," she said.

"Good evening," Vincent returned.

"DeVilbiss?"

"The same. Isn't this rather late to be making deliveries?"

"Not before the holidays," the driver replied. "I can't wait for December twenty-fifth! We haven't met before, have we?"

"No."

The young lady pushed her pad and pen forward, indicating the line for Vincent's signature. "Gift?" she asked.

"What? Gift? Yes." Vincent took the package. "I wonder where that word came from. Did you know that in German 'gift' means poison?"

"No, I didn't," the woman admitted, still holding her affable smile. She pointed to the package. "That isn't perfume, is it?"

Vincent hefted the square parcel, wrapped in brown kraft paper, with no return address on it. "No. Why do you think that?"

"Oh, I thought it'd be funny if it was. There's a perfume called 'Poison,' y'know."

"No, I didn't." Vincent dug into his pocket, came out with a five-dollar bill and handed it to the woman.

"You don't have to do that."

He stuck it under the clip on her board. "I know. Happy holidays."

"Thanks!" she said, then strode down the stairs toward the truck. Before she mounted, she turned and said, "I hope it's a *good* gift."

"The best," Vincent assured. He watched the truck rumble down the street and disappear around the corner before taking the package into the kitchen and opening it. Wrapped in raw cotton was a brown glass jar, filled with a yellow-green powder. Vincent glanced at the counter, where the last delivery's jar stood, and did a double take. He picked it up and held it only inches from his eyes. The night before, when he had drunk his nightly dose, he was sure that one full measure remained for the following day. What lay in the bottom of the jar was perhaps a third of a dose. His eyelids narrowed, then darted around the room. This was not something Nick would do. At least he never had before. Vincent decided that he must have seen wrong, a trick of light or whatever. At any rate, with the latest supply arriving, what would be the point in Nick's stealing less than a dose of the old elixir? Vincent unstoppered the old and new jars, poured the few grains of old into the new and stirred them around with a spoon. Then he dug the spoon into the powder and extracted enough to flatly fill the spoon's bowl. He transferred the mixture to an eight-ounce glass, filled it with tap water and drank it down. He carefully pushed the stopper down onto the neck of the new jar and set it far back from the lip of the counter.

Vincent went to the hall closet for his coat. He was unwilling to wait until after Mrs. Raymond's visit to leave the house. He needed fresh air immediately. He took to the sidewalk in a heavy, maundering manner, unable to expunge the missing grains of elixir from his thoughts. Several minutes later, he paused in front of a darkened antiques store, to look at the image he cast in the reflecting window.

"They don't know anything. You haven't done anything they could catch," he counseled his agitated face, under his breath. "If you weren't damned clever and damned careful, you wouldn't have survived five hundred years." His jaw set firmly. "But from now on forget mercy. Forget it! Do exactly what they ask. And give them those fucking scrolls for Christmas."

CHAPTER ELEVEN

December 22

❧

There is more than one way of sacrificing

to the fallen angels.

—*St. Augustine*

The telephone on Simon's desk rang. He could have sworn from the sound of its jangle that it signaled trouble. He toyed with the idea of ignoring it but knew that could lead to more problems. He answered with a cautious voice.

"Simon, it's Lynn." Her tone was artificially "up." "How are you?"

"Fine," he said, rolling back from the desk and pressing his palm against his forehead, as if to keep it from filling up with headache. "How about you?"

"Oh, okay I guess. Listen, I have a present for you. It's monogrammed, so it's not the sort of thing I can return."

Simon clenched his teeth and squinted. He saw precisely where the conversation was going.

"That's very thoughtful."

"I was something of a bitch about the J and J party. I apologize."

"It's okay. You had every right to be angry."

"I did, but that's not the point," she said. "When can we get together?"

"Not till after vacation. I'm gonna catch a train tonight and visit my folks," he lied, knowing it was a poor substitute for firmly denying to her that there was any hope of reconciliation.

"I see. That's nice. Well, I'll hold your present for you until you get back." She paused for a reply; when she got none, in a voice uncharacteristically subdued, she wished, "Happy holidays."

"Happy holidays to you," he said. He replaced the handset gently on its cradle. Barry the account manager had evidently been gobbled up alive already, or else had preternatural antennae and had fled the web before becoming hopelessly entangled. Simon cursed under his breath. He looked at the reverend, bent assiduously over his beloved scrolls, wishing he could disturb the man and pour out his troubles. He decided against it, picked up a six-hundred-year-old hand-scribed manuscript of St. Augustine's *The City of God* and concentrated as best he could.

Frederika walked through the doors of the Reference room and over to the foyer pay phones. She deposited her money and dialed a number by heart.

"Vincent DeVilbiss," said the sonorous voice.

"This is Frederika," she announced.

"Yes. So good of you to call. How do you feel?"

"I feel fine. Can I see you tonight?"

"No, I'm sorry. I have several clients. But soon, my lovely one. Do you have your purse with you?"

"Yes."

"Open it and look in the bottom. You'll find a prescription bottle filled with a yellowish powder. Do you see it?"

"Yes."

"Do you remember the last time you visited, when I walked you to your car?"

"Yes."

"I slipped the bottle into your purse. I want you to pour one level teaspoon's worth of the powder into a large glass, fill the glass with water, mix and drink it. It will make you feel good and strong. Do you understand?"

"Yes."

"You will do this every day at this time. Do you understand?"

"Yes."

"Good. Thanks so much for calling."

"You're welcome."

"I'd be very pleased if you called me again tonight. Would you do that?"

"Yes."

"Good. Now say good-bye."

"Good-bye." Frederika listened for the disconnection, then hung up.

She turned around and found herself confronted by Millie Townshend, one of the librarians who worked at the main desk.

"Boyfriend troubles?" Millie asked, with a face as solicitous as her voice. Millie was not one of Frederika's major detractors in the library, but she had as much prurient curiosity as the next person and could not resist the chance to eavesdrop on the notorious younger woman's private life.

"Yes," Frederika answered. A confused look animated her previously deadpan expression. "I mean . . . I don't know."

Millie cocked her head in the attitude of a domineering nanny. "Are you feeling well? I know you had that bad cold."

"I'm fine."

"You look kind of out of it." Millie peered into Frederika's glassy eyes. "Is that cold medicine?"

"What?" Frederika stared blankly at the prescription bottle in her hand. "Yes. It's my medicine."

Millie decided not to pursue her tack. She gestured at the phone just behind Frederika. "You have to make another call?"

"No. I'm sorry." Frederika stepped out of the way.

"Well, take care."

"Yes, I will." Frederika continued back to her desk. She wondered why Millie was the third person to inquire after her health. She wondered only for a moment, found she could not remember what she was thinking about and returned to her work.

Simon paused again from his document evaluation to watch Reverend Spencer's unusual antics. Until this afternoon, the old scholar had been as disciplined as a monk, sitting hour after hour at his stool, occasionally reaching for a reference book but otherwise reading and writing, reading and writing, reading and writing. Two hours earlier, when Simon returned from lunch, he had found Willy pacing in front of the scrolls, eyeing them as if they had magically transformed into the *National Inquirer*. Suddenly, Willy gathered up the reams of translations and hurried out of the room. Half an hour later he returned, burdened with three times the paper he had when he left. Simon watched with curiosity as Willy separated the sheets into three stacks, placed one stack into a large manila envelope and sealed it. He brought the envelope to Simon's desk and laid it directly atop the book Simon was evaluating.

"That guard who died here . . ." Willy said, abruptly.

"Tommy Wheeler. Yes?" Simon said.

"How long ago was that?"

"Ten days, I think."

"And the rare-book alarms went off," Willy continued.

"Right. They think Tommy kicked out at one of the emergency switches. Why?"

"You won't be here tomorrow or Christmas Day, I expect," Willy said, evading the question.

"That's right," Simon replied. Agitated did not adequately describe the way Willy looked and acted; he became agitated over all sorts of petty things. Unnerved was more like it, Simon thought.

Willy's bushy brows scrunched together. "When will you be in the library next?"

"Tuesday."

"Very well. If I don't come in by ten o'clock on Tuesday, open this and read the passages I've marked in red. This is a copy of everything I've translated; it's important that you have it all. The pages I'm talking about are toward the back."

"I don't understand," Simon told him. "Why are you doing this?"

"Insurance," Willy answered, patting the envelope. "I'm not going to say another word, Simon, because you'd think I've lost my mind. I already feel like the world's greatest paranoid."

"What do I do after I read the passages?"

Willy sighed. "Good question. Make sure the information gets to as many sources as you see fit. Use your best judgment. I've made another set. I'm sending it to Dr. Mustafa Elmasri, at the University of Athens."

"He's the one you worked with in Iraq?"

"Yes. He's actually more qualified to translate the scrolls than I."

"If you don't come in Tuesday, where will you be?" Simon asked.

Willy pushed his glasses up the bridge of his nose. "God only knows, Simon. God only knows. Do you have a safe place to store the envelope outside of this room?"

"Yes." Simon lifted the package. It felt heavier than it should have, given the amount of paper inside.

"Then hide it there."

"You can trust me—"

"I know I can," Willy interrupted.

"I mean with whatever you're worried about."

"That's okay." Willy hoisted an artificial grin. He patted Simon on the shoulder. "Just humor a crazy old man. It's really nothing. I'm sure I'll see you Tuesday." He turned toward the scrolls. "I'm locking them up for the day; want to get right to the post office."

Simon looked at the clock on the wall. It was barely past three o'clock. For the first time since he started the translating, Willy was quitting early. That, even more than the old man's unnerved condition and cryptic words, worried Simon.

The Conrail locomotive's headlight winked around the bend in the distant gloom, heading north. One by one, the dozen people on the Princeton Junction platform came out of their private thoughts and collected their belongings.

"Is that our train, Dad?" Liam McCarthy asked.

Martin saw that the train traveled on the track nearest their platform. He glanced at his wristwatch. It was 5:05, precisely when the local was scheduled to stop. "It must be. Ian! Nora!"

McCarthy's other two children ran from the edge of the platform, where they had been hunting up stones to throw. Martin McCarthy shook his head. Being dressed in some of their best clothes had not deterred them in the slightest. When they were also at his side, he handed each of them a ticket.

"Now remember: Aunt Polly stayed late after work to get you. The last stop is Penn Station. You get off and go up any of the stairs into the lobby. She'll be standing near the overhead sign that lists all the trains."

"What if she's not there?" Nora worried out loud.

"Ian's got my telephone number at the office. That's where I'll be. I'm sure everything will be fine." He put on his most confident face. "Okay. Here it is."

The train groaned and hissed to a halt. The twins, eleven, would have been mortified if their father had helped them with their luggage, so he took Nora's suitcase in one hand and his daughter's dirty little paw in the other. He herded all three onto the train and into seats. The boys seemed satisfied when he lovingly tousled their hair, but Nora insisted on throwing her arms around his neck and hugging him for all she was worth.

"I love you, Daddy."

"And I love you, Beanbag." Since his wife's recent death all three children had shown frequent signs of anxiety, checking for assurances of his love and that he, too, would not disappear. "See you all tomorrow night," he promised, backing down the aisle. Liam offered a thumbs-up sign. Nora's lower lip protruded slightly.

"Where are they getting off?" the kindly-looking conductor asked Martin, as the scientist stepped back onto the platform.

"Penn Station."

"I'll watch over them," he said, but before Martin could voice his thanks, the man had redirected his attention to signal the waiting engineer.

The passenger train moved away, sparks jumping brightly between its pantograph and the overhead wires. In the minute between the train's arrival and departure, night seemed to have dropped over Princeton Junction like an indigo curtain.

Martin waited until the train's red lights disappeared before quitting the platform and picking his way through the car-crowded parking yard. Only a few gaps showed in the long lines of metal roofs. The rush of weary, home-bound commuters would not begin for another few minutes. Meetings and seminars up and down the East Coast forced Martin to take a train about twice a month, and he was relieved that he never needed to worry about the severe lack of parking near the station. A few years back, he had done consulting work for POM Laboratories, which sat just across from the train station. The company president had invited him to park in their private lot whenever he needed.

POM Laboratories lay dark and still. As Martin walked by the front of the building, he took the time to examine the notice on the door. The company had closed at 3:00 P.M., in preparation for their holiday party. At the back of the building, the parking lot was completely empty, but for Martin's Honda Accord.

Martin opened the car trunk and took out a blanket and pillow. He would not return to his empty house this night. Since the robbery and Dieter Gerstadt's death, he had felt increasingly ill at ease and vulnerable. For a few days he told himself that the two misfortunes had been nothing more than coincidence. But then two facts occurred to him. The first was about Dieter's smoking habits. For years, Martin had been after his collaborator to give up cigarettes. Finally he had won a concession from Gerstadt; the old boy had stopped polluting their laboratory with nicotine and had promised he would stop smoking in bed. Gerstadt had many faults, but if you could nail him to a promise, he kept it. The second fact was that Martin's neighborhood had occasionally had daylight burglaries, but never one during the night. It was the sort of neighborhood where husbands and wives both worked, attracting teenage thieves with drug habits to feed. They would find a house without evidence of an alarm system, smash a window and go in. But this robbery, with the cut phone lines, carefully etched-out glass, and lack of fingerprints, had the earmarks of a professional second-story man's work.

The trouble was, no such robber would exert such effort or take such a risk to loot a middle-class home. It looked to Martin more like the work of a spy, searching for materials on his research. Many governments would pay dearly to know the details of his and Dieter's work. Fortunately, or unfortunately, neither Martin nor Dieter kept records of their work at home.

So Martin had changed his family's holiday plans, sending his children ahead to his brother, going so far as to bring all their presents to his office that morning so he would not have to enter the house alone. He planned to call his contact at CIA headquarters as soon as he reached his office, to see if they should investigate the break-in and the mysterious fire. Then he would finish the grant proposal, which required posting no later than the last day of the year. Whenever he became too tired to keep working, he would put his blanket and pillow on his office couch and sleep, confident in the protection of the physics building's many locks and patrolling security guards. He and his children would return home only when an agent of the federal government gave them an all-clear call. Maybe he was being paranoid, but then again maybe he had been luckier than Dieter and should not ignore his intuition. Better safe than sorry.

Martin climbed into the Honda, started the engine and tuned in the local classical radio station. He backed around to exit the lot, shifted gears and only turned on his headlights when the car began to move forward. When he toed the accelerator, the engine responded quickly, thrusting the machine toward the driveway.

Without warning, a human figure darted into the headlights. Martin jerked the wheel to the right, but the figure jinked that way as well. Then she was on the hood loudly, rolling up the windshield and off the roof. Martin jammed on the brakes. He had hit a middle-aged woman wearing a gray raincoat and carrying a shopping bag. With his heart thumping in his throat, he reached for the door handle.

Then Martin paused. What was the woman doing behind POM Laboratories? How could she have missed seeing him coming, the only car in the lot? Was he being set up? He reached behind the passenger's seat and grabbed the heavy metal locking bar he used to secure his steering wheel when he left his car in unsafe places. Then he reran in his mind's eye the woman flying over his car and felt supremely foolish. He threw open his car door and rushed out.

The woman lay in the posture of a broken doll, about twenty feet behind the car, unmoving. The contents of her bag were strewn about, barely visible in the red glow of his taillights. As Martin approached, he was relieved to see she was not covered in blood. Coming even closer, he saw that she looked Scandinavian, paled-skinned with wiry blond hair and angular features, big-boned and probably in her mid-fifties. One raincoat pocket hung almost completely ripped off, but the woman showed no visible sign of injury. He knelt beside her.

Simultaneously, the woman's eyelids popped open and her arms thrust out toward Martin. Subconsciously primed, he tumbled backward out of her reach, rolling away, then coming to his knees. Before he could rise, the woman was on him, soundlessly. He whirled around and caught her in the grimly set jaw. It was a well-delivered blow, and he expected to see her crumble from the pain of dislocation. Instead, after her head rocked back, amber eyes glaring, she grabbed his hair roughly and thrust him toward the asphalt. He resisted with the manic energy of panic, but she threw her weight upon him and thrust again. His face smacked down hard, and his body lost all tension.

The woman grabbed Martin's head once more and forced it hard enough into the rough surface that bone cracked. That done, she felt the pulse at his neck, assuring herself that he still lived. She was rewarded with the feeble pressure of his heart pumping.

She stood and walked quickly to the car, reaching into the driver's area and shutting off the headlights. In near-total darkness, she returned to her shopping bag and methodically gathered up the spilled contents. She brought the bag to the car and deposited it in the backseat, then went around and opened the passenger door. After surveying the area, she hoisted McCarthy onto one shoulder and carried him to the car, putting him into the righthand seat. She assumed his place behind the steering wheel, looked at her image in the rearview mirror, and reached back to the shopping bag, out of which she dug a towel. Spitting onto it several times, she used it to cleanse the dirt from his forehead. She buckled him in place, adjusting his seat belt so he would not collapse forward.

The radio station played a brass quintet rendition of "The Twelve Days of Christmas." The woman thumbed it off, relit the headlamps, and drove expertly out of the parking lot. The night before she had scouted out a nearby lake bordering a road. In one location the lake forced the road to take a sharp right turn. The curious thing about the spot was that neither a sign nor a guardrail protected it. It was a perfect place for a preoccupied college professor to drive off the road, smack his head into the steering wheel and drown helplessly when his car sank. Before she could complete her plan, she would have to hide for a time, while the rush-hour traffic died down. But waiting was one of her virtues; she had literally all the time in the world.

"How about a rematch of Got a Minute?" Simon suggested to Frederika, as she cleared away the dinner dishes. "You want to avenge that drubbing you took, don't you?"

"I don't think so," Frederika said. "The house is dirty. I'll clean the downstairs, take a bath, and go to bed early."

"I'd be glad to help you clean," Simon offered.

"No. You're a boarder, not hired help," Frederika said, sliding the dishes into the sink's sudsy water.

"I don't have anything to do," Simon persisted. "I could help you get done sooner. You seem drained."

"I feel fine." Frederika faced him. "I like to do my cleaning alone; it gives me time to think."

Simon got up from the table. "Fine. If you need help—somebody to lift the piano when you're vacuuming—just whistle. You do know how to whistle, don't you?" No recognition of the famous Lauren Bacall line altered Frederika's blank expression. "And stay away from the uncooked steak. I know iron and protein's supposed to be good for a cold, but you could get trichinosis or something." Her expression remained just as void.

Simon was no epicurean, but he knew there was more to steak tartar then cutting hunks off a thick porterhouse and shoving it in

215

one's mouth. He had caught Frederika doing just that, with the animal's blood dribbling over her bottom lip onto her chin. It might have been more disconcerting, had her color not improved so radically of late. She was the embodiment of the expression "in the pink." When he had observed that she seemed drained, he had meant it in the mental sense. Physically, she looked like an Olympic athlete.

Simon left Frederika standing in front of the sink, a wash rag clutched in one hand. He would have probed a little more at her apparent depression—such a flip-flop from her liveliness two nights earlier—if not for his meeting with her mother the next day. Once that happened, he might have a better idea what made Frederika Vanderveen tick. A casual observer would peg her as manic-depressive. Simon wondered if her normal unhappy condition was being worsened by Seasonal Affective Disorder—just a bad lack of sunlight. Maybe *he* was responsible for her sudden depression, bribing Vincent DeVilbiss into summarily dumping her. Ironically, after years of "vamping men" (as Neil Yoskin put it), then running away, she might have finally fallen hard for one who was doing the same to her.

As he reached the top of the staircase, a third possibility came to him. Perhaps the words he had used as an excuse to manipulate her mother were more true than he could have guessed; maybe she was having a very serious mental breakdown and right now staring down unblinkingly into that lightless oblivion called suicide.

"I guarantee it'll ease your arthritis within the week or you come back for your money, Mrs. Hornby," Vincent assured. His hand rested casually and familiarly on the woman's lower back.

Holly Hornby turned to face the handsome herbalist. "Maybe if it works well, I should come back anyway." The twinkle of lust was unmistakable in her eyes. Vincent judged her to be in her late forties, but she had taken remarkable care of herself. He envisioned the hours of self-indulgence every week, with makeup sessions, exercise classes, and low-calorie meals. He suspected the tummy tuck and face-lift, which were justified to her by psychologists, surgeons, girlfriends, and the adoring husband. She was a beauty holding down a twenty-four-hour-a-day job of staving off the ravages of time, and she wanted her rewards.

"Maybe you should," Vincent said, letting his hand drift down to rest on the upper curve of her buttock. It did no harm; if she came back to the house next week, he'd be long gone.

Mrs. Hornby patted Vincent lovingly on the cheek and sashayed through the front door. Vincent waved good-bye, closed the door and shoved the thirty dollars she had given him into his pocket. He thought of Frederika, of her beauty which so outshone Holly Hornby's. He could have taken the lusty-eyed woman to bed tonight if he had wanted to, but Frederika drained his desire for others as effectively as he had drained her of her will.

Picturing Frederika's naked splendor, Vincent felt his rear end pucker involuntarily. Mrs. Hornby had definitely made him randy. He longed to call Frederika and order her to come to him. But he had promised Simon Penn he would stay away from the woman, and he had no idea just how closely the intense young man kept tabs on her. Vincent knew that Simon's appeasement was crucial, so that the feisty little pawn would not be tempted to move from his position on the gameboard. Vincent admitted to himself that he had made several miscalculations of late, each because his passions had gotten the better of his logic. He would not blunder again, not when this most critical game of his long, long life was concluding so soon.

Reverend Willy Spencer had just finished his evening meditation and prayers when the telephone rang. He closed his Bible, leaned out of his easy chair and plucked the phone from his desk.

"Hello?" he said, brightly.

"Reverend Spencer, you don't know me," the precise, British accent began. "My name is Montague Fox. Can you spare a few moments?"

"Certainly, Mr. Fox," Willy granted, easing back into his tufted leather chair to hear the stranger out.

"A few weeks ago, while I was still in England, I read about the wonderful gift to Princeton University of the ancient scrolls of Ahriman. I also read how *you* would be the fellow leading the translation."

"That's correct," Willy admitted, keeping his voice even but tensing at the expectation of another request for an interview.

"Well, sir, I am in possession of a very old book. It has no title page, but from the date and the colophon, it would seem to be the translation of those same scrolls, printed in 1503 by Aldus Manutius. Do you know the colophon . . . the dolphin curling around the anchor?"

Willy sat up straight in his chair. "I know of the work, Mr. Fox," Willy said, carefully, then shut up so that he could hear the subtext as well as the spoken words.

"It's been in my family for generations, but nobody before me ever thought it was worth much. I did some investigating and found that it might be very valuable indeed."

"That's right, if it's authentic," Willy said.

"Which is precisely why I'm imposing on you, sir," Fox said. His voice was nasal and slightly whining. The reverend pictured Uriah Heep. "I took it to two different authorities. They each said it's probably a forgery."

"But you could verify its authenticity if I shared some of my translation with you," Willy filled in.

"Have you done any yet?" Fox asked.

"I have."

"That's wonderful. If it were real I could sell it. I'm not a rich man, Reverend Spencer. Its sale could help my position immensely, and no doubt provide a smashing addition to some great library."

"Perhaps even the Princeton University collection."

"Certainly. It would make perfect sense, what with the original scrolls there."

"Where are you now, Mr. Fox?" Spencer asked.

"Oh, right here in Princeton. My company sent me over to the States this week, and I thought I'd make this little side trip to kill two birds with one stone as it were. I'm ever so pleased to find you home."

"How long will you be in Princeton?"

"Only until I've seen you. I wonder . . . would it be too great an imposition to nip over to your home tonight?"

"I'm afraid it would," Willy answered.

"Oh," Fox said, his little voice growing even smaller in his disappointment.

"However, I could see you tomorrow afternoon," Willy said. "About two-thirty."

There was a slight pause. "Two-thirty you say?"

"Yes."

"That would be wonderful." Fox sounded happy again. "And do you live at the Mercer Street address in the current telephone directory?"

"Yes. Do you need directions?"

"No. I walked by your place just after supper. I'll bring the book with me, of course."

"Fine. And I'll make tea."

"Lovely."

"Oh . . . Mr. Fox," Willy said, as if he'd had an afterthought. "In case something comes up, where are you staying?"

"With friends here in Princeton. Their phone number's unlisted, but I'm sure they won't mind my giving it to you."

"Go ahead." The stranger supplied a number, but Willy did not bother writing it down. The man's reply was all he had been looking for. "I'll see you at two-thirty," Willy confirmed, then hung up. He rose slowly from his chair and looked around the room. He had hidden that money somewhere nearby. Yes, in the pewter mug. After all these years of saving it for a rainy day, perhaps it would provide more sustenance than he could ever have anticipated—and without leaving his hands. He had much more to scare up before he would be thoroughly prepared for the stranger's visit, he thought. The phone call portended the realization of either his fondest dream or his most dreaded nightmare.

CHAPTER TWELVE

December 23

Remember the old saying,

"Faint heart ne'er won fair lady."

—Cervantes, *Don Quixote, ch. 10*

W illy Spencer opened the door as far as the safety chain allowed.

"Good afternoon!" the man outside said brightly. His gloved right hand rested high against his chest, and in its grasp lay an old book wrapped in clear plastic. "Reverend Spencer?"

Willy squinted from the bright sunlight that filled the world just beyond the umbra of his house's eaves. "Please indulge me, Mr. Fox; kindly remove your hat and step back into the light."

The man pulled his head back in surprise, then without demur, turned around, marched into the light and took off his broad-brimmed fedora. His brown eyes blinked rapidly at the harshness of the winter sun.

"Take off your glove and let me see your hand and wrist," Willy ordered.

"I don't understand. Is there some problem?" the stranger asked, while he followed the reverend's direction as best he could, holding the hat and fighting back his overcoat, jacket, and shirt. Finally he showed a wrist nearly as white as a fish's belly.

"Not at all. I'm just a bit eccentric. Come to the door now," Willy said. "Smile at me. Biggest smile you've got." Once again, Mr. Fox did as he was asked. He was rewarded by having the door shut in his face. His generous smile vanished; the face transmuted into one of vicious rage. When he heard the door chain being slipped, however, he quickly reerected the smile and inclined his head to an affable angle. After several seconds, the door still remained closed.

"Come in," Willy's voice called, from deep inside the house.

DeVilbiss set the fedora on his head and cautiously walked through the doorway. The old theologian was nowhere in sight.

"Reverend Spencer?" DeVilbiss called out.

"In here." The voice echoed from the back end of the hallway, where a door stood ominously open.

DeVilbiss licked his lips apprehensively and walked forward with careful stride, noting the home's layout, the positions of the furniture, avenues of escape as he moved. He walked through the open doorway and found himself in a well-used study, where built-in bookcases lined two walls. Every inch of their space was being used, although not necessarily for storing books. Not too far from the door stood a tufted leather, high-backed easy chair and, beside it, a floor lamp and reading table. Angled catercorner in the room's center was a huge walnut desk of considerable age. Arrayed on the desk were an open Bible, a large "balloon" glass filled with a colorless liquid, and a purple liturgical stole. DeVilbiss's keen sense of smell detected the odor of garlic. He felt instantly more at ease.

Willy Spencer stood on the far side of the desk, next to a well-worn wooden study chair. Both his hands were invisible, dug deeply into the huge pockets of the bathrobe he wore. He had on a white shirt that looked none too clean. Upon the white cotton field, an enormous, gold-plated cross hung from a thick chain.

Baroque music played from a stereo system within the bookcases, a piece Vincent recognized from Bach's *Christmas Oratorio*.

"Welcome to my home, Mr. Fox," the reverend said, managing to convey no warmth with the invitation.

DeVilbiss hung his fedora on the doorknob. "Thank you. Interesting Christmas tree." There was a dwarf blue spruce root-bound in a pot on a corner of the desk, suggesting that the old man intended

223

to plant it after the holiday season. The tree was sparsely decorated, with a pair each of white Styrofoam fish, lambs, crosses, vines, and oil lamps.

"You recognize the decorations?" Willy inquired.

"I do," DeVilbiss answered. "Except for the Star of David on the top, every ornament is a symbol of Jesus."

"Are you a Christian?" Willy inquired.

"A lapsed Catholic," DeVilbiss answered.

"Ah. May I see the book?" Despite Spencer's casual attire, he seemed alert and tense. DeVilbiss noted the gloss of perspiration on his temples, even though the room temperature was cool.

DeVilbiss unwrapped the book and placed it on the edge of the desk. He stared fixedly at the reverend as he crumpled the plastic bag into a tiny ball.

Willy lifted his right hand out of his pocket. Three fingers and his thumb circled the grip of a revolver; his forefinger curled around its trigger. He extended his arm slightly and took aim at DeVilbiss's heart.

"Need I even bother looking at the book?" he asked.

DeVilbiss shrugged as he retreated two steps. "You might . . . for curiosity's sake. I found it diverting. The man who forged it was inventive, but he honestly didn't know much about the real Aldus printing. He'd made eight copies. I burned seven, but it was such a special souvenir I couldn't bring myself to destroy the last one."

"Yet you destroyed him, didn't you?" Willy asked.

"Regretfully. It's a long story."

"Sit, then. I'm sure you have many fascinating stories." This time, the man's invitation sounded sincere.

"I do," DeVilbiss affirmed.

"And how often do you get to repeat them?"

"Just so."

DeVilbiss noted the lack of quaver in the scholar's voice, the steadiness of his grip on the revolver. He admired both his opponent's control and his intellectual curiosity in the face of what he surely knew to be one of Death's preeminent executioners. The gold cross, the gun, the garlic, and the glass undoubtedly filled with holy water clearly gave the old cleric the courage to attempt a conversation. Vincent welcomed a learned dialogue. Never before had he encountered a man who knew not only the contents of the scrolls but also Vincent's true nature. For the first time since his transformation, he found himself with the opportunity to share musings on those who controlled him, with no less than a learned scholar of antiquities. There was no danger in such candor; Spencer would be dead within the hour. More important, the invitation afforded DeVilbiss the chance to trick the old man into revealing the vital information which he had dared daylight to obtain.

DeVilbiss sat. Spencer took his seat, resting the gun on the Bible, keeping it leveled at his guest's heart. DeVilbiss asked: "You feel confident that gun will protect you?"

"The scrolls mentioned no means of killing your kind," Spencer replied, "so I take it that destroying you isn't that difficult. The difficult part is learning that you exist and then having the faith to believe it."

"You must have read thoroughly into the passages about my kind," DeVilbiss said.

"I did . . . until there was nothing more to read."

"When did you come across that section?"

"Yesterday afternoon. I've been skipping around."

DeVilbiss made a tsking sound. "Just yesterday. My bad luck. How were you so sure that Montague Fox was such a creature, coming for you?"

"I wasn't," Willy admitted. "I almost believed your story, especially when you agreed to come out in broad daylight, then stood outside with your head and arm bare. That shine on your wrist and the back of your hand . . . is it from suntan lotion?"

Vincent made a polite little obeisance. "Very astute. The new, unscented variety. I hope its inventor gets rich from the idea."

"And your brown eyes—contact lenses?" Spencer inquired.

"Of course. Behind thin plastic they're as amber as the scrolls describe. Did the lotion give me away?"

"That, your pale skin, your good nature at my ridiculous demands," Willy imparted. "In fact, once I'd read those passages, the

225

very coincidence of being called with a ready translation of the scrolls. Shall I continue to call you Mr. Fox?"

"No. Call me Vincente."

"The invincible conqueror," Willy translated.

"Lui parla Italiano!" exclaimed DeVilbiss.

"Un po'." Willy transferred the gun to his left hand, keeping it trained on Vincent's heart.

"Let us return to the scrolls," DeVilbiss said. "The information about my kind appears in the *Metaphysics* scroll. Have you read the section about the reason for my existence?"

"I take it that you were once a normal man, like myself. You must have had little faith in God or an afterlife, which made you desperate enough to accept a pact."

"You're dancing around my question," Vincent said. "But very well. You know the specifics of the pact?"

"It clearly stated unending life on earth, in exchange for killing people."

"But why?"

"Because whoever controls you cannot operate 'in the good light of God's day.' Have I translated that properly?"

DeVilbiss crossed one leg casually over the other. "Yes, you have. And yet that doesn't go deep enough, does it? I've tried for so long to know why they're limited to darkness, but I've never been allowed to ask questions."

"You're telling me that you don't know who controls you?" Willy asked, incredulous.

"Precisely. I was hoping you'd tell me," said DeVilbiss. "The writer of the scrolls called them the Dark Forces, the Ancient Foe of Man."

The music ended. Reverend Spencer was unaware, caught in the discussion. "It's absolutely clear to me. It means the fallen angels. The Devil and his minions."

"Absolutely clear? Then why are these revelatory scrolls attributed to Ahriman—the Devil himself?" DeVilbiss asked.

Spencer waved the argument away peevishly. "The Ahriman attribution was an ignorant assumption. Simply because the writer of the scrolls took the religions of that time to task. Ergo, the complaint of the Devil. I'd say . . ."

"What?" DeVilbiss asked, truly interested.

"I'd say, the scrolls were written by exactly the opposite side. Either through an archangel or by the same divine inspiration given to the writers of the Bible, God caused the message of the scrolls to be delivered to earth. He did it precisely to offset the Devil's scheme to alter men and turn them against their own kind. Before Satan was cast from heaven, he was Lucifer . . . the bringer of light. After he and his followers lost their revolt, God made him the opposite: the ruler of darkness. He and his followers were suddenly unable to act in light or directly against mankind. So Satan used man against man . . . or whatever your species calls itself."

DeVilbiss relaxed back fully into his chair and folded his arms across his chest. "Couldn't the creatures who offered me eternal life just as easily be invisible but natural things, threatened by us? All mankind is by nature bloodthirsty . . . whether we actually drink blood or not. Once we emerged from the caves, the invisible ones knew we'd never stop advancing. One day we would learn the technology to detect them. And, being what we are, we would try to exterminate them."

"So, are you told to kill *only* men of science?" Willy said.

DeVilbiss's expression grew grim. "No," he admitted.

"Or are your victims people responsible for uncommon goodness? If so, you should know that you are a slave of Satan himself."

DeVilbiss's mouth contorted into a rueful smile. "There is *nothing* supernatural about me. Superhuman, yes; supernatural, no. Why should there be anything supernatural about those who control me? The Devil's existence would prove God's, but never once in five centuries have I found any other proof."

Willy had his retort ready. "That's because you've always looked with the eye of reason, not faith." His old eyes blazed with intensity. He had converted perhaps a score of people over the tenure of his ministry, but now he saw the chance to make the conversion of a lifetime. Beyond a pleasing exterior and cultured behavior, the figure sitting across the room did seem to possess strong vestiges of humanity. After all the evil he had committed, he still searched, still questioned. The chance to gather him into the fold existed, and Willy fairly panted with the opportunity.

"I've looked with *both* reason and faith," Vincent replied, calmly. "Five hundred years ago I was the same as you . . . a so-called man of God."

Reverend Spencer blinked. "I don't believe you."

In a deep and pleasant voice, Vincent began to sing.

> *Dies irae dies illa,*
> *Solvet saeculum in favilla.*
> *Teste David cum Sibylla.*

"Is a chant from the Requiem for the Dead enough for you? Would you like the saints' days in order? The Nicene Creed in Latin? Or precisely how confessions were heard then, and *what* I heard? And what I thought of my noble fellow men after twenty years of listening to their sincerely contrite *revel*-ations? Of course I could be lying. One needn't have been a Renaissance priest to learn these things. Just as you say: reason won't tell you the truth, Reverend. Look with the eyes of faith and despair that I speak no lies." He uttered the words with a dread irony that made the minister's condemnations sound like the hypotheses of a novice.

"Where were you a priest?" Spencer asked, after a long moment of assessment.

Vincent tucked the crumpled plastic bag between the chair arm and the seat cushion, rested his elbows on the arms of the chair and tented his hands, fingertip to fingertip, in an attitude of prayer.

"*Roma. La città eterna.* Later I became an abbreviator, then papal legate."

"For which pope?"

"Rodrigo Borgia."

"Alexander the Sixth."

"*Bene. Esattamente.*"

Willy nodded his understanding. "Not a good age for faith."

"You have a talent for understatement," Vincent answered, razing the steeple formed by his hands. "There was little room for faith, hope, or charity then. Not with all the political maneuvering from within the Vatican walls, the intrigues and betrayals, the nepotism and simony. The cold-blooded murders. Not with the Spaniard Borgia who bought the papacy outright. This man of God, this Vicar of Christ, Keeper of the Keys to the Kingdom, chosen directly through God's will, threw orgies in the gardens of de Bichi, fathered three bastards and the bitch Lucrezia by another man's wife. 'Not a good age for faith,' you say? And I had the misfortune to be born into the middle of it."

"When?"

"Anno Domini 1464. Christened Innocente Farnese."

"The innocent one," Willy translated.

"But not for long," Vincent declared. "Rome was the sick body of the Vatican's unsound soul. I saw pilgrims robbed at every gate, kings' envoys spat on and stripped of their clothes outside the walls of ancient glory. Every powerful family's palazzo was an armed camp of mercenaries. I stepped over bodies in the streets each morning, come there by disease, starvation, and murder, while inside palazzi walls three thousand ducats would be squandered on a single night's feast. And there was I growing up in it, loving life but so appalled by it. Wanting the wine, women, and song yet seeing that even the *earthly* wages of greed, lust, and gluttony could torment. When I was sixteen I turned to God for deliverance. I fought my desires, sublimated them in favor of eternal rewards. Like you, I tried to look with the eyes of faith and consecrated my worldly life as a bargain to win an everlasting reward. If I was unfortunate in the time and place of my birth, I was at least lucky in my family. My cousin, Giulia Farnese, became mistress to Rodrigo after Vanozza dei Catanei had grown haggard bearing his illegitimate brood. Through *Giulia Bella* I secured a cleric's position at Borgia's right hand. Each day, from the distance you are to me, I observed the man who had been elected *pastore* of God's earthly flock. Do you see the irony?

The Keeper of the Faith personally destroyed mine. If God could allow such a man to hold the keys to His kingdom, then why should He care if I received eternal life?"

The long-pent-up memories released, DeVilbiss collapsed back into the chair. "But Saint Joseph did."

"I don't understand," Reverend Spencer said.

"Neither did I. I thought I was going mad. Each morning I would retire to one of the Vatican's side chapels, to mend my constantly fraying faith with prayer. The statue in the chapel was that of Saint Joseph. It was almost life size, beautifully carved of wood, painted and gilt. About a month after I began pouring out my disillusioned heart, the statue spoke to me. 'You *can* have eternal life, and you don't even need to die to get it,' it whispered. When no other part of my life hinted at insanity, I began to think it must be the Devil. It whispered, over and over, that there was nothing behind my faith, that unending life had to be earned another way."

"How was it possible for a statue to talk?" Willy asked in fascination.

DeVilbiss shrugged. "After all these centuries I still don't know. But think, Reverend: Could mine have been an isolated experience? Why else have men all over the world created gods from trees, metal, and stone?"

Willy's forefinger relaxed around the trigger as he accepted DeVilbiss' proffered puzzle. His mouth hung open a moment, then he said, "It's because . . . most people find it difficult to deal with the abstract. They feel secure worshiping something symbolized in strong material."

"Or is it because stone, metal, and wood possess certain properties necessary for the dwelling places of these 'gods'? What does it say in the scrolls?"

"I've read nothing that touched on this," said the old translator.

"Then you haven't read far enough. The creatures' inability to survive in open air is clearly stated. So they hide in dense matter. But you have no doubt already read that Easter Islanders, Mayans, Egyptians, Hindus, Buddhists, Abyssinians, Phoenicians, Assyrians, and Sumerians all worshiped in stone. Moses destroyed his people's calf of gold. And in wood: Africans, Druids with their sacred oak and rowan, Northwest Indians with their totem poles. Perhaps *all* those wood and metal and stone idols talked to them."

"And your statue wanted you to kill in exchange for unending life," Willy said.

"No. If that were the original agreement, I would have refused. It demanded killing later, once I had proof of eternal youth and had glutted myself on the fruits of youth. At first the statue only required the same functions I performed for the Church. That's when I first believed it was something other than the Devil. Why would Satan reward me for merely continuing the ill I already performed? It turned out that these tasks created far more harm than if I had committed an occasional murder, but I couldn't see the enormity of the request."

"What tasks?"

"Ones that preserved the common man's ignorance, suppressing scientific knowledge that threatened the Church's supremacy. If man continued to suffer and die from disease, hunger, and oppression, so be it. That's the reason I was able to hunt down almost every copy of Aldus's translation of the scrolls; I had Pope Alexander's blessing. Not only did the scrolls deny the validity of all religions in general, but they specifically preached that the earth was not the center of our system. I had the Church's full powers at my disposal to crush the truth."

"You see? You do argue for the Devil." Willy's face suddenly brightened. "Now I understand the purpose of *two* scrolls! The scroll we call *Metaphysics* is so filled with unbelievable assertions that the giver felt compelled to offer a companion piece as well . . . a scroll with facts that could be proven in the physical world. You see? The beings that control you are indeed metaphysical . . . supernatural . . . fallen angels." Before DeVilbiss could reply, Willy added, "The second scroll says that you drink the blood of other humans, right?"

"Yes," DeVilbiss admitted. "But the thing that keeps me young is a powder, delivered from a secret place. After twenty years, they changed the formula, so that I needed blood as well."

"Is that when they first demanded you kill for them?"

"Yes."

"If that's not diabolical, what is? You see how they mock God?"

"Tell me," Vincent said.

"When you were a priest, at each Mass you commemorated the blood Christ shed by drinking wine. You did this *on behalf of* your fellow man. The reason Jesus chose wine was that it, not water, was the drink of life in his time. These demons make you drink the blood *of* your fellow man, on your own selfish behalf, your wine of life if you will. What else could provide such a powerful, subliminal reminder of the side you'd chosen?"

"An elegant argument, *pastore,*" Vincent granted.

"Compelling enough for you to see the light and end your ways?" Spencer asked.

"Which means to die."

Willy thrust out his hand. "Face facts, Vincente . . . either way you won't literally live forever. If Judgment Day doesn't come first, then eventually the sun will nova and engulf the whole earth. Long before that, chance will make a building fall on you or your plane crash into the ocean."

Vincent's chin lowered several degrees toward his chest. He looked past his eyebrows at the old man. "I am perfectly aware of that. I have never intended to live forever."

"But . . . ?"

"But neither can I ever contemplate dying tomorrow."

"Yet if you die in a state of grace, you *will* live on. God has promised it. If you were once a man of God you can be again. You can't go on slaughtering your fellow man."

"You don't understand. It doesn't matter who controls me. And whether God exists or whether he cares about what happens to me can't be allowed to control my actions. I'm very close to giving man the greatest gift possible. What I have done, I have done. What I do, I will continue to do. I kill because I must survive to bring this gift. Once that happens, I'll be free to listen to your arguments. Now listen to mine. I need your help in removing the scrolls from the university. I will *not* destroy them. I wish only to hide them and

232

prevent their translation, to protect myself until the time I'm free. I promise you this on my honor as a gentleman."

Willy laughed. "On your *sacred* honor? Why not swear on your immortal soul, since you have no fear of losing it?"

Vincent flushed pink in his anger. "Do you think I'd sit here staring at a gun so calmly if I felt I couldn't convince you?"

"What I think is that you're guile personified. The purest form of evil that can exist in a man's body."

Now DeVilbiss laughed. "Then pull the trigger: ensure your own destruction as well as mine. If you kill me, they'll send another within days . . . one who will not even pretend to my compassions."

"I can't let the scrolls be taken."

"You don't have to do anything," DeVilbiss assured. "Just let me have your security system key."

Willy's eyes darted down to the desk drawer in front of him. He caught himself an instant later and returned them to DeVilbiss, but not before his opponent had registered the all-important information.

"How many others hold keys?" DeVilbiss asked.

Willy reached out for the glass. "You lie," he said with conviction. "You've been destroying the words of the scrolls for centuries. You won't stop now." He lifted the glass and readied it for throwing. At the same time he inched his revolver forward, still pointed at DeVilbiss's chest. At last he seemed nervous. DeVilbiss knew that Willy was fighting his deep-seated aversion toward taking a life, no matter how monstrous. "I must kill you," he said, as if to himself.

"They'll lock you up for murder," DeVilbiss said, rising slowly and casually, as if ready to leave the room.

"Not when I prove you're what you are. Sit down!"

DeVilbiss ignored him, straightening to his full height, placing his left hand on his hip, his right gesturing, palm up. "How? With oversized incisors? They'll call them a genetic defect. My pale skin? A dislike of the sun. They'll find any explanation but the truth. Don't you understand? After all those silly movies, everyone knows what a vampire is. A shape-changer, invisible in mirrors, crumbling to dust when the sun hits him. Nothing like me. If you insisted on your story they'd institutionalize you. You'll never translate another word."

"Shut up!" Willy commanded, thumbing back the revolver's hammer.

DeVilbiss took a step forward, almost to the desk. " 'Thou shalt not kill.' "

"Silence!" Willy screamed. His arm jerked up; his hand retrained the revolver at the mouth that mocked him. DeVilbiss's eyes went wide with horror.

The gun boomed. The bullet entered DeVilbiss's open mouth, smashing through his upper wisdom tooth and exiting out his cheek, leaving a gaping hole.

Roaring his pain and outrage, DeVilbiss lunged forward and grabbed the huge desk by the edge. Seeing that his bullet had done so little damage, the minister threw the holy water at his attacker's face. DeVilbiss's head snapped back from the cold assault, but he was otherwise unaffected. By the time Willy Spencer realized his second failure and was about to aim his gun at the vampire's heart, DeVilbiss had the desk firmly in his grasp. He threw its huge mass over as if it were made of cardboard. Willy flew backward into the chair and then down in a crumpled heap, firing off a second shot as he collapsed. The bullet caromed off a brass telescope on an upper bookshelf and disappeared into a wall. The desk landed fully on the old man, burying him under its weight. DeVilbiss darted around it and wrested the revolver from the hand that stuck out from beneath a pile of papers. He tossed the weapon into a corner, then clutched his head with both hands and dropped to his knees, rocking back and forth, moaning his agony.

No wound had ever hurt as this had. His tongue found the jagged remnants of his wisdom tooth but could not reach as far back as the exit wound. Behind the tooth, it felt as if an army of angry hornets were trying to sting their way out of his head. His ear throbbed red-hot with every heartbeat. The movement of any muscle on that side of his face created a torment that had him weeping with pain.

Vincent fought the pain, as he had a thousand other times. He crawled to where the reverend's head lay, captured under the overturned chair. He grabbed the man's white hair and yanked on it until the old eyes popped open.

"You are a fool," Vincent hissed. "Like the idiots who invented wearing garlic and tying coffins shut. But I'll give you one more chance to live." He paused, to hawk up a thick glob of blood that had trickled down his throat. He spat it onto the still-open Bible. "When you read about my existence, you believed. Therefore, you feared for your life. Therefore, you would have entrusted your translations to others. Who are they?"

Willy gasped for breath. His face was red, as if he was in the throes of a stroke. "Go . . . to . . . hell," he answered.

DeVilbiss tore the minister's purple stole from under a corner of the desk. With demonic fury, he pulled Willy's mouth open and stuffed the material inside, inch by inch, until not another thread would fit. The remaining length he clapped around Willy's nose and squeezed. The old man did not struggle long.

DeVilbiss lifted the desk high enough to let the top drawer fall open. Among the items that tumbled out was a ring of keys. He staggered to his feet and stuffed the keys into his pocket. One of these shiny bits of metal had necessitated his extemporaneous tale of woe, all of it true except for his willingness to spare the minister and the scrolls. If he had been in Spencer's place, he would have hidden the security system key off the premises. Spencer had been less careful, pinning too much hope on legendary vampire banes. In Spencer's place, DeVilbiss would also have sent copies of his partial translation to at least two trusted colleagues. After destroying the scrolls he faced the tiresome task of researching all of Spencer's philologist associates, determining who had received translations and eliminating them.

Vincent gingerly explored the skin just in front of his ear where the bullet had exited. Blood continued to ooze out, and the hole felt as if it had not scabbed over at all. He kicked aside the Christmas tree, which lay on edge. Dirt spilled and decorations scattered across the carpet. He prized his cherished Aldus forgery from under the desk rubble and moved into the hallway, where a long mirror hung. The reflection confirmed Vincent's fears; the wound was not healing as it should. He ran his tongue over the remnant of the wisdom tooth. He had never suffered a broken tooth and had no idea if Nick's powder would reconstruct dentin. The jagged remainder sliced open his tongue. He cried out his frustration, ripped the mirror from the wall and smashed it on the floor.

The previous night, just as he had told Spencer, he had walked through the Mercer Street neighborhood and come close enough to Spencer's house to determine that it was connected to the gas company's utility line. DeVilbiss hurried into the basement, turned off the electricity that powered the heater's sensing devices, then opened the gas pipe. He flared his nostrils at the noxious odor the gas company mixed into the line to alert users to leakage problems. As he turned toward the basement steps his eyes fixed on Willy's workbench, where a torch lay connected to a small acetylene tank. Next to the torch sat one old silver dollar and the melted remains of another, as well as three bullets whose surfaces glinted piebald in brass, lead, and silver.

"Bastard!" DeVilbiss muttered, spitting out pink saliva. Throughout his existence only three people had suspected his dark secret and had the nerve to try to kill him for it. The first two had come after him in daylight, with wooden stakes. They had been laughingly easy to despatch. Only Willy Spencer had had the foresight and skill to fashion makeshift silver bullets. The pain continued to radiate through Vincent's head with each beat of his heart, although he realized with relief that it had abated somewhat. Perhaps, he mused, among all the ludicrous vampire superstitions, the one about a silver bullet through the heart was true. He was the last man to reject all folklore out of hand, if for no other reason than that his livelihood as an herbalist depended largely on "old wives' tales." He cursed the bad luck that made Spencer reaim his weapon from DeVilbiss's bulletproof-vest-protected heart to his face. Of late, the Fates seemed more and more allied against him.

DeVilbiss returned to the minister's study. On a bookcase shelf stood an arrangement of holiday candles and a book of matches. Vincent lit them one by one and stepped back to admire their festive glow. As he prepared to leave, his eyes chanced on what looked to be an old copy of Chaucer's *Canterbury Tales,* bound in leather. He plucked it from the shelf, for leisure reading after the scroll business was concluded. He intended to read it soon.

At 3:38 in the afternoon the Spencer house on Mercer Street ceased to exist. In a moment it transformed into light, heat, noise, dust, debris, and irreparable chaos. What the explosion had not instantly destroyed, the ensuing fire claimed.

Vincent DeVilbiss emerged from the evergreen-shadowed park across the street. Satisfied that the destruction was complete, he walked toward his rented car, a book clasped in each gloved hand. His walk was quick-march; both to avoid the sun and because he had killed a third member of the Princeton University community. Although he had made the deaths look convincingly like suicide, smoking in bed, and a faulty gas line, the weight against three mishaps in quick succession was sure to bring an investigative response from law authorities. At the very least, their presence might slow his progress toward eliminating the scrolls. Slowing meant more time, and time was for once definitely not on his side.

Simon came out of the Conrail Building and looked at the two-shopping-days-till-Christmas action in downtown Philadelphia. The French bakery where he and Alice Niederjohn were to rendez-vous lay not far to the east. Anxious that he not miss the appointment, he had taken an early train. He strolled, peering into any store window that seemed remotely interesting. Turning away from one, he spotted the trim figure of a middle-aged woman, heading with grim purpose in the direction of the bakery. Despite the thirty years since her high school photographs, Alice was still recognizable and still beautiful. Her golden hair had aged to a handsome ash and her skin had lost the tightness and fat of youth, but the blue of her eyes sparkled wetly and her complexion was nearly as flawless a porcelain as her daughter's. Between her fingers she clutched a cigarette. She raised it needfully to her lips as she strode by.

Simon followed her for half a block, watching her body language as she walked, realizing that she carried her beauty with the same

237

introversion and shyness as Frederika. A well-dressed man who looked about thirty-five smiled at her as she approached him and then turned to admire her passing, but she seemed unaware. Simon increased his stride until he walked alongside her.

"Mrs. Niederjohn," he said, gently, just as she noticed his presence. Her step faltered.

"Mr. Penn?"

"Yes." He gestured toward the corner. "There's the bakery. Shall we go inside?"

Alice blinked nervously at his gentle smile. She dropped her cigarette to the pavement and ground it out, then allowed herself to be shepherded into the bakery, which doubled as klatsch-café by providing a half dozen cozy tables in the back. Alice maintained her silence while Simon helped her take off her black lamb coat and pulled out her chair. He noted the designer cut of her dress, the Piaget watch and the simply set half-carat diamond in each earlobe.

"Thanks for agreeing to meet," Simon opened, ignoring the fact that he had virtually blackmailed her into the meeting.

"You're a friend of Frederika," Alice said, repeating Simon's words from their telephone conversation.

"I am. I think I'm her best friend."

"How can I be sure of that?"

Simon described the Vanderveen mansion in detail, mentioning the furniture that seemed to have been there a long while, commenting on the line of patriarchal portraits on the stairs and concluding with the yearbook she had left behind in the basement, which had provided him the clues for finding her.

"I'm sorry I can't provide any of Frederika's reminiscences," Simon said. "She never speaks about you."

The woman seemed satisfied by his candid reply. As soon as he finished she asked, "Do you have a photo of her?"

"Sorry again. I don't keep pictures in my wallet." Simon was pleased to hear Alice's first maternal expression.

A waiter took their orders of coffee and left them alone.

"My husband knows about my first marriage and Frederika,"

Alice said, "But we both decided that we wouldn't let our children know about this part of my past."

"I see," Simon said, although he didn't. "How old are your children?"

"Fourteen and twelve." Alice produced a pack of Salems and tapped a cigarette out. "I'm willing to help Frederika, but only to the extent that my family is left out of this." She struck a match. Her hand shook as she lit the cigarette; her eyes fixed anxiously on Simon. He said nothing while she drew in the first puff.

"You've got nothing to fear from me," he assured. In two dozen well-rehearsed sentences he related Frederika's notorious behavior with older men, her lack of other friends, her increasingly morose attitude, and the bizarre efforts she had begun making to contact her dead father. As he spoke he analyzed Alice's expressive face and traced her concern.

"You love my daughter, don't you?" Alice asked, when he had finished.

Simon felt a sudden explosion of heat in the pit of his stomach. "Yes, I do," he admitted for the first time, even to himself. "But I'm only a friend. That's all I may ever be. It's certainly all for now. As she is, Frederika destroys any man who gives her power over him."

"I understand only too well," Alice said, smiling sympathetically. "You're wiser than I was. I married her father, and he nearly did destroy me. I was twenty-three when I met him. Even though I worked in New York City I was naïve. I hadn't dated much. I was swept away by Frederik's charm, his intelligence, his dominance, that great sense of purpose. Everything about him seemed positive. I had no idea the same attributes could prove so negative to a marriage."

The coffee arrived. Simon drained his cup much sooner than Alice did, allowing her to talk with little interruption. She too had her tale in ready order, but he wondered how long ago she had assembled the list of Frederick Vanderveen's trespasses against her. Once they were married, Alice had become Frederik's shadow. He kept her constantly at his side, displaying her beauty as proof of his seductiveness. She accepted the roles of hostess, traveling companion, and servant. He fed her his opinions on everything and expected her to echo them. Her life melded into his.

"And all the while I told myself that the good works he did justified his high opinion of himself and my having to live in the shadow of his career. I saw how everyone else adored him, and I thought, 'How can you do any less?' " A look of loathing marred Alice's face. "Only after several years did I come to understand that he took away more than he gave. He fed the stomachs of the world's poor all right, but their hunger repaid him many times over; it fed his insatiable ego. Until this became clear to me, I felt as if I was being sucked into a huge vortex but blamed myself for being a weak swimmer. I had to escape or drown."

"But why did you leave without Frederika?" Simon knew she would be ready for the question. Yet she winced when she heard it and drew in a long breath.

"My reasons were not simple. As soon as my daughter was a year old, Frederik began badgering me about traveling with him. I wasn't a bad or neglectful mother, Mr. Penn. I wasn't. But you may begin to understand Frederik's powers of persuasion when I tell you I left Frederika behind in spite of my personal desires. Not once but twenty times."

"Who stayed with her when you were both gone?" Simon asked, almost positive of the answer.

"Her aunt . . . an older sister of Frederik's who lived with us in the house. Whenever I came home I felt so guilty for being away that I indulged her, let her have whatever she wanted. The more I tried to show her affection . . . to buy her affection, the less interested in me she became.

"But Frederik was another story. She was obsessed with winning his love and attention. He knew he had a lock on the two of us, so he rarely bothered showing affection. Frederika wanted what she couldn't get. Her life centered on earning his approval, parroting his attitudes. The more distant he acted and the stricter he was, the harder she tried. I had no idea when we named her how appropriate it was; she became a little Frederik. I only understood these things later. At the time I couldn't think rationally. All I could do was feel, and what I felt was bereft. Like an outsider in my own home. What am I saying? That house was never a home and never mine. It was Frederik's alone, and always would be." There was a rancor in her tone unmitigated by the years.

"Didn't you think she'd change if you could get her away from her father?"

"You don't understand," Alice answered. "She rejected me and seemed perfectly happy with him. And I was convinced he'd never let me have her without a fight. The year before I left, I saw a psychiatrist, but the man was useless . . . should have had his license revoked. If I'd fought Frederik for custody he would have used the psychiatrist's testimony to have me declared mentally unfit." Alice sighed. "But the most important reason I left her was my own selfish needs. If we had shared her, I would have continued to be linked with the cause of my unhappiness. And he would have shaped her mind against me whenever he had her. He was very smart, and she would gladly have turned on me to please him. So I burned my bridges behind me." Her unhappy face finally brightened. "I also burned all three scrapbooks he'd assembled on himself."

"Why didn't you contact Frederika when you finally understood all this?"

"I tried to, when she was thirteen. I wrote several letters to her in boarding school abroad. In every one I apologized, but I also explained my side in great length. She didn't answer my first two. Then one day I got a response from her. She explained *her* feelings in great detail. The worst of it was a list of all my failures as a mother. She wrote that she'd been very happy until I started bothering her, that she wanted me to leave her alone, as I had years before, so she could . . . begin forgetting me again." The final words came slowly, as Alice fought them through a constricted throat. A tear escaped each eye. "So I honored her wish." She went to her purse, but Simon anticipated her need and handed her his handkerchief.

"I thought you'd severed all contact with the Vanderveens," Simon said.

Alice stopped daubing and looked at him in confusion. "I did."

"Then how did you find out that Frederika was at a boarding school abroad?"

"Oh. It took some time. Precisely because I wanted to have nothing to do with Frederik, I came up to Princeton one day in October and went to the junior high school I thought Frederika would be attending. The people in the office said she wasn't enrolled. I tried the other junior highs in the area, to no avail. I had used up the whole day, so I went home and immediately wrote to an old friend of Frederik's and mine, Stanley Krieger."

"Dean Krieger?" Simon exclaimed.

Alice smiled. "Is he a dean now? Good for him. He was kind to me."

"And did he write back?"

"Yes, although it took him almost two weeks. He was the one who gave me the address in Paris."

Simon reacted with such a start that the entire table shook. Alice drew her hands quickly from its surface.

"What is it?" she asked.

A brief aphasia overwhelmed Simon. Now he had the answer to why Krieger was so angry about Frederik's treatment of his family, why the dean belatedly was so protective of Frederika's well-being and insistent that Simon avoid the personal aspects of the Vanderveen family. During the interview, he had adeptly expressed how Frederik worked his ways with men of lesser willpower and intellect. One of those men had been Stanley Krieger. Whatever compelling arguments he had used, Frederik had convinced his friend to supply Alice with a false address.

"Frederika wasn't in Paris," Simon said.

"What?" Alice said, her face turning chalky.

"She attended the American School, in Montagnola-Lugano, Switzerland. I saw the proof. She's got six yearbooks from the school in the basement."

"My God!" Alice gasped, on the weak expulsion of air that escaped her lungs. Her hands had begun to shake again. Simon took them in his own.

"Your first husband was in Paris often, wasn't he?"

"Yes. Very often."

"He must have convinced an acquaintance there to accept letters on your daughter's behalf. I'll bet *he* wrote you the answer you thought you were getting from your daughter."

"But it wasn't his handwriting."

"But was it hers?" Simon argued. "You left before Frederika knew cursive handwriting. I'm sure you assumed it was her hand. My guess is that Frederik had some friend in Paris recopy his words and send them to you."

Alice sat up straighter, her eyes wet but no longer tearing. Her mouth worked for a moment, and then she said, "The bastard! I hope he's burning in hell." She drew her hands gently from Simon's grip and reached for her pack of cigarettes. Simon recaptured them.

"I hope the same. He did his best to ensure that Frederika wouldn't come looking for you either: a few years after you'd left, he told her you'd died." This time, perhaps from the previous shock, Alice's reaction was more restrained, although her face showed no sign of regaining its color. Simon recounted his conversation with Katerina Callahan and her verbal slip, the clue that began Simon's search. "Katerina backed her brother's lie," he concluded. "You'd cut yourself off so effectively from his world, it was an easy lie to maintain."

"I should have left him when he insisted I travel," Alice said suddenly. "That was my mistake. I should have left right then, with Frederika in my arms. I can't believe he got away with declaring me dead!"

"I'm sorry to say this, but you were his best accomplice," Simon said. "With his ego, I'm sure you wounded him deeply. Even eighteen years ago, abandonment and divorce were not looked on favorably. Especially for such a celebrated man. You were always at his side and then suddenly you were gone. Imagine the constant inquiries. Your leaving was one of his few public failures."

"He probably told everyone he had to have me committed," Alice said, bitterly.

"I wouldn't doubt it. And then, when it was clear you were never coming back, it was easier to say you'd died. Certainly an easier explanation to Frederika."

The color returned to Alice's face, along with a resolute expression. "What can I do now?"

"You can talk to her. Give her someone who loves her just because she lives," Simon suggested.

Alice offered a wan smile. "I think she may already have that someone."

"But, as you say, she's her father's daughter and wants what she wants. I'm certain she'll take great comfort from you when she learns you're alive, especially if you're loving and caring. She needs you to seal up the past she keeps slipping into."

Alice took a moment to think. "My husband and children are avid skiers. I hate getting cold and wet, so they're leaving me at home right after we open the presents Christmas morning."

"Do you want to come to Princeton?"

"Yes. I'm willing to see her. But I'm afraid to think of just walking into that house."

"I understand," Simon commiserated. "I haven't seen his ghost, but the place is definitely haunted."

Alice took a fortifying breath. "All right then; that's what I'll do." She reached for her cigarettes but thought better of it and folded her hands together. "Then we'll see where we go from there."

They parted company congenially. But as Simon hurried back to the train station, he had a gnawing doubt that the mystery begun in the Princeton cemetery could be concluded so neatly and so soon.

Simon stopped pacing and stared at the huge poinsettia he had carried back to the mansion from Nassau Street. Stuck with a sizable surplus close to the holiday, the florist was practically giving them away. Simon had sprung for the largest one, wanting to put Frederika in a positive mood before dropping the bombshell about her mother's return from the dead. He also knew that, even before Alice told her daughter of Frederik's shortcomings, Frederika would have to hear that her father and aunt had lied to her. She would also have to deal with the fact that Simon had been secretly delving into her private life on a monumental scale. In light of her already depressed state, Simon anticipated an emotional roller coaster of an evening.

The worst of it was the anticipation. He had fully expected to find her at home when he returned from Philadelphia. She had point-blank replied that she intended to be there after work when he had asked about her plans that morning. But when he got to the house, she and her car were missing. Where the hell was she, he wondered for the hundredth time. He glanced at the kitchen clock. It read 8:28. He strode to the hall closet. The filleting knife in his hand made it difficult to put his coat on, but he refused to relax his grip. It had rested there for the better part of an hour, ever since Simon convinced himself that Frederika had gone again to Vincent DeVilbiss's house. He tugged on his woolen cap and walked through the front door into the night, the knife now hidden in his coat pocket.

Frederika's car was nowhere on Park Place, and DeVilbiss's house lay dark. Simon told himself that a scoundrel like DeVilbiss would try to break his agreement and still get Simon's money. All he had to do was tell Frederika to park her car two blocks away and then keep the lights off while they . . .

Simon bounded up the porch steps and pounded on the door. He waited a few seconds and banged more forcefully. He got no answer. He walked down the alley to the back of the house. Angry heat rushed to his face when he saw the weak light escaping from one of the upper windows. Without weighing the consequences, he climbed a trellis running the width of the back porch and scrambled onto the porch's tin roof. From there he peered through the lit window and saw the bedroom beyond. No one lay on the bed. There was an answering machine connected to the telephone on the night stand. Its message light winked once, paused, winked once, paused, winked once.

The heat continued to pour off Simon's face. Frederika's missing car probably meant they'd gone somewhere. If they weren't together already, the phone message was hers, telling him where to meet her. Simon used his elbow to smash out the windowpane above the latch, raised the window and clambered inside. He knew absolutely that Vincent DeVilbiss was dangerous, and he resolved to make himself the man's equal.

The message was from a Sarah Potter, who had read DeVilbiss's advertisement in the local newspaper and "rather desperately" needed his services. Simon reset the answering machine and moved on. The dresser drawers and the closet held only clothing, not in great quantity but all of conspicuous quality. He found no hidden weapons there, nor under DeVilbiss's pillow or bed. The bathroom held nothing out of the ordinary, no illegal drugs or drug paraphernalia. Downstairs, in the kitchen, he found a music system. The components were expensive but very compact, as if all chosen for size, weight, and stowability. For all the expense, the man owned less than two dozen compact discs. Simon found a computerized chessboard, again very compact. On the kitchen table lay two books. The first was a very old edition of the *Canterbury Tales*. Simon examined it, to be sure DeVilbiss hadn't stolen it from Firestone Library. The second, with no title on the cover or inside, looked even more ancient. To his amazement, it was set in archaic cursive Greek type. The man seemed erudite to a degree, but much too worldly to waste his time on such an esoteric subject. Skimming the pages without bothering to translate, Simon thought of the Schickner Collection and asked himself without success what connection could be made.

Bundles of dried herbs hung from the walls, and the counters held various tools of the herbalist/channeler's trade. Next to the sink were two apothecary-style bottles. One stood empty except for a residue of yellow powder. The one beside it was filled to the top. Simon unstopped the empty bottle, lifted it to his nose and sniffed. The smell was unpleasant. He had no idea what it was and didn't particularly care.

A door in the inside wall of the kitchen opened onto stairs which led down to a basement. Simon turned on the bare lightbulb that dangled at the top of the steps. Descending, he found the basement dank and dreary, creepy with the webs and shriveled corpses of unlucky spiders. The many items stored there had too heavy a layer of dust to have belonged to DeVilbiss. The area was divided into two rooms. In the back he found a workbench with a collection of old and rusty tools, a team of antique gas and hot water heaters and the house's electric and water lines. He returned upstairs.

The dining room contained more of DeVilbiss's useless but showy accoutrements of the occult and a few classic books, but no other clues to his background. In the living room Simon found nothing out of the ordinary except the damnably unnerving French clown doll, which had been turned so that it faced him when he entered the room. Its eyes, which shone in the faint illumination from the kitchen, seemed to be fixed on him whenever he glanced at them. He retreated from the room and the glass stare.

Simon stood with his hands on his hips, glancing around the kitchen in a final sweep for clues. Whatever the man's sins, they were not easily detectable from his belongings. He took the two old books as hostages, shut off the light, opened the back door, turned the lock shut again and stepped outside. Walking back to the mansion he pondered other places where Frederika might have gone. She had no family in the area, no real friends, no current paramour except DeVilbiss. He hated the idea of waiting impotently for her to reappear, but he had no choice.

Lynn Gellman turned at her front door and offered a benign smile. "Thanks for a nice evening, Barry."

"It's still early," Barry said, hopefully. "Can I come inside?"

Lynn affected a rueful look. "That's not such a good idea. I'm driving up to Long Island in the morning, and . . ."

"Okay," Barry obliged. "Call me when you get back." He clutched Lynn by the upper arms, drew her awkwardly toward himself and planted a tongue-probing kiss on her. She allowed it to happen. He bounded lightly back down the walk toward his Saab, pausing once to wave.

Lynn stuck her key in the door lock. "The only thing I'll call you is asshole," she muttered. She locked the door behind her and threw the deadbolt. She had been careless about her safety when Simon had lived with her, but lately she felt a sense of defenselessness. She thought about the acidity in her stomach from one glass too many of Pouilly-Fuissé and trudged to the refrigerator for a glass of low-fat milk. As she poured and drank it she shrugged out of her scarf and coat, removed her belt, unzipped her dress and wriggled out of it. She kicked off her shoes on the way to the stairs and draped her dress on the banister. The woman who cleaned the townhouse was in Florida for two weeks and the place looked like Day Three of a bargain basement sale. Lynn promised herself she'd give it a lick and a promise when she returned from the for-once-welcome family holiday gathering. She had to set the glass on the stairs to wrestle out of her slip and panty hose. When she finished, she stuffed them between two stair spindles. She picked up the glass and flicked up the hall light switch.

The upstairs hallway remained dark.

"Shit," Lynn said, looking up into the blackness. There had always been something faulty about the townhouse's wiring; lights seemed to blow out after only a hundred hours. Before, when Simon replaced them, she never gave it more than a fleeting thought of annoyance. The light at the top of the stairs was a particular pain, since she would have to haul the stepladder out of the basement to get to it. She started whistling "Jingle Bell Rock," but the tune stuck in her throat. She blamed it on the milk. Taking a deep breath, she started up the steps.

The distance from the end of the banister to her bedroom door was less than ten feet, but the windowless hallway now seemed the length of a bowling alley. She ran her free hand along the wall to guide herself. When she reached the door she remained outside in the hall and ventured in only with her hand. Her forefinger found the light switch and lifted.

The bedroom remained dark.

Lynn gasped. The thought flashed through her mind that she was caught in the middle of a power outage. Almost as quickly, she realized that the refrigerator light had come on and that the foyer light still burned. She jiggled the switch desperately.

The hand that clamped around her wrist was incredibly powerful.

Lynn dropped the glass of milk. She yanked against the hand with all her might but found herself rooted in place. Her scream of terror hardly began before it ended, as her assailant hauled her into the room and slapped the noise out of her. The force of the open-handed blows stunned her into submission; little resistance was left in her as she was pulled down onto her makeup table chair. She was only half aware that her hands were being drawn behind her and bound with a soft cord rope. Even if the micro blinds had not been closed tightly, blocking off most outside light, her vision would have swum in a blur.

The moment sense returned, Lynn opened her mouth to scream. The palm of a hand clamped over her mouth; its thumb and index fingers pinched her nostrils shut.

"Screaming means dying," the man warned, as he finished securing her hands to the chair back. "Show me you can be trusted and maybe I won't kill you."

Lynn grew quiet. She was having too much trouble breathing around the palm of his hand to make noise anyway. Fighting the hyperventilation of fright was not so easy for her. He waited a few moments after she fell silent before he lifted his hand gradually off her mouth and nose.

"I'm not here to rob or rape you," the intruder told her. His voice was deep and incongruously pleasant. "But I'll do both if you don't give me the information I want. Nod your head if you understand."

Lynn was a survivor. She determined to master her panic and grasp at any hope of staying alive. She nodded.

"Good. One question and one question only: Where is Simon Penn?"

Lynn moaned. "I don't know."

The hand over her mouth tightened again, and his other hand grabbed her throat roughly, pinching her windpipe so that she coughed involuntarily.

"That's not the answer I want. He was your boyfriend only a short time ago. You must know where he is."

The hands relaxed. Lynn coughed several times, then whooped

in a breath. "He doesn't want me to know," she answered, in a raspy voice. "He moved out a few days ago, when I was away on a business trip. I can prove I was away. The charge slips for the plane and the hotel are in my purse downstairs. He took his furniture. You must have seen the empty spaces."

The man was unnervingly silent and motionless for a moment. Then his hands began roaming in parallel lines along Lynn's body, starting at her face, down her throat, along the prominences of her clavicle bones, and to her bra straps, with a seductively light pressure.

"Don't you want him back?" the man asked. "He's such a good-looking young man. Doesn't your body ache for him?"

Lynn fought the hysteria climbing out of her rib cage. "No. It's over between us. I have a new boyfriend."

"And you haven't been curious or angry enough to learn where he's gone. Perhaps to another woman?" The man's hands threatened just above her breasts.

"No."

"Have you spoken to him at all since he moved out?"

"Yes, but only on the telephone. At his work."

"And you didn't ask him where he was living?"

"I . . . yes. Yes, he did say something! He said he was staying with someone on the university staff. But he wouldn't give me the name."

"All right. Who are his closest friends on the staff?"

"His boss is Dr. James Gould. His tennis partner's Professor Neil Yoskin. And . . . oh, God, help me . . . Marty . . . Salkin, from the theater department. What's he done?"

The hands came away. "He's angered the wrong people," the voice said, from a distance.

"If this is about drugs, you've got the wrong Simon Penn," Lynn said. "The guy who used to live here is as straight as . . . he was a goddamn Eagle Scout!"

Lynn got no reply. She heard her closet door being opened and a few metal hangers clattering together. Then, suddenly, the hands

250

were back, now at her left leg, pulling a belt around it and securing it and the chair leg together.

"Stay quiet," the man warned, as he repeated the process on her right leg. Through the panicky jumble of her thoughts, she marveled at how swiftly and assuredly the man moved in the cave-black room. She had just begun to regain an atom of composure when a third belt snaked over her head and around her neck. She began to cry softly as he secured it to the back of the chair.

When the man had finished, he said, "Don't struggle or you'll choke to death. If you've given me the right name, I'll call this new boyfriend and tell him the sliding door's unlocked and you're waiting for him. Otherwise, I'll be back. Do you wish to improve your list?"

"I can't, I swear. I wish to hell I knew where the son of a bitch is," Lynn whimpered.

"I'm sure you do. Before I gag you, is your *new* boyfriend's listing correct in the telephone book?"

Lynn weighed the virtues of giving the intruder Barry's name or waiting for her parents to call the local police.

"Yes. His name is Barry Dietz," she said, through a deep sob.

As he approached his rented duplex, DeVilbiss slowed his pace to a trot. Dressed as he was in a stylish black warm-up suit and matching black ski mask, he was a beau example of the Princeton jogger out for a winter's eve run. He had not waived his private rule against running, however, simply because of his outfit. Brisk walking would have wasted time he did not have. Minutes, which normally stretched out before him like the sands of the Sahara, were now constricted as if into a mere hourglass.

Vincent rushed to overcome bad luck and a mental lapse. Reverend Spencer's house had been destroyed beyond expectations, obscuring the details of the minister's murder and incinerating any information about the scrolls Spencer might have hidden away. Vincent had also gloated over the ease with which he had manipulated the old scholar to gain his key. He had been so sure his plans for destroying the scrolls this evening were flawless. He was wrong. One poor assumption had blown his scheme apart with a psyche-shattering force as cataclysmic as the afternoon's gas explosion.

Vincent blamed his unfocused thinking on the silvered bullet he had taken in the face. The tooth was still broken, jagged and annoying to his tongue. Even though the exit wound had finally closed, for the first time the healing was not total. His handsome image was scarred by a raised bubble of flesh paler than his normal pallid complexion. Thanks to the gutsy minister, he would need both oral and plastic surgery. At least, he told himself, two valuable lessons repaid his pain and disfigurement: the scrolls must definitely be destroyed before another man of Spencer's mettle got his hands on them, and he must henceforth be prepared for any other adversary who might trust in the power of silver bullets.

But Vincent could not blame the bullet wound for his original miscalculation. When Frederika told him that Simon Penn had "just left his girlfriend," he had assumed the expression was figurative. Right after Penn had visited him and negotiated for Frederika's freedom he had checked the telephone directory and found a number and address beside the librarian's name. Too late, after a humbling shock, did he again consult the directory (this time under Gellman) and find the same telephone number and address. He had immediately called directory assistance and learned that Simon had no new number. The university's administrative offices were closed for the holiday, so he could not get Penn's new address from Personnel. Still, he should have had a source to learn the whereabouts of Simon and his security key, but he had let that source literally disappear. Maddeningly, he had been the very cause of her disappearance. One hour after witnessing the gas explosion he had called Frederika at her home.

"Are you alone?" he had asked, without bothering to identify himself.

She had said she was.

"I want you to leave the house now, with your suitcases, passport, and money. Do you understand?"

She had said she did.

"You will drive to a hotel or motel within half an hour of Princeton but not too close. You'll check in, then park your car where it won't be seen. You will not leave your room. At noon tomorrow you will call me at my house. If I don't answer, you will call every half hour until I answer. Repeat what I said."

She had obeyed perfectly.

And here was the fact whose frequent surfacing in DeVilbiss's mind nearly drove him insane: To be perfectly sure he could contact her at any time, he had said, "What hotel do you intend to check into?" She had told him of a Ramada Inn on Route 1, some ten miles north of Princeton. He let her go, certain she would follow his instructions to the letter. His intent was to give her enough time to get well out of Princeton, then call Simon Penn and offer to trade her life for the scrolls. At 4:48, when he dialed the number next to Simon's name, the commonness of his mind became crystal clear. He listened in shock to Lynn Gellman's recorded voice announcing that she was not able to come to the phone right now but that she would get back to the caller soon. At 5:10 Vincent telephoned the Ramada Inn and discovered that, due to holiday traveling and several Christmas parties, the entire hotel had been booked up days in advance. A woman of Frederika's description had just been at the desk, had been told the same thing, and had gotten into her car and driven away.

Vincent waited until 5:30 without expectation of Frederika's call. In her entranced state she could not be counted on to act logically, much less anticipate what he would expect of her under changed circumstances. He drove immediately to the Vanderveen house and found it dark and unoccupied. He bellowed his rage into the night. Outside lights winked on up and down the block as he climbed into his rented car. He drove the length of Route 1 from Princeton to New Brunswick, winding through every hotel and motel parking lot in search of a white Mazda sedan. The one matching car he found had an infant's safety seat in the rear. He accepted the futility of his search and hurried back to Princeton.

The situation looked so bleak that, for a minute, Vincent seriously considered how he might bring down the entire Firestone

Library. Then he set the notion aside because nothing short of several tons of dynamite would guarantee that the steel case in the heart of the structure would be totally destroyed. Ordinarily he would have rejected such a plan because of his reverence for books. This great library was worth all the lives he had managed to spare in this century. He had known that at least one other of his kind operated in Europe when the museum and library had been torched to destroy the copies of Manutius's book. Perhaps Little Nick had doled out those assignments to another minion precisely because he knew Vincent would have balked at such sacrilege. Now, however, when Vincent had so recently incurred the anger of the Dark Forces over sparing the widower scientist, even this library's existence balanced against his own survival did not seem such a difficult choice.

Yet there had to be a simpler solution. If he could not learn Simon's whereabouts from Frederika until the next noon, Lynn Gellman seemed a logical source. After entering her home and examining her personal phone book, her appointment book, and her wall calendar, he resigned himself to wait for her return, prepared to kill her and anyone she invited inside to save the night. Yet once again, despite his recent promise to himself to act ruthlessly, he had shown her mercy. Profound as his terror was of angering those who controlled him, a new impulse vied for control of his actions. Something that made him feel so good, so—impossible as the word might seem—rejuvenated, could not be called a weakness. Could it?

At least, Vincent reflected, he had three more leads, each of which he would follow as soon as he played his answering machine and learned whether or not Frederika had called on her own. He entered the old duplex house and went directly upstairs to his bedroom. He saw the red light winking on the machine and hastened to rewind the message.

"It's only a prospective customer," the whispering voice informed, causing Vincent yet again to jump in surprise. "She called twice, but her first message was erased."

Vincent became aware of the draft from the window. He saw the broken glass and the open lock.

"Your visitor erased it after he listened to it."

"Who?" Vincent demanded, resigned to playing Nick's cat-and-mouse game. A profound and rare shudder shook him. In spite of his long-held determination never to show fear in the voice's presence, he could barely control his agitation.

"The man who visited you and demanded you leave the woman alone. Does he know about us?"

"No, of course—"

"Does he know what you are?"

"No! He just wants his girlfriend back."

"You told us that you had him under your control."

"I have. This is the worst he can do," Vincent asserted, working as hard as he ever had to make a lie sound positive.

"Will he get you the scrolls tonight or will he not?"

Vincent abandoned the idea of finding Lynn's three leads to Simon's whereabouts. His uneasy presentiment about the librarian had come to horrible fulfillment. Penn had surely received a copy of the translation from Reverend Spencer. By now, Vincent assumed, he had also heard about the old man's bizarrely fatal accident. The ineffectual-looking young man had to be armed with the scrolls' information and the knowledge that Spencer's precautions had failed. Penn was, therefore, highly dangerous. Wherever he had lain his head the night before, Vincent was convinced Penn would not be there tonight.

"The night is young," Vincent evaded. "I will have this done by tomorrow night, if not before. The scrolls' translator is dead already."

"Yet another death?" the voice said, and, before Vincent could reply, "The translator can be replaced."

Vincent turned a full circle in his rage. "If you're so fucking smart, why don't *you* get the scrolls?" he screamed. He plucked his hairbrush from the dresser and hurled it at the picture of The Seven Ages of Man, shattering the glass across half the room. He took several deep, composing breaths. "I've never failed before, and I won't now. Is there some special reason this must be done tonight?" he asked. "Is there?" The room stood silent as a sarcophagus.

CHAPTER THIRTEEN

December 24

༼ↄ༽

He that finds his life will lose it.

—Matthew 10:39

Simon woke with a start, features frozen in alarm. The Christ-mas tree still glowed beside him. He struggled up from the couch and loped to the base of the mansion's ornate staircase.

"Frederika?" he called. The house felt as empty as when he had drifted off to sleep. He guessed that hour had been about four A.M. He hurried to the back of the house and looked out the utility room window. The garage doors still hung open, exposing a dark, hollow space. He was not surprised, not after the answer to DeVilbiss's identity had come to him as his mind ascended from sleep. Now all he needed was to find the exact biography and confirm the details. The facts of the account he recalled only vaguely, but his emotional memory registered clear alarm.

While Simon wolfed down a stale doughnut, he stared at the two books he had stolen from DeVilbiss's house, thinking what a puny, useless act it had been. Just as he gulped down the dregs of a con-tainer of orange juice, the telephone rang. He grabbed it on the second ring.

"Yes?" he said, disguising his voice in the bottom of its range.

"Simon?" the caller asked, hesitantly.

"Good morning, Rich," Simon greeted with relief.

"It didn't sound like you," the physics grad student said. "Have you by any chance been listening to WHWH this morning?"

"No. Why?"

"The announcer said there was a gas explosion yesterday on Mercer Street. I heard the boom, but I didn't know what it was till now."

"When?"

"About four o'clock."

"I was in Philadelphia," Simon said, looking anxiously at his coat and cap, hanging on a hook near the back door.

"That explains it. I called you a little while after the explosion, but you weren't—"

"What blew up, Rich?"

"Reverend Wilton Spencer's house."

Even as the shock electrified his nervous system, Simon accepted the news. Willy had not been a paranoid after all. And Simon finally knew DeVilbiss's connection to Firestone Library.

"Isn't he the guy you said was working on those old scrolls?" Rich asked.

"Yes, he was," Simon managed. "Was he inside?"

"They think it was him. There was one body, but it was . . ."

"I get the picture," Simon said.

"Incredible! First I lose my advisor, now you lose somebody working in your area. What the heck's going on?"

"You wouldn't believe it."

"Wanna try me?"

Simon dropped the last of the doughnut in the garbage. "Sure. After I do some research at the library."

Rich snorted his perplexion. "The library? I don't—"

"Hang loose, pal. I think at least one of these deaths wasn't an accident. You gonna be around this afternoon?"

"Sure."

"Then I'll call you later. I may need some help."

"Count on it, buddy."

Simon hung up and knelt in front of the kitchen hearth's decorative woodpile. One piece of oak looked ideal for sharpening into a stake.

★ ★ ★

The biography proved almost as elusive in the library's stacks as it had been in Simon's memory. He had forgotten the author's name and had to hunt it down through the subject of "conjury." The author was a little-known performer, celebrated only as the chronicler of the Britannic Brotherhood of Magicians. It was an elite group of prestidigitators who not only enjoyed royal cachet but also controlled the bookings in theatrical halls throughout the British Isles. Simon had found the author, "The Grand Gilliam," tedious, xenophobic, and a braggart, but the Victorian world of legerdemain he described was fascinating.

Simon walked slowly out of the maze of stacks toward a window-lit reading cove, scanning the pages for the passages he needed. No one stepped in his path, nor was anyone seated in any of the couches or easy chairs. A Sunday that also happened to be Christmas Eve attracted few researchers, even during the library's reduced hours of operation.

Simon dropped into a heavily stained and tattered plush chair and continued flipping pages. Finally he saw the name that had so long eluded his memory. His eyes swept slowly through the lines, wanting to miss no clue to combating the creature who was neither magician nor herbalist.

In the winter of 1898, the club suffered an incident that reminded its members of the true magic which surrounds us, the magic which we pretend to duplicate by purely human agencies. For some time, the BBM had been assailed by an Italian who averred considerable repute in his homeland and the south of France as a conjurer but of whom not one favourable report had reached our hearing. He went by the name of Signore di Bussolotti, a puerile play on the Italian name given to cup and ball players, which invoked among the members a prejudicial antipathy. He had doubtless heard of the memberships we had bestowed on Herrmann the Great of Germany and Harry Kellar of the United States and thought that a foreign name provided some sort of easy entrée. His persistence and the claim to several unusual illusions finally convinced us to audition him.

On the twelfth of December, the requisite four members necessary to grant membership, along with assistants and cognoscenti of magic—numbering altogether, I believe, ten persons—assembled at St. George's Hall. The gas lights were lit, and we dispersed throughout the house to observe the Italian's skills. He was handsome in a Mediterranean way, rather tall for his race, and most especially striking in his pale rather than swarthy complexion and the unusual amber colour of his eyes. He looked to be about forty yet maintained the thinness of youth. He wore expensively tailored evening dress of the style popularized by Robert-Houdin, in which he cut quite a dash.

He began with card tricks, and I immediately was struck by the man's strangeness. Whereas many lesser magicians will have personality and patter aplenty to divert and misdirect, they will fail to mystify through lack of dexterity. This person evinced exactly the opposite, appearing somewhat ill at ease and slow in his speech but exercising manual skills with a speed I had never before seen. As all good magicians understand, no quickness can compensate when the audience's eyes have not been redirected or their minds not been prepared to expect something distinct from the illusion. Whispering among ourselves, we credited his difficulty with our tongue as a reasonable impediment and bid him continue.

I was also struck by the fact that, again as the immortal Robert-Houdin had done, Signore di Bussolotti worked without the aid of confederates. For his first major illusion, he called upon two of our group to assist him. He produced seven overlarge playing cards, which he asked to be shuffled. He stepped to the back of the stage with one of my assistants, whom he enjoined to hold his hands fast and prevent him at all costs from moving to the footlights. He bid the lights in the theatre be totally extinguished. Need I tell you what an unnerving experience it is to be possessed of your faculty of sight in one moment and to be utterly deprived of it in the next? The blackness was complete. He commanded Mr. Petrie-Jones to shuffle the cards one more time, then to place one in a special holder, to turn in a complete circle holding the card outward until he again faced the audience, then to pull the card forcibly from the holder. I listened to Mr. Petrie-Jones inserting the card, heard di Bussolotti call out 'Jack of Clubs,' waited a moment and saw the card illuminate in an eerie blue glow sufficiently bright to allow the audience to see that it was indeed the card the Italian had called. Twice more, the trick was repeated, the second time with much laughter when Petrie-Jones lost his bearings in the dark and faced stage left instead of straight outward. I was impressed, but David Devant correctly pointed out that no town's fire marshall would allow a period of total darkness during an actual performance, rendering the trick unusable.

The Italian moved on to pigeon killing, that heinous trick devised by another of his blood, the infamous Bartolomeo Bosco. Bosco it was who first convinced audiences that he was decapitating the heads of white and black pigeons, switching the heads and restoring them to life, when in point of fact he was pulling other pigeons out of his false-bottom boxes and assassinating birds at every performance. The revival of this sadistic illusion sat poorly with our crowd and had already decided the opinions of several.

Di Bussolotti performed the 'Sands of Egypt,' then trundled out two large box illusions, both known to us. He smiled with disarming charm at the two ladies in our audience, producing his desired effect, but I could discern a trace of panic in his eyes. He left the stage for a minute and returned with a delicate table on rollers, atop which sat a large, black lacquer box decorated with silver moons and stars. He knocked on the box and stepped away from it. Under its own power a harlequin doll appeared, being about two foot in height. The doll he called Pierrot Lunaire. It was very much the duplicate of the great Robert Heller's automaton, which sprang in and out of its box, smoked, whistled, and answered questions. This one, however, was somewhat larger. More importantly, di Bussolotti's willingness to allow minute examination of the table proved that there were indeed no helpers. Up close this Pierrot was a marvel of creation, having glass eyes that roamed back and forth as if through an independent will and fingers so delicately articulated that it could pass a pen from one hand to the other. Like Heller's machine, it did a handstand; it also whistled. But here the Italian appeared to surpass the old master. His Pierrot, he declared, performed mathematical calculations, and he invited us to pose it any problem. Having said as much, he stepped back and seemed to let the doll work on its own. We obliged with a few simple additions, which the doll supplied, along with such written derisions as 'Are your brains not as nimble as your hands?' Thus challenged, we began demanding square roots, then the answers to quadratic equations. Its answers, in florid script, were always swift and perfect. Just when we began to murmur our total perplexion, the doll froze in place and would not respond further. Di Bussolotti tucked him back in his box, explaining that his mechanism had, unfortunately, wound down.

The four members retired to the back of the house and argued membership. David Devant pointed out that the calculating doll was perhaps the most amazing trick any of us had ever seen, but Reginald Stephens rightly remonstrated that such a machine was properly the province of watchmakers. The Italian's other failings could not be made up by this one capital feat. It was no more acceptable to our theatres than the bizarre moving picture magic of the Frenchman Méliès to whom some of our number had been exposed.

I had the onerous task of informing the Italian that his magic was not up to our standards. Instead of skulking quietly away or else hurling bitter invectives, he merely smiled and said, 'What, gentlemen, is the most dangerous trick in the world?'

'Why, the bullet-catching trick,' Devant answered.

'Has it not killed at least three of our profession?' the Italian asked.

'More, I think,' said I. 'Do we not all recall the fellow who was killed recently, not by the false bullet but by the piece of the ramrod broken off in the barrel?'

'What would you say, then, if I did not catch the bullet in my hand but rather in a pail behind myself, allowing the bullet to travel through me without harm?' the petitioner asked. 'Would not such a trick be worth a two-year contract?' Speaking above the murmurs of astonishment, he went on to challenge our powers of observation and our credentials as master conjurers.

Petrie-Jones turned red in the face. 'Will you allow us all up on the stage?'

'Certainly,' he said.

'But,' spoke up one of our guests, a man occasioned to carry large sums of money on a regular basis, 'what if the gun were not yours?' He drew from his pocket a small calibre pistol. Here the conversations broke into an uproar. Di Bussolotti himself silenced the group by waving his hands.

'I accept these conditions if the Brotherhood promises absolutely that I shall have a *three*-year contract to play in your halls,' the Italian said.

We were stymied by his answer. Our conclusion was that it was only sporting to accept his proposal. A sturdy bucket was found, to be held aloft some two feet behind the man. First he and then each member of the Brotherhood examined the gun and bullets minutely. Seeing that the weapon was indeed real, none of our number was willing to murder a man whom we clearly thought insane. At last, the Italian suggested a solution. In case the trick did not go according to his plan, the one shooting should direct the bullet through the left extreme of his chest, missing his heart, so that he had a decent chance of survival. The bullets were further to be dipped in alcohol (which he had ready), to destroy bacteria on their surfaces. That decided, I volunteered to pull the trigger. The bullets were prepared and reloaded, without his handling them in any manner, then replaced in the pistol. Di Bussolotti took his place, and Petrie-Jones held the bucket out. I paced back three long steps, turned, aimed and fired.

The crack of the gun was authentic, as was the disturbance of the Italian's tails, the rending of his dress shirt fabric and the blood that sprang out and besmirched it. Most terrifying was the man's recoil from the impact of the bullet and his cry of pain. The women screamed; a few of the men shouted out. A moment later, Petrie-Jones cried out as well and dropped the bucket.

'I've been hit!" he said, his voice little more than a whisper.

The Italian straightened up, looking a bit pale but miraculously fit considering his state. 'I'm fine,' he assured. 'Attend to your friend.'

We found that Petrie-Jones had been struck in the forearm and the bullet lodged inside. He had felt the impact simultaneous with the firing of the gun and wondered aloud if it had not hit one of the Italian's rib bones and angled off course, missing the bucket and finding his arm. When we determined that Petrie-Jones would survive until we bore him to hospital, we turned our attention to the Italian, who stood over us as if a casual observer.

'Taking a real bullet through one's body hardly qualifies one as a magician,' I snapped at him.

'But it did not go through me,' di Bussolotti affirmed hotly. We told him he was ridiculous, that we clearly saw the evidence, no matter how bravely he stood before us. His coat was pierced in front and back, the rear hole in fact closer to his arm. In answer, he very slowly undressed, peeling off the coat and then unbuttoning the shirt. He wiped a cloth over his hairy chest, cleaning away the blood. 'See for yourself,' he invited.

Examining as closely as gentlemanly decorum, the rather dark theatre and the shadows of his chest hairs allowed, all we found was a closed-in and red dimple of flesh where a gaping hole should have been.

'The result of a first failure with the trick, a year ago,' di Bussolotti explained, as he attempted to close his damaged shirt.

'Really?' David Devant asked. 'And may we see the damage to your back?'

'You may not,' the man said. His face took on an angry pallor. 'You have seen no bullet wound beneath the front holes in my clothing; I stand before you as healthy as when I entered the stage. That is sufficient to hold you to your promise.'

At that instant, a chilling premonition overcame me. 'Hold him, fellows!' I commanded. Five of our number, including myself, fell upon him and attempted to wrestle him to the floor. We found his power of resistance incredible, beyond that of two men his size. In the melee, his coat and shirt were again pulled away from his chest. To my astonished eyes, the supposedly old wound had formed over even more perfectly. Its angry red hue had faded to bright pink, and I could swear that the puckering of the skin had even smoothed somewhat. And then the creature was free, throwing the lot of us off him. But not before I had seen his prominent incisors. I knew then that my premonition was correct. We were auditioning not a man but a truly magical creature: a vampire!

Quick as thought, the one who called himself di Bussolotti vaulted to the valves that controlled the gas lights. The theatre was plunged in darkness. Some of us found matches and struck them, but by that time the creature had moved with perfect ease across the pitch-black stage, reclaiming his box with the doll and disappearing out a side door.

Afterward, my observations were held suspect, owing to the emotion of the moment. My theory was found to be, despite the evidence, too incredible to bear credence. But I know what I saw. The man was a vampire. His petitioning of our club and desperation to join was in my mind absolutely logical. The guise of a magician is exquisitely suited to such a creature. He and we are both denizens of the night, doing our work after the sun's dying. He and we are both required to travel often—we to seek new audiences, he to seek new victims, so that he will not commit too many murders in any single place. He and we require large boxes—we for our large-scale illusions, he for his native soil and the coffin he must inhabit during the day. What better excuse to transport bulky boxes than a magician's life? But he had no assistants, no animals, because his life is that of the unholy and perpetually lone predator.

I challenged my fellow members to explain in scientific terms how the Italian's clothing was torn, where the blood had been concealed, and how he was left unharmed by the bullet while Petrie-Jones, behind him, was hit. Theories were advanced, but none offered a better explanation than my supernatural one. Nevertheless, the Brotherhood would not allow me to go to the authorities with my story, fearing that it would be perceived as a cheap publicity stunt to increase ticket sales. I succumbed to their wills. Notwithstanding, I know now irrefutably that there exists a real, sinister magic, in which relation our conjurers' art is a mere pale and harmless shadow.

For months we searched the Empire's newspapers and all our connections for news of the vampire/magician, but he had vanished from the British Isles apparently as totally as he had from St. George's Hall. It was a disappearing act as clever as any I have ever witnessed on the stage.

Simon closed the book and took it back to its place on the shelves. He went from there to the library employees' time clock and examined Frederika's card. He found an isolated room with a phone and a Princeton directory, looked up a number and made a call. The man he called had rotating shift hours, so Simon had a good chance of reaching him.

"Hello?"

"Ray?" Simon asked.

"Yeah. Who's this?" Ray was a local policeman who had a gift for acting. He and Simon had earned Equity wages together in a couple of McCarter Theatre productions.

"Simon Penn. We worked together in *A Christmas Carol* and *A Phoenix Too Frequent.*"

"Sure. What can I do for you?"

"I need some advice. Say a woman's been missing since four-thirty P.M. yesterday, when she left work. She—"

"You writing a play?" Ray asked.

"I'm thinking about it, and I'm sure you can help," Simon said, switching to the safer hypothetical mode.

"Glad to. Go ahead."

"Anyway, she promises to come directly home, but she doesn't. She's still missing by the middle of the next morning."

"How old is she?"

"Twenty-four."

"And who did she promise she'd be home to?"

"A guy."

"Is this guy a husband or boyfriend?"

"Neither."

"Does she have a boyfriend?" From the background sounded the cries of children squabbling. "Hey, girls, be quiet! Go ahead, Simon."

"She's seeing this other guy, who's very good at hypnosis. The guy's a no-good character."

"Has he got an arrest record?"

"I don't know. I mean, I haven't thought about it yet."

"She lives with the one guy but dates another one?" Ray asked.

"The first guy rents a room from her. He's worried the other one's done something to her. Can he call the police?"

"Not unless he wants them pissed off at him. First she's not even gone for a whole day. Secondly . . . wait. Is this gonna turn out to be a kidnapping or a murder?"

"A kidnapping."

"There's no ransom note at this point?"

"No."

The little-girl noises grew more vociferous. "Hey! I'm on the phone here. I don't care who hit who first. Alison, go upstairs. If I were Santa I'd fly right by this house tonight. Sorry," Ray apologized. "So your fictional lady's of age. No sign of foul play. The police wouldn't touch it with a ten-foot pole. If the guy who rents a room from her is your hero, have him go to the bad guy's place and confront him. That would make a better scene anyway, right? You want to work on it, Simon, and get back to me? I gotta go."

"I understand. Thanks, and Merry Christmas."

"Same to you."

Simon recradled the telephone handset. So he was on his own. He realized he had left the wooden stake lying on the floor by the old stuffed chair. He made no move to retrieve it. The more time passed, the more he doubted his acceptance of an ancient bloodsucker's presence in Princeton. And yet DeVilbiss was far beyond the ordinary. Simon hunted up a scrap of paper and a pencil. He wrote down everthing he knew. First, the description of the Italian magician and his Pierrot Lunaire exactly conformed to DeVilbiss and his doll. From the date mentioned in the passage, the man had to be at least a hundred and thirty years old, but DeVilbiss still looked forty. But he moved in daylight, and he owned no coffins filled with native soil. Simon knew so firsthand, from having minutely examined DeVilbiss's house. Frederika had eaten and drunk with him, so he didn't exist solely on blood. Then again, he slept during the day, and he had a grip of steel. And amber eyes. He haunted the library. Tommy Wheeler, the guard, had been killed and the alarms had gone off right right after Simon first saw the man there. He was evil and somehow ancient. And, for some reason, he wanted the Ahriman scrolls badly enough to kill for them.

Simon had hidden Willy Spencer's bundle of notes within the library's B level, behind a storage room's air return grate. Simon rode the elevator down and shut himself in the tiny space. As he cut open the envelope and pulled out the pages of translation, his mind labored to prepare itself for a description of a similar amber-eyed creature, not hundreds but thousands of years old. Spencer's beautiful penmanship did nothing to soften the profound shock he received on reading the final pages.

These instrumentalities of evil may no longer walk the earth, as they did when they were beings of the light. The blessed air is to them as the sea is to man; if they enter it for any time they may perish. The air protects man as the ocean protects fish, an ever-present refuge. Nevertheless, the legion of darkness are an enemy of vastly superior intelligence, who will devise methods of harvesting despite the hazard.

Their most diabolical method is to turn man against his own kind. This they do by finding those who do not fear God, offering such ones unending life in exchange for doing their bidding. To help these venal creatures in their tasks, they change them into something more powerful and vicious than their kind, as a shark is to a sturgeon. For their own sake, they cause these supermen to drink the blood of their own kind to survive, and to move in the same darkness to which they themselves are confined. Such servants of evil are known by their pale skin and the amber hue of their eyes.

Simon searched the pages in vain for instructions on killing this foe. Obviously, whatever weapons the forwarned Willy Spencer might have devised had proven useless. Or perhaps DeVilbiss's expertise at murder, his willingness to kill and vast experience at survival had overcome the wily old man's preparations.

Simon closed his eyes and vigorously massaged his lids. Even if logic insisted he disbelieve the words of both the magician biographer and the scroll's author, he knew in his gut that true evil was at work in Princeton. Firsthand, he had learned that DeVilbiss slept in the daytime. He had also personally felt his superhuman strength. A guard of the scrolls had been found swinging from a rope. Then the nervous translator of the scrolls had died in a gas explosion. Then Frederika had disappeared. Simon realized he would be at a fatal disadvantage unless he allowed himself to suspend his disbelief. By his meddling in Frederika's life and because he worked in the Rare Manuscripts section, Simon had become part of DeVilbiss's plan to reach those scrolls. If Frederika were safe, he would have hopped the next train out of Princeton Junction, security key in his pocket. With her survival dependent solely on his decision, he had no choice but to fight.

Climbing the stairs to the main floor, translation in hand, Simon remembered with disquiet the sweatshirt an old athlete had once sported on an adjacent tennis court: *Old age and guile defeats youth and skill every time.* As he walked off the campus, he reviewed the pitiful amount of information he possessed. His feet turned automatically toward the Vanderveen mansion. When he thought about his destination he stopped short, changed direction and found a sidewalk telephone. He dialed the number from memory and, while he waited for the connection, consulted his watch. The time was eight minutes before noon.

"Vincent DeVilbiss."

"Simon Penn." Simon pictured sharp incisors, millimeters from the phone's mouthpiece.

"Mr. Penn!" DeVilbiss exclaimed brightly. "Where are you?"

"Near enough. Where's Frederika?"

"Not here—as you know firsthand."

Simon felt a panicky loss of advantage, then told himself DeVilbiss's list of suspects for breaking and entering his house could not have been that long. "But you do know where she is?" he pushed on.

"I do."

A frisson rippled through Simon, icing down his hot panic, as he listened to the affable facade of evil. "Then you admit to breaking our agreement."

"I only said I would consider it," DeVilbiss reminded. "At any rate, I don't want your money."

"But you do want my key and my help to get the scrolls," Simon anticipated.

After an assessing silence, DeVilbiss said, "We need to speak in private."

"Wrong," Simon answered. "First you prove to me that Frederika's under your power. I don't believe you have her."

"And why is that?"

"Because otherwise she'd have told you I'm staying at her house, and you'd have paid me a return visit last night. Wouldn't you?" Simon listened to a second silence. He felt a rush of relief that his opponent's intelligence was not as superhuman as his strength.

"I can prove my control . . . very soon," DeVilbiss answered, his voice sounding like a steel spring under high tension.

"Then I'll call back . . . very soon," Simon replied. A police car had appeared at the corner and waited for the traffic light to change. He wanted to run to the man in the black-and-white, but his conversation with Ray had told him what he could expect.

272

"We're at something of an impasse," DeVilbiss noted. "Let me suggest an alternate proof: pose a question only she can answer."

Simon understood the delicacy of their negotiation. He was unwilling to reveal his location and DeVilbiss was equally unwilling to produce Frederika. "All right," he acquiesced. "Ask her what I bought my father for Christmas."

"What present you bought your father?"

"That's right. I'll call again at two o'clock." He thumbed down the switchhook, denying DeVilbiss opportunity to refuse. He stared across the street at the sprawling university library, wondering as he did what price Frederika had paid in keeping his sleeping place secret from her captor. Simon walked briskly in the direction of Richard Chen's garret.

DeVilbiss opened the back door to his duplex, found Frederika huddling without a coat in the shadows of the porch, and yanked her roughly inside. Almost an hour after Simon Penn's call, his blood still boiled. Mental lapses and ill fate continued to befall him, crushing him inexorably under their accumulated weight. In all his years he had never been forced to labor under such a combination of adversities. When Frederika reported that Simon had rejected her sexual advances, it had never occurred to Vincent that the two librarians might be sharing the same roof. He feared the possibility of creeping senescence, that though Nick's powders and human blood kept his body perpetually youthful, the human mind could not so easily be preserved. Perhaps, he thought, no elixir could hold senility at bay more than five hundred years. But what explained the barrage of bad luck that teamed with his mental failings? Why, in the time he had known Frederika Vanderveen, before he hypnotized her and reduced her to a purely responsive automaton, had she not volunteered or at least let slip the fact that Simon lived with her? Had she not wanted him to suspect that there was a rival for her affections?

For all his troubled musings, the one possibility Vincent felt unwilling to consider was that his cerebral matter had been common and fallible since the day he arrived squalling into the world. Vincent

DeVilbiss, born Innocente Farnese, had long ago forgotten the mediocrity of his mind, soon after the powers of his body had been augmented. Reveling in heightened senses, speed, and strength, he fell willing victim to the assumption that his thinking had also improved. His invulnerable body had survived numerous mental mistakes that would have killed a normal man, lessons learnable only by the Undead. And he never considered how easy the demands of his existence were. His victims rarely expected attack; few owned weapons; virtually none were trained in self-defense. Those he preyed upon for blood were despatched at random, in situations advantageous to him. The simple truth behind Vincent's recent bad fortune was the inaccessibility of the scrolls. Before he had been able to overcome the defenses of the academic fortress, two of its employees had come to know him for what he was. Self-doubts, bad luck, true adversities, and the hectoring voice of the Dark Forces combined to whip up his fear. When the woman finally arrived at his back door, he was ready to vent his full fury on her.

Frederika winced from the talon grip around her wrist, but she made no protest. DeVilbiss spun her into the kitchen and slammed the door shut.

"About time," he fumed. "Did you park your car away from here?"

"Yes. At the Choir College."

"Where does Simon Penn live?" He had purposely refrained from asking her over the telephone when she checked in at noon, determined to see her face when he posed the question.

"He rents a room from me," she replied, without hesitation.

DeVilbiss exhaled loudly and struck the kitchen table a resounding blow with the heel of his hand. Frederika flinched and looked frightened.

"It's all right," DeVilbiss soothed, sucking in his anger with a mercurial lack of effort. "If he were in trouble and not at your house, where would you look for him?"

Frederika thought. "He eats with a friend named Rich."

"And where does Rich live?"

"I don't know."

"Rich's last name?"

"I don't know."

DeVilbiss mastered his urge to slap her but could not resist sarcasm. "For someone who is such a good friend to you, you know very little about Simon, don't you?"

"Yes," Frederika admitted. She seemed to think about the meaning behind his words, found the task too taxing and gave up.

DeVilbiss sighed. He pulled out a kitchen chair and sat, looking up at Frederika, who stood before him like a schoolchild awaiting discipline. "What Christmas present did Simon buy for his father?"

For a moment Frederika's eyes went wide and blank, and DeVilbiss feared that Penn had somehow tricked him. Then she said, "A fishing reel. Flycasting reel."

DeVilbiss merely nodded. His awareness centered instead on the image before him, the angelic-looking woman standing so defenselessly, waiting for his next order. She had not bothered to apply makeup, which only emphasized her natural beauty. Lynn Gellman's near-nude body the night before had ignited his libido. His loins ached for a release that would, at least temporarily, lobotomize him of his fears and frustrations. He sought to mask his impotence over destroying the scrolls with an act of sexual vehemence.

"Come closer," Vincent commanded. Frederika's eyes narrowed, as if in mistrust. "Come closer I said!" Vincent repeated. When she had, he slid his hands under her skirt and ran them up the outsides of her thighs, luxuriating in the feel of the firm flesh beneath the sensual nylon.

"Take off your panty hose and panties," he whispered.

Frederika's hands stayed at her side. The blade of her tongue rose slowly to the roof of her mouth, as if to say "no," but, locked in the hypnotic stare of DeVilbiss's amber eyes, she obeyed in silence.

Standing, Vincent removed his shirt, unbuckled his belt, opened his trouser clasp and pulled down his zipper. He sat again. "Sit on my lap," he directed.

"No," Frederika said, in a small, unsure voice.

Vincent's hand flashed out and grabbed her belt and the top of her skirt. To his surprise, her reaction was almost as quick, taking his hand in both of hers and wrestling with it. As he pulled toward her, she pulled back with astonishing strength. Vincent had forgotten that she now had several doses of elixir coursing through her. With his free hand, he delivered a powerful backhand to her face, stunning her. He ripped her skirt up to her belt and pulled her down onto his lap, so that she straddled him.

Frederika's hands rose together and descended on his back, raking his flesh with her nails. He screamed in pain as he found both arms and pinioned them behind her back. Then he managed to grab her hair and hold her head steady long enough to catch her eyes with his. She blinked once, then stopped struggling.

"You will never speak to your father without me," he told her, in a calm voice. "Without me, you will be lost forever. Do you understand?"

After a long moment, she told him that she did.

"You need to go into a deeper level of rest. Watch my eyes and relax. You need to find peace. Relax. You will listen to every word I say and obey. Do you understand?"

Eyelids half lowered, Frederika assured him.

"Good. Now prove it to me. Move closer!" He sighed with pleasure at her contact. "Now move back and forth, slowly. Good girl, good." Her body and motion were so stimulating that he forgot the continuing pain across his back. Vincent was oblivious to the knowledge that the parallel tracks of claw marks had not only just begun to close, but that blood continued to ooze from the wounds. A week earlier, such scratches would have nearly vanished in the same time.

Vincent took Frederika's exquisite but blank face lightly in his hands, leaned forward and offered his mouth. Just as she had done on both identical occasions, she averted her lips and nuzzled his ear and the angle of his jaw.

"You little vixen," Vincent said. Despite being subjected to his most potent hypnotic trance, she still managed to exert some will of her own. He determined to test his will over her, and to learn the reason why she so forcefully and cunningly avoided kissing on the lips. He also wanted the sex to last more than a few strokes. To divert his arousal, he began an intermittent interrogation, to expose not only the cause of her sexual quirkiness but also the secret reasons she had for seeking his alleged necromantic skills. While he hardened and wriggled himself inch by inch inside her, she regressed to the age of five, and the long-closed floodgates were opened. He struggled to expose her innermost thoughts chronologically, but her memories had no order of time. Six and sixteen were stitched side by side by misery and the same haunting, unanswered question. She was becoming again the only child whose parents were so often away and, even when at home, distant from her. She revealed from her child's perspective an uninterrupted stream of primal thoughts: how all too infrequently her handsome father whom everyone obviously loved paid her attention, stroking her hair, hugging her tightly, rubbing her bottom, telling her that she must not kiss others on the lips because of germs but that she could kiss only him since he was her Daddy and she was exactly like him and they shared the same good germs and praised her to the heavens whenever strangers came to parties at their house and other times shoved her peevishly from his study because he had so many important things to do for other children of the world who needed him just as much and screamed at her when she forgot as she frequently did and ran or sang enthusiastically through the house and teased her at breakfast but was never there at night to tuck her in, how her mother tried to hug her often but proved her true self by letting her be stubborn and whiny and willful and capricious and even a thrower of tantrums and a liar, never caring enough to scold or discipline her for her own good, protesting her love for her but always away when she was sick or frightened of lightning and then finally going away for good without even saying good-bye, proving absolutely her nonlove and then, not long afterward, her father telling her that her mother had died and her trying desperately to be good so that her father wouldn't also abandon her so that she would be like Oliver Twist or Heidi or Little Orphan Annie and wanting to hurl herself at her father's knees each time he prepared for a trip, wanting to beg him to take her along but holding it all inside for fear that her whining would drive him away for good like her mother, and when she misbehaved or failed to get a lesson perfect or committed unknown sins which upset her father how he invariably would sigh and say, "No wonder your mother left."

By the time Frederika had revealed this much, tears streamed down her face, tiny jewels of liquid that made her all the more vulnerable. Vincent could no longer use his questions and her answers to damp his excitement. Circling her back with his forearms, he swung around and deposited her atop the table, stoking furiously into her the instant her weight was supported, sawing back and forth until he was a blur between her bent-back legs, screaming out his climax with abandon and collapsing over her motionless body. When he had regained his breath, he withdrew and cleaned himself with her panties, coaxed her off the table with silent pressure, and placed her standing again before him.

While he recovered, DeVilbiss guided Frederika back in remembrance. Now, however, her words did not cascade out, but slowed from unending run-on phrases to sounder, discrete sentences. Her body had showed no signs of pleasure during the sex, and yet it seemed as if her mind had experienced a climactic release. She talked on, answering his questions, anticipating them, moving past, but not with the previous urgency. Her eyes were wide, as if she beheld some natural marvel.

Whenever her father was upset, Frederika repeated slowly, he would invariably sigh and say, "No wonder your mother left," but he never answered what it was about herself that caused her mother and father to act as they had. Her father refused to specify what had ultimately driven her mother away. She spoke deliberately and repeatedly about his words, recalling instance after instance of their use, until DeVilbiss realized that the mystery of her innate and unforgivable infant failings had become a pathetic *idée fixe*. Finally, in her thirteenth year, she weighed the prospects of loss against insanity and confronted her father, demanding to know what was wrong with her or what she had done and forgotten that both drove her mother away and made him so harsh and demanding with her. She demanded to know what it was about her that forced him to periodic flight, so that he would not have to leave her forever. He

278

replied that he left her only because of his job and that her difficult nature was something too complicated and technical to explain to a girl just entering adolescence. Instead, he promised faithfully to explain it all three years hence, when she had matured to her sixteenth birthday. Then he had promptly punished her effrontery by packing her off to a private school in Switzerland. He completed her punishment twelve months later by keeling over from a swift, fatal heart attack, fully two years before fulfilling his promise, leaving her spirit and mind imprisoned by an endlessly playing subconscious loop that told her she was fundamentally unworthy of love even from the two people on earth who should by all laws of nature have loved her simply because she was theirs. She spoke in flat, inflectionless tones, mirroring the void she felt. She despaired of joy, found no comfort in the men she conquered with her body and mind and no courage to attempt a platonic friendship, had despaired for so many years that she determined either to rend open the curtain dividing this sphere and the afterworld and demand of her father his answers or, failing that, to commit suicide and confront him face to face.

"And this is why you want me to reach your father," DeVilbiss said.

Frederika stared off into space, even though she looked directly into his eyes. "Yes."

"Enough!" DeVilbiss commanded. His expression was a grimace of distaste. Frederika's eyes and nose were bright pink from the truths she had unburied. Tears still weaved down her cheeks along well-laid channels. He tossed the panties on the table. "Bring me a glass of water, a teaspoon, and that jar filled with yellow powder. Be careful with the jar! And don't say another word! I'm tired of hearing you speak." Vincent had made too many mistakes already; he was not about to have Frederika make some innocent remark about the powder looking exactly like the stuff she was taking, in case Piccolo Niccolo dared daylight and listened as invisible voyeur. He scooped up the panty hose from the floor to clear her path to him, dropping them beside the panties. Frederika set the glass, the spoon, and the jar in front of DeVilbiss. He thumbed the stopper out of the jar.

DeVilbiss sighed dramatically. "Poor Frederika. Such a difficult youth. You've been seriously damaged. *Quel dommage!*" He chuckled at his pun. He turned and faced Frederika, who remained obediently silent. He rubbed his forefinger back and forth across her barely parted lips, shaking his head with a grave expression as he did. "Looking at this perfect facade, who would believe how tragically flawed the masterpiece is? But we'll get those scrolls and make it all better, won't we?" He glanced at the wall clock. Ten minutes until Simon Penn called again. "Come with me, *ma belle,*" he beckoned seductively, taking her by the hand when she failed to move. There was just enough time to take care of her before he concluded, revitalized, the bloody business of destroying the scrolls.

"That's all of it," Simon told Rich. He sat on the edge of the grad student's unmade bed, staring at the obliterated pattern in the oriental rug under his feet. "Now tell me I'm crazy."

Rich spat the gum he had been clacking for almost an hour in the direction of the trash basket. It struck a book, a landing place almost assured, since the tiny garret apartment was stuffed from floor to ceiling with reading materials, the sort that spoke in the international language of equations. The few areas of free wall space were covered with posters demanding democracy in mainland China and the famous photograph of the lone Chinese man defying the line of tanks in Tiananmen Square. Although he was Amerasian and born in the United States, Rich had a vocal affinity for his ancestral homeland. Everything but the bed, the posters, and the photo was coated with a layer of dust, and everything seemed—despite the torrid dryness of the attic rooms—to be stuck together. Rich adored his squalor.

"The guy who's crazy is this DeVilbiss," Rich declared. "Maybe he's deluded himself into thinking he's the real vampire from that British book. What he really is is a dangerous man . . . maybe a killer. He obviously thinks he can force you to help him steal some priceless scrolls by kidnapping your friend, and *that's bad enough* without bringing the supernatural into it. I'm a scientist, ferchrissake; I can't believe in anything like that."

Simon picked Willy's translation off the bed and handed it to Rich. "Okay. Well, do me this favor anyway." He dug into his wallet and pulled out two twenty-dollar bills. "Make several sets of photocopies. I don't have the time to dope out who should read them. You'll have to do that. Just mail off a bunch, to philologists, archeologists, people serious about the supernatural and the occult. But make sure one copy goes to Reverend Spencer's superior. I know you're a scientist, but try your best to write a cogent letter of explanation. Will you do all that?"

"Sure," Rich said, although he looked perplexed.

Having gotten one concession, Simon said, "I need something else from you."

The slight, bespectacled physicist set the translation on top of a pile of papers and folded his arms. "What?"

"In case this guy turns out to be a real monster, I need a surefire way to destroy him. Willy Spencer told me point blank he might not survive the holidays, and he didn't."

Rich grimaced. "You're willing to *murder* this guy, on the possibility he's a *vampire*?"

"Whatever he is," Simon affirmed, "he needs stopping."

The physicist scrunched up his face. "No way. I can't help you murder somebody. For one thing, I'm your friend; for the other, I might become an accessory."

Simon glanced at his watch. "Look, I'm gonna call him in a few minutes and arrange a meeting. Nine chances out of ten he'll be able to explain the weird stuff."

"Ten out of ten," Rich said.

"I hope so. We've got three minutes to kill. Let's see just how good a physicist you are. Purely hypothetically, if you were faced by a vampire how would you destroy it?"

Rich signaled his acceptance of the challenge by removing his glasses. "You said 'surefire.' Well . . . supernatural or not, if he operates in this world he's gotta be subject to physical laws. I'd do him in with thermodynamics."

"Specifically?"

"Trap him in a confined space and drop a thermite bomb on

him . . . you know, powdered aluminum and iron oxide. Toss a match and it'll reach a couple thousand degrees in a wink. Flambé the fucker."

"You're more dangerous than you look. But, just for argument's sake, let's say you could only trap him in a place too valuable to jeopardize with flame. Someplace like Firestone Library."

"Okay. Then opt for the other extreme: lower his temperature until he crystallizes. You've seen what happens to rubber balls when they're immersed in liquid nitrogen? I'd bathe him in seventy-eight degrees Kelvin for a minute, then whack him with a tire iron and watch him turn into ice cubes."

Simon stood to stretch his legs, moving to the unapologetically filthy window that looked through a barren oak's branches onto a junkheap of a backyard. "Where do you get liquid nitrogen?" he asked, noting through the window the brutal effects of mere natural cold.

"You couldn't. But I can. We've got several tanks of it down in the fabrication labs."

"Are they portable?"

"Well, sort of. They're heavy, but they're on dollies."

"But how would you get one out?"

Rich laughed. He brought his hands down from behind his neck and began gesticulating. He was evidently warming to his own idea. "Are you kidding? Security in the main part of the building is tight, but there's so much going on in the labs at all hours, loading in and out, that the emergency doors are propped open half the time. We let the alarms clang on and on. Campus Security treats us like the boys who cried wolf."

"It's time to call him," Simon said, unburying the telephone. Rich fixed his attention in a bird-dog attitude while Simon dialed.

"Vincent DeVilbiss," the plummy voice answered.

"What's the gift?" Simon asked.

"A fishing reel. Flycasting, I believe. Satisfied?"

"For the time being," Simon answered. "Now, let me understand this with absolute clarity: all you want are the scrolls."

"What I want is to meet with you in person," DeVilbiss said, pointedly. "No more telephone talk."

"Then we'd better meet soon," Simon told him. "The library closes tighter than a drum at five o'clock. Nobody but security gets inside after that."

"I've been outside far too much of late," DeVilbiss said. "The closest place you'd feel safe with me is the Catholic church at the top of my street."

"St. Paul's. When?"

"As soon as possible."

"Ten minutes," Simon answered. "But I warn you: I won't have my key with me."

"Ten minutes," DeVilbiss confirmed. "You alone. No hidden microphones either. If you involve the police, this will end unhappily for both of us." He disconnected.

Simon put down the phone and reached for his coat.

"I think you're wrong, man," Rich said. "I'd call in the cops and let them sweat where Frederika is out of him."

"Maybe after the meeting. In the meantime, would you get those copies made?"

"Right." Rich rose from his chair, then hesitated and looked sheepish. "Uh . . . I haven't been able to find the keys to my truck. Did you return that second set?"

"Sure. I put them on the windowsill a couple of days ago."

Rich got down on his knees and began searching through the rubble. "One of them's got to be here."

Simon slipped silently out the door.

St. Paul's pews were empty, but the church reverberated richly with the harmonies of sixteen singers, rehearsing Palestrina's *Missa Hodie Christus natus est* from the choir loft. A cherubic altar boy moved confidently around the ornate apse, replacing the candles for the Christmas Eve Masses.

Vincent waited in the shadows at the rear of the nave. His forefinger swished idly over the surface of the holy water filling a wall niche stone basin. His eyes moved not at all, riveted on the ten-foot-high wooden Christ on the central cross. His mind's eye focused on the even larger marble statue of St. Paul just outside the narthex. All the old saints' true features having been lost to the ages, Vincent had observed that their sculpted countenances took on a beatific sameness. And yet, eerily, the stone face of St. Paul looked identical to that of the St. Joseph that had spoken to him in the Vatican, as if in seeing this second sculpture he had finally come full circle. He assumed that this unnerving coincidence was responsible for the cold sweat he found himself bathed in.

Encountering the familiar statue was but one added element to the crowning irony of his life, Vincent reflected, as he stood once again under the shelter of God's house. The irony was the return of his faith that God cared about mankind. In 1503, very soon after he had become Undead, he was ordered to destroy the Venetian printed versions of a Latin manuscript supposedly copied from a Greek manuscript, taken from some ancient Akkadian scrolls, called *Physics* and *Metaphysics*. A few decades later, he learned that at least the Latin manuscript was genuine, as he had been directed to the house where one was located and told to destroy it and the family who owned it. Such stern measures to eliminate mere words had piqued Vincent's interest, to the point that he had skimmed one copy of the book. The *Physics* section was divided into forty-nine "evidences." To Vincent, it had seemed so much insanity. It began by stating that "God's language is numbers," followed by incomprehensible formulae. The descriptions touched on such topics as the nature of gravity, the roundness of the earth and other planets and their orbits around the sun, the elements from which the universe was built, and two notions that Vincent could never forget, precisely because of their impossibility. The first stated that time was a relative measurement; the second that the secret to all life and to its continuance was contained on infinitely small yet enormously long spiral ladders, which broke apart to reproduce themselves.

The second book, *Metaphysics,* contained an accounting of the creation of the universe and the world, far less picturesque than that in the Old Testament. Much of its body contained accounts of the nature of God's angels and their roles. Lucifer had been God's favorite but had rebelled and been confined to the realms of darkness, whence he visited trials and temptations upon God's living creatures. Vincent had read much the same cant in the Bible and credited it as primitive superstition, a way to fix the blame for all man's baser traits on a malevolent outside agency. The one section of *Metaphysics* he could not dismiss, however, was that which accurately described him and the pact he had made in order to gain unending life. In the years that followed his reading of the book, he had developed several theories. One was that the author was a crackpot who had heard about Vincent's kind or else had been befriended by one. Another was that the author was in fact identical to Vincent and, like him, had grown tired of serving an enemy of his race. Perhaps before ending his life, he had written the text as a warning to mankind. There had been no proof in those centuries of the writing's ancient origins. Such ideas as a round world and a heliocentric universe had been advanced by several thinkers before Vincent's time. One way or the other, it was all explicable with no divine authorship. The one thing Vincent was sure of in 1503 was that the Creator didn't give a damn about mankind or its salvation. The world and the Church proved that to him. Thus, evidences and warnings could be nothing more than a hoax, to fool those who desperately wanted to believe.

But then, over the centuries, more and more of the incomprehensible ideas of the *Metaphysics* section were proven. Vincent often wished he had saved a copy of the Manutius translation, because his exact memory of the writing had grown so vague. Nevertheless, he retained enough to prove to him the intent of the forty-nine evidences. They, like the Ten Commandments blasted into the tablets on Mount Sinai, were tangible evidence of the laws of the universe—proof behind the invisible, infinite intelligence of the Creator.

Vincent was precisely a hundred years old when William Shakespeare was born. If in his 'youth' he had read the genius's works, he would have made a pilgrimage to Stratford. But Vincent had not learned English until the end of the eighteenth century. Even as soon after Shakespeare's death as that, scholars were doubting the man's authorship of many writings. Yet once Vincent truly knew the English language, he knew Shakespeare's handiwork whenever he saw it. Reading with painstaking deliberation, given his handicap with the language, he came to recognize the Bard's inimitable stamp, his sorcerer's magic at combining simple words into powerful images, using the laws of meter, rhyme, simile, and metaphor to the purpose of his immortal creations. His belief in Shakespeare the author could not be shaken.

And so it was with the evidence of *Metaphysics*. For more than three hundred years Vincent had stubbornly held to the argument he deceitfully offered Willy Spencer: that invisible creatures who feared man shared earth but on another plane of the senses. Bizarre as it had been, it at least involved no demons, no angels, no God. Then, slowly, Vincent realized that both parts of the scrolls told the truth. And that these scrolls were no less than a Third Testament. Raised as scholar and priest, his Latin had never failed him. *Testamentum* meant nothing less than a covenant from God to man. The translations Vincent had so dutifully destroyed were copies of a companion to the Old and New Testaments, more important by far than the Dead Sea scrolls. In the first scroll, God's existence had been indirectly proven; in the second, by extension, the existence of Satan and his minions.

Ironically, the advances of science that led to the duplication of Vincent's elixir and hence his freedom were the same advances that verified *Metaphysics*. Immutable, mathematical laws (God's language) proved a never-completely-forsworn belief on Vincent's part that, even given the eons since the beginning of time, nothing so wondrous as this world could have evolved by chance.

Yet even though he once more believed that God cared about mankind, DeVilbiss would destroy the scrolls (after looking on them for the first and last time). The New Testament of the Christians promised eternal life to the faithful; the Old Testament of the Hebrews only occasionally hinted at it; the Third Testament promised nothing. The fact that God existed and cared did not in itself assure that He would grant man immortal life any sooner than He would to a crab. And even if He might, after all these centuries of Vincent having served "the Ancient Foe," would He forgive one who had sinned far beyond seventy times seven? In the end, despite everything else, the love of life won out over faith.

Vincent wiped the holy water off on his pant legs.

An aisle door from the narthex opened. Simon entered the nave, aware of the choir singing above and behind him. When he looked down, he found himself directly in front of the niche where DeVilbiss waited. He sprang back, uttering a small gasp.

"Don't worry; I won't bite." DeVilbiss smiled broadly. "Not you anyway." He wore a tweed sports jacket and a plaid bow tie.

Simon was not reassured by the calculated Caspar Milquetoast costume. He kept his right hand deep in his coat pocket, wrapped around a metal cross he had just purchased. "All you want are the scrolls," Simon stated, once more.

"Isn't that enough?"

Simon took a step back, bumping into the pew behind him. "I don't give a damn about them," he asserted. "But you won't get them without my cooperation, and I won't help you until Frederika's free."

DeVilbiss was sizing him up, even as Simon did the same. "I understand the bargain. How do you suggest it be completed?"

"You say she's nearby?"

"Near enough."

"I have a friend who'll pick her up."

An old woman entered the nave, pushed past DeVilbiss and took a sprinkling of holy water. She moved to the end of the back pew, genuflected and sat. DeVilbiss nodded toward the altar and began walking. Simon followed, through the softened shafts of stained-glass sunlight. He noted a pale scar at the rear of DeVilbiss's jaw, a blemishing bubble of flesh he was sure had not been there the last time he had seen the man.

"You've got to get inside the library before four-thirty," Simon instructed as he walked. "Do you have an access card?"

"Yes."

"Pass through the turnstile. Someone will come in through the employees' entrance and go out the front for me, so the exit count agrees."

"Is it so strictly watched?" DeVilbiss asked over his shoulder.

"It is now," Simon said, "thanks to you." He realized that the conversation could be turned to a tactical advantage, even while he was reminded of DeVilbiss's sensitive eyes, seeing them squinted almost shut against the soft natural light. "Go down to B floor and find Room B9F. I'll be sure it's open. Lock yourself inside and wait until I call to say all is clear. There's a telephone on the desk."

DeVilbiss moved into the front pews' shadows, near the outside wall, pivoted the movable kneeler up and slid along the pew, leaving ample room for Simon. "Continue," he said.

Simon glanced up at the huge central cross, while the sixteen voices filled the vaulted space with the glorious sounds of the *Credo*. He envisioned a vast graveyard of crosses, created by the murderous acts of the man beside him. Unbidden, the familiar but spectral face of the night guard, Tommy Wheeler, floated into his memory.

"Thanks to you, the security at the library's been doubled," Simon reported. "They suspect a link between the deaths of the security guard and Reverend Spencer, done by somebody determined to steal the treasures of the Schickner Collection." He saw no sign of incredulity on DeVilbiss's face, so he embellished his lie. "It's valued at over twenty million dollars, and there's been a rash of university library thefts all over the country. I assume you've read about them."

DeVilbiss nodded. "My bad luck."

"I saw the schedule of security's rounds for the holiday," Simon lied. "We'll have one full hour after closing when nobody's inside."

"Plenty of time."

"Not if Frederika isn't in town," Simon countered. "I'll telephone you in B9F right after closing. You give me her location. I telephone my friend. He gets her and calls me. I call you, then let you get to the scrolls."

"No," DeVilbiss said firmly. "I'll find my own hiding place. At five after five I come up to your section door. I'll tell you where she

288

is. *Then* you call your friend. It'll save time and telephones ringing inside the building."

Simon recalculated furiously. Storage Room B9F had been well known to him. For some reason, when its door was completely closed from the inside it couldn't be reopened. He had learned the fact the hard way, two months earlier. After ten minutes of yelling for help, he had climbed on the desktop and used his Swiss army knife's screwdriver to remove the return air grate. Plenty of light came through the grate slits from the room directly across the air duct. The other room was entered from the stair landing between Levels A and B, six feet higher than B9F. Simon had climbed through the opening easily and escaped through the upper room. His plan against DeVilbiss had been to somehow get a liquid nitrogen tank into the adjacent upper room and let DeVilbiss isolate himself in B9F. As soon as the library closed he would have kicked out the grate and hosed the monster into nonexistence, worrying what to do with the body once it had proven vulnerable. Now he could think of no good reason why DeVilbiss had to conceal himself in that one particular place.

"All right," Simon agreed. "But come up by one of the two back elevators. They'll have the stairs blocked off."

"You're a bright young man, Mr. Penn," DeVilbiss said. "I've faced brilliant men in my lifetime and never been defeated. My lifetime, of course, is a staggering span. Cross me . . . and you, Frederika, and your library will suffer the most dire consequences."

"This is all so pointless," Simon replied. "Reverend Spencer sent copies of his translation all over the world."

"The preliminary scribbles of a dead scholar are meaningless without the actual scrolls," DeVilbiss countered, closing his eyes. "Especially when he's translated so little of the work. Besides, I'm not free to walk away. You must understand that."

"You say your lifetime is a staggering span," Simon said, carefully. "Exactly how staggering is it?"

DeVilbiss smiled. "However long it's been, it's just beginning. Leave me now, please; I have meditating to do."

After the young librarian had gone, Vincent's lips moved for a minute without sound. His head sank slowly into a bowed posture. The singers began the polyphonic *Agnus Dei*—"Lamb of God, who takes away the sin of the world, have mercy on us." Vincent had heard the work only one other time, when Palestrina himself had conducted it in the Julian Chapel. The composer was dead almost four hundred years, but his work lived on, as did mankind's cry for mercy. Vincent realized that, without thinking, he had begun to recite the prayer. Lips frozen in mid-word, he fled from God's house.

The chromed steel cabinet surface gleamed coldly in Simon's shifting perspective. He stepped slowly around it, staring at the scrolls resting below the double thickness of shatterproof Plexiglas. He thought of the Constitution of the United States of America, sealed inside a similar cabinet down in Washington, D.C. Considering the message of the scrolls and mankind's ignorance of their earthshaking revelations, the elaborate security measures seemed not so ridiculous after all. Simon realized that he was staring at the compass capable of reorienting the world's direction back to God. The scrolls had to survive.

Simon watched the wall clock's red hand sweep away seconds of his life, dragging the minute hand inexorably up to twelve. Among the curiosities that had passed through the Rare Manuscripts Preparation section was an 1818 Bible the pages of which had been hollowed out to create a hiding place for a wealthy drug user's stash. Simon had claimed the ruined book for his desk but had never put it to use. He checked one last time to be sure the security system key rested inside it and squeezed the book back into a line of reference works.

Faintly, from beyond the room, came the loudspeaker announcement that the library closed in five minutes. He felt a sudden desire to pick up the phone and call Ohio, hear the voices of his family and tell them that he loved them. In the same moment he wanted to join his fellow librarians in a final holiday rush from the building. He could do neither. He locked the section up tightly, walked to the rear pair of elevators and pressed the UP button.

The righthand elevator arrived. Simon entered and studied the full bank of buttons—the above-ground Main, 2, 3, and 4 and below-ground A, B, and C. As soon as the doors closed he got his feet on two of the handrails, lifted the emergency escape hatch and wriggled through. Already atop the elevator roof sat the capsule-shaped liquid nitrogen tank and hosing equipment. He had used the unreturned set of keys to drive Rich's pickup to the physics labs and transport the weapon Rich had so innocently suggested. When he rolled the tank into the library receiving section, he silenced his lone challenger by declaring that the tank resupplied inert gas to the rare manuscript containers.

In his undergraduate days, Simon had become adept at "elevator surfing"—a risky sport involving leaps from the roof of one moving elevator car to another, with side diversions of using the auxiliary roof controls to stop cars from above and trap unwary riders inside, sometimes water-ballooning them through the emergency hatch. Simon had resurrected his skill at cracking the elevator doors to load the tank.

At precisely five minutes after five o'clock, Simon used its roof controls to stop the other elevator of the pair on A Level, then rode his car up to the main floor. When the lift mechanism stopped and the hollow echoes died away, the shaft lapsed into an ominous silence, punctuated only by occasional moans of air descending from the winch room. Simon slipped into his coat, loaded its pockets with equipment and tugged on one of the insulated mitts tied to the top of the tank. He opened the tank valves and braced himself against the elevator's sudden start-up. Although his eyes had ample time to adjust to the darkness, he could barely see. Little natural light penetrated from the rooftop machine room, as the sun had almost set. He reached into one of his coat's generous pockets for a tool borrowed from Rich's truck. It was a hand spotlight, an instrument that Rich assured him threw as much candlepower as a 747 jet's main landing light. Its tungsten bulb was powered by a series of nickel cadmium batteries, and it was encased in ABS plastic, which Rich swore could withstand the wheels of a Mack truck. Simon thumbed on the switch and directed the spotlight up through four stories of shaft. No sounds other than the sough of the wind came to him. Vast as the library was and peopled virtually twenty-four hours a day, this night of all the year was the one when the building might be unoccupied for hours. Despite his words to DeVilbiss he had heard nothing of doubled guard rounds, doubted if anyone would patrol the floors until midnight. He might as well have been facing his adversary in a dark, uninhabited space station a hundred miles above the earth. He turned off the light and tucked it back into his pocket.

Simon waited patiently for what he judged to be three minutes, with impatience for another minute, anxiety the next and finally frozen panic, able to hear the pounding of his heart within the silence. He forced himself to review the facts he knew about his opponent. DeVilbiss could see in near-total darkness. He was swift. He was strong. But he could be wounded. Both the magician's biography and the fresh scar on his cheek—probably inflicted by Willy Spencer—proved it. He healed in time, but perhaps not quickly enough to survive an overwhelming attack, with a weapon such as liquid only 78 degrees above absolute zero.

Simon was forced from his thoughts by several muffled pops like those from an air pistol, and by the crunching of something brittle. He knew the sounds were unusual and therefore ominous. Before he could place the noises or decide how to react, his elevator plunged downward, responding to a call.

Simon lowered his center of gravity and groped blindly for the hose attached to the tank. He watched the doors rise in front of him—Main, A, and B. The elevator bottomed at C. He heard the doors open. The floor creaked. The doors closed, and the elevator began to rise. Simon let B doors pass, then A. When Main came almost in line with the elevator roof he stabbed the emergency cutoff switch down, bringing the machine to a groaning stop. He transferred the hose to his mitted hand and threw back the emergency hatch.

Simon saw no one.

He angled around, to take the back of the car into view, the trigger already half depressed. The elevator stood empty. DeVilbiss's words echoed mockingly in his head: *brilliant men in his time, and never defeated*. Simon's legs jellied. Could the vampire have reversed the roles of prey and hunter so quickly?

From below came the buzz of someone summoning a car. The relays clicked impotently. Simon flicked the power switch back on. But his elevator, instead of descending, continued to climb, past Floors One, Two, and Three. So DeVilbiss was acting offensively; he had purposely sent Simon's car to the top of the building, planning to take the second elevator in case Simon had boobytrapped the first.

The doors opened on Floor Four, shut almost as quickly, and the car plunged downward again, straight toward the jaws of Hell. Simon sidled to the edge of the car's roof, eyes straining to make out the second elevator—the one he had earlier disabled. Its dark shape emerged from the blackness. He hopped onto it, slightly unbalanced by the bulk and weight of his coat, catching the cable for safety's sake. He unlocked the mechanism and sent the second car shooting down in pursuit of the one holding the nitrogen tank. The first car had stopped at C Level. Simon halted his car two feet higher, before it had aligned with the floor, making it impossible for DeVilbiss to open its outer doors. Simon reasoned that this would leave DeVilbiss only one path if he wanted to get inside the shaft—he would have to come up through the first car's emergency hatch. Simon hopped down onto that car's roof now, as lightly as he could, and searched out the liquid nitrogen nozzle. The car beneath him rattled periodically, revealing that DeVilbiss had shoved something substantial into the path of its automatic doors, making them open and half-close over and over, imprisoning the car in place.

Simon prayed for the opportunity to shoot one long, immobilizing spray into DeVilbiss's face, so he could methodically hose him into oblivion. His hands were palsied as he waited, feeling the seconds piling up into yet another impotent minute. A new noise vibrated through the shaft. It had the same timbre as that of the elevator doors, but its sound was continuous rather than periodic.

Simon knew the meaning of the sound; DeVilbiss was struggling to pry open the second elevator's C-Level outer doors. Despite even the vampire's supernatural strength, Simon relied on the system defeating him. With the elevator stopped too high, the immediately adjacent doors locked the same way file cabinet drawers did when one of their number was opened, to prevent accidents. Simon and three other hearty sophomores had once failed at the same maneuver. He dropped the hose and stood. As he straightened, his ears told him the noise sounded not from the C-Level doors but from those on B—a set of doors that would allow DeVilbiss through.

There was no time to wrestle with the heavy tank. Gasping out his terror, Simon leapt back up onto the higher elevator, unlocked it and punched the Main Floor button. It started smoothly upward. Just above him, the B-Level outer doors were being wrested apart. From out of darkness emerged the blacker shape of DeVilbiss as he fought the doors. As his elevator continued upward, Simon swung around behind the cables. An arm thrust through the door opening into the shaft, catching the hem of Simon's coat, threatening to rip him from his perch. Simon hugged the cable and kicked out blindly at the hand. He missed, but the roof of the rising elevator saved him, forcing DeVilbiss to release his hold. Simon listened to the outer doors bang shut again, accompanied by no outcry of pain or rage. The elevator reached, then stopped at the Main Floor. His brain seethed with life-or-death calculations. He lifted the hatch and jumped down, landing awkwardly and crumpling to the floor.

As Simon came up, his hand punched at the Floor Three button. Before the doors began to close, he dashed out and toward the side entrance to the Rare Manuscripts Preparation section, hand digging for keys as he went. Each slap of his foot on the oak floor sounded like a cannon shot to him. He reached the unmarked double doors, grabbed one of the knobs to stop his momentum, and stabbed the key into the lock. Throwing back the door, he was confronted by the illuminated button system that controlled the metal gate. He pushed the red button once, the green button twice, the yellow button once. The gate popped open. Simon swung past and slammed it closed. It latched in place a split second before an inky form hurtled into it, making it clatter raucously. The steel mesh bent slightly inward, but the thicker bars were unaffected and the lock tongue held fast.

Simon stood wide-eyed and riveted to the floor, betting his existence on the door's strength. DeVilbiss threw himself against the gate again, then laced his fingers into the woven metal and yanked backward. It gave only so much, then held firm.

DeVilbiss released his grip, refocused on Simon and took two steps backward. His dress was uniformly black, from leather jacket, to turtleneck sweater, to woolen pants, to what looked like crepe-soled espadrilles. He sucked in several short breaths, followed by one large one, drew himself up very straight and folded his arms across his chest.

"This is so stupid," DeVilbiss declared. "If the Reverend Spencer had handed me his key he'd be alive right now. I didn't want his blood on my hands; I don't want yours. All I want are those damned scrolls." Simon glowered at him in silence. "You tried to kill me," Vincent went on. "So would I have in your place. But you failed. We must go on with our original agreement. It's the only way Frederika will live."

"Go to hell," Simon said.

DeVilbiss lowered his arms. "Those were Spencer's last words." He backed into the darkness until it swallowed him. Simon dared to bring himself close to the gate, but he could not see far around the outer door. Nor could he hear anything.

Simon retreated down the storage passageway, into the section's main room. He had hoped to save Frederika but conceded that he would be more than fortunate if he could save himself and the scrolls. Switching on lights as he passed, he hurried to his desk. He lifted the telephone handset, to call security.

The phone was dead. Simon sprinted to the only other phone in the room. It also had no dial tone. He took the cut lines as proof that DeVilbiss had no intention of letting him live. Isolated in the virtual inner sanctum of the library, he had no windows to break, no grates he could remove for easy escape. He looked up to the high ceiling. Across the length of the room ran two sprinkler pipes. If he got a flame close enough to one of the heads, he believed the fire alarm would be tripped. But he had no means. He did not smoke and, fire being the great enemy of books, matches and lighters were never left around. He wracked his brain for some way to create a spark.

From beyond the main door to the section came deep, vibrating noises. Simon was not particularly worried about that direction, as DeVilbiss would have to penetrate a set of thick oak doors and another wire gate before invading that way. But as he listened, Simon realized the significance of the sound. The old card catalog cabinets stood just outside the doors. Any one of them, filled with thousands of oaktag cards, had to weigh at least a ton. DeVilbiss was moving a cabinet to block the door, denying Simon any avenue of escape but the doors through which he had entered.

While the heavy scraping sounds continued, Simon rushed across the room and down the corridor to the side door. He hit the inner access buttons in sequence, releasing the gate. He could have saved precious seconds, in fact might have guaranteed his escape, by leaving the gate open and the scrolls unprotected, but he had judged their worth to mankind and could not bring himself to sacrifice them. There was no way to lock the gate without making noise. He prayed it could not be heard around several corners, even by superhuman ears. He yanked it closed behind him and ran for the back stairwell.

As soon as Simon pulled open the heavy metal fire door to the stairwell he knew what the strange popping and crunching sounds had been. DeVilbiss had knocked out lights, determined to increase his advantage if Simon tried to get out that way. The noises he had heard in the elevator shaft could not have reached him from this stairwell. Evidently, DeVilbiss had blackened the entire path to the loading dock, Simon's only reasonable means of escape. The stairwell loomed dark as obsidian beyond the feeble illumination from the Exhibition Hallway.

Simon took the spotlight from his pocket and thumbed it on. The stairwell filled with light as if a magnesium flare had been lit. Simon rushed down one flight and threw open the next door.

DeVilbiss stood in the hallway, waiting. His evil smile of triumph vanished when he saw the spotlight. He threw himself toward Simon.

Simon swung the light upward, directly at DeVilbiss's eyes. As the Undead one rushed at him with frightful speed, he held the light in the same place but jumped suddenly to the side, as would a bullfighter. DeVilbiss stumbled blindly forward, arms outthrust to bat away the instrument that apparently inflicted so much pain. A split second before he reached the light, Simon yanked it away. DeVilbiss, finding no solid body in his path and knowing instinctively that the stairs lay directly ahead, attempted to halt his headlong dash. For a moment, he teetered precariously on the lip of the first step. Then Simon's foot found his rear end, and he hurtled blindly downward, crumpling as he went, striking his head and arms hard.

Simon did not wait to assess the damage. He lowered his shoulder to the closing fire door and muscled through, increasing his speed as he drove it back, thrusting the light ahead of him into the darkness. He played the beam down the length of the corridor, did a quick calculation of how long it would take him to escape the building, and made a righthand turn down one of the twenty or so rows of shelves between himself and the far wall, moving away from the loading dock. The row was less than thirty feet long. Only when he had run its full length did he switch off the light, concealing himself in absolute blackness.

The B-Level stairwell door burst open, striking the wall with force. In the absence of light, the noise seemed magnified greatly. Simon shuddered but refused to be shocked into paralysis. He repocketed the light, then removed both shoes. Clutching them in his right hand, he used his left to guide himself along the wall, doubling back in the direction of the library's center. He knew the vampire had hypersensitive eyes, but he hoped no creature, superhuman or otherwise, could see in such total absence of light. He moved slowly but steadily, skimming his feet along the cool surface of the concrete floor.

DeVilbiss gave out one howl of rage, then lapsed into silence. Although he also sought to move with silent stealth, he neglected to remove his shoes. Simon caught their passing along the far end of the

297

row, moving toward the loading dock. Simon continued slowly but steadily in the opposite direction, picturing the area in his mind's eye, reorienting himself when a door appeared sooner than expected in the wall. Some fifty feet ahead, around a corner, the farthest spill of a single lightbulb created dim shapes in the tenebrous surroundings. Simon headed for the light, moving with ever-greater assurance. He had lost DeVilbiss's position in the library. For all he knew, the vampire was just then hurtling noiselessly toward his back. His skin crawled with the idea, but he pushed steadily toward the light without turning.

Simon reached the end of the rows, where a large corridor ran at a right angle to his path, across the middle of the library. He turned right and edged along one book-filled set of shelves, until he was confronted by a yawning and well-lit intersection. On the opposite side lay a door and, beyond it, the central staircase. Simon drew in a deep breath and stepped into the open. He looked right, into the blackness leading to the loading dock entrance. From far down its length, faint footfalls raced in his direction.

Simon sprinted toward the central staircase, pulling a book re-shelving cart into the opening as he passed. He took the cold marble steps two at a time, swinging wildly around the turn, bursting into the library's grand foyer, leaping the turnstile, skittering around the corner into the Exhibitions area, zigzagging around the exhibit cases with the assurance of long acquaintance, finding the Rare Manuscripts side door with no trouble, stabbing at the sequence of buttons, charging through the gate and slamming it shut.

Again, less than two seconds behind, DeVilbiss threw his weight against the gate. This time he hung on, shaking it like a great ape outraged at capture. Getting no farther than he had the previous time, DeVilbiss stepped back. Simon noted that he no longer wore his leather jacket. His black turtleneck sweater had ridden up slightly in front, exposing what looked like a quilted fencer's chest protector beneath. With affected dignity, he stood erect and straightened his clothing. A goose egg bump swelled prominently from his right temple.

Simon looked at the luminescent hands on his wristwatch, then

298

through the wire mesh at DeVilbiss. "Half an hour gone and you're still outside. A security patrol will come through in a few minutes," he bluffed. "Five minutes after that, half the police in Princeton will be in here." As he said his final words, he withdrew the spotlight and shone it on DeVilbiss's face.

DeVilbiss took a step backward and shielded his eyes. "You're a fool, Penn."

"I know," Simon agreed. "But there's no fool like an old fool, and there's no one older than you." He angled the light away and saw in the reflected light that, considering his insult, DeVilbiss's expression was remarkably calm.

"You may be right," the vampire said. And then he vanished into the darkness.

Simon stood for a moment, shining the light into the empty Exhibitions area. His words might have frightened DeVilbiss out of the building, but he could not take the chance. He had to remain in the Rare Manuscripts Preparation area until help came, defending his position however he could. He dropped his shoes and scudded his feet into them. Then he backed down the wire-mesh-lined corridor, repocketing his spotlight as he came into the room's full brightness. Attached to his keys was his old Swiss army knife. He took it out and exposed the larger blade. It looked puny in his hand. He glanced around the room for something potentially more lethal. His eyes fell upon a long-handled push broom, leaning in a shadowy corner. He stepped on the broom bottom and twisted the five-foot handle out of its socket. The wood was dense, probably oak. He began whittling the upper end, shaving off curling pieces. Within five minutes, he had fashioned a good, conical point.

As Simon looked around, to expand his arsenal, he heard a deep, resounding clang from the Exhibitions area. He set the makeshift lance upright against the end of the mesh corridor and moved toward the door to investigate.

DeVilbiss turned into the door's alcove, holding a hose in one hand and the cryogenic tank in the other. He smiled as he had when Simon opened the B-Level door.

"Turnabout is fair play, Penn." When Simon made no reply, he said, "One last chance. We have between us the keys necessary to open the scroll cabinet. Let me in and use your key, and I promise I'll let you go. I truly shall."

"Truly?"

DeVilbiss sighed. "We shall discover the depth of your pluck once I've breached this gate."

"The scrolls will still be locked up," Simon reminded him.

DeVilbiss raised the hose and curled his finger around the trigger. "One challenge at a time." He released the liquid nitrogen. A white cloud enveloped the gate. Metal groaned from superfast contraction. Simon retreated to the end of the corridor. DeVilbiss paused his spraying for a moment and kicked at the gate. Chunks of white mesh burst away and skidded down the corridor. He had created half the opening he needed to pass inside. He lifted the hose again and fired the liquid at the metal. An icy, masking fog rose again.

Simon took his lance in both hands and moved toward the crumbling gate. He could see virtually nothing of DeVilbiss as he advanced. He paused ten feet from the gate and waited. Finally, the hissing spray stopped. Simon charged, lance lowered. By the time he reached the gate, the fog had dissipated enough so that he could make out the black form beyond. DeVilbiss already had one leg lifted, to kick out the last of the mesh. Simon aimed below the place where he had seen the quilted vest, trying to catch DeVilbiss just below his navel. Instead, he speared the crease between thigh and torso, ramming through until the oak point collided with hip bone.

Screaming, DeVilbiss collapsed backward through the ruined gate. The buried lance arched toward the ceiling. Simon retreated several steps, hardly able to believe he was capable of such violence, even to defend his life. DeVilbiss rolled slowly from side to side in his agony, then lay quietly in the dissipating nitrogen fog. Simon held his ground, waiting. It was too much to hope that he had defeated DeVilbiss with a simple piece of wood. He saw a pooling of blood under the man's thigh and felt simultaneously revolted and elated, until DeVilbiss reached to the lance with both hands and yanked it out of his flesh, moaning deeply as he did.

Simon fell back farther as DeVilbiss first sat up, then pulled himself into a stooped position, using the broom handle for support. The pointed end, aloft, showed darkly stained with blood. Unbelievably, DeVilbiss took a small step, then another. Simon backed into the Rare Manuscripts Preparation chamber. His adversary pursued on his makeshift crutch, almost as quickly.

"Better regroup and attack right now," DeVilbiss mocked. "I won't be completely healed for minutes."

Simon's back collided with the stainless steel coffin that held the scrolls. He spun around it and hastened to the far end of the room, to heed DeVilbiss's admonition. While he searched frantically for another weapon, DeVilbiss reached the sealed steel cabinet. He peered through the Plexiglas.

"So this is the cause of all my trouble," DeVilbiss said. He looked up at Simon, his face seeming, impossibly, paler. "You know, for all the centuries they've plagued me, I've never seen them before."

Simon glanced down from DeVilbiss's chalky countenance to the floor. The vampire's path to the scrolls had been traced by a stream of blood. Around his left leg formed a widening red pool.

DeVilbiss followed Simon's eyes downward. He looked calmly at the wound area. But then he turned and saw the size of the red trail, and his eyes went wide with horror. He dropped the broom handle and grabbed hold of the steel cabinet, to keep himself from falling. Laboriously, he lowered himself to the floor. The side of the metal cabinet where his dark trousers had touched was beaded in scarlet. DeVilbiss grabbed his left pantleg with both hands and ripped it open at the crotch, exposing his wound. A spray of blood spurted from it with each beat of his heart. He pressed his hand hard to the spot, but it continued to seep through his fingers. He looked up at Simon and gave out a tiny, bitter laugh.

"I had a bad feeling about you all along," he said. His jaw hung slack as he gasped for air, like a fish out of water.

"I must have hit your femoral artery," Simon said quietly. "Nothing can stop the bleeding."

"A tourniquet . . . high on my leg?"

"The wound's mostly in your torso. It wouldn't help."

DeVilbiss's amber eyes flashed up at Simon. His jaw regained its tension. "They took out the healing factor. But my body must have residual strength." He lifted his hand for a moment. The blood spurted as vigorously as before. "It will staunch soon. It must!" He looked suddenly again at Simon. "You have to save me."

"What?"

"We're on the same side, dammit!" He gestured at the trail of blood. "This proves it."

"I . . . don't . . ."

DeVilbiss inclined himself urgently toward Simon. "You saw what the reverend translated."

"Yes."

"Then you read about the demons who control me. The landlords of Hell?"

"Yes, but—"

"I'm their unwilling slave." His words tumbled out now. "I don't just drink blood to live. They supplied me with a powder that kept me young and invincible. As long as I obeyed them."

Simon's brow unwrinkled. "The glass jars in the kitchen."

"Exactly. They've discovered my treachery and abandoned me. The last delivery had no invulnerability." He touched the scar on the back of his jaw. "Your friend, the reverend, gave me this. Shot me with a silver-coated bullet. I thought the superstition must be right, but silver had nothing to do with it. My infernal lords took the invulnerability factor out. *You must understand.* This *proves* I'm no longer on their side." He groped into his pants pocket. "But I've got good powder . . . in my car." He held up the keys. "Get it for me!"

Simon stood his ground. He couldn't push from his mind the images of Tommy Wheeler, Professor Gerstadt, and Willy Spencer.

Reading Simon's face, DeVilbiss clawed himself up to a standing position. He took two steps toward the exit and fell. He crawled several yards through his blood, until he was forced to accept the futility of escaping the room. He rolled over onto his back and stared up at the ceiling.

"Where's Frederika?" Simon demanded.

DeVilbiss laughed. "You should worry about yourself. Forget

the scrolls and the girl. Run as fast and as far as you can, and hide until the scrolls are destroyed."

"I can't let that happen. If you're really on my side, tell me what I need to do to survive."

"After you've murdered me? Give me a better reason."

Only DeVilbiss's lips moved. His body was stretched out as if on a bier, with one hand at his side, the other still pressed to the bleeding wound. His eyes fixed, unblinking, on Simon; his chest barely rose and fell. Looking at this man who appeared dead, who by all rights should have died centuries before, Simon had difficulty framing his reply.

"Revenge, then."

"What will I care about revenge in half an hour?"

Simon dropped his arms impotently against his side. "That's all I can do for you."

DeVilbiss's eyebrows rose slightly, and a strange look of calm came to him. "Perhaps not. You realize what the scrolls are worth to mankind."

"Yes."

"So, you've appointed yourself their guardian, little man. If that's the case, then you must remove them from here and have them translated. Very few people possess such skills. Every one of them will be watched." DeVilbiss sat up with effort and tore off his turtleneck.

"Tell me where Frederika is before you pass out! You don't have much time."

"I . . . am the expert at bloodletting," Vincent growled. "I will inform you when my time has come. Now listen!" He ripped open the Velcro fasteners that held the bulletproof vest in place, at the same time muttering, "Useless thing. You'll need to travel and to leave no trace with credit cards. I have money in the trunk of my rented car." He took the keychain from around his neck. "And I . . . I kept diaries. They'll tell you about how I killed, and my powers, so you'll be prepared to face others like me. Also . . . what I learned about the Dark Forces." DeVilbiss's eyelids fluttered

303

briefly. "My current diary is also in the car trunk. It's . . . in code . . . based on that day's headline of the most important newspaper in the . . . the country where I was at the time. You understand?"

Simon nodded vigorously, wanting the man to impart as much as possible.

"You're smart; you'll figure it out. You see, one key is same as yours. Reverend's . . . to the security system. The others are to safe deposit boxes. Amalgamated Eurobanque and Credit Banque de Suisse, both in Zurich. Code numbers are engraved on the keys. You can learn to forge my signature from . . . my passport. It's also in . . . car trunk."

Simon was aware of the continuous growth of the blood pool around DeVilbiss. He watched anxiously as the man's eyelids fluttered and his eyes rolled upward. "Stay with me!" he shouted.

DeVilbiss jerked alert.

"It will take time to get your diaries and read them," Simon said. "Tell me the demons' weaknesses!"

"Can't be in light."

"That's in the scrolls. What else?"

DeVilbiss shook his head. "Don't know."

"What? After centuries? Maybe I *should* just run."

"No!" DeVilbiss thrust the keys outward.

Simon made no effort to take them.

"Fool. Don't you realize you have no choice? Your only salvation is to get the scrolls published and believed. As long . . . as you are one of the few who know what they contain, you have a . . . death sentence on your head. You must act." He pushed the keys the full length of his reach.

Simon took them with a wary snatch.

DeVilbiss lay back, into his blood. "Good."

"Why should this mean so much to you?"

A sly grin curled DeVilbiss's bluish lips. "Because part of me will still be immortal. If you succeed in passing this gospel on, it will be through my help. My memory . . . will live on . . . blessed . . . like St. Francis. Like Schweitzer. And He will forgive."

The apparent non sequitur convinced Simon that DeVilbiss's

brain was becoming oxygen-starved. "Where is Frederika?" he asked, urgently.

"Do you know the last rites?"

Simon humored the bizarre question. "No. I'm Protestant."

"It's all right. Just witness this." Forcing his eyelids open but staring at nothing, he began mumbling Latin rapidly to himself.

Simon refrained from asking how this servant of Satan not only believed in God but also knew a sacrament of the Catholic church from memory. It would all have to be pieced together, once he, Frederika, and the scrolls were safe. He dug into his pocket and handed his newly purchased cross to Vincent, who seemed grateful to receive it. Vincent clutched it to his chest. His lips barely moved; his face had become the color of paraffin.

"Vincent." Simon knelt and fixed the dying man's eyes with his. "It's time. Tell me where Frederika is."

DeVilbiss's head lolled back and forth slowly. "Too late to save her. She's been sentenced . . . like me and you. When I don't return with the scrolls, they'll kill her. If they let her go, she'd remember too much, even if someone . . . broke my hypnotic spell."

"Where is she?"

Vincent looked abruptly alarmed, and Simon thought he had felt his final pain. Instead, DeVilbiss said, "Your old girlfriend. I tied her up in her house. Left her back door open so she could be rescued."

"Fine. I'll see that she's safe. Where's Frederika?"

"So *cold,*" Vincent murmured, now trembling all over. "This is what they all felt." He lifted his hand from the large wound. The spurting had stopped; only the faintest welling of blood remained.

"Frederika," Simon insisted.

Vincent sighed. "The basement . . . of the house."

"The house you rented?"

Vincent nodded.

"What words will release her from your hypnosis?"

Vincent struggled to recall. " 'Your . . . your lost teddy bear.' But don't go inside without the police. She's doomed. You will be, too, if you go alone." His hand rolled off his stomach onto the floor. "My death . . . my own fault. Hope . . . turned me human again.

305

Compassion is not weakness, as long as He cares. His mercy will save . . . even me." A spasm shook his chest. He looked directly at Simon. "I told you I knew when." His breath came out softly, once. His chest stopped moving.

Simon put his hand to the white neck and felt for a pulse. DeVilbiss was as cold as the marble floor. Simon reached up and closed the fixed eyes. He wiped the blood on the turtleneck and looked around, thinking hard. Wincing at the ghoulish act, he checked DeVilbiss's pants pocket and found a wallet. Then, patting his own coat to be sure of the spotlight, and checking his pants for his knife, he moved toward the side door. He wrestled the liquid nitrogen tank through the ruined gate and set it in the corridor. Incredibly, though the center of the gate lay in little pieces all over the floor, the alarm buttons continued to glow as if the system still offered protection. Simon stepped through, closed the doors and locked them. Security, when they finally did come by on their rounds, would only make sure the knobs of the outer doors wouldn't turn; if left on the floor, DeVilbiss's corpse would not be discovered until the day after Christmas. Switching on the spotlight, Simon hurried down the back staircase and out the loading dock into the welcome Christmas Eve night. He started to run at full speed, headed for DeVilbiss's duplex, only three bocks away.

Simon had an image of how DeVilbiss's demonic controllers would kill Frederika: another gas explosion, which would cremate her and also eliminate every trace of DeVilbiss's presence. Perhaps the house was already filled with gas. He saw no sign of the police and was unwilling to lose any time in summoning them. His feet churned on in his own version of supernormal speed. He reached the house whooping for air but still pushed himself down the alleyway, looking in vain for a basement window. He recalled none from his previous night's visit. For several seconds he agonized over the thought that both front and back doors might be boobytrapped. Rejecting normal entry, he vaulted over the back porch rail and kicked in a kitchen windowpane, routing out the remaining shards with his spotlight. He thumbed the light on (afraid that even the tripping of an electrical switch would blow the house apart) and

306

played it around the room, making the space midday bright. While he caught his breath, he let the light skim slowly over the counter-top. Caught in its beam were the twin glass jars he had seen on his last visit, one empty but for a glimmering yellow powder residue, the other almost filled. A thin trail of the powder ran away from the jar across the Formica, glowing eerily in the light. He swung the beam to a grouping of table and two chairs in the center of the room. On the table sat a glass, a spoon, and what looked to Simon like a small, crumpled pile of woman's underwear. He sniffed the air, smelled no trace of gas, and climbed cautiously inside. His spotlight fell on the basement door. Around the doorknob hung a piece of string and, at the bottom of its loop, an old-fashioned key.

Simon pulled the knife from his pocket, removed it from his keyring and opened it. He inched toward the basement door, swinging the spotlight back and forth in a searching pattern. As he came around the table, he saw DeVilbiss's doll, lying on the floor on its side with one arm under it and the other behind at an awkward angle, as if its owner had hurled it there in a rage. The spotlight caught one open and unblinking eye, which shone as wetly as a living eye. Simon flashed the beam along the hallway, then to the right, into the empty dining room. He continued toward the base-ment door. As he reached for the knob, he heard a small noise from nearby. His head jerked around. He played the light into every corner. Nothing moved. And then he looked down on the floor. The French clown now lay on its back, with its trailing arm out to its side. The arm that had been hidden was now partially exposed. The tiny hand held tight to something that looked like a piece of wire. Simon told himself that his footsteps must have shaken over the precariously balanced doll. He moved closer, shining the light on the mannequin. The thin object in its hand glowed with the reflection of a red crystalline powder coating.

Simon leapt onto the closer chair and then to the tabletop. He swung the spotlight back down to the floor. The doll had disap-peared.

"Shit!" Simon cried. If a biography of magic, a translation of ancient scrolls, and a former member of the Undead had not just convinced him of the supernatural, he would have bent to examine the doll and gotten an ice pick in the throat. DeVilbiss had not wound it up for the British magicians, had not helped it do its amazing computations. The thing had a life of its own and was even quicker than its supposed master had been. Simon had not left it unlit for more than three seconds. Now it had disappeared without a sound, on tiny leather soles.

Simon shone the light all around the kitchen and down the length of the hall. He had no idea what manner of poison was in the red powder on the ice pick, but he was sure the homunculus needed only to scratch him. Simon threw his beam fleetingly on the utensil rack that hung on the wall above the stove, to reassure his memory of the tools there. He bent swiftly and scooped from the tabletop the glass and the woman's underwear. He wrapped the material lightly around the glass and dropped the bundle over the edge of the table, far enough out so that he could see it land. As it fell he caught the fleetest flash of red-coated metal, appearing and then disappearing quickly back under the table.

Simon hefted the knife in his hand. Even twenty years back, quite a few Ohio boys still mastered the art of knife throwing; in his neighborhood, Simon had been mumblety-peg king. Finding its center of gravity, he took the blade between his thumb and forefinger. He circled the edge of the table several times with the light beam, then fixed it on the chair on the side nearest the back door. His left foot struck out, sending the chair skittering against the stove. He circled the table again with the light and inched farther and farther toward the hallway, until he felt the table starting to tip. Screaming his most blood-curdling Indian war cry, he backed to the edge of the table, rode it down as it tilted and gave it a final shove as it struck the floor. He stumbled for an instant against the second chair, but found his balance and rushed to the table. The clown lay on its back, still clutching the slender ice pick, its shining eyes fixed on Simon, its painted smile wicked. Without hesitation, Simon flung his knife at the clown's chest. Incredibly, the doll lurched to the side before the knife reached it, but the flowing material of its costume was pinned by the blade, just above the elbow of the hand that held the pick. Simon threw aside the table. As he stumbled toward the utensil rack, the doll swung itself over, stretching with its opposite hand to wrap its delicate fingers around the poison-laden weapon. Simon ripped the steel meat fork from its hook, took it in both hands, dropped to his knees and drove the fork down with all his might, piercing the doll between its shoulder blades. He leaned his full weight onto the fork, willing its points into the floor's ancient linoleum.

The doll uttered a shriek like an electric guitar at full volume. Simon fell backward and watched it, transfixed. For several moments its feet and hands beat the floor. Then it stopped dead. Absolutely silent. Much as DeVilbiss had after he had been speared. Again, Simon refused to believe his opponent could be stopped so easily. Whatever it was, it was certainly not merely a thing of porcelain, glass, wood, and cloth. And certainly not of flesh and blood. He snatched up the chair and swung it over his shoulder, not willing to wait for a twitch before he continued to destroy its clown's form. Before his arms swung down, a red light burst from the wound. Smoke began curling up around the fork's tines. Simon dropped the chair, grabbed the still-lit spotlight and retreated toward the basement door. Working blindly with his fingers, his eyes riveted on the smoking, glowing doll, he fitted the key into the door, unlocked it and swung it open. A tongue of orange-red flame shot out of the doll's back, enveloping the fork in a conflagration that looked as if it must start from below floor level, perhaps from the depths of hell itself. As each second passed the tongue of fire widened, consuming more and more of the doll.

Simon flipped on the basement light and hurtled down the stairs, stuffing the precious spotlight lens-side-up in his coat pocket.

Frederika was not in the front area. He threw open the door to the back room and found her alive. She stood on tiptoes but bore most of her weight on her wrists, which were bound by a pair of sturdy-looking chromed handcuffs that had been slung over a water pipe. She looked sedated, but when she saw him, her forlorn face showed recognition.

Simon examined the handcuff lock. He pulled DeVilbiss's keys out of his coat and searched desperately for one with a perfectly circular tip. Neither those from DeVilbiss's chain nor from his pocket conformed.

"Frederika, you've got to help me," Simon said, taking her jaw in his hand and aligning her eyes with his. "Where are the keys—"

"Can't help," she said. "Must stay here."

Simon would rather have had Frederika hypnotically drugged until he got her out of the house, but he understood that she would not cooperate until released from DeVilbiss's spell.

"Frederika, listen. I've found . . . *your lost teddy bear.*"

For a moment, she seemed not to have heard. Then her eyes relit with intelligence.

"I've found your lost teddy bear," Simon repeated. "And now I've come to take you home."

"Home, yes," Frederika said.

A sudden racket of objects being thrown around echoed from upstairs. Frederika looked up. Simon forced her face to focus again on him.

"Where's the key to these handcuffs?"

"I . . . I don't know."

The noises continued and grew louder.

"Shit, shit!" Simon swore, dashing to the workbench.

"Have got to get loose," Frederika said. She yanked down on the handcuffs.

"That won't do any—"

Simon stopped in mid-sentence. Despite being on tiptoe and having no leverage, Frederika was bending the water pipe and drawing its strong fasteners out of the dry wood. He watched in amazement as she pulled again, and several links of the handcuffs thinned and lengthened. She pulled once more, and the water pipe burst at the joint nearest her. Cold water gushed in a steady stream onto the floor. Mastering his amazement, Simon helped her guide the handcuffs off the open pipe. Once she had her arms in front of her, she crooked her elbows and finished the job of bursting the links that joined the cuffs. Her legs buckled. Simon caught her in mid-fall and scooped her into his arms.

"Time to go," he said, kicking open the door and turning the corner to the basement stairs. Even before he looked up, he knew the battle had not ended. The kitchen was filled with a hellish red glow.

And then the frame of the door at the top of the stairs was filled. The figure was the epitome of every race's and tribe's timeless incarnation of evil. It had the size and shape of a man, but there the resemblance ended. Its legs were spindly, backward-kneed and ended in cloven feet. The upper appendages were thin and tipped with curving claws. Behind the wedge-shaped torso rose what looked to be wings, and below it hung a lancet-tipped tail, which whipped back and forth. The head was supported by a long, thickly corded neck. Its face thrust forward into a snout, nostrils little more than gaping black holes and teeth triangular and three rows deep. Its eight eyes shone like backlit rubies. In its left hand it held a pitchforklike instrument. All of it, including the pitchfork, was surrounded by a translucent aura of unholy scarlet.

Simon turned Frederika's face into his chest as he watched the thing descend slowly. It moved as if it was burdened by an unaccustomed gravity. With each movement, its breath escaped metallically.

"What's that?" Frederika asked, as Simon retreated toward the backroom door.

"Something's after us," he said huskily, amazed that his voice worked at all.

"Some *thing?*"

Simon set her down and slammed the door shut.

"You know the demons the grimoires describe?"

Frederika gasped and backed from the door. She looked suddenly more alert.

The door had no lock. Simon rolled a barrel in front of it. "Help me barricade this until I can figure out what to do!"

Simon moved a heavy dining room chair and pinned its back under the doorknob, turned and saw Frederika carrying its maple dining table as if it were a jewelry box. She rammed it forward into the pile, compacting everything in front.

"Did I bring it here?" Frederika agonized, listening to the descending footsteps on the stairs.

Simon shook his head. "It was all DeVilbiss's doing. He had you in a trance, and I . . ."

Simon's sentence trailed off as he searched for a potent means of protecting them. He recalled something from the scrolls about creatures that were "at sea" on the earth—the very reason they had created vampires. He could hear the approaching demon's breathing, but the red glow did not yet show under the door. He whirled around and studied the workbench filled with tools.

Frederika was oblivious to Simon's staring, busying herself with piling the last of the room's big items against the door.

Simon strode to the workbench, through the expanding pool of water cascading from the burst pipe. He picked up an old hatchet and a pair of rubber gloves and took them to the house's master service panel. It was a relatively new box, with circuit breakers instead of fuses. Out of it ran the 110-volt line, encased in only plastic, and the 220 line, shielded in steel cable.

From the opposite side of the door hissed a new sound, like a welder's torch being ignited. Frederika backed toward the workbench. Simon tugged the gloves on, took the hatchet in both hands and struck the 220-volt cable with all his might, just above the service panel.

The hollow-core door exploded into a forest of slivers. Frederika gave a yelp, and Simon saw that a large splinter had pierced her upper arm.

"I'm all right," she said, gesturing with her good arm for him to return to his business.

Hunks of burning wood floating on the water and the fire that licked off sections of door still clinging to the hinges masked the blue light arcing from the cable's exposed wires. Simon grabbed the cable as high up as he could and tugged it toward the door.

"I can help!" Frederika cried out.

Before Simon could reply, a beam of red energy streaked through the ruined doorway, blowing much of the barricade backward and bathing it in fire. The old boxes and dry furniture took flame

312

quickly. Simon doubted now that the creature would bother to advance into the burning deathtrap, but he tugged the cable in the direction of the doorway anyway. It resisted tenaciously, fastened securely to the concrete wall in several places by metal U clamps. Frederika dashed across the little room.

"Don't!" Simon warned. "You might be elec—"

Two things stopped Simon cold. The first was the sudden transformation of the room's color as the red beam drew closer. The second was Frederika's left hand curling around the cable sheathing with no apparent harm. Simon removed his hands from the cable to find a better purchase. The next thing he knew, he lay sprawled on the floor. He looked up and realized Frederika had shoved him away. Before he could exclaim, she ripped the cable from the wall with one fierce tug and swung around to face the door.

The thing Vincent DeVilbiss had dubbed Nick filled the door frame in terrible satanic splendor. Simon lay near the workbench, in its direct line of vision. It pointed its pitchfork at his head.

Frederika whipped the cable around and threw it toward the creature. The cable's mooring on the wall stopped it a good foot short of the demon's red aura, but it fell into the pool of water filling the floor around the doorway. The exposed wires popped and sizzled, making the water's surface dance with hot blue arcs. The demon's eight eyes bulged; so did the protective glow surrounding it. Then the aura collapsed with a sudden *whumph,* like an enormous vacuum-sealed jar being opened. Jittering from the pulse of the electricity, the creature nevertheless managed to straighten and to point its weapon at Simon. No beam came from it. A furious noise issued from the demon's throat, like a thundering express train. Although it stood as if at home amid the flame, smoke, and sparks, it dropped its weapon and clasped its claws to its throat. Its pink color was quickly draining to white. Its wings fanned out behind, until their tips touched the ceiling. Suddenly, they beat downward, and the demon disappeared.

The creature's beam had blown much of the flaming barricade directly under the broken water pipe. As flames were extinguished a great mass of smoke rose, filling the space under the low ceiling.

While Simon crawled toward the doorway, Frederika bent low and used a plank of wood to draw the wires from the water and onto dry concrete. She reached behind her, grabbed Simon's wrist, and led him in a duck-walk to the basement stairs.

Coughing to rid their lungs of smoke, they entered the kitchen. Tendrils of smoke escaped from the air vents, around the floor moldings, and out of the floor cabinets. To Simon's profound relief, he saw the ashes of the doll lying on the linoleum where he had left it. As Simon raced out the rear entry alcove, Frederika darted back briefly to grab her purse from the countertop. Despite his lead, she passed him before he had reached the neighboring yard. She had to turn around and wait for him on the sidewalk of the next street.

For a time, they both concentrated on catching their breaths and filling their lungs with clean air. Then Frederika said, "Thank you."

"You're welcome."

"I'm sure I owe you my life. What are you doing here?"

"It's a long story."

"I believe you. I hope you know all of it. Was that thing from hell?"

"I think so."

"And Vincent brought it here?"

"Indirectly. He—"

"Why?"

Simon realized Frederika was shivering. "Is your coat back in the house?"

Frederika's eyes blinked as the question shoved DeVilbiss and the demon from her thoughts and gained sudden primacy. "No. It's . . . in . . . my car. I left it there this afternoon."

"You were hypnotized then," Simon said, stripping off his coat.

"Yes. But I can remember. I can remember it all. My God."

As Simon moved forward to drape the coat around Frederika's shoulders, he looked at her upper arm. The spike of wood was gone; so was the wound it had made.

"Did DeVilbiss make you take any powder?"

"Yes. What was it for?"

"Look at your arm."

314

Frederika gasped.

Simon finished wrapping the coat around her. "It's for strength, speed, and invulnerability. And for eternal life. But the price is that it'll turn you into a vampire."

If he had been in her place, Simon was sure he'd have fainted at the words. Frederika stood firmly, eyes darting in thought.

A rowdy little band of carolers turned onto the block, singing "Joy to the World." Simon quickly stripped off the rubber gloves and shoved them into his coat pocket, then curled his arm familiarly around Frederika's waist and started toward them at a slow pace, through the snowflakes that had begun falling.

"Ah, young love," the eldest man among the carolers gushed as they passed. "Merry Christmas!"

Simon and Frederika returned the wish. When they were out of earshot and under the glow of a streetlight, Frederika turned around.

"Where are you going?" Simon asked, grabbing her by the arm.

"Back into the house."

"Are you crazy? That thing might come back."

Frederika looked calmly at Simon. "The powder's in there."

"But it's no good. That jar was poisoned or something. No invulnerability in it. That's how I was able to kill DeVilbiss."

At last Frederika seemed stunned by news. "He's dead."

"Yes."

Her expression hardened. "Good."

Frederika's sangfroid combined with the winter night cold to thoroughly chill Simon. He rubbed his upper arms vigorously. "Do you know if your car's nearby?"

"Yes. It's two blocks that way."

Simon gestured for Frederika to take the lead. "Let's get to someplace warm. I'll start this long story from the beginning."

CHAPTER FOURTEEN

December 25

❦

Penetrating so many secrets, we cease to believe in

the unknowable. But there it sits nevertheless,

calmly licking its chops.

—H. L. Mencken

O ne last time about the diaries. They're in Switzerland and tell about his whole life."

Frederika had the point of her pen poised over a note-filled paper napkin. Six similar napkins had been laid neatly to her left. She looked alert, exactly the opposite of the way Simon felt. The clock on the diner wall read one minute past midnight.

"I don't know if it's his whole life," Simon answered, wearily. "And they're in code."

"But he gave you the key to the code."

"He did. But I'm not sure I understood him completely."

Even though the hour was late, at least Frederika was calm and no longer grilling him about his actions. When he had unfolded the first third of the tale, speaking of DeVilbiss's true nature, the messages of the scrolls, the murders, and how Frederika had gotten enmeshed in the vampire's quest, she had digested the information with appropriate awe and not interrupted too often with questions. During the second part—when Simon explained how he had chanced on her in the cemetery and purposely involved himself in her life—she remained outwardly calm, but he could feel the upset below her quiet surface. Once he had gotten that far, there was nothing to be done but to plunge on to his discoveries of her past, of her father's behavior and her mother's flight. His conversations with Neil Yoskin had prepared him to expect Frederika to flee as well, unwilling to hear anything bad about her father. To his amazement, she sat and listened, signaling that she heard him only by an occasional tear. The revelation that her mother lived and that Frederika would see her within hours produced the deepest shock of the night, but this, too, she weathered. And with little comment. Too relieved to have gotten through his entire confession, Simon did not press her for her feelings regarding Alice Niederjohn. At the same time he felt great disappointment at no explosion of emotion, no cathartic release that promised to improve her day-to-day mood and behavior. Frederika instead refocused on the scrolls and on the undeniably urgent matter of their survival.

The hours flew by, from early evening to midnight, with dinner a partial punctuation and then two pots of coffee to fortify them and provide an excuse to keep the booth. Finally, at two minutes past midnight, Frederika set down her pen and stared at Simon.

"You got into all this for a hot fudge sundae."

"No," Simon answered. "For a life. It was past time for me to get off the dime."

"But you couldn't have hoped for this. How many times have you cursed spotting me in that cemetery?"

"Never. I've been waiting years to find something really important to do. By chance, accident, or fate, you gave me that opportunity. I may regret it in an hour . . . or a day . . . but I don't think so. DeVilbiss said, 'You must act.' Well, I will."

"*We* will," Frederika corrected.

The waitress, who had been hovering conspicuously since a quarter to twelve, approached the booth, check in hand.

"Listen, we're closing."

Simon glanced around the diner and, for the first time, noticed that he and Frederika were the only customers left.

"I thought this was an all-night diner," Frederika said.

"Not on Christmas Eve or New Year's Eve, honey. We got lives, too." The waitress struggled with her smile.

"Sorry," Simon said.

Frederika opened her purse and peeled a fifty-dollar bill from a thick roll of currency. "Here, keep the change."

"And a Merry Christmas to you!" the waitress said, pocketing the bill and the check, grabbing the cups and coffee pot and rushing away.

"How much money have you got there?" Simon asked.

"A little over twenty-two hundred."

"Don't be throwing it around. We're gonna need it." He rose from the booth and plucked Frederika's coat from the hook.

"Let's talk more about that," she said. "Our plan's not good enough yet to beat the Devil."

Simon sighed at her words. She grabbed her napkin notes and began putting them in order as they left the diner.

"I'm sorry, but I can't think more right now," he said. "I slept very little last night, and today's . . . yesterday's exhausted me."

"But we can't go home in the dark. Vincent warned you about others of his kind probably being around. I still need to think." They reached Frederika's car. "I can do it while I drive. The passenger seat tilts back. Do you think you can sleep with all that caffeine in you?"

"I'll try."

When Simon woke, the dashboard clock read 6:58. He might have slept longer, but for the cold. The car was parked with the engine turned off. The fog of his exhalation coated the windshield. Frederika studied him from the driver's seat. Her expression was placid; he thought he read the trace of a smile on her lips.

"Finished thinking?" he asked.

"For now. I got stuck on a question: Why would you go through so much trouble for me? I was a stranger. If somebody kept lying to *me* and trying to raise the dead, I'd have run the other way."

Simon thought about telling the whole truth, but after her unexpected reactions to his news the previous night, he said, "I told you; my life needed change. Helping you was the most positive thing I could do at the moment."

Frederika stared hard at him another moment, then turned the key in the ignition. "I've made some improvements in our plan. You drive; I'll tell you while we head back to Princeton."

When they reached Park Place, dawn was fanning pinkly over the horizon. Simon drove past the duplex without slowing.

"The water must have put out the fire," Frederika speculated. The duplex bore no signs of smoke or fire damage.

"Then why isn't water pouring out around the foundation?" Simon asked. "And why didn't the neighbors hear or smell anything last night? Very strange."

"Drive around the corner and let me out," Frederika said. Simon had agreed that her speed and strength would serve better in case of danger. She already had in her hand DeVilbiss's ring of keys. "Since the place is still standing, maybe I should risk going inside. That demon's pitchfork could still be there. What a fantastic bit—"

"No!" Simon said emphatically. "Stick with the plan. We stay in the light."

"You're right." "God Rest Ye Merry, Gentlemen" played on the radio as Frederika got out of the car and walked back around the corner of Moore Street onto Park. A layer of dark clouds was dispersing. Simon watched the dashboard clock flash off two minutes. He put the car in gear and drove around the corner to where Frederika stood, beside the beat-up Escort. The rented car's trunk lid was up. He noted that no one else stood on the street; he saw no faces peering from windows. Frederika slammed down the lid. Her free hand held a large, black gym bag. He stopped the car, and she climbed in.

"Paydirt," Frederika said. "The diary, a couple thousand dollars, in several currencies, three passports—British, Swiss, and Italian—and a set of little tools." She held one up.

"For lock picking."

"And an extra bonus." Frederika produced a filled brown glass jar. "*Good* powder."

Simon thought of dinner the previous night. "Do you always eat hamburgers rare?"

321

"Not always," she said.

Simon steered into a parking space on a side street near Firestone Library.

"Now for the real fun," Frederika said. She stepped briskly from the car, striding with purpose toward the library. Simon locked the car and followed.

At the loading dock they encountered one of the security guards, a man who recognized them both. Simon explained about the inert gases that needed tending, and the man nodded them through without hesitation. They sealed themselves behind the privacy of Rare Manuscripts' doors and walked down the narrow fenced-in corridor into the room proper. Both their attentions fixed on the floor near the special cases.

DeVilbiss lay where he had died. Other than the natural effects of rigor mortis and postmortem lividity there were no visible changes to his body. The lake of blood around him had largely congealed. Simon looked for Frederika's reaction and found her regarding the corpse with a mortician's detachment. When she caught Simon staring she smiled.

"Good," she said, echoing her reaction to the news of his death the previous night. Neil Yoskin had been right; deep down, Frederika was a woman with a cold steel backbone.

They went about their work with the precision of a bank robbery team. Simon took his system key from the hollowed-out Bible; Frederika already had in hand the one DeVilbiss took from Reverend Spencer. They inserted their keys and turned them in tandem, opening the case that held the priceless scrolls. Simon lifted them out carefully and placed them in the metal tubes in which they had arrived. First using a special machine in the corner of the room to evacuate the air from the tubes, he reversed the process and filled each with inert gas. He cautiously exited the room and carried the tubes to the B-Level air duct where he had hidden Willy's translation. Strapping the tubes securely in place with duct tape and replacing the grille took two minutes. Barring an all-consuming fire, they would be perfectly safe. Even if he and Frederika failed in completing their plan, actions Simon had taken the previous day and would soon take were sure to make the scrolls even more notorious. One day they would be found again, and the memory of those actions would protect them while the translating began anew.

By the time Simon returned to the Rare Manuscripts chamber, Frederika had used a desktop computer to produce a letter to the authorities. The letter contained four paragraphs. The first argued that the body in the room was that of a vampire and urged an exhaustive chemical as well as physical autopsy to prove the declaration. The second described the vampire's quest for the Ahriman scrolls and his killing of the security guard and Reverend Spencer to reach his purpose. The third stated that the scrolls had been removed for their protection, since others of DeVilbiss's kind were believed to exist. It closed by affirming that the reason for all the deaths and the scrolls' disappearance would very soon be made clear. Frederika lay the sheet of paper in the open case, beside documents of great antiquity but much less import.

Neither Simon nor Frederika signed the letter. They knew their failure to report to work the next day would do that for them. Simon shut the lid and placed the two security keys on top. As his final act, he took as decoys two empty metal tubes in which other precious scrolls of the Schickner Collection had arrived.

While Simon locked the room, Frederika patiently held the heavy liquid nitrogen tank. She refused to let him share its burden as they walked to the elevator.

"You're not going to take any more of that powder," he said.

"If I did, I could protect us better."

"You could also die from it. You aren't taking another vital ingredient, remember: human blood?" Frederika offered no more argument, but Simon doubted the disagreement was over.

The remainder of their plan involved meeting Frederika's mother at the mansion, packing, returning the nitrogen tank to the Physics Lab, returning the pickup truck to Rich, and getting from him a copy of Willy's translation. With the translation in their possession and multiple copies going out to scholars, the theft of the scrolls themselves would create a worldwide stir. Within twenty-four hours they would be in Europe, to retreive DeVilbiss's diaries and visit Professor Elmasri, the Akkadian scholar. From there, their goals generalized to getting the rest of the scrolls safely translated and averting something like biblical Armageddon.

Since it was still early Christmas Day, they drove by Lynn Gellman's townhouse and were relieved to see a police car beside a sedan with New York license plates. Frederika was the first to break a mutual silence as they headed to the mansion.

"He wasn't that smart. Not as smart as he thought anyway." DeVilbiss's name was unnecessary. "But we can't assume all their servants are like him. Whenever we travel or go out in public, it has to be in broad daylight."

Simon nodded. Frederika spoke of "we" so easily. She had made them a team with no formality, not even a passing remark. He was not pursuing; she was not running. He liked to think he was different from the other men she had known.

After Simon pulled the car into the driveway, he suggested that they make use of the new-fallen snow and circumambulate the mansion. They found only the tracks of rabbits and squirrels; no human footprint approached the house.

"Maybe we're safe for a while," Simon hoped aloud. He gestured for Frederika to open the front door. "Let's take down the Christmas tree; we'll be gone long past New Year's."

They had finished undecorating and were carrying the tree out to the curb when a late-model Lexus pulled up in front of the mansion. A woman sat behind the steering wheel. She turned off the engine and stared at Simon and Frederika, who stared back. No one seemed to want to move first.

Alice emerged slowly from the car. Her expression was pinched with anguish. As soon as she closed her door, Frederika started toward her, closing the distance between them. They hugged for a long moment. Then Frederika took her mother's hand and led her inside, with Simon trailing slowly in grateful silence. By the time he entered the house, they were both releasing tension by chattering about the layout of the furniture when Frederika was small. Frederika took her mother's coat and gestured toward one of the living room chairs.

"I think I can make this easier for us," she said to Alice, her face growing suddenly serious. "I was recently put under deep hypnosis by a very talented professional." Her eyes darted to Simon, to be sure he was listening. "He regressed me, so that I was able to remember how it truly was in this house."

Simon finally understood why, at the diner, Frederika had been able to take his news about her father with such equanimity. As Frederika spoke about her youth, Alice glanced at Simon with embarrassment. He determined to hear the revelations privately at a later time, and excused himself to brew tea. Mother and daughter were speaking with far less tension in their voices as he set the tea out, but he excused himself again, to clean out the refrigerator, set back the thermostat, cancel the newspaper delivery, and begin packing.

Nearly an hour had passed before Frederika came into Simon's bedroom. She wore her placid persona; still impossible for him to read. She placed herself within inches of him, took his face lightly in her hands and kissed him fully on the lips. When he finally mastered his shock and responded, she did not turn away, but returned his passion with interest. Finally, she drew back and regarded him with one eyebrow cocked.

"You lied to me," she said.

"When?"

"When you promised you weren't going to mother me."

"I won't do it again," he said, "now that we both know you've got a real mother."

"The question that was puzzling me all night; I'm pretty sure of the real reason you stayed and fought for me. Some day, when you decide to admit it, I promise I won't run away." With no pause to allow reply, Frederika glanced at her wristwatch and said, "You all packed?"

Simon laughed, then nodded in the direction of a single medium-sized piece of luggage. "Ready."

"Would you go down and keep my mother company while I throw a bag together?"

"Of course," Simon said, knowing that he had given her the power to ask almost anything of him.

"We're even," Frederika declared, her smile fetching a pair of dimples. "I was responsible for your new life, and you were responsible for mine."

"And," he replied, "it seems to continue."

"It seems that way." She ran her hand along his cheek. Then she was gone, rushing out of the room.

When Simon entered the hallway carrying his suitcase, he expected to hear Frederika packing in her bedroom. Instead, he saw that the door to Frederik Vanderveen's sanctum sanctorum lay open. Frederika sat at his desk, rolling a sheet of paper into an old manual typewriter.

"I'm giving my mother power of attorney," Frederika informed, "in case we're longer than we expect."

"Good idea," Simon said, looking around the room.

"There's more money over there." Frederika gestured toward one of the shelves. Simon found an enormous brandy snifter stuffed with African and European currencies, no doubt accumulated from the diplomat father's many trips abroad. Simon felt deep satisfaction as he plundered one of the room's treasures, as if Frederika had invited him to help exorcize her father's potent ghost. He left her typing at good speed and went down to keep her mother company.

"I can't thank you enough for what you've done," Alice told Simon.

"You're very welcome."

"I think she knows what she's got in you." Simon felt one of his characteristic blushes rising. Before he could offer a response, she looked at his suitcase and said, "So, you two are flying off to England this afternoon."

"That's right." Frederika had been wise enough not to tell even her mother the truth of their destination. He patted his pocket, making sure his passport was there. "It's only part vacation. Did she mention why she might be gone awhile?"

"Yes. The job offer." Alice looked a bit sad. "I frankly hope she doesn't get it. Now that we're getting back together, I'm selfish enough to want her near me. I don't know how I'm going to explain this to Tom and the boys."

"Would you like me to get your old yearbooks for you?" Simon offered. When he returned to the living room with the books, Frederika stood in her coat, beside a large suitcase. She handed her mother a key. "Thanks for having the courage to come here. I love you." They embraced. "And look," Frederika added, "don't feel like we're pushing you out just because we have to catch a plane. Hang around as long as you like . . . and take whatever you want."

"Okay. I might catch my breath before heading home."

Simon smiled at Alice and led Frederika through the foyer toward the back door.

"You took my phone number?" Alice called out.

"Yes," Frederika answered. "We'll do some real catching up when I return. 'Bye!"

Alice listened to the back door closing. She moved to one of the living room's side windows and watched the two young people loading the car in the bright Christmas Day sunlight. They were transferring a black gym bag and a pair of dark metal cylinders from the passenger compartment into the trunk. Oblivious to her watching, they dumped their suitcases in the trunk and climbed into the front seat. She stood at the window for a full minute after the white Mazda had backed down the driveway and her daughter had driven out of sight.

Alice broke her reverie and gazed around the room. There had been a number of things she had regretted leaving behind. She struggled to recall them all. Some of it was old sheet music and books. And then there was a box filled with loose family snapshots, dating back to the turn of the century. She opened several built-in cabinets, searching.

The front door knocker banged twice. Alice opened the door. Standing on the porch was a big-boned woman with wiry blond hair poking out from under a Russian-style fur hat. It was difficult to judge her age, as much of her face was covered by enormous sunglasses. In her gloved hands she held a large gift basket of fruit.

"Good morning," the woman said, pleasantly. "Is this the residence of Miss Frederika Vanderveen?"

"Yes, it is."

"This is for her. Is she home?"

"No. You just missed her."

"Oh. Too bad. She'll be back later then?"

"As a matter of fact, she won't for some time," Alice said. "She and her boyfriend are flying to England."

The woman's mouth turned down in disappointment. "Oh dear! I'm sure the person who ordered these won't want them left here. Do you . . . do you mind if I use the phone and call the shop?"

"No, of course not. Come in." As the woman walked inside, Alice was struck by a thought. "Your shop is open on Christmas Day?"

The woman smiled. "We never close."

As Alice shut the door, she was sure she smelled the odor of suntan lotion.

About the Author

Brent Monahan is the author of *DeathBite* with Michael Maryk, *Satan's Serenade,* and *The Uprising*. He lives in Yardley, Pennsylvania, close by the novel's setting. Both his daughter Caitlin and son Ian were born in Princeton, New Jersey, making them True Princetonians.

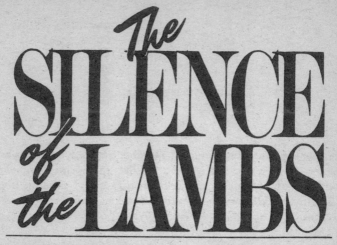

The SILENCE *of the* LAMBS

THE ELECTRIFYING BESTSELLER BY

THOMAS HARRIS

" THRILLERS DON'T COME ANY BETTER THAN THIS."
—*CLIVE BARKER*

"HARRIS IS QUITE SIMPLY THE BEST SUSPENSE NOVELIST
WORKING TODAY." — *The Washington Post*

THE SILENCE OF THE LAMBS
Thomas Harris

———— 92458-5 $5.99 U.S./$6.99 Can.